The Progress of Julius

Daphne du Maurier was born in London, and was educated at home and in Paris. Her first novel, *The Loving Spirit*, was published in 1931, since when she has written many highly successful novels, including *Rebecca*, *My Cousin Rachel*, *Frenchman's Creek* and *Jamaica Inn*. Disliking town life, she lives in Cornwall, and her favourite pursuits are walking, gardening and sailing. Her most recent novels include *The Flight of the Falcon*, *The House on the Strand* and *Rule Britannia*.

By the same author in Pan Books

Rule Britannia
My Cousin Rachel
The King's General

Daphne du Maurier
The progress of Julius

Pan Books Ltd London and Sydney
in association with William Heinemann Ltd

First published 1933 by William Heinemann Ltd
This edition published 1975 by
Pan Books Ltd, Cavaye Place, London SW10 9PG,
in association with William Heinemann Ltd
ISBN 0 330 24368 3
Copyright Daphne du Maurier 1933

Printed in Great Britain by
Richard Clay (The Chaucer Press) Ltd, Bungay, Suffolk

Contents

Part One (1860–72): Childhood

His first instinct was to stretch out his hands to the sky. The white clouds seemed so near to him, surely they were easy to hold and to caress, strange-moving things belonging to the wide blue space of heaven.

They floated just above his head, they almost brushed his eyelids as they passed, and he had only to grasp the long curling fringe of them with his fingers and they would belong to him instead, becoming part of him for ever. Something within him whispered that he must clutch at the clouds and bring them down from the sky. So he held out his hands to them and they did not come. He cried out to them and they did not come. They passed away from him as though they had never been, indifferent and aloof; like wreaths of white smoke they were carried away by the wind, born of nothing, dissolving into nothing, a momentary breath that vanished in the air.

Nor yet did he understand, for a queer puzzled look crept into his eyes, and he would frown his ancient baby frown of an old man; while from the innermost part of his being came the long-drawn pitiful wail that can never be explained, the plaintive cry of a child born into the world who knows not what he wants, the eternal question of the earth to the skies – Who am I! Where from? Where to? The first cry and the last. The sigh of the baby, the sigh of the old man.

The white clouds had gone, and now others appeared over the rim of the world, coming into his little sphere of sight; so that the frown went from his face and the look of longing came upon it once more, and again he must stretch out his hands and call to them, the lesson unlearnt, the question in his eyes. A child newly born and he must know the answer – continuing from this first moment until the last for ever seeking, a bright spark rising in the cold air.

The Progress of Julius

Julius Lévy was born in Puteaux, at that time little more than a village on the banks of the Seine. The street and the house in which he lived – now demolished and built over by large factories, their tall chimneys belching smoke into the air – was in his childhood the Rue Jean-Jacques, a long twisting cobbled street leading downhill from the village towards the high road to Paris. The houses were grey-coloured and drab, leaning forward, nearly touching, the air coming with difficulty to the dark rooms.

The last house in the street, cramped and unhealthy like the rest, possessing two rooms and another space scarcely more than a cupboard, was owned by Jean Blançard the grandfather of Julius. Here he lived with his daughter Louise and his son-in-law Paul Lévy. Beyond the house were rough uncultivated plots of ground, as yet unbuilt upon, where the people of the quarter threw their waste and rubbish. This waste was never removed, and here dogs and cats came to scavenge; lean, wretched animals who would prowl at night and disturb those who slept with their thin hungry cries.

In the daytime children played on the rubbish heap; squatting on their behinds they delved amongst the filth and sewage for hidden treasure, and often they would find odds and ends of food, half an apple thrown away or a crust of bread, cheese rind and peelings, and these they would thrust in their mouths with squeals of delight, relishing the joy of forbidden food.

Once he was able to walk, Julius found his way here too, and he would batter open the lids of old tins and thrust his little nose inside, working with his tongue round the edges to catch the last lingering taste of what had been, and then, scratching his body with one hand, he would glance slyly out of the corner of one eye to find the whereabouts of the nearest child, who might, if he were not careful, snatch the tin from his grasp.

Gradually and naturally from the timid shrinking bundle of flesh and nerves that was a baby, Julius grew to be a child, possessing feelings and intelligence, who used his senses, who began to realize that the faces about him were those of his relatives, that the house and the street and Puteaux were his home.

Supper would be ready, and they would sit to the table, Julius with a napkin tied around his throat, his black eyes opening wide as Mère placed before him the bowl of steaming soup. After his soup Julius ate pieces of garlic sausage off the end of Grandpère's fork, and he would taste a lump of cheese from the finger of Mère, and to finish off he would drink his fill from the glass of red wine handed him by Grandpère, the old man rocking the whole table with his laughter as the child's head nodded foolishly, and his eyes rolled; and to Julius this would seem the essence of peace and plenty, to sit there at the table, his body fully nourished with food and drink, already swaying in his chair as he longed for sleep, and half-consciously he would be aware of the food smell, the drink and tobacco smell, the voices of Mère and Grandpère jabbering through a haze, these people who were part of him and part of each other.

And just before his head sank down upon his chest, and Mère picked him up and carried him to bed, the door would open once more and Père come in, white-faced, lean, and silent, Père with Julius's eyes, Julius's hair, Julius's long pointed nose. Then the family broke up, they would not be themselves any more, Grandpère would swear and grumble, shaking his shoulders, and Mère would begin to scold shrilly, complaining of this, complaining of that, until the room was full of her and the old man, but in a new key, different to what had been before.

Père would be silent, like a lean wolf, caring for none of them, and sitting down in the corner he would eat by himself, goading them to fury by his imperturbability; and when he had finished he would reach to a shelf for his flute and sway backwards and forwards in the rocking-chair, his eyes closed, a lock of black hair falling over his face. Sometimes he gazed at Julius, who, with stained pinafore and swollen eyes, cried for his bed, and then he turned to Grandpère and Mère, his teeth bared in a strange smile, more like a wolf than ever, and he said: 'You want to make a brute of him, do you, a glutton, a little pig? You wish to teach him to live like a beast?'

They looked back at him, their faces flushed and resentful, Grandpère with his mouth wide open in surprise, his pipe hanging from his lips, and Mère, one hand on her hip, the other picking a piece of meat from her tooth with a brooch.

'What do you think you are doing, mixing yourself in matters

9

that don't concern you?' she scolded. 'Can't he enjoy himself, poor little soul? Hasn't he the right to eat? Who pays for his food? Answer me that. Is it you?' and Grandpère added his voice to hers, rumbling, jeering, letting forth a flow of words pointed and coarse. 'Stay quiet in your corner and leave your brat alone. Aren't we all beasts, my poor boy; weren't you a beast when you lay with his mother? Would the child have been born but for that? Let him learn to enjoy his belly and to enjoy other things, like his father before him.' Then he laughed, a vast roar that shook the table once more, laughing until he choked and his daughter had to lean across and pat his back while he spat on his plate, she too laughing, her breasts shaking.

'Go on with you,' she said; 'you're nothing but a filthy old man.' They looked at each other, both red, both fat, fair-haired, blue-eyed, ridiculously alike, and once more she filled her mouth with the garlic sausage, and he smacked his lips, a thin trickle of wine dribbling from his chin to his blouse. The old man waved his fork in the direction of his son-in-law. 'Jew,' he sneered, 'nothing but a miserable Jew.' Then Paul Lévy stretched out his legs, closing his eyes once more, and lifting the flute to his lips he breathed upon it, calling forth a queer plaintive tune that rose in the air like a cry from the wilderness, and Julius, half asleep on his mother's lap, would gaze across at his father, so white and strange in the candlelight, and it seemed to him that the song was his, and the cry was his, and these things and the face of Père vanished into nothingness, and were Julius himself. The music went into him and sent him to sleep, carrying him away to some distant place belonging only to dreams and not to the waking day, and he would be aware of an enchantment known only to himself and to Père. Unconscious of the world he was carried to bed, fast wrapped in his secret city, and later when he awoke in the middle of the night, and listened to the harsh splitting snores of Grandpère, asleep in his cupboard of a room, the city would be forgotten, and turning on his side he felt for the large comforting breast of Mère, physical and tangible, nearer to him now than the faint music lost in the air; and the still figure at the other end of the bed was not a magician who called to him and who understood, but only the limp body of Père, a poor thing and a Jew. So Julius smiled to himself in the darkness, curling himself round the body of his mother, and it seemed to him as he fell asleep once more that this feeling of her was more satisfactory than the whisper of a dream heard at odd moments, not fully understood. There were many things to puzzle the mind of a child, and the relationship of these people who belonged to him and cared for him was never clearly defined.

Grandpère was the most distinct; large, red-faced, broad-shouldered, he belonged to the daily scheme of things, he was a man like no other man would ever be. He was the richness and the pageantry of life, he was a riot of colour and of glory – eating, drinking, laughing, singing, he was a superb figure of incredible dimension in the massed shadows of a small boy's mind. Even when senseless from drink, when he had to be laid flat on the bed in his cupboard room, washed and undressed like a monstrous child, he lost none of his power, and Julius crept to the edge of the bed and saw before him a full-length portrait, stamping itself upon his brain, Grandpère, a god, his blue blouse stained, his velvet trousers patched, his large and comforting hand limp on the white sheet like a juicy steak, the breath, smelling of cheese and wine, coming in long-drawn sighs from his open mouth.

And Grandpère was god and Grandpère was life to him.

His snores were music in their own way, a fuller, more familiar music than the thin wail of the flute, and his loud voice shouting when he awoke, his curses, his laughter, the wild excitement of his very obscenity, they were things that Julius counted upon as part of his daily bread. Mère also belonged to the rich atmosphere, her laughter was pleasure and so was the feel of her body and the touch of her hands, she was colour and movement, but in some incomprehensible way she was mixed up with Père, and this was something that could not be understood. It was as though Père dragged her away from life and would take her to his secret city, it was as though he played to her upon his flute and she had to follow him. In the day he was a Jew, a poor Jew, a good-for-nothing, worse than a mongrel dog, he was wretched Paul Lévy who could not earn a *sou*, who lived on his father-in-law, who had no country, who insulted the presence of real live people by his existence, because Grandpère, Jean Blançard, was alive, and

Mère, Louise Blançard, was alive, but Père, Paul Lévy, was a dead thing, was a Jew.

Then at night he played his music, and the candlelight flickered, and the laughter ceased, and the sound of eating and drinking, the clatter of plates and voices, were lulled into silence.

Grandpère lost his god-head, Grandpère became old Jean Blançard nodding in a corner, drowsy, a fool; and Mère became a woman, her hair brousy about her face, her flesh soft, no more the ruling dominant Mère scolding in her shrill voice; and Père was no longer Paul Lévy the Jew, but a man who whispered, a magician who called, a white still face of beauty crying in the darkness, a spirit with his hands on the gates of the secret city.

So these things Julius could not piece together, neither the eyes of Père bending to the eyes of Mère in the strange quiet of the night, he a tiny boy beside them on the bed, and the murmur of his voice and hers in answer, two other people in another life; nor the contempt of Mère in the daytime, the ruler, the chief, the anger she had for this pallid, thin, miserable specimen of a Père who shrugged his shoulders at her, saying nothing, crouching over a book, a poor thing who could not fight for his rights, a Jew by day, a king by night.

This very word of Jew grew to be a thing that Julius feared.

'Jew,' spat his mother, when she wished to scold him; 'you miserable little Jew. You are your father's son. You are not my son today.'

And his Grandpère, in angry teasing mood, would seize hold of a lock of his dark, sleek hair, would pinch his little pointed nose between thumb and finger, and slap his pale cheeks so that the blood tingled. 'Jew,' he roared, 'you wretched stinking piece of Jew-lust. Got by a Jew – born of a Jew – you aren't a Blançard – you're a Lévy.'

For to be a real Blançard was the highest praise to which a small boy could attain, he laughed loudly as they laughed, he straddled his legs apart as Grandpère did, he stuck out his little stomach, and glancing triumphantly in the direction of Père he jerked his thumb to his nose and spat 'Jew,' he said, 'you Jew.' Then Grandpère picked him up on his lap, his vast shoulders heaving in merriment, and he danced the boy up and down on his knee, while Mère stood beside him, her hands on her hips, her cheeks bulging with the sweets she sucked first and then gave to the child, and Julius screamed in delight and turned his face away so that he should not see the strange white face of Père in his corner, who had not said a word, who stared at him with his burning black eyes, who made him feel ashamed.

He had tried to show off before Père, he had wished to prove to him in triumph that he was a Blançard, that he was not a Lévy, not a Jew, but in his child's heart he knew he had failed. His laughter and his rudeness had gone for nothing, he had not won after all, he, and Grandpère and Mère were coarse, gross creatures for whom his cheek burned in humiliation, and Père, silent, aloof, his thin nostrils quivering in contempt – he had won.

'Let me down, Grandpère, I'm tired. I don't want to play any more,' he whispered, his voice fretful, his heart sick and his belly too from the sweets he had eaten, and they put him down to grub on the floor. When they were not looking he edged nearer to the bench where Père sat in the corner, and slowly he leant against his knee, waiting for the hand to stroke his hair softly, gently, in the way he did; and clasping his knee he stared up into the face of Père, who stared back at him, and losing himself in the strange depths of those dark eyes, he was lifted up to another world that the Blançards could never know.

Suddenly, without warning, these moods would come upon him, and he would sit quite still, his chin propped on his fist, his eyes staring straight before him, and 'What are you dreaming, you creature?' scolded Mère, and 'Come and play,' called Grandpère, but they could do nothing with him.

'Leave me, I don't want to play,' said Julius, his lips pressed together, and in these moments he knew he was greater than they, he knew that the Blançards were only people, and he was someone apart, taller than before, someone who stood alone with Père, scornful of the pitiful world, someone who lived with dreams, and beauty and enchantment, who conquered by silence, who dwelt in a secret city – a Lévy, a Jew.

When he was four years old, life began to develop day by day in regularity, up to that time it had been a question of eating and drinking, petting, scolding, and sleeping, but now life was shown to him from its true angle, the business of produce, of buying and selling. Five days a week the Blançards sold at the market. Because of this Julius was clothed and fed, and slept in a warm bed. That much he had learnt. And now, the market took the biggest place in his mind, it looked larger than the drab home at Puteaux, it meant life, and the world, it meant the land beyond the bridge. Every evening of the five days Julius would be awakened at midnight by the light of the candle, and see the figure of Père drawing on his trousers, while Mère talked in a low whisper, shading the child's eyes from the light; and outside on the cobbled stones came the sounds of hoofs, and the wheels of a cart, and Grandpère stamping up and down to keep warm, whistling to his horse, blowing upon his hands, calling to the closed window, 'Are you coming, Paul? You lazy hound, you sluggard – can't you leave your wife in peace?'

And in a moment or so the candle would be blown, and Père himself stumble from the room, and later the cart would rumble away down the street, Grandpère cracking his whip, urging the animal forward with his hoarse, rough voice. Julius closed his eyes once more, pressing next to his mother, glad that he had her alone with him, and he knew that Grandpère and Père had gone to the Halles to fetch the produce for the market. The Halles was a mysterious place which he had never seen, and many times he awoke, half surprised at the absence of Père in the bed, and the silence from Grandpère's cupboard.

'Where are they, Mère?' he whispered, and she snuggled him close to her, muttering in her voice swollen with sleep, 'At the Halles, little one; hush, go to sleep.'

In the mornings they rose early, before the sun had risen, and the sky was grey and cold, and Mère would draw on her clothes hastily, without washing, frizzing her fair curling hair round her fingers, tying her petticoats, wrapping a thick shawl over her woollen dress, slipping her felt slippers inside the wooden clogs. Julius wore a little black cloak on top of his pinafore, and he too had a thick scarf wound tightly round his body, and covering his mouth so that the air should not come to him.

He wore black clogs, and a woollen cap pulled down over his

ears. If his face was dirty she took her handkerchief and licked it, scrubbing his cheeks hard until the dirt was gone. When they were dressed they went out into the street, Julius holding on to his mother with one hand and eating his bread in the other. His bare legs would be blue with the cold, and the tip of his nose too, but his body was warm because of the scarf. They clattered down the muddy hill to the high road, their breath coming in gasps from their mouths, a thin stream of smoke in the frozen air. They crossed the bridge, the Seine flowing beneath seeming pale and treacherous, and before long, when Julius's legs were beginning to drag and his small feet trip in their heavy clogs, they came to the long line of stalls in the Avenue de Neuilly. These stalls would be ranged along the *trottoir*, in front of one another, reaching for ever, it seemed to Julius, and the carts were pulled alongside of them in the gutter, the horses with their noses dipped into food-bags, the backs of the carts open as the market folk lifted out their produce and staggered heavy-laden to the stalls.

Before long Julius and his mother would come to the Blançard stall, and the boy would leave go of her hand and run to pat the legs of the horse who swished his tail, and shook his head until the bells jingled.

Then Grandpère would appear from behind the stall, his mouth full, his sleeves rolled up above his elbows. 'So it's you, is it, you imp of mischief?' he cried, and picking up the child he held him so that he could catch hold of the horse's ears.

Père was setting out the stall, a dumb mediocre figure, a white apron round his waist, a little black skull cap on the back of his head, but already Mère had pushed him to one side, already she was altering the things that he had placed, arranging them differently with swift, capable hands, letting forth a torrent of abuse at his inefficiency. 'Is it like that, you would sell food?' she screamed, 'you big lump of stupidity, you poor rat. Do I have to show you how to do everything?' And he let her scream, saying no word himself, moving to the other end of the stall, his nostrils quivering. He would lift Julius, by this time grubbing on the ground under the stall, and put him high up on a barrel, covering his knees with a coat, and he would look at him for a moment with a ghost of a smile, laying one long thin finger on his cheek.

15

The Progress of Julius

Julius sat there, perched above them all at the back of the stall, his legs tucked under him, clapping his mittened hands together to keep warm. Soon the stall would be ready, and his eyes bigger than his stomach, he would gaze down at the good things spread before him, the smell mounting to him, delicious, strong, sending a quiver of pleasure and anticipation through his body. Oh! the smell of the market, the wonder it was to him, never to be forgotten, stamped for eternity upon his eager child's mind open to impressions. The high pile of butter, rounded and smooth, the great slabs of Gruyère cheese, poignant and keen, studded with little holes, and other cheese too, the red shining Dutch changing to yellow when it was cut, the Camembert, squashy like juice, the fat white cream cheeses bulging through their thin paper, the crate of eggs, brown and white and speckled. Adjoining the Blançard stall, part of it almost, so close it was, came the sight and the smell of green vegetables, of great flowery cauliflowers, stout cabbages, and a multitude of brussels sprouts, carrots rough and red like the hands of Grandpère, celery white and hard, the lovely odorous leeks hanging from their green stalks, and little lumpy brown potatoes smelling of wet earth.

From the stall opposite sausages clung to one another, brown and grey and black, long twisting sausages, short stumpy sausages, rolls as thick as a boy's arm, rolls as thin as a boy's finger – rich, red, garlic-flavoured sausages. A little farther down grey fishes gleamed on a white slab, their sleek fins wet from the tub of water, their mouths running blood, the whiff of salt sea upon them still. Somewhere the carcass of a bullock hung from an iron nail, the pungent smell of good fresh meat, liver blood-coloured and flabby, a calf's head, the lips bared strangely over the dead teeth. And somewhere the odour of silks and stuffs, carpets and furs; and somewhere the bright vision of a little girl waving bunches of yellow mimosa and deep purple violets, the dust of the cobbled streets, the feeble sun showing through a grey sky, the cold wind, the ceaseless cry of voices filling the air. All these things merged into one, hopelessly intermingled, a riot of sound and smell and colour, and there floated up to Julius, perched on his barrel, a snatch of smoke from a cigarette, a tang of Gruyère cheese, the great hearty laugh of Grandpère as he waved his hands, the shrill cry of Mère wrapping a pound of butter in white paper.

Grandpère was the real merchant, the true salesman; he watched the faces of the people as they pressed against the stall, as they hurried past, rubbing shoulders with one another, and his blue eyes twinkled, his mouth widened, and a woman would turn, laughing at him over her shoulder. He had a word for everyone, a nod here, a joke there, a whisper somewhere else. They flocked around his stall, buying as he suggested; he played with the fringed shawl of an old woman who gaped at him coquettishly, showing toothless gums, he kissed his hand to a dark-eyed girl whose slim ankles showed beneath her petticoat.

And Mère smiled too, with her fair frizzed hair, her tiny ear-rings, the dimples at the corners of her mouth, her full breasts shaking. 'Get on with you,' she said, 'get on with you,' and she looked boldly at a young man whose cap was pulled on one side, who passed his tongue over his lips. As the morning passed the cries became more shrill, the clamour more deafening, and the smell of the produce pungent and strong. Folk did not linger so long over their choice, they bought hastily, scrappily, elbowed from their place by newcomers, their bags bulging open, their hands fumbling for the *sous* in their purses. Julius, lifted down from his barrel, played now round the legs of the stalls. He found clippings of cheese and put them in his mouth, he sniffed about like a little dog amongst the scraps, his eyes darting here and there, and already his sharp ears noted the passing of time as the prices fell, as the voice of Grandpère became hoarse and strained, as the smiles of Mère became more artificial, her hair escaping from its pins, and when she lifted her hands to arrange it, large patches of perspiration showed under her arms.

The child was cold now and tired, scarcely hungry because he had fed himself from scraps here and there, but the bustle and clatter were now too much for him, the scene was no longer fresh and exciting, it was stale and familiar, the very sight of the food itself unappetizing and high.

Grandpère and Mère, those shouting noisy Blançards, jarred upon his nerves, he crept to the back of the stall where Père was counting money, he whined pitifully, pulling at his knee, begging to be taken up. Then Père took him in his arms, first tying the *sous* carefully in a little bag with a string round it, and Julius was carried to the cart and laid to sleep on an old coat and a box for a pillow.

When he awakened *midi* would be striking, the deep boom echoing strange and hollow in the cold air, the sound of the bell taken up by other churches, and Julius would climb to the opening of the covered cart and look outside.

The last stream of buyers straggled away from the market across the Avenue, their shawls over their heads, their shoulders bent, scurrying over the cobbled stones like black beetles, and the people of the market were packing away the remains of their produce, unhinging the boards, unfolding the overlapping stalls.

A group of small boys in cloaks and *casquettes* came hurrying along, their cheeks glowing red, and Julius watched them as they slipped past him, chattering shrilly, a fat sinister priest bringing up the rear, his stomach protruding from his gown, his beady eyes darting to right and left.

Flakes of snow were falling from the sky, soft and white they melted on Julius's hands as he lifted them, and he held up his face too that they might linger for an instant on his cheek, wet and gentle, then vanishing to nowhere. The sky was full of snow, it fell from the heavy clouds like scraps of paper, strangely silent, covering the street and the remaining stalls, blocking the hitherto uninterrupted view of the Avenue stretching back to the bridge, and in the other direction widening and rising, to the distant gates of Paris.

Julius watched the snow fall, and listened to the deep tolling bell of a church; he saw the trail of little boys disappear with the priest down one of the streets branching from the Avenue, he heard the horse stamp impatiently on the cobbled stones, and another cart rumbled by. The market smell was still in his nostrils, he was no longer tired, but hungry.

'Mère,' he called from the cart. 'Mère, I want to go home.'

Soon the last basket was packed, the last box shut, and they climbed into the cart ready to return to Puteaux, Julius high in front beside Grandpère, forgetting his hunger, drumming his legs against the ledge in excitement, begging to hold the whip.

'Hué-dada, Hué-dada,' he shouted, and the horse plodded forward, the wheels moved, and they were being carried along the Avenue towards the bridge, the sight of the flowing Seine looming faintly through a mist of falling snow.

When Julius was older he was allowed to sell in the market. He was sharp, he knew how to tackle the customers.

His quick eyes detected the shadow of hesitation on the face of a passer-by, and he leaned forward, touching her arm. 'What's the use of going any farther, Madame? Don't you want value for your money?'

The woman smiled at the eager face of the boy, but she drew her shawl tight around her, shaking her head in doubt. 'It's too dear,' she said, 'I can't pay that price for butter.'

Julius shrugged his shoulders, turning from her in contempt.

'The stuff that is sold in the market cheaper than this is not butter at all, it is vomit. You are welcome to poison yourself.'

Again the woman hesitated, looked regretfully at the slab of rich yellow butter.

'Even a beggar would afford twenty centimes to nourish his children,' muttered Julius, and the woman fumbled in her purse, producing the coins. 'Here, all right – give me a pound then,' she said.

'Thank you, Madame, thank you,' and Julius was wrapping the slice in a piece of paper, forgetting her already, his eyes once more searching the faces of those who pressed around the stall. 'Come on, come on,' he called, 'is everybody asleep? Does nobody want to spend a *sou*?'

Grandpère was just behind him, coughing and choking.

'Oh! it's always the same now,' he grumbled; 'you can spare your voice, my poor boy, no one will put his hand in his pocket because of this stinking war.'

'Everyone must eat, the war makes no difference to stomachs,' said Mère impatiently, and she stood with her hands on her hips, red in the face because of the heat, and the dust and the flies.

There was no denying that business was bad. People were timid of spending, they bought small quantities at a time and then hoarded. It was all the fault of the louse-ridden Prussians.

19

The Progress of Julius

Nobody knew when the war was going to end or how or what it was all about. Things were little better under the Republic than they had been during the reign of the Emperor.

The only thing that mattered to the market folk was for prices at the Halles to touch normal again, the quality and quantity of produce to resume their usual standard, and above all for the purchaser to throw aside mistrust and open his purse once more with confidence.

'Let all governments go to the devil,' laughed Jean Blançard' 'it's their affair, isn't it? Nothing counts but that people must eat to live. Come on, messieurs, mesdames, come and empty your purses and fill your bellies. The good times are just ahead. Ah! Ha! you're laughing, my little lady with the scarlet petticoat – what are you laughing at? Don't you need good butter and cheese to make you round and plump? Come and see, then, I'll sell cheaper to you because of your smile. Well, what about it? That doesn't please you, eh? You don't want any cheese today. . . . But what do you want, my mignonne, my flower? Go to the *légumes* at the next stall, it's a kilo of carrots you'll need before you're satisfied.' He stood with his arms folded, his head thrown back, a colossal figure of self-confidence and scorn, his prices were the fairest and his produce the best in the whole market, if people were not pleased, let them go elsewhere and poison themselves, he did not care. They would always come back to him in the end. That little woman in the red petticoat, wasn't she smiling at him over her shoulder? 'So you've changed your mind, my beauty? It's cheese after all and not carrots – Here you are, then, half a pound and no more. Anything else today? Hoo! I know what you'd like me to show you. . . .'

She scuttled away, blushing and confused, and he shouted with laughter, winking a blue eye at his friend the butcher opposite. 'They're all the same, aren't they? I know them. What a trade, what a life! Come and see, messieurs, mesdames, come and see. Impossible to find anything better in the market. Well – haven't you hands – haven't you mouths?'

Julius looked up at his grandfather and smiled. What a figure he was, what a grand fellow! He over-topped the world, he made the other market folk seem dwarfed and pallid with his great strength and health, his vigorous personality. White-haired, blue-eyed, red-faced, was he really sixty-five and an old man? Père, in the corner of the stall, thin and drooping, he didn't exist beside him. Julius stuck out his chest and folded his arms. Wasn't he a Blançard too, even if he was only ten years old?

'Come on, come on. It costs nothing to throw an eye over the stall. But I can see you, monsieur, with your hungry glance at the crate of eggs, are you paralysed that you can't put your hand in your pocket? New-laid eggs, fifteen *sous* the dozen. . . . Yes, mademoiselle, this is the best quality butter in the whole of Paris. Am I a robber, am I a liar? Try it, mademoiselle, such butter is made for young women like yourself – it is fresh, it is clean, it has taste. . . . No, I'm not cheeky. I'm not a child – I tell you I know a thing or two. . . . You'll take a pound, then? Thank you, mademoiselle.' Julius threw back his head like his grandfather, he winked at the butcher's son. Oh! it was good to hear people laughing at him, it was fine to feel them slap his shoulder and tell him he was a young rascal.

'I'm a Blançard – I'm a Blançard.'

The smell of the market was good too, the sight of the stalls, the familiar cries. Cheese, leeks, carrots, sausages, liver, fat over-ripe plums – all of these mingled together, and a blue silk hand-kerchief, a coloured carpet, green glass beads jingling on a string, white dust of the cobbled stones, a cart rumbling by. A packet of straw blowing past in a litter of paper, somebody laughing, a large-breasted woman shaking her hips, a whiff of cigarette smoke borne on the wind, workmen in their blue overalls clattering by on clogs, smiling at a dark girl with gold ear-rings, blue sky, and the white clouds flying. 'I'm happy,' thought Julius. 'I'm happy,' and his hands closed over a pile of *sous*, round and small, chinking together, his own *sous* that belonged to him. 'Will it always be like this? Will there be other things? Shall I be old one day?'

He closed his eyes, the better to breathe, the better to smell – the better to feel the rough edges of his money.

'Which is best to handle,' he wondered, 'the chinking hard coins or the warm furry body of my cat? That is a very difficult question. Whom do I like best? What do I want most in the world? Why was I born at all?'

But the voice of Grandpère broke in upon him. 'Wake up, you slacker, you dreamer. Those who do not work cannot expect to eat, and those who do not eat will never grow tall. Don't you hope to be a man one day?'

So Julius must lean forward in the stall, his eyes sharp, his hands busy.

The days went past the same as they had always done, and then in a flash as it seemed to Julius there came a morning that for the first time in his life was different to all other mornings, a morning when Grandpère and Père came home from the Halles at seven o'clock, instead of going straight to the market, came clattering over the cobbled stones of the narrow street, the cart empty of produce. Mère, ready dressed, fastening the pin of her petticoat, thrust her head out of the window, Julius beside her.

'But what is it?' she called in amazement, 'what in the world are you doing here at this time?' Then she trailed off in the middle of her sentence, she saw Paul Lévy shrug his shoulders, indifferent and resigned, she saw Jean Blançard stare up at her with his big blue eyes bewildered like a child, his mouth open, his hands outstretched.

'They've turned us away,' he said, 'everywhere there are soldiers, nothing but soldiers. The Halles are guarded, nobody was allowed inside – soldiers with bayonets stood there. In Neuilly, in Courbevoie, in Boulogne – in all the villages the people are flying from the Prussians, leaving their homes. The soldiers could not tell us anything. All we know is that the barriers are guarded – every gate in Paris will be closed. Soon nobody will be allowed to go in or come out. There are soldiers, I tell you, soldiers everywhere. None knows what it is all about or how long it will last.' He broke off into a torrent of curses and abuse, curses against the Government, against the soldiers, against the people of Paris themselves.

'Can't they leave us in peace?' he shouted. 'What do they want to meddle with us for, what have we to do with their dirty bloody wars? How are we going to live? What is going to happen to us, to Julius?'

Mère still leant from her window, frowning, perplexed. She twisted her hands, looking from one face to the other.

'Still I don't understand,' she said, 'why all this fuss, all these precautions? The wife of the baker told me yesterday the Government were going to send the Prussians away. I don't understand.'

Then Julius watched Père climb down from the cart and walk towards the window, taking no notice of Grandpère, of the old man's fury and string of words, but he came to where Mère was leaning from the window and he put his hand on her shoulder.

'Don't be afraid,' he said. 'We must none of us be afraid – it can't do any good. The baker's wife told you wrong. Paris is being barricaded everywhere – and the Prussians are marching to Versailles.'

He spoke softly, slowly, never raising his voice, but Julius knew that these were words he should never forget, that would stay in his memory should he live, for ever and ever, words that sank deep into his boy's brain and remained like letters of ice – blocked and frozen. 'The Prussians are marching to Versailles.' And even as Père's voice was silenced, and they stared at one another, bewildered and lost, it seemed to Julius he could see the long line of the enemy coming towards Puteaux, he could see their spiked helmets, their grey uniforms, he could hear the slow tramp, tramp of their boots upon the cobbled streets, the gleaming steel of their bayonets striking the air. Already men and women were collecting at the street corners, on the doorsteps of houses, already folk ran to and fro in groups, calling excitedly, and a baby cried pitifully, his thin cry rising in the air.

Somewhere, away to the left, hidden by the towering fortress of Mont Valérien and the thick trees of Meudon, the enemy would be marching, their feet echoing hollow on the road; somewhere, beyond the hills, muffled and strange like distant thunder on a summer day, would come the low mutter and rumble of a cannon, and the siege of Paris would begin.

Every day more houses were deserted, more families fled from the villages into Paris. Always the line of carts crossing the bridge, the wheels rumbling on the cobbled stones.

'Yesterday the baker sent his wife and sons into Belleville to his cousin,' said Mère; 'he told me it is no longer safe to stay outside Paris.' 'Today the coal-merchant shut up his house,' said

Père; 'he has found accommodation for his family in Auteuil. Once inside the fortifications he will lose his fear.'

'The *blanchisseuse* at the corner of the street is packing up to-morrow,' said Julius, 'her son told me this morning. They are going to relations in Montmartre. They are leaving their dog behind to starve – who is going to feed it? Can I feed it, Grandpère?'

And in every one of their hearts rose the same unspoken question: 'And us? When are we leaving Puteaux? Where are we going?'

Jean Blançard watched the stream of villagers troop down towards the Seine, cross the bridge, march side by side, bundles over their shoulders, trailing children by the hand. 'Go on, you cowards, you poor crawling fools,' he shouted, 'go on and shut yourselves up behind the barriers of Paris. I was born in Puteaux, and my father was born in Puteaux, and not all the louse-ridden Prussians in the world will turn me from my own house and my own village.' He watched them, his arms folded, his cap on the back of his head, a cigarette hanging from his lips.

And the booming cannon of Mont Valérien would bark suddenly, a mutter and a rumble of thunder, and Grandpère would take his cigarette from his mouth and smile, jerking his thumb in their direction.

'D'you hear the fortress?' he said. 'They're ready up there; they'll send the vandals back to hell. We're ready, aren't we? Let 'em come – let 'em all come, every stinking Prussian mother's son.'

No one could make him move, he would stay in Puteaux until the very stones of the streets were blown up beneath his feet, and his blind obstinacy influenced his daughter, she would not leave her house and her belongings, she was a Blançard, she was not afraid.

'I have a gun,' said Grandpère, 'it belonged to my uncle who fought at Austerlitz. I can use it, can't I, if the Prussians come to Puteaux? They shan't take my house, not a stone – not a brick.'

And Julius helped him clean his gun, he soaked an old rag in oil and polished the barrel, but he was thinking: 'What about our money, will the Prussians take that? Oughtn't we to tie our *sous* up in bags and bury them in the ground?'

The daily journey to the Halles, the market in the Avenue de Neuilly, these were things that belonged to the past, and the

Blançards lived as best they could by selling country produce to the few folk left in Puteaux and the nearest villages. It was only October, and already food was scarce; careless of danger and a possible encounter with the Prussians, Jean Blançard would take his cart every morning and drive round the country roads to bargain with the peasants living in hovels on their own plot of ground, in search of a few overblown cabbages, potatoes run to seed, a dead horse perhaps to sell in portions, or an old sheep.

Julius set snares to catch birds, he fixed lines on the banks of the Seine below Puteaux in the hope of finding fish.

Soon it would not be a question of selling meat to feed others, but of finding meat to feed themselves.

Any day the Prussians might take it into their heads to descend upon Paris, and might not they march through Puteaux, down the wide, high road towards the Pont de Neuilly, burning and destroying as they went? 'Would they kill us?' asked Julius, 'we who are not even soldiers and cannot fight?' And nobody could tell him. Nobody knew how long they must wait, how soon the evening would come.

They drove in the cart along the high road, Grandpère and Julius, leaving Puteaux and Courbevoie behind them, striking out towards the village of Nanterre over the brow of the hill. The road was rough, the wheels of the cart kept sinking into deep ruts, and there were puddles everywhere, and mud, and from the pallid sky a wet sun shone into the puddles, reflecting a space of blue no longer than a man's hand, and a loose, straggling cloud.

'Ha! Ha! my beauty,' called Grandpère, cracking his whip, and the horse flicked his ears and sniffed at the air. It was cold, sharp autumnal weather. Julius blew upon his hands.

'In Nanterre we shall find meat,' said Grandpère, 'there is a fellow there who used to own a couple of strong mules. They will make excellent eating, and will fetch a good price in the fortress.'

'Perhaps he won't want to destroy them,' said Julius. 'Who would kill animals that have served well and worked hard?'

'It isn't a time for sentiment, my darling,' said Grandpère, 'when he sees my money he will slaughter everything he owns. I can bargain better than he. He is a peasant, he knows nothing. I shall sell the meat for treble the sum in Puteaux.'

25

The cart splashed through the puddles. The sun peered once more through the grey clouds, and shone upon the bare, white head of Grandpère. He smiled, cracking his whip, and sang – swaying from side to side in his seat:

> ' Bismarck, si tu continues,
> De tous tes Prussiens il n'en restera guère;
> Bismarck, si tu continues,
> De tous tes Prussiens il n'en restera plus.'

Grandpère loved the sun, the fresh morning and the crisp air.

'When this war is over we'll amuse ourselves, eh, my Julius? Soon you'll be a big boy, you'll go shares in the market. You're going to be heavy and strong, a real Blançard. Even though I'll be an old fellow when you grow tall, I'll show you things. We'll laugh, won't we? we'll trick the world.'

'Yes, Grandpère, my dear.'

'You won't forget me when I'm good-for-nothing. You'll come and tell me when you're angry, when you're happy, and when you want to run and shout, and when you want to go with women.'

'Yes.'

'It's mornings like this that are good, Julius. The sun and the cold air. Open your lungs, boy, and breathe. That father of yours is a queer fellow now. He sits with his thoughts and his music, he doesn't care for this. You must learn to live with your body, my little one, and laugh and sing, and fill yourself and take everything you want. But don't be a dreamer.'

'I don't know what I want, Grandpère.'

'No – not yet – how should you, you silly midget? But when you're a man – ah! I tell you, living is a great game. Don't let people do you in. You be the one to win, always, always.'

'Something for nothing – something for nothing,' sang Julius.

'Go on, laugh at me, you miserable chicken. One day you'll stretch yourself and wink an eye at the sky, and you'll do someone down for a hundred *sous*, and you'll pocket the money and walk out and have a woman. That's life, Julius – and you can tap your nose and say: "Ha! – Ha! – Grandpère Blançard, he knew me, he understood." '

'Shall I do that, shall I then?' laughed the boy. And Grandpère cracked his whip once more, and threw back his head.

> 'C'est là qu'est l'plan de Trochu,
> Plan, plan, plan, plan, plan,
> Mon Dieu! quel beau plan!
> C'est là qu'est l'plan de Trochu:
> Grâce à lui rien n'est perdu!'

'When you are sixty-five, will you have lived as fully as Jean Blançard? I wonder, my little son, with your dark eyes and your white Jew face, where will you be, what will you have done?'

'Give me the whip. Let me crack the whip too.'

Julius flicked the reins, the horse trotted fast along the high road, and Grandpère sat back with his arms folded, smoking his pipe.

When they came over the brow of the hill and turned to the left down the road to Nanterre they saw a little white cloud of dust far ahead, the road dust that is made by the hoofs of many horses, or the tramping of many feet. It was not the ordinary surface dust raised by a rumbling cart. There was a sound, too, a distant murmur – the movement of people blocked in a mass, foreign, queer. Grandpère flushed, his eyes narrowed, and he swore under his breath.

'What is it?' said Julius, but not waiting for an answer he gave the reins to Grandpère, and he knew.

Jean Blançard backed the cart and turned his horse round in the direction of Puteaux once more. 'If they have seen us,' he began, but he did not finish his sentence, he cracked his whip on the back of the horse and no longer in the air. The cart jolted over the ruts, flinging them both from side to side. The old horse galloped, his ears laid back. Julius kept looking back over his shoulder.

'They're coming, Grandpère,' he said.

The cloud of dust was drawing nearer, he could see soldiers on horseback, and the leader was shouting out something, waving his arm in the air.

Jean Blançard chuckled. 'Go on, my beauty, go on,' he cried, and he handed the reins to Julius. 'Drive straight, keep in the

27

middle of the road – don't look to the right or left.' The boy obeyed.

'What are you going to do?'

'I'm going to have a shot at them,' said Grandpère, and he turned in his seat and reached for the old gun in the back of the cart.

The sound of the clattering hoofs drew nearer, there was shouting behind them, the movement of men, and a voice calling loudly: 'Halte – Halte.'

'Drive, my darling, drive like the devil,' laughed Grandpère, and he raised his old musket to his shoulder and fired. The staggering report frightened the horse, caring nothing for the light hands of Julius on the reins he took the bit firmly between his teeth and bolted.

The cart rocked, pulled first one side then the other, by the terrified, maddened animal.

'Take no notice of me, little fool, keep in the middle of the road,' said Grandpère, and he lifted his musket and fired again.

'Got him – the stinking vandal, got him!' he shouted, and now there came the sound of another shot, from behind, from farther away, and the clattering hoofs coming nearer, nearer, and Julius looked at Grandpère, and saw blood coming from his eye, running down his cheek.

'You're hurt,' whimpered Julius, and he felt a cold shiver go through him and began to cry.

'Drive, you silly idiot – get home, get back to Puteaux,' said Grandpère, and there came another shot, and the blood ran all over his face splashing down on to his blouse. It was not Grandpère any more, it was a strange inhuman thing of torn flesh and streaming blood, it was someone who rose high in the cart and shook his fist in the air, who raised his old gun and fired again, who threw back his head and called in a voice of thunder: 'Go on – go on – try and split my guts, you louse-ridden Prussian bastards' – it was someone who flung his gun away, who fell upon his face into a ditch and died. And a little Jew boy white with horror clung to the reins of the maddened horse, thrown from side to side in the tottering, jolting cart, seeing nothing but the dust of the high road, the stones flying, the sudden rain falling from the sky and beating his eyes, washing the blood on his sleeve, hearing nothing but his own child's voice crying in the cold air: 'The Prussians are coming . . . the Prussians . . . the Prussians.'

Now Père was looking into his eyes, was whispering softly, and Mère was shaking his shoulder, her hair falling over her face, and she was calling to him: 'But where is Grandpère, tell us, where is Grandpère?' And he pushed them away from him, bewildered and frightened, pointing towards the high road but murmuring nonsense, inarticulate, running to a corner and snatching his little cat in his arms, stroking her, burying his face in the fur.

Why must they ask him questions? Why could not they leave him alone? He was tired, tired. . . . Mère gave him a crust of bread and he chewed it hungrily, crying softly to himself. Did not they understand that Grandpère was dead and the Prussians were coming? He could not tell them any more than this.

Mère was rolling a heap of things into a blanket, she gazed about her wildly, a strange, distracted figure, grasping at odds and ends of no value or use, a pair of slippers belonging to Grandpère, a frying-pan, a mat from the floor, the pillow from the bed.

'The Prussians are coming – the Prussians are coming –'

Père made a bundle of clothes, he found sticks, too, for fire-wood, and a small sack of potatoes. He piled all these things on top of one another, the cart was bulging, there would only be room now for themselves. Julius watched them from his corner, he knew now that they were going away from Puteaux because of the Prussians, that if they had gone before Grandpère would not be dead.

'Where are we going, Père?'

'We're crossing over the bridge to Paris.'

'But the gates are all shut.'

'They will let us in.'

'Where shall we live?'

'We will find somewhere.'

And Julius looked around the room he would not see again, the dirty, untidy floor, the table stained with wine, spilt long ago by Grandpère, an old pair of clogs on the hearth, the dull smouldering fire.

'When shall we come back?'

Nobody answered him, they were out in the street now surrounded by a little cluster of people, who also carried bundles, who also loaded their carts.

'The Prussians are coming – the Prussians are coming . . .'

The bedroom was not swept, the mattress lay turned on its side. Père came in and carried it away, lifting it into the cart. There was some dirty water in the basin. Would it never be emptied away? Would it stay there until the war was over? And the grey ashes in the grate, and the bowl of thin soup – cold and congealed – on the table?

'Why are you looking back, Julius? What do you see? There is no time . . .'

He didn't want to leave the house, he did not want to leave Puteaux. It was his home and his room, those dingy walls, that dirty floor, the creaking tumbled bed, the ticking clock, the queer familiar stuffy soup smell. He did not know anywhere else but this.

'But you cannot take the cat with you, you must leave her behind, she will find food,' said Mère, plucking at his arm, her large, frightened face close to his.

'No – no, my little Mimitte, my sweet. I will not leave her to the Prussians, they will hurt her.' He clasped the cat next to his heart, he beat his mother away with one hand.

'They won't touch her, you child, why should they harm an animal? Someone will take her and give her milk,' Mère scolded impatiently. There was no thought in the mind of anyone but to fly, to run.

'The Prussians are coming – the Prussians are coming.'

An old woman stroked the cat's head, she bent down to Julius.

'I am not going, I'm staying in Puteaux, little one. Give me your cat to look after, she will be happy with me. Don't cry, my poor little one.'

But Julius shook his head, he wiped his eyes on the sleeve of his coat.

'No,' he said, 'no, she is my own cat. No one will ever have her but me.'

Now they were climbing into the cart, the faces of people gaped up at them, white masks, shadowy and distorted, a girl with a handkerchief tied over her hair, an old man with a long beard.

They were driving away from Puteaux down the muddy, twisting street to the bridge, and somebody trudged beside them, a bundle over his shoulder, and somebody ran in front, hitting a donkey with a stick, a donkey laden with sacks and pillows.

From the fortress of Mont Valérien came the boom of the cannon, a low rumble of thunder. 'The Prussians are coming – the Prussians are coming . . .'

Somewhere on the high road to Nanterre Grandpère lay dead in a ditch.

They came to the Pont de Neuilly. They looked back over their shoulders, up the high road to the distant brow of the hill. No time – no time. On, on towards the deserted Avenue de Neuilly, the rattle of carts, the trudging of footsteps.

When they came to the other side of the bridge Julius pulled at Père's arm.

'Will my little cat starve in Paris?' he asked.

'I don't know,' said Père. 'I don't know who will take us in or where we shall go. Cats are never happy in strange places. You ought to have left her behind. She would have fed herself. Someone would take care of her.'

'No,' whispered Julius, 'no – never, never anyone but me. What is mine cannot belong to another person. Père, do you understand? Tell me you understand.'

He looked up at Père, his thin face white, his nose pinched, and he was shivering from the cold and the rain.

'Yes,' said Paul Lévy, 'I understand.'

He stopped the cart and Julius climbed down. People passed by, bending low under their packs, and another cart rattled over the cobbled stones, and another.

'Why do you wait? The Prussians are coming – the Prussians are coming –'

Julius picked a stone from the gutter and folded it in a handkerchief. He tied the handkerchief round the neck of the cat. The animal purred, arching her back, patting the boy's face with her paw. He buried his face in her fur and closed his eyes. Then he ran to the rail of the bridge and threw her over into the Seine.

Mère cried out in horror, clutching the side of the cart. 'Oh!

poor little Mimitte, poor little beast. How could you? You cruel hard-hearted child, someone would have fed her – someone would have taken care of her.'

Julius said nothing. He climbed up on the cart once more beside Père and he did not look back. The rain mingled with the tears on his face, they splashed down on his sleeve, they became part of the stain that was Grandpère's blood. Julius was indifferent, caring no more, heedless of the people who walked along the avenue, heedless of the murmur rising from them like the echo of a cry: 'The Prussians are coming – the Prussians are coming . . .'

He sat with blazing eyes in a white face, silent, proud, his small arms folded, a Lévy – a Jew.

And so they came to the Porte Maillot and the barriers of Paris.

Paul Lévy of Puteaux and his wife and son were refugees. They lodged in one room, on the seventh floor of an old house in the Rue des Petits Champs. Instinct had taken Paul Lévy to this quarter, close to the Halles. This warren of narrow streets was the only part known to him, a villager from Puteaux, a poor market salesman. And they were not alone in their comfortless garret. They must share it with an old woman and her son, Madame Tripet, toothless, half-witted, who mumbled to herself in a corner, and Jacques, a big, hulking brute of twenty-two, apprentice to a butcher, handsome in a coarse, bold way, his mass of red hair standing up on his head like a bush.

Mère and Jacques Tripet fought at once, she scolding in her shrill voice, protesting at the small space of the room, and he grinning contemptuously, letting forth a flood of meaningless jargon, sending her to the devil.

Père said nothing, he laid down the big mattress he had brought from their bed in Puteaux, he arranged it in one corner with the pillow, the blankets; he even fixed up a spare blanket, pinning it to the wall to serve as a screen.

The fireplace Mère must squabble over with half-witted Madame Tripet, they would have to eat in common, but at least there could be some small measure of privacy behind the blanket screen.

Firewood was scarce, Paul Lévy saw that they would have to

ration their sticks. Mère argued at once, hysterically, ready to hit her husband. 'My limbs are numb and chill, and the child too. Do you want us to freeze?' She shivered, glancing at the crack in the window. Somebody had covered it with a rag, but even so the draught whistled through, and when it rained, drips of water crept down the wall and spread in a pool on the floor.

Julius blew on his fingers and thumped his little body, hell – but it was cold in Paris, colder in these huddled, twisting streets than back in the country at Puteaux. He was hungry too, it seemed as though he was always hungry now. He longed for the rich good smell of the market, for Grandpère's face smiling at him, breaking off a piece of cheese. The room in the Rue des Petits Champs smelt of Madame Tripet's bedclothes, of Jacques Tripet's red hair, of his feet in the boots he never took off. Stuffy, high, unwashed – and yet all the time the cold air blew through the crack in the window.

'How long must we stay here, Père, how long? When can we go back?'

'I cannot tell you, my Julius. When the siege is over, when the war is finished. Nobody knows.'

Like almost every citizen, Paul Lévy enrolled in the Garde Nationale. He was put into a uniform, he drilled, he marched; he was stationed on the fortifications at different hours during the day and night; he received one franc fifty centimes a day for his services. He was seldom in the Rue des Petits Champs, he returned at odd hours, chilled and tired, flinging himself on the mattress with his uniform splashed with mud.

In the morning Mère wrapped herself in a shawl, stuffing her shoes with paper against the cold, and she took up her station in the queue outside the butcher's. Sometimes she waited there in the crowd two hours, sometimes three. Soldiers guarded the door of the shop. Snow fell on to the cobbled streets from the leaden sky, at her side a little girl crouched, the skin drawn tight over her bones, whimpering from the cold. At the end of the three hours, numbed and almost senseless, Mère received her portion of meat – thirty grammes of horse-flesh for each person – and she stumbled back to the room through the maze of little streets, the snowflakes brushing her face. Two members of the Garde Nationale whistled

The Progress of Julius

to her as she passed, they were lounging against a wall, yawning, drunk. The Garde Nationale were always drunk. What was the use of one franc fifty unless you spent it on liquor? Besides, there was nothing else to do but drink in a besieged city.

The Prussians would not attack – they waited on the hills.

'Mère, I'm hungry, let me have another piece, just a little piece.'

'No, my darling boy, there will be none left for tonight – tonight you will be hungry again.'

Jacques Tripet came in, reeling a little, smelling of spirits.

'Look here, why are you such a devil to me, Madame Lévy? I don't harm you, do I?'

'Oh! go on with you – I haven't the mood for silliness.'

'I bet you're a hot one, when you feel like it, eh? With those eyes and that body. Tell me, eh?'

'Maybe – go off, don't breathe at me and keep your hands to yourself, young fellow. When a woman's limbs are cold and her stomach is empty she does not want to be bothered with men.'

'You're a devil, you are, you're playing with me, you're putting me off. You shouldn't smile at me as you do. Listen, I know a fine way to warm those limbs – don't you want it?'

'No, you puppy, you fool. Leave me alone.'

Julius nibbled at his nails, his little belly empty.

'Mère, give me a *sou* – give me a *sou* to buy some bread.'

'I haven't any – you must wait till Père comes home.'

'Here, young fellow – here's a *sou* for you. Run and play, maybe you'll find something with your sharp eyes and nose, Jew-baby. Go on, leave your mother and me to talk.'

Julius went out in the streets. Most of his time was spent in the streets now, away from the cheerless room and the moans of the old woman in her corner, away from Jacques Tripet harping at Mère. He was beginning to know the quarter. He found his way through the maze of the Halles to the wider streets, and out on to the Place du Châtelet. Here a bridge crossed the Seine to the Île de la Cité. He wandered along the quays, his mind working hard, peering into the holes and crevices, feeling with his hand up the pipes that led from the sewers. In a scavenge heap on one of the quays he found the remains of a stale crust of bread. He stuffed this at the end of a sewer pipe and waited, a heavy stone in one

34

hand, crouching behind the pipe. In twenty minutes or so he saw the bright eyes of a rat peering from the edge of the pipe. The rat hesitated a moment, sniffing the air, and began to nibble the crust. Julius raised his hand slowly, then hurled the stone, crushing the head of the rat. When he lifted the stone he saw that the creature was dead. Julius smiled, a queer, pinched smile in his thin face, and he rubbed his hands together, gloating, wishing that Grand-père was not rotting in a ditch but was standing by his side, laughing at him.

'Something for nothing,' said Julius, 'something for nothing.'

By the end of the afternoon he had caught six rats in this way. It was getting dark, and a fog was rising over the Seine. The houses loomed drab and gloomy through the mist, the streets ill-lit. People with their heads low hurried home to their cold rooms. There were no shops open, even the churches were closed. The streets were bare of *fiacres* and carriages, the horses had been killed for food. Only one or two omnibuses plodded their customary route, half empty, along the dark silent streets.

Julius swung his rats by the tails, beating his feet on the pavement to keep warm, humming a little tune to himself. He walked down the long Rue St Antoine to the Place de la Bastille. He knew his quarter – he knew the poverty-stricken queues of starving work-people who would be grouped there, waiting outside the butcher's for their thirty grammes of horse-flesh. They would be tired, frozen, their bellies aching for food.

He pushed his way amongst them, holding up his rats for all to see.

'Forty *sous* a rat, Messieurs, Mesdames, forty *sous* a rat.'

On Christmas Day old Madame Tripet died. She had been lingering for over a fortnight, suffering from dysentery brought on by starvation and the cold. No one was sorry to see her taken away. Her groans had been too irritating, the dirt and the smell she caused had become unbearable. Jacques Tripet bought a wooden coffin for his mother, but the thought of burning the wood for fire proved too strong for him, and the old woman was buried in the common ditch.

The room could be heated at last. The Lévys and Jacques

Tripet spread out their hands to the blaze and sighed for sheer luxury, the incredible pleasure of self-indulgence. Even Père drank wine that first evening, wine supplied by the bereaved son, and Julius wondered to see the colour rise in his pale cheeks, Père, thin as a corpse himself, in his uniform that hung on his bones. He played upon his flute, his eyes closed, his black hair falling over his face, and as the sound of his music fled and was lost in the air he smiled to himself.

Mère also closed her eyes, she was drowsy from the wine. She breathed heavily, her sensual mouth half open, and she leant against the shoulder of Jacques Tripet. They were friends now. People could not be enemies for long living in one room. Jacques Tripet listened to her breathing, his green eyes hot and silly, and he ran his hand up her leg under her petticoats. Julius thought him a fool, ugly with his red hair.

Julius yawned, stretched his arms above his head. He went close to Mère, and curled himself up against her, glad of her warm body, pillowing his head on her lap. She smiled in her sleep and sighed. Jacques Tripet stroked her gently, secretly, watching Paul Lévy out of the tail of his eye, and Père slept with his face in his hands, never moving, scarcely breathing, lost in his secret city.

The days dragged by, endless and wretched, the January mornings were bitter cold, and to stand in a queue for rationed meat became physical torture.

Still the guns rumbled, and the shells fell on defenceless citizens, still the pathetic efforts of the imprisoned troops to pass the Prussian batteries continued, always in vain – back they came wounded, bleeding, faith and courage gone from them. The strictly rationed food was practically uneatable, nor would the tough horse-flesh, the black bread, nor even the rats last much longer.

It was the beginning of the end. The surrender of Paris, inevitable, fatal, loomed into the minds of the people. On the fortifications of Auteuil, Paul Lévy stood on sentry duty, his hands clasping his bayonet, his head bent low. He had not slept for twenty-four hours. He had no other thought in his brain, no other desire in his body, but to lie down, anywhere, in a ditch and sleep. His feet were like two solid lumps of ice, frozen in his leaking boots, he had lost the feel of them and the feel of his fingers, blue knobbly bones sticking out from his hands. Paul Lévy was no longer a magician who breathed music, who dreamed dreams, he was a senseless thing of no will, who could not even raise his head to watch shells whistle through the air from the Prussian batteries. He wanted to sleep, he wanted the warm body of his wife next to him, her arms to cradle him, her breast to pillow him. He wanted to lose himself, he wanted to sleep.

In the room in the Rue des Petits Champs, Louise Blançard was preparing supper. She had stood for four hours outside the butcher's and when her turn had come the doors were shut in her face and a soldier, his face a wooden mask, told her the rations were finished for the day.

'But we have nothing in the house,' she pleaded, clutching his arm, 'what are we going to eat? My little boy is hungry.'

'I'm sorry,' said the soldier, pushing her away, 'it's not my fault, is it?'

She climbed the seven flights to the cold room, her shawl over her head. There was no fire now, and a trickle of water ran down the wall by the window. One flickering candle was stuck in a bottle.

Jacques Tripet knelt by the fireplace. He had three sticks of green wood which he was trying to light.

'I took them off a peasant who had been scavenging outside the gates,' he said, 'they are damp, they will not give much warmth. Have you any food?'

'The butcher's were shut,' she told him, 'we shall have to make wine soup. We must have something inside us.'

Julius looked up from his corner. His skin was drawn tight over his bones. 'I don't like wine soup,' he said fretfully, 'it gives me a pain. I always have a pain now.'

'There is nothing else,' said Mère, 'you must bear with it. Wine soup is good, it puts warmth into you.'

The boy began to cry, the tears slowly rolled down his cheeks. He brushed them away so that no one should see. He was ashamed to cry. He did not know it was weakness. He stuffed his fingers in his mouth. The nails tasted good.

'You will feel better when you have had some wine soup,' said Mère.

Jacques Tripet produced a flame from the green sticks. Mère put the saucepan on top of them, and began to stir slowly, a soft watery mixture.

Julius could not manage more than half a bowl. It made his head muzzy and gave him a pain in his belly.

'When Grandpère used to give me wine I felt fine,' he complained. 'I don't see why this soup should disagree with me.'

'It's because you have nothing solid inside you,' laughed Jacques Tripet, 'it goes to your head at once. That's why it's good – it makes you forget you are hungry.'

He and Mère had two bowls and could have wished for more. They smiled at each other, Jacques Tripet kept laughing for no reason. He breathed heavily as though he were hot; he opened his blouse.

'You know what I want, don't you?' he said to Mère, 'and you want it too. I can tell, don't try and put me off.'

Mère made a face at him.

'What if I do?' she said. 'You're only a big bumping boy.'

He shook his finger at her, smiling foolishly. 'You didn't say that last time, did you?' he said, 'you told me a different story. You were pleased enough, I know.'

'Shut your silly mouth,' she said.

Julius rubbed his hand on his stomach.

'Go outside in the street. The air will do you good,' said Mère.

Julius went out of the room. When he came on to the landing he began to cry again, softly to himself. He could not help it. It was that beastly wine soup. After a little while he felt better, but his head still ached. The air was bitterly cold. He thought perhaps if he walked fast his headache would pass away. He found his way down through the maze of streets, scarcely looking where he went. Hoo! But it was cold. He stamped on his feet and bit his fingers. He had walked some way and the moving had not warmed him at all. He would like to be inside again. He found himself in a square surrounded by cloisters. There was comparative shelter here, the sleet did not blow in his face. Somebody was knocking at the door of one of the houses. After a moment the door opened and the person went inside. Later one or two other people came to the door and knocked and were also admitted. There was an old man with a white beard, there was another man, and then another. A woman came carrying a child. Julius was puzzled.

'Can they all live there?' he wondered. Perhaps food was being given away free. He went and knocked on the door. A face peered at him through a little grille. The face of a man whose dark eyes stared from a white face, whose black beard came to his chest. The eyes smiled at him, and the door opened. Julius found himself in a stone corridor, looking up at the bearded man. He wore a queer-shaped cap on his head.

'The service is just beginning,' said the man, 'push open that further door into the Temple.'

Julius obeyed, curious, wondering what it was all about. When he went through the further door he saw that he had come into a church. At least, the first impression was that of a church, but in a few moments he realized that it was quite different, it was more friendly, more intimate, it was like a meeting place for people who knew one another.

There were rows of pews the same as in church, and here men were standing or sitting, shaking hands with each other, smiling, talking in low tones. There was something about their faces that was curiously familiar to Julius, it was as though he knew them all, as though he had met them long ago, and they smiled at him too and they understood. At first he thought there were no women but when he looked about him he could see some sitting in separate pews, like creatures apart.

He smiled to himself, it was just, it was right. Instinctively he approved of this. Creatures apart.

He leant against the pew, trying to catch snatches of conversation. The men were speaking a language that was not French, and this too was strangely familiar to him, words he knew and understood, that were part of him, that were connected in some way with his life.

It was peaceful here and simple. There were no painted figures of saints, no crucifixes, no decoration. The walls were plain, the roof rose in a high dome, and two galleries stretched one above the other round the building. Instead of an altar there were high black gates, and in front of them stood a golden candlestick, bearing seven candles.

'All of this has happened to me before,' thought Julius, and he felt happy, queer. A man bent down to him and gave him a book of prayer. Julius looked at the letters, he saw words that were known to him, *Yöschev Besseïsser, Adonoï Mo-Odom. Alenou, Kadisch,* he saw the word *Israélite*.

Then he knew, then he understood. It was as though something warm took hold of his heart, clasped him softly, loved him, murmured to him. He was amongst his own people. They saw with his eyes, they spoke with his voice; this was his temple, those were his candles.

They were poor, ill-clad, ill-fed, their temple was tucked away in the heart of the city, but they came there to be together because they all belonged to one another. Their minds were alike, they shared the same longings, their blood was too strong for them – they were bound hand and heart, they would never break away.

That was the Rabbin who bowed before the golden candlestick, who chanted in his soft sweet voice. He turned to the people, and lifted up his voice, he cried to them, he whispered, he echoed the prayer in their heart. It was not the Rabbin only, young, pale-faced, who stood there, it was Paul Lévy, it was Julius, it was child and boy and man, it was Père's mind in Père's body, it was Julius's eyes in Julius's face. And the psalm he chanted was Père's music, the song that rose and whispered and lost itself in the air, the voice cried out like the music had cried, it pleaded and wept, it sorrowed and rejoiced in his sorrow, it quivered immeasurably high as a bird hovers, beating his wings to escape, it travelled away, beyond the gold sun, flinging itself against the stars, exquisite, trembling, a song of beauty and pain, of suffering and joy and distress, the cry of one who searches the sky, who holds out his hands to the clouds.

Julius sat huddled in the pew, his chin propped on his hands, and the chanting was food to him, was eating and drinking, was peace and consolation, sleep and forgetting.

The young Rabbin was himself, the seven candles were the symbols of his song and the iron gates were the gates of the secret city.

Julius was lost in a dream, he was nothing, he was no one, nor any longer a little starving boy whose bones showed through his clothes. He had no more tangibility than a measure of music and the tremor of a song; he was as abstract as the sound of wings in the air, of a running stream, of the wind in the trees. He would never be touched, he was the flight of a bird, the shadow on a flower; he was the river-bed and the desert sand and the snow upon the mountains.

When the Rabbin ceased from chanting it was as though Julius could feel his body falling through space, hurtling through the air, striking once more the cold hard ground. The people stood up in the pews shaking hands with one another, the Rabbin leant over the rail and talked to them, the iron gates were closed. Julius had come back into the world again, he was a poor, hungry boy in a besieged capital. Everyone was leaving the Temple. He followed the rest of them, looking over his shoulder for the last time at the seven candles before the gates. Then he was in the cloisters once more and the heavy door banged behind him.

The sky was clear, the grey sleet was not falling, but the night was cold.

'When I grow up I will be a Rabbin, too,' thought Julius, 'and I shall lose myself in the singing like he did. I shall make music and dream dreams in front of the golden candlestick.'

As he walked home he wondered why the air was so silent and the streets so still, and he realized that the rumble of the guns that had continued now incessantly for a whole month had ceased at last.

'Perhaps the Prussians have used up all their shells,' he thought; 'perhaps they are tired of firing and are going back to their own country. Anyway, none of this matters to me. I am going to be a Rabbin. I am going to make music.'

He turned down into the Rue des Petits Champs, his hands deep in his pockets, his head poking forward.

'I shall go back often to the Temple,' he said to himself, 'I will learn Hebrew properly with the young Rabbin, and I shall never go to Mass again.'

A smile of satisfaction came over his thin little face. 'Besides,' he reflected, 'there was no collection that means there is nothing to pay . . .'

He turned into the house in the Rue des Petits Champs and began to climb the staircase. He wanted so much to tell Père about the young Rabbin and the visit to the Temple. He did not know how he was going to put into words all the things he had felt and seen and already he was making up little sentences in his mind – 'You do understand, don't you, Père? You know how I felt when I saw the seven candles and the writing in the book of prayer? His voice was your voice when you make music, it cried in the air and was sorry and was lost. You understand, don't you, don't you? I'll never be a glutton again – I'll never be a glutton again!' – The voice was still in his ears and the golden candlestick before him. Père and Julius were bound to one another, other people did not matter at all. The singing in the Temple had taken away his headache and his bellyache, he was not tired any more or sick from the wine soup, he wanted to run to Père and tell him he was happy.

When he tried to open the door of the room he saw that it was locked. He rattled and shook at it and still it did not open. He began to kick the panel.

'Be quiet,' called Mère, 'I am resting, I am not very well. Run and play a little longer and watch for Père coming home.'

'I'm cold, Mère,' cried Julius. 'It's dark and horrid out in the streets. I want to come in and warm myself.'

'Don't plague me,' she scolded back, 'after waiting nearly four hours to get you food can't I rest one moment? Run away and meet Père, you can't come in just yet to worry me with your clatter and noise.'

Julius slowly let go the handle of the door. Mère was unkind, she did not care if his fingers were blue with the cold and he could no longer feel his toes. He did not see why he should lie in the street just because Mère was tired. He would be very quiet, he would sit in a corner and dream about the Temple. Why did Mère have to rest so early in the evening? He did not see. Perhaps Père would be home soon. He pushed open the window on the landing and leant out to watch the passers-by in the street. It was dark, though, and difficult to see. He balanced himself on the sill and drummed his feet against the ledge. What was the young Rabbin doing now, he wondered. *Yöschev Besseïsser*. Julius would never forget him. Who was that moving in the room? It was Mère murmuring something, it was Jacques Tripet talking in a low voice. Well – that really was not fair, that really was unkind, it was too much. Mère would not allow Julius to be in the room while she rested, but she did not mind that fool Jacques Tripet. Julius slipped down from the window-sill. The candlelight flickered from the grating in the wall of the room. Julius had an idea. He would climb up the ladder that led to the roof and if he swung himself against the wall and held on to the ladder with one hand, he would be able to peer through the grating and shout to Mère how unkind she was. Perhaps she would let him come in then. He climbed up the ladder and clinging to the ledge below the grating and hoisting himself up into position with his elbow, he managed to catch a glimpse of the room. He gazed below him in astonishment. Why, Mère was lying on the mattress with Jacques Tripet, she was not resting at all. She should not do that, it was Père's thing, it had nothing to do with Jacques Tripet. It was horrible of Mère. She must know it was wrong of her, otherwise she would never have locked the door. She was afraid Julius would come in and see, and she would have been ashamed. She was beastly. He hated her. He hated to see her with Jacques Tripet. He wanted to break through into the room and beat her, and beat her. She deserved to be beaten, she deserved to be whipped. To see her lying there with Jacques Tripet made him feel hot and furious for Père. He shouted to them through the grating: 'I can see you – I can see you. You weren't resting at all, you told me a lie. I'm going to tell Père and he will beat you.'

They stared up at him in terror. Jacques Tripet leapt away from Mère and she tried to cover herself with the blanket.

'I see you, I see you – you can't pretend to me,' shouted Julius. He jumped down from the grating, his heart nearly bursting he threw open the window of the passage and leant out, peering down into the street. Yes – there was Père two steps away from the door. He could see his tall figure in the dim lamplight, drooping, weary, dragging one foot after the other. He could scarcely walk, he was so tired. Poor Père, how angry he was going to be. Julius trembled with rage, he leant far out of the window and called down into the street.

'Père, Père,' he shouted. 'Come up at once, run, quickly, quickly. Mère is lying with Jacques Tripet on the mattress.'

He saw Père lift his head, he saw the white face gaze up at him, bewildered, not understanding.

'Be quick, be quick,' Julius screamed, kicking his legs in a fever of impatience, 'they are lying together on the mattress. I've seen them through the grating.'

A hand was laid on his hair, pulling him back from the window. It was Jacques Tripet, his face red and podgy.

'Be quiet, you little fool, be quiet, can't you?' he whispered, shaking him backwards and forwards like a rat. 'I'll give you a hundred *sous*. I'll give you anything . . .' Then he dropped Julius, he turned in alarm and peered over the banisters. There was a sound of feet, running, running, there were footsteps climbing the stairs, someone was shaking the rail of the banister.

'It's Père,' yelled Julius, 'it's Père. I've told him I saw you and Mère. He's going to beat you.'

Jacques Tripet crouched against the corner of the wall. There was not any colour in his face now. He looked queer. Père came into view at the foot of the staircase. His uniform was streaked with mud and rain, wherever he trod on the stairs he left splashes of dirt. There was sweat pouring down his face. There was nothing to see in his face but the sweat and his blazing eyes. He pushed past Jacques Tripet, he did not look at him at all. He went straight into the room and Julius followed him. Then he locked the door. Julius heard Jacques Tripet give a funny sort of sob, he heard him clatter down the stairs as though he were afraid, as though he were going to run through the streets and lose himself. Mère was bending over the mattress, she was doing something to the blanket, pulling it straight. Her hair was untidy and her face blotched. She looked like Grandpère used to look when he had been drinking.

'She can't pretend,' said Julius, clutching at his father's hand; 'she was lying there with him. I know, I saw.'

Père pushed him away. He went over to Mère without a word and took hold of her. She held out her hands to defend herself, she retreated backwards to the wall.

'No,' she called out. 'No . . . No . . .'

Père put his hands round her throat, he bent her underneath

him, and she curved strangely, her legs twisting. Père's hands tightened round her throat, her face grew purple, she choked and coughed, and her eyes became big and startled.

'Go on, go on,' shouted Julius, 'it serves her right, it serves her right. Go on, hurt her, squeeze her.'

Père could swing Mère backwards and forwards now as though she were a dummy thing. Her shoes fell off and her heels drummed on the floor. She choked hideously, the noise she made was terrible. With her bent body and her popping eyes she looked ugly.

'Go on, go on,' shouted Julius.

Then Père dropped her suddenly, she fell heavily on to the floor her legs spread open. Her tongue came out of her mouth and her face was black. She lay very still. Her lips were parted over her teeth. She looked like a rabbit that Grandpère had strangled once in the fields outside Puteaux. Père sat down in a chair, he was breathing heavily. He wiped the sweat from his forehead. Julius touched Mère with his foot. She did not move.

'I shouldn't be surprised if you've killed her,' he said.

Père did not say a word. He got up from his chair after a while and poured some water into a basin. Then he dipped his face inside, he dipped his whole head. Some of the water ran down his neck and underneath his tunic.

'I expect you feel warm,' said Julius.

Père wiped the water away from his face with a towel. He poured some of it into a glass and drank it as though he were very thirsty. Then he stood and looked down at Mère on the floor.

'Is she dead?' asked Julius.

'Yes,' said Père.

Julius wondered what he should say. It really served Mère right. She deserved to die after going with Jacques Tripet. He could understand why Père had killed her. He didn't want his thing to be spoilt. He would not allow anyone else to have it.

Julius knew it had hurt Père very much to kill her, but there had been nothing else to do. He would be very, very unhappy, but it was the only way out. Julius knew – Julius understood. He had thrown his cat into the Seine so that nobody else ever in the world would be able to feed her and stroke her little body. Père had killed Mère for the same reason.

'It's really a good thing she is dead, don't you think?' said Julius.

'Yes,' said Père.

'I mean, you couldn't have gone with her again, could you?'

'No.'

'Her face looks awful, shall I cover it up?'

'Yes – put the blanket over her.'

Julius took the blanket from the mattress and arranged it neatly over Mère's body. 'It's still a bit early for me to feel sorry she is dead,' he thought. 'I haven't given up being angry with her yet.'

Père looked very weary and strange. His face was still the colour of a sheet. Julius felt old and grown up, he wanted to look after Père.

'I expect this business has made you tired,' he said; 'why don't you lie down on the mattress and go to sleep? Sleep will do you good. After I had thrown my little Mimitte into the Seine I was glad to lie down that evening and go to sleep.'

'I'm all right,' said Père. He sat down again, he seemed queer. Julius went and leant against his knee.

'You're bound to feel sad at first –' he said. 'I suffered so much when I killed my Mimitte I felt I could not talk to anybody. Even now I cry sometimes at night when I go to bed. I miss stroking her warm fur and feeling her paws on my face. I expect you will miss going with Mère. But it can't be helped, can it? It is better for her to be dead than for other people to have her.'

He leant his cheek against Père's face.

'I shall miss her badly, too,' he said. 'When I've stopped being angry, I shall cry.'

Père hugged him tightly, so tightly he could scarcely breathe. He kissed him too, on his eyes and his mouth.

'You are my own little thing, aren't you?' he said.

'Yes,' said Julius. He longed to tell Père about the Temple and the young Rabbin, but perhaps it was scarcely a good moment. He would wait.

'It's not very cheerful having Mère lie there in the middle of the room, is it?' he said 'It's going to be cold too, sleeping tonight without the blanket.'

Père got up from his chair and began to button up his tunic.

'We shan't be staying tonight,' he said 'we're going from here at once. You had better put a warm scarf under your coat and make a bundle of your clothes.'

'Where are we going, then?'

'I don't know – anywhere – it doesn't matter. We can't stay here.'

'Could we go home to Puteaux?'

'No.'

'Why not, Père? I'm not a coward. I'm not afraid of the Prussians if they are camping there. They don't seem to fire any guns tonight.'

'There's going to be an armistice.'

'How do you know?'

'There are notices on the walls. Tomorrow it will be official. Paris has surrendered.'

'Then the siege is over and the Prussians have won?'

'Yes, little one.'

'Why can't we go home, then?'

'Because Puteaux isn't our home, it belonged to Grandpère and Mère. We have not got a home, you and I. Paris is not our city, France is not our country. We are Lévys, we are Jews.'

Julius was silent. There was no argument to this. He did as Père had told him and began to pack his clothes into a bundle. He was glad to leave the Rue des Petits Champs.

'I suppose someone will bury Mère,' he said. 'Jacques Tripet is going to get a fright when he comes in, anyway. I shouldn't care to be him, would you?'

Père did not answer. He was changing from his uniform of the Garde Nationale into his old suit. It was odd to see him dressed like that again.

'Nobody would recognize you,' laughed Julius; 'look how thin you've got since the siege. Your clothes scarcely fit you at all.'

Père opened the window and looked out. Then he blew the candle.

'All quiet,' he said, 'there is nobody about.'

Père unlocked the door and listened. No sound came from the passage.

'Come on, are you ready?' said Père. Julius wondered if he had any money in his pockets.

'Mère had a purse tied round her waist, shall we take it?' he said.

'No,' answered Père, 'don't bother about that. I have money enough for the moment.' He began to walk down the stairs, his boots creaking.

Julius hesitated. It seemed a pity to think of the purse tied round Mère's waist when she was not going to use it any more. He knelt down by her body and began to fumble under the blanket. Good – there was the purse. It seemed full too. The coins jingled nicely. Mère was warm to touch. He pulled aside her dress and kissed her breast. He had always loved the smell of her skin. The only way to prevent himself from crying was to think of her lying on the mattress with Jacques Tripet. He kissed her once again, and then pulled the blanket over her. He jingled the money next his ear.

'After all,' he thought, 'there must be at least ten francs here, maybe more. In a way it's something for nothing.' He ran down the stairs after Père, his hand in one pocket clutching on to the purse.

That night the Lévys slept in a side chapel of the church of Saint-Sulpice. Julius broke off the ends of altar candles and hid them in his pocket with the purse. One never knew. He rattled a box that was nailed to the wall, a box that was marked: 'For the Poor', with a cross beneath it. But it was locked. He was not able to take the money. They had to leave early for fear some priest should come and ask them their business.

Near a week ago Julius had pocketed three francs after selling pieces of shell as souvenirs of the siege here. 'It's a pity the Prussians are not firing today,' said Julius, 'we might have done business and made profit.'

But the guns were silent, the last Prussian shell had fallen. In the streets little groups of people formed, red-eyed, silent, their heads low as though some calamity had befallen them.

Paul Lévy pushed his way amongst them, and side by side he and Julius read the proclamation on the wall signed by all the members of the Government and dated Paris, the twenty-eighth

of January, 1871. It was the terms of the armistice and the surrender of Paris, the siege had lasted four months and twelve days.
The crowd read it in silence, no voices were raised in hostility or
defiance, nor was there a single expression of agreement or content. They stared at the printed letters, dumb and unresponsive,
it was as though all the suffering and the horror and the anguish
of what had been and which would always remain deep in their
hearts, could not be put into words, not now, nor ever. There was
a man in a blue blouse and a cap on the back of his head who
looked like Jean Blançard. He stood with his arms folded, his face
hard as a stone. He did not seem to be reading at all, he stared in
front of him, his eyes dry and cold. When he spoke his voice was
like one coming from far away.

'It's over,' he said.

Nobody spoke in answer. From the back of the little group a
woman sobbed and then was silent, putting her shawl over her
mouth. Then the crowd broke up and dispersed. They melted
away as though they had never been. Julius looked up at Père,
and he too seemed dumb like the rest of them, dazed and queer, he
stared at the letters like a sleeping man. Julius tugged at his hand.

'It's over,' said Père.

He turned on his heel, and began to walk up the street in any
direction.

'Where are we going?' asked Julius. But Père did not answer
him at all. And the day they passed was muddled and confused,
one moment here, one moment there, and this was followed by
another day and another day. At night they slept in churches. In
the daytime Père would leave Julius, and he himself would try to
find out whether people were free now to leave Paris or whether
they must wait for the peace. To leave Paris it was necessary to
obtain a pass from the Préfecture de Police, there were various
formalities that must be gone through. Technically every citizen
was a prisoner of war. By making such a demand Paul Lévy
would be discovered. He did not know what to do. He was a
dreamer, unpractical, inexperienced, without initiative, all he
knew was that he must get away from Paris and even France if
possible. The idea was fixed in his head. It stood before him like
a light that he could not grasp.

He and his son sat huddled together in the entrance of a church. Père looked ill, his dark hair was matted, for three days he had not been able to wash.

'We must get away,' he kept repeating, 'we must get away.'

He sat with bent head, his white hands drooping over his knee.

Julius was turning his cap inside out, looking for bugs. He caught one and squeezed it between his finger and thumb.

'Can't we find a train?' he asked, 'there must be trains leaving the stations now that the siege is over. The soldiers are going home to the provinces.'

'One must have a pass,' said Père. 'They will never let us enter the station. And even once a train is in motion it is obliged to stop now and again, and the Prussians search the carriages. Again, I am not sure of the price of a ticket. It will cost dear to travel far.'

'Where do we want to go, Père?'

'South,' said Paul Lévy, and he made a vague gesture with his hands.

Julius knew that in the south living was plentiful and the sun always shone.

'It is a pity to waste money on a ticket,' he said, 'we ought to be able to go south for nothing.'

Père did not know how this could be managed.

'No one can travel without a ticket,' he said, shaking his head. He seemed to have lost hope. He looked shrunken and desolate. He was changed from the Père who had shaken Mère like a rat and killed her. There were hollows in his cheeks and his eyes were sunken. It seemed to Julius that Père was only splendid by moments, and at other times he was a poor creature. He understood why Grandpère had despised him. 'I am a Blançard as well as a Lévy,' thought Julius, and he wondered how they would be able to get away from Paris by train without anyone knowing and without paying a *sou*.

It was Julius who nosed his way into the Gare d'Orléans and discovered the departure of a goods train for Dijon was due at two o'clock on Thursday morning. An official was talking to a soldier, and the soldier turned to another official, and nobody bothered to notice a little Jew boy biting his nails.

'There are still blocks everywhere,' said one of them, 'the Prussians are holding up all traffic. What time the train will arrive and on what day, no one can tell. We must hope for the best.'

Julius strolled away, his hands in his pockets. 'At two o'clock it will be dark,' he was thinking, 'and no one would be foolish enough to search every wagon that leaves a station. Besides, people do not travel in goods trains.'

He went and told his father what he had heard. 'We shall be discovered and arrested, little love,' said Père. 'It is one chance in a million.'

'The first time I caught a rat during the siege I had only a crumb of bread and a heavy stone; that was a chance in a million too,' said Julius.

At half past one on Thursday morning they crouched in the shadow of a deserted signal-box amongst a mass of intricate lines, just outside the Gare d'Orléans. It was dark, the lights of the station loomed dimly in the distance. There were trucks blocked everywhere. It was impossible to distinguish letters on any of them. Some might be moving that night, others might be shunted there to remain for weeks. Paul Lévy felt his way along the lines in the direction of the station, Julius creeping at his heels like a dog. There was something a little farther on that might be the train destined for Dijon, a line of trucks but no engine. Père dared not strike a match for fear he should be seen. He looked up and down the line, there were no other trucks to be seen on the same line. These must be the Dijon trucks. Suddenly there came a blast of a whistle from the station, and the shriek of steam from a funnel. An engine was coming towards them. Père hoisted Julius on to his shoulder and threw him into the nearest truck, following himself, climbing hand over hand. Julius fell on to his face amongst a heap of stones. They lay side by side, listening for the approach of the engine. In a few minutes it came, striking the last of the line of trucks with a rude jolt. A voice called out from somewhere: 'We shan't be leaving until half past two, there is a delay.' And another voice answered: 'Who is certain whether we go at all? Anyway, we shall be stopped at Châtillon by the Prussians.'

The voices grumbled, they became fainter, and then moved away up the line.

'Lie still,' whispered Père. 'At any rate, we are due to leave some time. We must stay where we are.'

They tried to make a position of comfort amongst the stones, but it was impossible. They were not hard bricks, they were the ordinary small road stones, rough-edged and multitudinous. The minutes passed, interminable, and suddenly there was a grunt and a jolt, a voice called from somewhere, and the trucks began to move.

They could only have gone three hundred yards or so when the train stopped. Another whistle blew and then there was silence. The delay lasted for twenty minutes.

'What's happened?' whispered Julius. Père did not answer, it was useless. How should he know what had happened? And the trucks jolted and clanked, and then moved on again. They were going slowly, making no pace at all. Every few minutes they would stop, the line being blocked. A thin drizzle began to fall and it was cold. Julius was glad of his shawl, but even so the rain trickled down his neck. They were not yet past the Prussian lines. After over two hours of jolting and shunting they came to a stop once more, and here there must have been a station, for they could see lights reflected, and there was much noise and movement.

Men were walking along the line, and somebody began to curse in a shrill voice.

'I tell you we have the necessary authority,' shouted the voice. 'This train goes through to Dijon by way of Orléans. They would not let us go by the shorter route, it is not our fault.' The answer was short, authoritative, spoken in a guttural voice. 'Nix, Nix – *pas* passer.'

Père stretched his hand and touched Julius on the shoulder. 'The Prussian lines,' he whispered, 'we must be at Châtillon.'

'What was he saying?'

'He is not going to let us pass.'

Julius's heart began to throb, and a lump rose in his throat. Would they be sent back to Paris again, would it all have to be started once more? Paris, the Gare d'Orléans, the bare church of Saint-Sulpice, and Père being taken away to prison? The voices came very near now, they passed by close to the truck, the driver arguing and pleading, the Prussian speaking German which nobody could understand.

More footsteps came tramping along the line, more guttural voices, arguing. An hour passed. The Prussians had moved away. Everything was silent, except for the pattering of the rain on the roof of the station.

'Père, I'm hungry,' whimpered Julius.

Paul Lévy gave him a cigarette. 'Be quiet, my little one, try and sleep,' he said.

Julius could not sleep. He felt tired and hungry and evil-smelling and cold, but he could not sleep. At any moment the Prussians might come along and discover them. He closed his eyes, ugly shapes and distorted images danced before him, like the beginning of a nightmare. Slowly his head sank and his mind began to lose itself, in five minutes now he would be asleep from very weariness.

Then he was brought to himself again with a start. The driver was coming back again along the line, grumbling and cursing still, muttering to some companion.

'At last,' he said: 'what a delay and commotion – the lousy idiots. They are like thick brutes, these Prussians, they cannot understand a word one says. At last . . .'

Once more the whistle was blown, the steam shrieked from the funnel and the trucks moved again over the rails. Julius could hear Père whispering, he listened to hear what he was saying, but he could only catch a word now and again. Père was speaking Hebrew. He was praying. Julius prayed too. He prayed to the young Rabbin who bowed before the golden candlestick, he murmured the few words of Hebrew that he knew and understood.

The train increased its pace. Now they were clear of the Prussian lines there would be no further delay, and every effort would be made to make up for the lost time. Julius was shaken against the stones, his small body was hurled from side to side. The jolting trucks would not let him lie, backwards and forwards he was thrown against the rough-edged stones, the whole of his body bruised and tortured, his hands and his knees and his face were swollen and raw.

'Tell them to stop, tell them to stop,' he screamed. The train went faster still. It was roaring now through a tunnel, the air was thick with soot and smoke, the night was black as a pit. There was no breath left in Julius's lungs, he was beaten and broken.

'Père,' he whispered. 'Père – don't let me die.'

Paul Lévy felt for him in the darkness, he stretched out his arms and found him. He drew off the wet clothes and put Julius close to him upon his own naked body, underneath his clothes, next to his skin, so that his own warmth should go to him and their flesh would be together; he held him tight in his arms that Julius should feel only his body and not the jolting stones, while he himself lay on his back, shaken and bleeding, his head against a great jagged-edged stone. And Julius slept.

For five weeks the Lévys tramped the country between Dijon and Marseilles. They begged, borrowed, and stole; they rested at nights upon the charity of peasants, or in churches, and even sometimes under the stars in the shelter of a hedge. The month of February was mild, and farther south the sun shone all day from a blue sky bare of clouds. They fed when they could, Julius taking upon himself the business of procuring food, and it was a delight to him to trespass upon the hospitality of the peasants, clutching the while in his pocket the purse of *sous* he did not need to spend. He kept secret from Père the existence of the purse, for Père was scornful and Père was proud, he suffered much from this constant reliance on the charity of strangers, he was unable to appreciate the joy and the thrill that it was in life to obtain something for nothing.

In the towns it was not so easy. In Lyons Julius persuaded his father to play his flute and Paul Lévy let himself be pushed into position on the edge of the pavement, weak, unwilling, the poor Jew of the old days in Puteaux, ruled by the dominant Louise Blançard, while Julius stood at his elbow, his cap in his hand, digging his father in the ribs – 'Go on – go on.'

The boy grew during these weeks of outdoor life. He became tanned and ruddy from exposure, his chest broadened and his legs filled. Not so with his father. Paul Lévy was as thin and as pale as ever, the hard times of the siege had left their mark upon him, nor had he ever recovered from the agony of those ten hours in the jolting truck of stones. Julius had not realized what his father had suffered for his sake, and now the sight of his pallor and his visible fatigue awoke irritation in the boy's heart as it had done in his mother's. Physically strong himself, he could not understand the weakness of others. He put it down to laziness, to incapability. Grandpère and Mère had always said that Père was lazy.

'Only eight more kilometres to Avignon, Père,' he would protest; 'surely we can step out a little faster. You rested an hour in the sun this afternoon. If we arrive late in the town there may be a difficulty in finding food. As for me, my stomach is gaping. You are never hungry, you do not care.'

Père would look at him with gaunt eyes. 'I am coming, little one, don't be so impatient. You shall fill your poor stomach, I promise you.' And he would follow his son, his long legs dragging wearily on the rough road, the veins showing blue on his thin white face.

'Come on, come on,' shouted Julius.

In the town Julius would insist upon bargaining with the shop-keepers, and argued when Père would have paid what they demanded.

'No – no, it is ridiculous, you cannot give four *sous* for those oranges, they are not worth more than two. Listen, Madame, my father is a fool, he is not strong in his head, we will give you ten centimes for the pound. It is a matter of take it or leave it – Ten centimes? Good. Here is the money.'

'You are a rascal, you are not honest,' said Père, too tired to argue.

'Who cares? I have made a profit. Leave me alone.'

Paul Lévy and Julius came to Marseilles on the tenth of March. They had been exactly five weeks on the road. They found their way to the port, where ships were anchored near the cobbled quays, and sailors strolled, burnt and tattooed, sailors from every corner of the world. The sun shone all day in Marseilles, the streets were white with dust and there was a good smell like the old market smell, food and wine, tobacco and ripe fruit. Women leant over balconies yawning, flashing a smile, stretching lazy arms above their heads.

Père lounged about the quays, his eyes for ever amongst the ships, and he made inquiries, too, whither they were bound.

'You do not want to sail in a dirty ship,' protested Julius. 'We should be better off at Marseilles.'

'We should be warmer,' said Père, and he shivered in the soft wind that blew from the sea. He was always cold now.

'Where do you want to go then?' asked Julius.

Père hesitated, then he looked down at Julius and smiled.

'At the end of his life a man returns to the land where he was born,' he said. Julius did not understand.

'You talk as though you were old with a beard; what do you mean?' he said.

'I was not born at Puteaux,' said Père. 'I am not a Blançard and a little French town-bred thing like you. My people came from Algeria, my mother carried me on her back. I remember nothing of all this. But now the time has come for me to go back.'

'Where is Algeria?'

'In the north of Africa, right away there, across the sea. I must find out when there is a ship to take us.'

A cargo boat was due to sail at the beginning of the following week. A certain number of passengers would be taken, but there was no definite accommodation for them, they must berth for'ard on the deck in the open air, making shift for themselves. A small space was ruled off for them, and the passengers must crowd into this, herded like animals in a pen. Paul Lévy and Julius were amongst the group of passengers. They were a poor wretched crowd, the dregs of Marseilles who could not earn a living, and low-caste Arabs from the towns in North Africa. There were no sanitary arrangements on the deck of the cargo boat, and no privacy, for the miserable sum they paid these people could not expect comfort. The stench and the dirt were appalling, there were women too on the same deck; no attempt was made to separate them or rig some shelter.

The sea was very rough. The crossing took five days, which was considered good time with such weather. Julius suffered much from sickness, he was ill most of the time.

The Arabs made no effort at cleanliness, and Paul Lévy would clear up their filth himself, and scrub their corner of the deck, slipping and staggering on the sloping deck himself, suppressing his own sickness, peeling oranges for Julius who stretched out his arms and cried.

It was not until the day after he had landed in Alger, when the horror of the flight from Paris, the long weary weeks on the road to Marseilles and the vast misery of the crossing to Africa had been left behind him for ever, that the reaction seized hold of Paul Lévy and he gave way. He and Julius had spent the night in a humble lodging-house on the quays, and had awakened to the lovely brilliance of a southern morning, the sun as hot as when it shone on Paris in May, but stronger, with a deep intensity. He opened the window and threw aside the shutters, gazing at the blue sea beyond the port, and the vivid glare of white houses and dusty streets in the full rays of the sun. The sun warmed his thin body, it brought a smile to his pallid, sunken face, and he leant against the rail of the window, his head resting on his arms.

'This is the end,' he said. 'I cannot go any farther.'

Julius stood beside him and laid his hand on Père's arm.

'We must look around and see the best way to live,' he said. 'Alger seems a big place. I should say there is good trade to be done here.' He was excited and intrigued by this strange city. There were a hundred streets to explore, and hills to climb; there was a long boulevard leading uphill to a higher quarter where white houses gleamed amongst tall trees. Somewhere there were gardens and flowers growing, the rich scent of tropical plants buried in deep moss, perfume of honey and heavy sweet purple blossoms, and another smell too, a market smell of spices and leather, and scarlet fruits and people with dark skins who slept in the sun. Julius opened his nostrils and closed his eyes. The knowledge of all this floated up to him from the hot street.

Paul Lévy allowed himself to be dragged out under the full strength of the sun, he made no protest, he too would have intimacy with the atmosphere of Alger. He did not know how ill he was. They were climbing the hill towards Mustapha when he reeled suddenly as he walked, and clutching at Julius's shoulder, was shaken in a paroxysm of coughing. His face was green, his eyes were glazed. Then he fainted, crumpling to his feet like a dead thing. Julius bent over him, a child, lost and scared. A passer-by crossed to the other side of the road. Nobody wished to show charity. Julius was helpless, a small boy in a strange country. Then a sudden thought flashed into his head, he left Père propped against the wall, he ran and touched the passer-by. 'Please,' he said, 'my father is very ill. Can you tell me if there is an Israelite Temple in Alger?'

The man looked down on him, his handkerchief against his lips, for fear he should contract a disease. 'There is a synagogue somewhere for the Jews, I could not tell you where. You had better take your father to a hospital.' And he went his way.

It was not until he had inquired of three people that Julius was given the address of the Temple. He helped Père to his feet, he saw in the distance a *fiacre* at a standstill. 'I shall have to open Mère's purse at last,' he thought, and he wondered how much the driver would ask. Père was too ill to realize where he was. The *fiacre* took them downhill again, they turned east through a maze of narrow streets, streets where tiers of steps led to the roads above, where houses touched one another, so close they were. These streets smelt of spices and leather, a queer, dusty, warm, mysterious smell. Veiled women peered from the windows of houses, and dark, hook-nosed men stood in the doorways of their little shops. The driver stopped before a humble white building, almost hidden, squeezed between two projecting houses.

'This is a synagogue,' he said, and he spat disdainfully, holding out his hand already for his money. Julius paid him with rage in his heart. There was no time to argue. He knocked at the door of the Temple. The man who opened was old, a flowing black beard reached to his waist, streaked with silver. His dark eyes smiled at Julius, and the boy knew that here was the help he needed, that no more need he fear nor tremble, all care would be lifted from him and he and Père were safe. He was amongst his own people. This man was a Rabbin.

'I have brought my father,' he said, and the tears welled up in his eyes and ran down his cheeks. He could not speak. The Rabbin understood. He put his arms round Père. There was no queer southern smell here, no mystery, no heavy purple flowers. The atmosphere was peaceful, silent, a place of security. They went inside and the door closed behind them.

The Rabbin Moïse Metzger fed and nursed Paul Lévy with his own hands.

Julius was given clothes and shoes, food and drink in plenty. Did these things appear from behind the closed iron gates of the Temple?

'When will Père be well enough to move?'

'He is not going to move,' answered Moïse Metzger. 'Have not you understood, my little son? This is your home. You and your father are the children of the Temple.'

'For how long?'

The Rabbin laughed, and stroked his beard. 'Until your father is strong enough to move the Atlas mountains. Now, there is a problem for you.'

'Père will never move a mountain,' answered Julius. 'I am not so stupid as to believe that. I understand now. We are going to live here for good. Alger will be our town the same as Paris was once, and Puteaux before that. But tell me one thing: we are poor, Père and I – will there be anything to pay?'

The sick man flushed and put out his hand. 'You little low thing,' he said. 'He is an evil boy, Monsieur le Rabbin.'

Moïse Metzger pinched Julius's ear. 'He has the quick mind of his race,' he smiled; 'you must not scold him for it.'

'I know how to make profit in the market,' boasted Julius.

'That is very clever of you, my child. But to make a soul fit for the Temple – can you do that?'

'Julius hopes to be a Rabbin,' said Père eagerly. 'He knows his Hebrew and I have explained to him many things. It is my dearest wish that he should become a Rabbin.'

'Do you want to be a Rabbin?' asked the old man.

'Yes,' said Julius; 'it would be beautiful.'

But growing to be a man and having his full strength and using that strength, travelling away from Alger and seeing all the countries in the world, all the cities, all the seas, and new things and new people, and other men and other women, and living and loving, and being more powerful than those other men – and getting farther than them and further than anyone, not a Rabbin in a Temple, but he himself – he – Julius Lévy – was not that beautiful too?

He felt the need of escape, he knew not where, to get free from the quiet dead atmosphere of the Rabbin's house and to lose himself amongst streets and people. It was as though Père's room smelt already of decay, of tepid warmth and closeness, of the stale breath of a sick person. It was as though Père did not belong to the world any more.

'I don't care,' said Julius to himself. 'I don't care. I'm going to forget all this. I'm not going to think about Père any more.' He ran through the streets, defiant in his misery, putting away from him the dark blazing eyes in the white face. He came to the market-place. He always found his way here, as though the sense of the market was born in him, deep and inherent, something that would cling to him for ever. There was more variety here than in Neuilly, more colour and life and movement, the cries and smells of a strange race. The Arab smell, amber and dust and leather, the rubbing together of warm dark skins; great scarlet fruits, oversoft, over-ripe, a purple flower with its petals crushed by a naked foot, a fellow pushing his way through the crowd, carrying carpets, a little old man kneeling on the ground arranging a row of brass pots and jugs, a veiled woman fingering bright silks spread out on an open stall, and amongst the legs of everyone a crippled beggar wormed his way, crawling like a dog with his hands in shoes, his face the thin pointed face of an idiot under his scarlet fez. The stir of the market excited Julius, he felt restless and impatient, he could not bear to listen to the merchants bargaining with one another and he not able to bargain himself. He belonged to the life of the market, he could not keep away. He remembered the first day he had sold at Neuilly, picking up faded flowers from beneath a stall, and he knew he must do it again, that nothing and nobody would prevent him.

He pushed his way in amongst the stalls, he grubbed in the litter and found fruits that had fallen, crushed blossoms, odds and ends of market produce that had slipped from the stalls unperceived. He clasped them next his blouse and went with them to the lower end of the market where the street sloped downhill, where the houses touched, where the narrow passages and steps intermingled with one another like a spider's web. A poor quarter, a quarter of beggars. He knelt on the dusty street, spreading out his handkerchief and he lay his gathered pickings on the top. Then he put his hands to his mouth and called: 'Who would fill his belly and save his purse? Come and buy fresh fruit at the lowest price.'

An old woman heard his cry; she bent down to him and fumbled amongst his goods; a man passing turned on his heel and waited, then bought a bunch of flowers scarcely faded, another woman pressed against the first woman's shoulder.

'Save your purse – save your purse,' shouted Julius, and he held up two oranges, round and smooth, hiding the black mark where they had fallen with his thumb. 'Would you pay double the price up the market?'

Julius smiled; his sharp eyes darted amongst the faces of the crowd choosing his victim.

'A sweet cake for you, little girl? Look at this – how rich, how plentiful. What about the *sou* your mother gave you to spend? Thank you, thank you.'

A blind man approached, tapping on the ground with his stick. Julius thrust a bunch of dusty flowers under his nose. 'Only a *sou* for these fresh buds – smell them, my friend, smell them. They came this morning from a garden in Mustapha.' He jingled his money in his pockets, he wiped the sweat from his forehead. By selling off the dead flowers to the blind man he had cleared his stock. He rose hastily and disappeared in the crowd before the market people should find him and beat him. He laughed, his hands clutching the coins in his pocket.

'I shall never be a Rabbin, it's no use. I was not meant to sing in the Temple. This is my thing, selling to make profit. Something for nothing, something for nothing.'

He kicked a stone before him as he walked, whistling a tune, smiling to himself. He had forgotten Père on his bed, the stale atmosphere of the sick-room, the grave, bearded face of Moïse Metzger the Rabbin.

The Progress of Julius

Julius made his way down to the port. He spent his day watching the loading of ships and listening to the cries of sailors, he rubbed shoulders with little half-caste boys and sewer rats, he had food and drink at one of the cafés on the quay.

He breathed it in, the clatter, the noise, the movement, the heat and the sweat of humanity, the scorching, dusty, amber, Alger smell.

The sun was setting when he returned to the house of Moïse Metzger, and the sky was flaming gold. A muezzin wailed from the mosque, a little dark figure crying with his hands to his mouth.

At the corner of the street an Arab crouched with his face in the dust. Soon it would be dark, the night coming swiftly with no twilight like a black cloak over the white city, and there would rise a murmur from the closed houses, queer, mysterious and the throbbing of music.

Julius knocked on the door of the Rabbin's house. Old Amédée the servant let him inside. He laid his finger on his lips.

'All day Monsieur le Rabbin has waited for you,' he whispered. 'No one could say where you had gone. Your father is dying.'

Julius stared at him without speaking. Then he ran upstairs to Père's room, he stood with his ear against the door. He could hear the low droning murmur of Hebrew prayer, moaning and monotonous. It was the Rabbin praying. Julius turned the handle of the door and crept into the room.

The Rabbin was kneeling by the bed, his head bowed in his hands. Père lay still with his eyes turned towards the open window. The setting sun had dipped below the roof of the last house, and the sky was still lit with a dusky shadow of gold. Julius knelt beside the bed and watched the eyes of Père. They were like two glazing onyx stones in a dead mask. He did not seem to be listening to the prayers of Moïse Metzger. He was wondering how long it would be before he should die. He did not turn his eyes away from the flaming sky.

The muezzin from the mosque had ceased his wail to the setting sun; outside the street was hushed.

The Rabbin continued his low monotonous prayer. Suddenly Père made a little movement with his hands, he was fumbling with something on the counterpane. It was his flute. He lifted it to his lips, never taking his eyes away from the sky, and he began to play. It rose in the air, soft and mysterious, the whisper of a cry that would lose itself in the air, the call of someone who would leave his bed and escape. Higher and higher it rose, trembling, exquisite, the fluttering song of a bird borne on the wind, like an arrow sped through the sky to the sinking sun, a last question, a last appeal, the messenger who whispered at the gates of the secret city.

And as Julius knelt and watched Père go from him, little by little, on the breath of his song, it was as though part of Julius himself was taken also, the child who listened in the Temple, the child who leant against his father's knee, the child who lay crushed, flesh to flesh, in the jolting truck from Paris, the child who whimpered and loved and stretched out his hands.

Père smiled, and his last note was like a note of defiance flung into the air, bearing him away to nothing and to no one, and as he went he took with him something that would never come again, the lost boy, the frightened happy child – he took something of Julius himself – something that was tremulous, and pitiful, and young.

Part Two (1875–90): Youth

The hot sun shone through the drawn curtains, it forced an entrance through all the glass window-panes and the curtain stuff into the little book-room, dark and silent, and the sun cast golden patterns on the carpet and caught the leather bindings of the books in a sudden circle of light. There was no sound except for the steady scratching of a pen, irritating and harsh, and ever and again the little dry cough of Moïse Metzger as he paused to dip his pen in the ink, and to balance his spectacles more firmly on his nose.

Julius glanced up from his book and watched him, the pursed lips above the long beard now streaked with grey, the lines that ran from his nose to his mouth, the high, placid forehead that never wrinkled in anger, the round shoulders bent over the manuscript he was writing, heedless of the hot sun that would make its way in, caring nothing for the close fusty atmosphere of the room.

Julius loosened his collar and ran his hands through his hair. He sighed heavily and moved in his chair to attract the Rabbin's attention, but either Moïse Metzger did not choose to hear him or he was deaf, for the old man continued his writing and gave no sign to prove that he had heard. Julius fluttered the leaves of his book, the Hebrew writing stared up at him as though they were no longer words of beauty but so much nonsense calculated to rouse fury in the heart of a boy, and slowly and stealthily Julius drew a thin paper book from beneath the cover of his Hebrew History, a book shabby from constant use, the pages crinkled and dirty, the lettering, *Principles of Mathematics*, almost obliterated by the tell-tale marks of sweetmeats and chocolates. He opened the book at random and began to jot down calculations with the stub of a pencil. 'Marcel Hibert owes five francs and fifty centimes, borrowed by him the first of June. Interest at the rate of

65

ten per cent a week, fifty-five centimes; three weeks brings it to one franc sixty, making in all today, the twenty-first of June, seven francs ten centimes that he owes. Pierre Falco borrowed two francs a fortnight ago, he can only pay three per cent, his father is poor and keeps him short, that makes eleven *sous* interest, or two francs sixty – total of both borrowings nine francs seventy centimes. If I do not press Pierre for one more week his interest will bring the sum up to ten francs. . . . With ten francs much can be done; I can bargain with Ahèmed for those two carpets when he is tipsy, and get them at a low price, say fifteen francs for the two, and then sell them up at Mustapha as genuine for thirty francs each – sixty minus fifteen, forty-five francs. Forty-five francs profit and almost something for nothing. . . .'

Julius mopped his forehead with his handkerchief, and fanned himself with his book. He looked at the chink in the curtains that betrayed the sun, and he could picture the glare upon the white houses and the cobbled twisting streets, the hard glaze of the blue sky and the intolerable burning heat that he loved.

Finally the old man closed the book and laid aside his spectacles. 'That will do for today,' he said. 'We must not tax the brain beyond its strength. Go and rest yourself.'

Julius went from the room, laughing under his breath. At fifteen he was tall and slim, with Paul Lévy's face, Paul Lévy's narrow hips, and his long beautiful hands, but his shoulders and chest were broad like Jean Blançard's had been, and he carried his head high, aggressive and confident, as his grandfather had done.

He stood for a moment sniffing the hot air, the amber and the dust, the sweat of a sleeping Arab lying against the wall taking his siesta, the whiff of steam on linen that blew down the street from the window of Nanette the *blanchisseuse*, and these things seemed good to him, part of the life he was leading, and he fumbled in his pocket for a cigarette, glancing behind him at the house to see if the Rabbin was watching. He inhaled deeply, satisfied with the smoke and the intake of breath, and in his pockets he found a petal of bougainvillea flower and a eucalyptus leaf pressed together that he had picked up in Mustapha some days ago, now faded and crushed, but the scent still strong as ever. He bit the flower so that he should taste it as well as smell it, and he strolled along the streets, his hands in his pockets, his cigarette hanging from his lips, whistling a song. He went to the street corner where he knew he would find the other fellows. There they were, Marcel Hibert, Pierre Falco, Toto the freckled madcap son of a coiffeur, Boru the half-caste. Julius at fifteen was the leader, younger than any of them. 'I couldn't get away before,' he said. 'Come on, there's no time to lose.'

It was a long climb from the town of Alger to the hills, where the road to Constantine stretched over unbroken country. A hot walk too, in the full glare of the sun.

It was two hours or more before they had left the last village clinging to the fringe of Alger and were standing by a belt of trees that screened them from the road.

'Phew! what a trudge!' grumbled Pierre. 'I thought we should never get here. Let's hope we shall have some success.'

'It'll be a lark even if we get nothing at all,' grinned Toto, and he winked at Boru and snapped his fingers.

'Have we ever failed yet?' said Julius; 'would I have brought you here if I hadn't been confident?'

'Come on, what's the plan of attack?' said Marcel. He was the eldest, sometimes he resented this leadership by the youngest boy.

'You owe me money, my friend,' said Julius; 'have you made any reckoning?'

Marcel reddened and shuffled his feet. 'You might give me till tomorrow,' he muttered. 'We shall see what happens today.'

'The three weeks at ten per cent interest are up,' said Julius; 'after today my interest is fifteen per cent.'

'Oh! very well, you shall have it now. I cannot afford more interest.'

The coins changed hands.

'Meanwhile, I've decided our plan,' said Julius. 'The merchant will soon appear along the road. There's a stretch of three kilometres or more he has to cover before he reaches the shade of these trees. He'll be tired from the sun. He will want to rest his feet. You must hide here and I'll begin conversation with him. When I give the signal you will burst from the trees and run to the mules. Boru is used to managing animals; he will take charge of two. The rest of us will take one apiece. Then ride like the devil, shouting at the top of your voices. This will scare the mules, and they'll bolt. Hold on tight and don't let yourselves be thrown.'

'Supposing the merchant tries to follow us?'

'He'll not follow us, I shall see to that,' said Julius. The boys glanced at each other, half excited, half scared.

'What will you do?' asked Toto.

Julius patted his pocket. 'The same as David did to Goliath,' he said.

They blinked stupidly, they did not understand. Julius laughed and turned on his heel. 'I am a Jew, I know everything,' he said. Then he walked away from the belt of trees to a high position where he could watch the long winding road and the dust from a merchant travelling with his mules.

Julius crouched in a ditch by the side of the road, his chin resting in his hands, and an hour had passed before he finally saw the little cavalcade approaching in the distance. The five mules were harnessed one behind the other, a gap of four feet or more between them, and the Arab merchant himself brought up the rear on the sixth mule, lopping backwards and forwards in the high saddle, his head bowed over his breast in weariness.

Julius rose from his hiding-place in the ditch and walked slowly along the road to meet him. When he came within hailing distance he lifted his hand. 'Good day to you,' he shouted. 'May Allah protect you and your sons and your grandsons. Can you give me a cigarette?' The merchant gazed down at him with sullen eyes. 'I've travelled ever since noon, I'm weary and pressed for time. Let me get on with my business.' He cracked his long whip, he called out to his mules. Julius backed aside from their hoofs, he fumbled in his pocket. 'You are the seventh merchant to pass this way,' he said; 'they were all driving mules. You will find the market glutted when you reach Alger.' The Arab turned in his saddle exposing his full face in astonishment. 'Impossible . . .' he began, but he did not finish his sentence, for the boy had taken careful aim and the stone spun from the catapult and struck him between the eyes. The Arab fell into the road with a groan, kicked a moment and lay still. Julius darted to his side and fumbling with his belt he took the heavy purse from the stunned merchant and

68

tucked it hastily down his own shirt; then glancing around him he propped the man into a humped sitting position at the side of the road and stuck a cigarette between his lips. From a distance he might have been taken for someone resting, overcome by fatigue.

Only then did Julius give his signal, and the boys ran out from behind their clump of trees, each one seizing the bridle of a mule and cutting the rope that bound them together. They flung themselves on to the backs of the frightened animals, shouting at the pitch of their lungs, and the mules kicked and plunged in terror, shaking their heads and bolting in a cloud of dust down the long white road.

Julius bent over the Arab. Still he had not moved, but sat hunched and motionless, a deep cleft between his eyes where the stone had struck him. Julius climbed into the saddle of the sixth mule, and clinging to the high supports he dug his heels into the creature's sides, shouting, and pressing with his knees.

The mule bolted after the others, and Julius was flung up and down in the saddle, his nose bumping the arched neck of the mule, his hair falling over his face – shaking with mingled laughter and pain, the dust blowing up into his eyes and the sweat becoming part of it, grimy and caked. The scared animals would not stop now, they galloped as though possessed by the devil, and it seemed to Julius there was no breath left in his body, so shaken he was and exhausted, the heat rising in him like a clammy, suffocating blanket, yet he could not stop laughing as he reeled in the saddle, hysterical at the sight of the other boys each as helpless as himself on the backs of the strong mules, and in spite of his bruised flesh and his agony of fatigue there was something exhilarating and grand in this mad screaming gallop in the dust under the burning sun, something splendid in the way his blood pounded and his heart throbbed, in the fierce motion itself, in the smell of sweat and dust, in the tearing clatter of hoofs upon the hard road.

It was joy and it was hell at the same time; the pain, the intolerable thirst scorching his throat, the warm flesh of the mule against his nose, and a vision of trees and sun and sky flashing past him, the black scared face of Boru beside him, showing the whites of his eyes.

The road began to slope, they were coming to the outskirts of

The Progress of Julius

Alger – Marcel pointed ahead jabbering meaninglessly, and as the bend in the road brought them up against a wall the mules shied nervously, unseating the boys, a couple of them pitching head-foremost into the ditch, Boru clinging on to the reins of his two animals and being dragged for fifty yards or more, Marcel landing on his tender parts into a cactus bush screaming with the pain. Julius lay with his face in a dung-heap helpless with laughter; it was Toto who pulled him out and brushed the filth from his clothes. Boru and Pierre had secured all the six mules, and the boys stood in a group panting, heaving, grinning at each other, the breath and the laughter exploding from them like a steam engine.

'Marcel in the cactus bush,' yelled Julius. 'I shall never forget it, never – nor Boru split in two between his mules, one foot on the ground – oh! what a glorious life.'

'And you,' pointed Toto, 'your face covered in dung; what d'you think you look like?'

Julius crumpled in the ditch once more, helpless with mirth. 'What are we going to do with these blasted animals?' asked Marcel.

'Soon, my friend, soon,' said Julius weakly. 'Let's go and drink somewhere just for the love of God. The cattle market must wait.'

Toto helped him to his feet once more, and gathering the reins of the poor animals, who still sniffed about them in terror, the boys went down the hill into Alger, laughing and lurching over the stones, brushing the dirt from their coats and shaking their caps. Three little Arab urchins, begging for *sous*, looked after the mules while Julius and his companions went into a café to quench their thirst.

Julius, filthy in his dusty dung-bespattered clothes, demanded a wash. It was good to plunge his head and shoulders into the cold water, to shake the drips from his hair and to feel the water trickle down beneath his shirt to his streaming body. He opened his mouth wide and gasped, he drew his head up from the basin snuffling like a wet puppy. His ribs were bruised, his arms nearly pulled from his sockets and his legs black and blue from bumping against the side of the mule, but he felt fine – strong, somehow.

He lit a cigarette and tied a soaking handkerchief round his head to keep cool.

The boys were leaning against the bar, clamouring for attention, thumping with their fists.

Julius pushed his way in amongst them and flung down a five-franc piece.

'Come on,' he said, 'we're pressed for time; we've got to sell half a dozen animals in the cattle market before sundown. Be sharp or we'll take our custom elsewhere.'

In less than twenty minutes all the boys were drunk except Julius. He was used to drinking and could carry more than this, but he was burning inside and if his hand was steady and his eye was clear, there was a reckless something within him that made him care for nothing and for no one.

'Come on, you dribbling bastards,' he said, and the older boys followed him, flushed and stupid like so many sheep.

'We'll ride to the market in style,' said Julius carelessly, and he hauled himself up into the saddle once more and jerked savagely at the reins. He clattered through the streets of Alger scattering the people to right and left, waving his hand to an old fellow who shook his stick at him and cursed, nearly running down a woman who screamed in terror, clutching her children by the hands.

'We'll have the soldiers after us if we're not careful,' shouted Pierre, but Julius laughed, caring not at all, and he charged his animal into the square cattle market packed with people, knocking into a flock of sheep as he did so. He looked around him, smiling; this was the sound he liked, the jabbering tongues of merchants bargaining with one another, hands spread wide, fingers tapping upon an open palm; nods and whispers, the clink of coins passing from one to the other. He made his way to the side of a tall fellow in a cloak and wearing a fez, who was feeling the legs of a thin poorly-fed horse. This man had a loose, protruding underlip and big eyes like a fish, but his clothes were good. He looked wealthy and a fool. Julius had picked his man.

'Half-starved beasts don't give service,' he said boldly; 'anyone who sells such an animal is robbing the purse of the honest. Are you an expert in beasts?'

The fishy-eyed fellow shook his head. 'I don't mind about looks, it's strength and carrying power I'm after,' he said.

Julius nodded, twisting a cigarette.

'I can see you know your business,' he said; 'you have already agreed that such a horse is only fit for pasture. What you need is a mule, hefty and powerful.' He bent and whispered in the man's ear. 'Listen, this is between ourselves. There is an animal here, Arab stock, arrived in Alger this morning from Aumale. His owner has asked me to sell him cheap, you understand?' He laid his finger against his nose and winked.

The man in the fez was lost, but no matter. He winked too, as though he understood. 'Don't let this go any further,' muttered Julius, 'the demand will be greater than the supply and the price will be raised automatically. But because I want no questions asked I am prepared to sell you this animal at the lowest possible price. For eight louis he is yours – cash down at once, take it or leave it.'

The fellow took off his fez and scratched his head. 'That is double the price I meant to pay,' he said.

Julius laughed. 'For a starved, bloodless pony, you're right, my friend. But for a mule, a thoroughbred straight from the stock of the Sheik Abdullah Ben-Ahmed – eight louis is nothing, it is less than a jet of spittle. Look here – feel his shoulders; look at that head. You are a judge, I can tell that. You know a bargain when you see one.'

The man fumbled with his purse. 'You are right, the mule is worth more than eight louis. Here is the money, I'll take him at once.'

Julius's hand was already outstretched. 'An animal of his build will outlive you and your children,' he said, 'even your children's children. Good evening to you,' and he laid the reins over the man's wrist and slipped away into the crowd.

The boys were not doing so well. Perhaps it was the drink or perhaps it was natural inefficiency, but a dealer had noticed them from the start and was rapidly persuading them to sell up all five mules at a low price in order to clear.

'I will take them off your hands for fifteen louis,' he said, thrusting his fingers into his palm, glancing from one to the other. 'I can see the beasts have been stolen and you don't care to be caught. Come now, I have made you an offer.' Marcel shuffled his feet, red and awkward.

'Hold on,' interrupted Julius, 'I have just sold my animal for five louis, and he was the smallest of the bunch. If we ask six louis for these it's giving them away. Nor were they stolen, sir, they were part of my father's legacy. You have had dealings with him, no doubt, El Taza of Aumale?'

'El Taza is not dead?' exclaimed the dealer.

'He died at sundown yesterday, Allah rest his soul,' lied Julius coolly, thinking of the stunned merchant on the road to Constantine. 'I am his illegitimate son and I was the love of his heart. Will you give me six louis apiece for these animals?'

'I will take three at five louis each, youngster.'

'Five and a half and the bargain is yours.'

'Done.'

The money exchanged hands and Julius nodded to the boys to follow him.

'We've only two left,' he said. 'The best plan for us now is to put these beasts in the auction ring. I'll give the fellow five francs to sweeten his gabble and to lay it on thick.'

The boys were too dazed and stupid with drink to take in a word of what he said.

'Here – leave it to me,' said Julius, and he led the two remaining mules to the auction ring. The salesman had just disposed of a flock of sheep and was wiping the sweat from his forehead. Julius slipped a five-franc piece into his hand.

'Spin them the goods,' he whispered. 'I want you to get rid of these beasts for me. Don't knock them down beneath four louis.'

He stood at the man's elbow while the mules went up for sale; he listened with approval to the cheap claptrap. In fifteen minutes the mules were sold, one for five louis, the smaller for four. Julius pocketed the cash and strolled back to the boys.

'Both knocked down for three,' he said carelessly; 'that crowd weren't wasting anything. Come to a café and let's settle up. I've got a thirst.'

They pushed their way to a café on the square, and sitting round a table Julius ordered drinks. He spoke rapidly and the boys could not follow his meaning.

'We'll turn it into francs for shares,' he was saying; 'first mule a hundred francs, and three at a hundred and ten, four ten, and two at sixty, five hundred and sixty francs. D'you agree? five hundred and sixty francs, which gives us an equal share of a hundred and twelve francs each, minus my three per cent commission, which works out at sixteen francs.'

'Commission?' began Pierre stupidly –

'Yes – three per cent for running the show and selling the beasts. Any complaints?'

'Oh! all right.'

'Here we are, then, a hundred and twelve, not so bad. Better than I expected.'

Julius pocketed his share and then, well satisfied with himself, stretched out his hand for a drink. He had sold the first mule for eight louis and the last couple for five and four; he had swindled the boys out of an extra hundred and twenty francs besides his three per cent commission and the well-stuffed purse he had stolen off the Arab merchant, who was probably dead. He tilted on his chair and laughed at them over the rim of his glass.

What fools they were, not an ounce of brain in their thick heads. Even sharp little Toto was stupid from drink.

Fools! Wine was a good servant but a bad master. Fill yourself to the brim by all means, but don't lose hold of your senses. Be a glutton, but don't be sick from your gluttony. Grandpère Blançard used to lose his brains and his body; Julius was determined never to lose anything at all.

He was hungry now as well as thirsty. He wanted food and plenty of it.

'Give us something to eat, for the love of Allah!' he said, and he smiled when a bowl of thick curried chicken, rich and garlic-flavoured was put before him.

Marcel had fallen asleep with his head on the table, his mouth wide open. Boru the half-caste had gone down the street to be sick. Little Toto's head was nodding and Pierre was staring stupidly before him.

Julius crammed his mouth and then paid for another round of drinks.

'O! que j'ai mal aux dents,
    Il faut aimer . . .'

he sang. He had drunk more than all of them put together, but his head was clear.

'Let's go home to bed,' began Toto sleepily.

'Too early,' said Julius scornfully, and he swaggered out of the café, sniffing at the night that had fallen swiftly, soft and tropical, and he wished there would be a fair in Alger and a whirling painted horse to ride.

A cart was rumbling down the street. He swung himself on to the back of it and dangled his legs, still singing, waving his hand triumphantly to the boys left behind on the pavement, who rubbed their eyes and yawned.

The smell of Alger was good, the deep moss that lay at the roots of the trees, the thick leaves, the folded flowers, the hundred and one scents intoxicating and disturbing wafted down on the air from Mustapha. The cart was carrying Julius downhill towards the port. He could hear the inevitable hum and throb from the distant Kasbah, the murmur of voices and a thread of music, the tune that was no tune and the beating of a drum.

Not the Mustapha scent now but the odour of a little dark street, spices and amber, a naked painted foot beneath a silk gown, a whiff of cigarette smoke curling in the air.

Julius swung off the cart that disappeared in the direction of the quays.

He went to the house of Ahèmed, the carpet seller, and climbed the rickety stairs to the dancing floor above. The place was packed, he had to wedge himself tightly between two old men to be able to see at all. They hunched their bent shoulders, moving irritably, cursing that a boy should force his way amongst them.

He squatted on his heels, his eyes round. The music continued, stupid and monotonous, like one who banged with a stick on a tin kettle.

The atmosphere was thick with smoke and breath, and the pungent smell of dark-skinned people.

Naïda the dancing girl moved slowly round and round in a little circle, shaking her hips and her stomach. Her finger-nails and her toe-nails were painted. She wore a girdle round her waist.

As the tin-kettle music thumped louder and the beating quickened, so did her step quicken and her heel tap louder on the floor.

Her breasts and her stomach moved up and down, and she held her arms above her head, the heavy bangles jingling on her wrists.

Julius watched her critically, she was too thin to his taste, and her hips stuck out. He was amused at the old men next to him; they were counting money between them to see who should muster the most and would have her. One old fellow was clutching at the other, his eyes starting out of his head.

When Naïda had finished her dance, Lulu the fat woman took her place. A roar of laughter went up from the crowd. She was well over fifty and her hair was dyed bright red. She had great pouches under her eyes. But she was very popular. 'Lulu makes more money than the rest of the girls,' whispered someone behind Julius. 'She never has less than fifteen every night. They say she is good for anyone suffering from shivers or staggers.' 'Oh! Lulu is experienced,' came the answer. 'You know Ali, who could not give his wife a child? He lay with Lulu five summers ago and now his wife has four healthy boys.'

The fat woman stamped on the floor and clapped her hands. Julius did not care for her much; she was funny for a moment, but she bored him for long. He hated her little beady eyes in the rolls of flesh; besides, she smelt too strong, even for him. He began to feel sleepy. His eyes were closing in spite of himself, and he knew it was getting late. The tin-kettle music droned on and on like a drug. It throbbed in his ears as though it were part of him. He waited to see Elsa, the little French girl, smuggled over to Alger from Marseilles three months ago. Elsa was only ten, a lovely slim child with jet-black hair and enormous eyes. She ran on to the floor stark naked, her nails painted too, and she clapped in time to the music, smiling and wriggling her little behind. The men shouted in admiration, and when she had come to the end of the dance they took her upon their knees and petted her, but she was too young as yet to work with the others. She would have to wait until she was twelve. She smiled over her shoulder at Julius. He liked to watch her dance; she was beautiful and sexless, she did not shake herself at you. She was quiet, too, with grave manners. Sometimes he met her in the mornings at the market, and he would show her how to bargain and where to find the best produce. It flattered him to see the adoration and hero-worship in her eyes. It made him feel fifteen and very grown up, and she was only ten.

'I made some money today,' he told her carelessly, and pulled out a handful of coins. Her black eyes grew round.

'How clever you are!' she said.

He laughed; he felt generous.

'Here, you can have five francs if you like,' he said, and he pressed the coin into her hot hand. Then he pushed his way out of the room and down the stairs into the street.

Supposing the Rabbin was waiting up for him? He would be punished, of course. It was nearly midnight.

Julius looked towards the house of Moïse Metzger at the end of the street.

There were no lights and everything was dark. The Rabbin and his old servant must have gone to bed. Sleeping was a waste of time, thought the boy; it didn't give you anything. Now he was free of the atmosphere of the dancing-room he did not feel so tired. He could still hear the throbbing music muffled from behind the walls.

Julius picked up a stone and threw it gently at the shutters outside the window of Nanette the *blanchisseuse*. In a minute or so she opened them, yawning, stretching her arms.

'Have you got anyone with you?' he called.

She looked down at him lazily.

'No, baby – what are you doing here? Why aren't you in bed?'

'I've had a glorious day,' he said. 'I've sold six mules at the cattle market. Stole 'em off an old merchant. I made the boys drunk, too.'

She laughed, her white teeth gleaming.

'Come on then and tell Nanette about it.'

He vaulted up to the window and landed with a thud inside her room. She was ready for bed; the sheets were turned down and the candle was lit under her crucifix. She settled herself yawning in the armchair and Julius sat on her lap. She fumbled with a box of sweetmeats and put one in his mouth.

'Well, it was all owing to me,' boasted Julius, his cheeks bulging. 'The fellows were scared stiff. They hid in the trees and I waited in the ditch for the merchant to come.

'"Hullo, you old flapdoodle," I said, and I stung him one in the eye with a stone. Down he fell like a wounded turkey-cock. Off we galloped on the mules, thundering down the road for dear life, and when we came to the top of the hill everyone fell off except me. We were thirsty as troopers, and the boys got roaring drunk. Mind you, I'd put away double the quantity they had, but it don't make a whit of difference to me.'

'Oh! little chatterbox,' teased Nanette.

'May I be struck dead if I'm not speaking the truth!' swore Julius, his eyes turned to heaven. 'Well, to continue, I took the beasts myself to the cattle market and seizing the hammer from the auctioneer, I sold every mule for ten louis apiece. The crowds gaped up at me. I'd had enough by then. I went and swallowed another drink, took some hashish, and spent the rest of the evening with the dancing girls.'

Nanette laughed and fumbled for a sweet; she did not believe a word of it.

'You're a fine fellow, no doubt,' she said, 'but it's time you were in bed! What do we look like if Monsieur le Rabbin comes over to fetch you?'

Julius wriggled impatiently.

'Moïse Metzger is in bed and asleep,' he protested. 'Nobody is coming to fetch me.'

He settled himself more comfortably and laid his head against her shoulder. Nanette was lovely all over. She had a rich smell.

'Let me stay, Nounounne,' he pleaded.

She grunted lazily, pushing away his hands. 'No, baby, go home.'

'Please, please, Nounounne, I want to so badly, like last time, you remember.'

'Oh! You're a pest, aren't you?'

'No, I'm not. I'm a man, I'm fifteen.'

He clung to her, blotting himself against her, burying his face in her warm flesh. She caressed him gently, feeling his narrow hips, his hard thighs.

'You're a bad boy,' she said.

He bit her ear, murmuring nonsense; he rubbed his cheek next hers and tugged at her hands, whimpering impatiently like a spoilt, greedy puppy.

'Please, Nounounne,' he begged.

'Go on, then,' she said. And she blew out the candle and crossed the room to close the shutters.

Julius was growing up. Already at sixteen he was as tall as the Rabbin, Moïse Metzger; he shaved every morning, he smoked innumerable cigarettes – he thought himself a fine fellow. Daily the Rabbin perceived that his pupil was getting beyond him: this boy would never be a minister in the Temple, he was made for the business of life itself, for gain, for success, for men and for women.

Julius would sit now in the reading-room with his legs crossed and a smile on his face, not even troubling to hold his book before him, but the smile on his face said: 'I know all this and more. Why am I wasting my time on you?' The Rabbin would wonder, watching the curving nose, the thin lips, the black eyes set in the pallid face, and he thought: 'To what end? Where is he going? What will he make of his life?' Sometimes he would bring himself to ask Julius what his plans were for the future. 'Have you decided? Are you always willing to become a minister of God?' But Julius would put him off, would frown and bite his fingers. 'I'm only sixteen – there's time enough, isn't there?' And to see him in attendance at the Temple, his silence, his attitude of worship, his utter denial of the world when in the presence of God, the Rabbin would be puzzled once again, would stroke his beard in bewilderment. 'Does he mean it; is it only his youth that makes him arrogant and rebellious?' Perhaps his brilliance and his insolence were part of his business of adolescence. He would grow out of them into a sound wisdom, a wisdom that rejected life for the service of the Temple. To see him at prayer, he could not be anything but a student in preparation for the ministry, this boy with his hands folded over his book, his head low, his lips murmuring the soft Hebrew words as he swayed backwards and forwards in a strange ecstasy, and he would offer nothing but worship in this atmosphere of peace and restraint as though nothing would ever exist but the vision of the iron gates, and the golden candlestick, and the Rabbin himself chanting the Kadisch. 'That is the real Julius, there, standing at prayer,' said Moïse Metzger, and in his ardour he would cry out to God to look down upon this young servant Julius, to hold him, to cherish him; and when the service was over after sundown he would see the boy sitting at his table with his books around him, his face eager, intent, and 'That is the real Julius, too,' he would say.

But later, much later, when darkness had come and the moon had risen, the table would be lonely and the books scattered, and there would be the window open wide filling the silent room with the scent of moss and eucalyptus, and the Rabbin in his narrow bed sleeping the sleep of God's chosen people would be unaware of the significance of that empty room and that open window; would neither waking nor sleeping have any knowledge of Julius, his real Julius, swinging his legs over the ledge and dropping to the ground below, nor the hasty flight across the dark street, nor the thrown pebble and the candle flickering behind the shutters, nor the lazy tread of Nanette the *blanchisseuse* as she unfastened the latch and stood for a moment, her arm upraised, black and mysterious, outlined against the sky. Nor would the Rabbin recognize his real Julius in the boy who lost himself in the night, who forgot the world as well as the Temple, who cared little for profit and less for dreams, and whose secret city was surely to be found in this furious intimacy, this building and breaking of power, this victory that was no victory but a sharp death, poisonous and strong.

There was the Julius who, curling like a child at its mother's side, slept with his cheek in the curve of her back and did not dream at all; and a Julius who woke when the sun rose making patterns through the chink of the shutters, who sat up in bed and demanded sweetmeats, who laughed at nothing because he was young and healthy, pulling on his clothes anyhow, who slipped from the window and back to the house of the Rabbin before the old servant had put one foot to the ground and rubbed the sleep from his eyes.

A different Julius, he who sat in the little low room of Oudà the cobbler, who weighed a packet of hashish in his hands, who leant forward and said: 'Yes, but look here – this packet only goes to someone who can give useful information. I'm tired of Ahèmed's carpets on which one cannot make more than ten per cent. Something new, my friend – something new.'

And Oudà, his beady eyes gleaming, his skinny hands plucking at the packet: 'Try Ab Azra in the Rue du Bac; he's a receiver of stolen goods, and his brother Menkir runs a vessel along the coast. But I tell you, I know nothing.'

Julius in a little café on the quays, with a swinging lamp above his head, a half-caste Arab merchant listening to him, fingering his greasy nose with his thumb, nodding his head: 'Yes, I can get rid of that for you. I can give you two louis for those ear-rings, no more; it would not be worth the risk,' and the boy whistling scornfully, sticking his hands in his pockets.

'I could get double that price up in Mustapha. I tell you I am giving nothing away.' Then the pretended consultation, the nods, the whispers, the two fat Arab brothers muttering together, the final 'Very well, we will give you the four louis,' and the passing of the ear-rings, the chink of coins, Julius tying his canvas bag round his waist, ordering a couple more drinks, and swinging out of the café, rolling a cigarette between his fingers. The hot night, the sound of the sea upon the distant shore, and a little half-caste urchin brushing against his knee begging for a *sou*. 'When I was his age I sold in the market,' thought Julius, and he flung ten centimes to the child, and went on his way that led from the sea and the port to the narrow winding streets and the terraces and the tall houses built against the hill.

And later, Julius leant against the window of Oudà the cobbler, who lifted his head and said: 'Why don't you leave Alger and shake the dust from your feet? Why do you linger with Moïse Metzger if you wish to be free?' Julius would reply: 'Moïse Metzger thinks I'm going to be a Rabbin, and meanwhile he clothes me and feeds me, and gives me his brain, and there is nothing to pay.' And, 'Tell me,' he went on, 'which is the most prosperous country in the world?'

Oudà smiled and laid a finger against his nose. 'You will do well anywhere,' he said, 'but England is a rich country. Besides, they are a nation of fools.'

'Is English difficult to learn?'

'How should I know? Go to the pastor up in Mustapha and pull him a story.'

'If I set my mind to it I can learn a language in six months.'

So Julius went to the house of Martin Fletcher, the English pastor, who lived in Alger because of his asthma, and when the middle-aged clergyman perceived a tall, pale boy with dust on his shoes knocking at his door he took pity on him because of his soft voice and his humility, and because he was forcibly reminded of somebody he had imagined long forgotten and buried in the past; and Martin Fletcher thought with a pang of that reading party à deux in Greece and the sun setting behind the hills of Athens, these pictures helping most forcibly the cause of Julius Lévy, who would learn the English language without paying for his lessons.

'And so you work in a draper's shop and you have no one to care for you, no one at all?' asked Martin Fletcher gently, without listening for the reply but searching in his mind the verses of Keats, who painted so subtly the charms of the sleeping Endymion. And, 'No, sir,' said Julius. 'Since my mother died I am entirely alone; the only things in the world are my books,' in a flash sizing up his man and turning a conscious profile to the window, drooping a little, as one who is troubled aesthetically and will never know maturity.

Then silence, and Julius sighing somewhat to deepen the atmosphere, and fingering the cover of a book as though he loved the very texture, a lock of hair falling most appropriately over his forehead, until Martin Fletcher moved in his chair, exquisitely disturbed, and went and laid a hand upon his shoulder and said: 'I am free from five to nine every evening if you are really anxious to learn English. . . .'

'Oudà said they were a nation of fools,' thought Julius. 'Is it always going to be as easy as this?' But aloud: 'If only there was some way I could show my gratitude,' and taking his hand and kissing it in grave humility, playing the boy, the starved genius.

It would mean four hours every evening in new company, four hours' extra study instead of roaming the streets and the cafés, but then it was useless to dream of the most prosperous country in the world unless the language became like second nature.

'You say you have had no education – do you know I can scarcely believe it?' Martin Fletcher smiled after the first lesson. 'It's quite extraordinary, this thirst for learning: you might have trained your brain for years. It is astonishingly receptive, intuitive, the way you grasp the very essence of my teaching.'

And Julius, thinking to himself: you couldn't sell produce for profit when you were ten and remain ignorant, nor sap the brain of Moïse Metzger for five years without getting somewhere, would reply softly, a little sadly: 'My mother and I used to read together in the evenings.'

Martin Fletcher, watching the expression in his eyes, the imagined shadow, 'Poor Julius, how you must have suffered,' and getting away from the lesson to the interest of an intimate conversation, the light dwindling in the room, so that it might almost be twenty-five years ago in St John's.

'You remind me of a very dear friend. . . .'

'Do I?' said Julius, caring not at all, and hearing with impatience the sound of the clock striking the half-hour, and seeing the time of his lesson slipping away – a good thing it cost no money or he would not be having his full value. 'By the way, I wrote that page of translation; would you correct the faults? I did it without a dictionary,' but careful to hide his impatience, to smile shyly as behoved the character he was playing, and to add: 'You make me want to work – it's as though you understood.'

And when it came to studying there was no pretence, for Julius was thirsty of knowledge as Fletcher had said, and he gave his whole mind to this learning of English, sparing no pains to perfect the grammar and the accent, already in his mind seeing the vision of England – the nation of fools.

'I should like to show you my England,' said Martin Fletcher, once more going off in the thread of his own thoughts, dipping his pen in red ink, the page of translation waiting to be corrected. 'I should like to show you Cambridge, and the Backs, and evensong in King's – if it wasn't for my wretched health, exiled here in Algiers. Julius, you more than anyone would appreciate the quiet beauty – none of this flamboyancy, these purple flowers, this exotic sky, but the grey shadows after the sun has set and the clear air.'

'Yes.' But Julius had bought a geography book, and Cambridge was only marked as a small town; if one wanted to make money one went to London. 'Yes, sir, it would be wonderful if we could go together.'

'Of course you are young, absurdly young. Only seventeen, aren't you? I was very much like you at your age, innocent, appallingly sensitive. You mustn't get hurt, you know – you mustn't spoil yourself. You know what I mean, don't you? There are so many temptations, especially in this country.'

'He's mad, of course,' thought Julius, but he turned a trusting face with wide-open eyes and he said: 'I can't bear anything ugly,' striking instinctively the right note so that Fletcher should keep his image of the pure Endymion.

'We won't do any more work tonight, Julius; you look pale – you must go to bed. Sure you are not lonely in those wretched lodgings?'

'No, sir – it's all right. I shall read a little and think about you. You help me so much.'

'Nonsense – I have done nothing. Tomorrow, then. Sleep well.'

'Good night, sir.' Not to a lonely bed and a dream of evensong at King's, side by side with the Reverend Fletcher, but to throw a pebble at closed shutters and swing his legs over the sill. 'Oh! Nounounne, my lovely, what price four hours hand-in-hand with a grey-haired English pastor – haven't you got anything for me? I've the devil of a thirst, but it isn't a drink I'm wanting.'

'You've got to go in, baby, I've someone coming along at ten.'

'The devil you have. Nounounne, tell your fellow to come another night.'

'Yes, that's likely, that's very fine. And d'you expect Nanette to go on washing shirts all her life? Scrub – scrub – whoof! the heat over a basin and the soapy, sticky water. Ya – I'll show you some dirty linen, if you like. Make you sick.'

'How much'll he give you, your fellow?'

'Fifteen – twenty – twenty-five francs, I dunno.'

'That's a hell of a lot, Nounounne. They only ask you ten in the Rue Maroc. I've never paid more, and there's dancing there too, thrown in.'

'Go on, liar, eat your words.'

'Well, anyway, I'm not going for half an hour. That's a settled thing.'

'What are you going to do, baby?'

'I'll show you.'

'Now, I tell you I don't see why I should spoil you as I do. What'll you say if I ask for fifteen francs?'

'I wouldn't pay it.'

'Wouldn't you, robber, hyena?'

'No – you're my own Nounounne and you love spoiling me. Get up out of that chair, you lazy old bitch.'

England did not matter, nor the lesson that must be learnt before daylight, nor the Rabbin, Moïse Metzger, waiting in the dim sanctity of the reading-room, nor the little cross given him that day by Martin Fletcher, 'making a bond between us, Julius' (which surely was eighteen-carat gold and could be sold to old Benjamin Ulmann the jeweller in the Rue Cambon for a good price), nor the life that was to come, London, profit, something for nothing – something for nothing, nor anything at all beyond this moment that was Alger, the warmth, the flesh, the scent and the darkness; losing himself in Nanette who was Alger, who was the amber smell and the dust, the white houses, the twisted streets, the throbbing of a drum – who was not even the whole of these things but something which was gone, the hot breath and the dizzy lights of the foire de Neuilly, the eyes of Jean Blançard, blue and hazy from drink, and the body of Mère curling towards him in her sleep, her hand about his thighs.

The time came when Julius thought of very little else but his plan of leaving Alger and going to England. It seemed to him that he had grown beyond this life he was leading, it held no longer any element of excitement or interest; he had had what he wanted out of Alger.

The Progress of Julius

His tricks of swindling, of dealing in secrecy, his adventures, his scrappy love affairs, they were all boys' games, and he did not feel like a boy any more. He knew he was spoilt, things had been made too soft for him. It was easy to make money in his own little way, to get the better of a carpet dealer, to sell a stolen article for double its value. There was not any fighting in that sort of business, he had only to undertake something and it happened as he wished. He knew now about the hot sun and the dusty streets, the smell of an Arab market and the cries of the people; he knew about amber and leather and silks and cooked rice; he knew the jingling bangles and the scarlet-painted heels of the dancing girls. He wanted to get away from all this now that it had been absorbed by him and drunken and digested; he wanted different things, a new life, and other men and other women.

Yes, he had had what he needed out of Alger. There was no more to be gained from the mind of Moïse Metzger.

Martin Fletcher was pompous, was a fool; he lived in a world that had no existence beyond his own imagination. He was only good for teaching English.

What was Oudà now but a crippled cobbler who lived for hashish, who was not even intelligent?

And of the group of boys who had been his companions, Marcel was a Spahi posted down in the Sahara somewhere, Toto helped his father the coiffeur, Boru was a porter, Pierre served in a restaurant. They were dull and unenterprising with scrubby chins and vacant minds; they would not get anywhere.

Even Nanette, what was she but a lazy Negress prostitute, who sucked sweets all day and yawned over her wash-tub? She was only good for one thing, anyway. It was hopeless to talk to her: she laughed and yawned; besides, she was getting too fat.

There was but one person in the whole of Alger who mattered at all, and she was scarcely more than a child, but she listened with wide eyes and open mouth of wonder when she was spoken to; she was quick, too, in her way; she wasn't a fool, she understood things. Julius paid ten francs for Elsa when he went to the house of Ahèmed. He did not care for any of the other girls. She said she would go with him for nothing, but Ahèmed would not allow this. He had to make his house pay. Elsa was getting old: she was nearly fourteen. In a way she was better than Nanette, because she told Julius he was the most wonderful person in the world. She made him feel important; she was willing and eager to please.

'I'm going to England, Elsa; I'm going to make my fortune,' he would say, lying stretched out on her bed, his hands beneath his head, drumming his feet on the rail, watching her face for the effect of his words. She would sit up and shiver, glancing at him with scared eyes – eyes as large as saucers, and then pull at her kimono to wrap round her shoulders. 'I shall go with you,' she said, and struck at him with her nails when he laughed.

'I don't want anyone,' he told her; 'a man cannot saddle himself with a woman in a big town. It means another mouth to feed. Besides, if I wanted girls there are plenty in London. Smart, too, and clever.'

He hid his smile as he saw the tears come into her eyes.

'I suppose I must seem very ignorant to you,' she whispered, her head low. 'I'd learn soon, though. I'd work like a slave if you took me with you. I'm not a child; I'm fourteen.'

'Pooh! That's nothing,' scoffed Julius. 'I can remember back in Paris girls of your age played with dolls. It's the same in all civilized places. You mustn't go by Africa; it's only a country for savages.'

The shoulders of Elsa began to shake, and her head bent lower and lower. Julius had to cover his mouth with his hand to prevent himself from laughing. He had discovered a new thing, of hurting people he liked. It gave him an extraordinary sensation to see Elsa cry after she had been smiling, and to know that he had caused her tears. He was aware of power, strange and exciting. In a way it was like the desire to make love. The two longings were very close together. To say something bitter and cruel, to watch the smile fade from Elsa's lips and the shadows come into her eyes, to taunt her until she put her hands over her face, it made his heart beat and his blood race the same as when he held her and loved her. To change swiftly too was good. To follow the stinging blow with a caress, to kiss the tears he had summoned, until Elsa did not know where she was, and would peer into his eyes to learn the truth. Sometimes she would lose her patience, fighting with him like a little animal, using her nails and her teeth, but he won in the end by saying how different she was to Nanette, how skinny and immature and ignorant; then she would lay her cheek against his shoulder and ask to be forgiven. He would strain his muscles to keep a straight face. Not that he cared how she felt, whether she was humble or proud, but he liked to see her crawl. It was a definite pleasure; and the fact that he was fond of her added to this pleasure. It did not affect him with a sense of power when other people gave way to him. He despised them, seeing them as fools.

In his opinion Martin Fletcher, the English pastor, was rapidly approaching senility.

'Why don't you make your home with me, Julius?' he would say. 'Are things always going to continue like this between us? Sometimes I feel you are keeping something back from me, we haven't the real intimacy I would wish,' sweeping his thin grey hair with his nervous hands, his eager chin thrust forward, the whole of him, pointed nose and ears, suggesting some monstrous hungry bird. Until Julius was aware of a profound dislike for this man who had taught him perfect English, who offered him comfort and security, and the longing grew keen within him to say or do something incredibly violent or coarse, so that Martin Fletcher should be shocked and disgusted and wounded. He would like to bring Nanette to the house of the pastor and lie with her on the floor before his very eyes, and then to say: 'What do you mean by intimacy? This? It's a question of take it or leave it.'

No, he was finished with Martin Fletcher; he had learnt the English language, and that was all he had needed.

He ceased abruptly his visits to Mustapha, and the little notes that reached him at the house of Oudà the cobbler – his false address – were unopened and used as paper spills. 'Why, Julius, is this a deliberate action on your part, this breaking up of our friendship? What has come between us? Is it a woman? If only you will believe in me and trust me, I shall be able to cure you,' word upon word in neat spidery handwriting that Julius could not even bring himself to decipher. Besides, he was too busy now counting his store of money put by day by day since he had first come to live with Moïse Metzger as a child of eleven. He was not going to let himself starve and go in rags in London, not he.

So Julius let the months pass and still remained under the Rabbin's roof. 'I am past nineteen and shall play for the last time; at least I will have my summer,' he said to himself. And the Rabbin asked him no questions, but allowed him to go his own way, knowing that the Temple was lost to Julius now and that his very presence in the house would endure but a little longer. And it was a good summer, with the preparations ready for slipping away in the first days of autumn; no need to worry with money and plans put by and close to hand, long weeks of laughter and loving under a burning sky, no prayers in the Temple, no English lessons up in Mustapha, but the life of a Blançard who would squeeze the utmost pleasure and joy and sensation out of this place Alger, forgetting everything but his body, money, power, property, profit gone to the winds till he should have need of them again. Every moment was to be grasped because it would not happen again. 'This I have had, and this, and this,' to taste life and smell it and grasp it, to have it even if he could not hold it, knowing that he was aged and wise beyond his years, for 'When I am twenty I shall be old and then I shan't want these things,' said Julius. And every song he sang was an adieu, and every movement a gesture of farewell. He sought exhaustion in all its forms, deliberately he made a fetish of sensation and the enjoyment of unbounded health became a sensuous experience. 'If I do everything when I am nineteen I shan't want to do anything later,' he thought. If he had never known what it was to be a child, at least he would know how a boy should live; and while he plunged headlong into every folly of mischief and adventure and vice, it was as though part of him stood aside, watching the figure of himself with his hands to his lips, waving good-bye to his own boyhood.

The autumn came suddenly with a storm and a wind overnight, the heavy rains falling from a blown sky bringing up all the moss-scents from the ground, the great trees in Mustapha bent backwards with the change, the clustered foliage shivering and drooping to the rich earth that sucked at the roots of the trees like a streaming sponge. The oranges and lemons had lost their beauty, and the eucalyptus stood stripped of its bark naked and pale.

The Progress of Julius

The white dust was scattered in the streets, rivulets forming in the dry gutters and running from the hills. An angry turbulent sea broke on the far shore where yesterday the beaches had been golden and the water blue. People lifted their faces to the rain and were thankful after the parched months with nothing but a burning sun in a burning sky, but Julius knew that his play-time was over and Alger was dead to him.

One moment he had been in a café with Toto, the last of his friends to retain some instinct of boyishness, the pair of them worn out after a long night in the closed houses of the Kasbah, Julius with his head pillowed in his hands, the ghost of a smile on his lips, and the next moment autumn had come and the day had broken, and Toto was only a curly-haired little coiffeur snapping his tongs over a flame, an apron round his waist, and Julius was down by the docks paying money for a third-class passage in the steamship *Timgad*, sniffing the wind, his nose turned to the north. Good-bye to Alger, where he had come as a child over eight years ago; good-bye without a regret and without a tear. Nanette, who had taught him how to make love, was like a coat he had outgrown, was a game left to rot in a play-box.

'I'm going to England, Nounounne,' but she was not impressed. She laughed at him over her wash-tub; she flashed a smile and waved her hand. And it came to him with a pang of fear and a thwarted inexplicable sense of frustration that never again would he have what she had given him, that he had known at fifteen what many crave in vain during a lifetime. However much he sought and whatever women it should be his chance to know, they could not equal her, his first, a lazy, good-for-nothing coloured washerwoman. No one would escape comparison; they would be judged by her standard and fall like pitiful lifeless toys of no value, so much so that as he climbed from her window for the last time it seemed to his merciless judgement that one part of his future was doomed to be sterile and empty, that nothing further in this sense existed for him, and he found himself bareheaded in the street watching the chink of light behind the shutters, and he was thinking: 'She has spoilt all that for me; I have had it too young.'

The parting with Elsa was trifling after Nanette. The memory of the older woman was still with him. The child plied him with questions which he answered at random, smoking a cigarette, scarcely listening to her words, and it was only when he had left Ahèmed's house that he realized with sudden surprise Elsa had neither wept nor clung to him. Perhaps she had not understood that he was leaving Alger for good; she would weep tears enough when she knew. He dismissed her from his thoughts, easy to him at all times about all people, and he ate his last supper under the roof of Moïse Metzger, his teacher and his guardian, wondering at the peace and deep wisdom that lay behind the eyes of the old Rabbin, wondering at his calm happiness and sense of security.

He went up to his room to pack his few things into a bundle, after bidding Moïse Metzger good night without a word of his departure, feeling no sorrow and no shadow of distress.

He pushed Père's flute amongst the clothes in his bundle and, 'What do I care?' he thought. 'Père was a miserable specimen who couldn't tell ten *sous* from twenty, who died without a rag to his back;' and he laughed at the memory of Paul Lévy as he had laughed as a child pointing a derisive finger to his nose in imitation of Jean Blançard, but he climbed from the window hastily, without looking back, suddenly filled with the longing to be rid of the old phantoms of childhood and boyhood that might cling to him if he stayed; and he ran away from the house, crouching in the shadow of a wall – like a thief, afraid of the darkness.

The *Timgad* was due to sail soon after midnight. Loose scurrying clouds blew across the dark sky, and an ill moon showed her face from time to time behind the black edges of a gaping hand. The wind came strong from the north-east, the waters of the port were ruffled and angry, while outside a tufted, high-crested sea swept towards the shore. The *Timgad*, one of the new steamships, iron-built, wet and uncomfortable, groaned and creaked at the side of the quay.

The little crowd of passengers shivered by the gangway, reluctant to leave the firm ground for this grey prison that awaited them, but Julius found his way on board at once and down to his cramped third-class quarters, where he must bend his head to the low bulkhead and steady himself against the cheap mahogany-coloured wainscoting – already the floor sloping to the roll of the ship, and the close atmosphere breathing of coal-dust from the furnaces and grease and fried fat from the cooking quarters.

Even so, this was luxury compared with the square patch of deck in the open air reserved for the steerage passengers that Julius could remember eight years before. Now he was a person of status, with his ticket in his breast pocket, no longer a tramp or a poor half-starved refugee. 'I am Julius Lévy, travelling to London on business,' he said to himself, and he stood with his arms folded against the rail of the ship watching the lights of Alger rising above each other on the hills, no feeling of regret in his heart for this city he was leaving and the people he would not see again, as calm and unmoved as when he had left Paris, and his mother dead in the house of the Rue des Petits Champs.

An old fellow stood by his side with tears in his eyes as they drew slowly away from the coast of Africa, and a woman, a half-caste, probably, with dark colouring, put her shawl up to her mouth and cried.

'They mind because Alger is their home,' thought Julius; and he wondered at them as though they were strange curiosities of nature interesting to the observation; but he knew he could never feel what they were feeling because he had no country and no home, and these things were not part of him.

He thought of Moïse Metzger now asleep in his bed, his last prayer on his lips, and Martin Fletcher pacing the floor of his library or turning nervously the leaves of a book, Oudà drugged with hashish, Nanette rocking in her chair, her heavy lids closing over her eyes. Little Elsa in the arms of some Arab shopkeeper; Toto, Marcel and the other boys drinking in some café: he would remember them, perhaps, but they would not matter to him.

He wondered if he would always be like this, making use of men and women for his own purpose, but sufficient unto himself and definitely alone.

He was turning to go below to his own quarters when a steward touched him on the arm.

'Monsieur Lévy, third class?'

'Yes – that is my name.'

'There is somebody inquiring for you in the steerage, monsieur. A young fellow.'

92

'Impossible, there must be some mistake. I don't know anybody on the ship.'

'As you wish.' The steward shrugged his shoulders. After all, a third-class passenger was little better than steerage.

Julius hesitated. There might be another Lévy on the *Timgad*, and the message would be for him. All the same, it was strange. He gave in to his curiosity and found his way across the deck to the railed-off steerage. Already the ship was rolling abominably, and a sea had left some of itself behind. A terrified old woman was praying out loud, and three little children were crying, huddled against their mother. It was something of pleasure to Julius to see them suffer, and to know that he too had suffered once, but was now superior to them. He turned up the collar of his overcoat and blew on his hands.

'Cold on deck,' he said loudly to a passing sailor. 'I guess I'm better off in the warm saloon below.' He cupped his hands and lit a cigarette, his back to the wind. A steerage passenger gazed at him with mingled hatred and envy. Julius laughed and threw away his match. Poor devils, condemned to a passage in this weather; but he did not care. Somebody put his hands over the barrier and clutched at him. A boy, with a cap pulled down over his eyes. Was this the lad who had been asking for him? Only one of the street urchins from the port?

'Here – what do you want? Leave me alone, can't you?'

But the hands would not let him go, and the boy peered up into his face.

'Julius – don't be angry with me.'

He looked closer into the boy's eyes, great eyes like saucers in a thin face, but the hair cropped short, the lips free of paint.

It was Elsa. For a moment Julius was too astonished to speak, and then he said: 'You damned little fool; what on earth are you doing here?'

She shrank as though he had hit her.

'I had to follow you; I couldn't let you go without me.'

He whistled irritably, glancing to right and left.

'You know what'll happen if they find you out? You'll be put into prison or sent back.'

'Not if you take me with you; you can say I am your brother.'

'You must be mad, Elsa. Why should I burden myself with you?' He had never heard such nonsense.

'Oh! Julius, dear Julius, please don't be so cruel to me. I can't help loving you. I've always loved you. I don't mind how you treat me; you can scold me and beat me and kick me, but please let me stay with you.'

She clasped her hands pitifully; she looked a child in her boy's clothes. Julius frowned; he longed to be brutal to her.

'I don't want you, you whining little idiot. You ought to have known that. You'll be sorry for this. A steerage passage is more like hell than anything on earth. It's your own fault, and now you'll have to lump it.'

The ship lurched violently. Elsa turned very pale and he saw she would be sick.

'Well, good-bye, I'm going below,' he said carelessly, and watched the misery in her pinched face.

'No – you can't leave me,' she cried, her hands pressed against her small stomach. 'Oh! Julius, I feel so ill, and I'm cold. . . . What am I going to do? I'm afraid.'

'Your fault, you shouldn't have come. What did you think I would do, anyway?' he asked.

She shivered, crouched against the barrier, and glanced away from him ashamed. He waited while she was sick, and then, as she fumbled for a handkerchief, he said:

'Well, what did you think I should do? I can't wait here all night.'

'I thought we would be together,' she whimpered.

He pretended to lose his temper.

'D'you think I have the money to buy you a third-class ticket?' he shouted. 'It's as much as I can afford to keep myself. What colossal impudence. Not likely. I'm going straight to tell the captain the whole story. He'll have you put in the hold in irons.'

He walked swiftly back across the deck, shaking with laughter, leaving her crumpled up in the steerage. What a strange thing that she should care for him as much as this. He would not have believed it possible. Should he take her or leave her? It was a question of whether she should prove expensive. It was a nuisance to have to buy her a ticket. Perhaps if she shared his bunk they would be charged less. Her sex must not be discovered, though. Funny Elsa, she looked attractive, unhappy and ill in her boy's clothes. After all, he could not go for ever without a woman, and if she was with him there would be nothing to pay. She must make her own clothes, and she needn't eat much. If she became dear he could send her away. She would not starve; she had been a prostitute since she was ten.

So Julius bought another ticket for Elsa, and spun a story about a young runaway brother. Then he went back to the steerage to fetch her. She was so weak from sea-sickness now that he had to carry her in his arms, and he dumped her down like a sack of potatoes in his bunk, shoving her up to the side to make room for himself. The atmosphere in the cabin was appalling, nor was it improved by the presence of the eight other passengers who shared it, all in various stages of sickness and undress.

'My young brother is very ill,' said Julius, pinching Elsa in the arm not to give herself away; but as nobody listened to him, he decided they were safe for that night, anyway, and he closed his eyes and prepared himself for sleep.

Elsa wrapped herself against him, whimpering softly to herself, and he put his arm round her and held her tight, content suddenly with the warmth she brought to him. It was as though he were re-minded of something long ago in his childhood, something that had loved him and warmed him in this fashion, curled next to him for company. He searched back in his mind to discover what it should be, and as he did so he ran his hands up and down her body in a caress that came naturally to him, that was suggested by some subconscious instinct, a caress that belonged only to this thing who clung to him and breathed against his cheek.

When she stirred it broke the wandering train of thought that would have solved his riddle, and 'Go to sleep, can't you?' he said, but she whispered in his ear: 'I want to tell you something.'

'Well, what is it?' he said, and she came closer to him, touching him with her fingers, her hair brushing his chin.

'All this time in Ahèmed's house I've never had anyone but you,' she said. 'You thought I went with men like the other girls, but it wasn't true. I only danced for them. You were the first – there will never be anyone but you.'

He grunted; he was too sleepy to answer.

'Aren't you glad? Tell me you are glad,' she said.

He undid her clothes and felt for her, this warmth that he knew now and understood; and 'Fancy,' he muttered. 'Yes, of course I'm glad; go to sleep.' But he was thinking: 'As if I care whether she's been with a hundred men; it's all the same to me.'

But as they slept locked in each other, two children at rest, it came to his mind in a dream that it was not Elsa the dancing girl in the Kasbah who curled upon him, but his own little Mimitte who had been lost to him so long, his own little drowned cat with her soft fur and her smooth paws, sleeping once more her heart against his heart.

Clifford Street was but one of the tangle of slum streets to be found branching away from the Euston Road. Number thirty-three was every whit as shabby as its neighbours, dirty area steps continually fouled by the droppings of cats and dogs, drab lace curtains in the front windows never opened, a dingy passage and narrow stairway covered with strips of torn oilcloth leading to the floors above. A smell clung to the house that not even the rapid opening and shutting of the front door could relieve, nor the bitter draught of cold November fog: a smell of undusted furniture, of stale food, of families herded together, of unclean lavatories. This smell had its foundation in the basement, where the landlady lived with her crippled son and her three cats, and the feel of these things would float upwards to pervade the staircase and the other rooms, even as far as the little back room on the top floor. Perhaps the smell crept through the cracks – the door being ill-fitting and shaking from moment to moment in the lock; but however it came, it took possession and mingled comfortably with the musty close atmosphere of the little back room itself. The window would be kept tightly closed night and day, because once opened it would swell with the damp and could not be shifted, and then the air blew coldly down upon the creaking bed against the wall. That the chimney smoked without ceasing, covering the scanty furniture with great flakes of soot, was something more easily to be borne, and it was not really difficult to become accustomed to the lingering smoky taste that pervaded with great intensity every particle of food, from tea to the scraggy meat bones. The one fault of the fire was its lack of heating power; it could smoke most gloriously and cook after its fashion, but any warmth it would gather to itself and expend far up the chimney, so that not even its sooty flavour nor the firmly-closed window could keep the November fog outside the walls. The cold air would make its way unobtrusively but unmistakably, and lay a clammy hand upon the walls and the strip of threadbare carpet on the floor.

To Elsa, all her life accustomed to the warm and sub-tropical temperature of a southern climate, this cold was like some gigantic force of unbearable brutality; she wilted and shrivelled like a little plant.

Julius was sorry for her, but he could not understand the measure of her suffering. Amazed at his own generosity, he bought her a woollen coat during the first hard days after they had landed, but when this did not seem proof against the cold, he shrugged his shoulders and dismissed her as incurable.

'Why, in Paris,' he said, half vexed at her stupidity and disagreeably surprised at his own concern for her. 'Why, in Paris that was a different matter altogether. You could say it was cold there. I've seen folk die of it in the streets during the siege, their lips turning blue and their hands and feet numbed like stone. I lived in a garret, and the snow came in through the cracked panes. That was cold, I tell you. But this isn't much; you ought to feel lucky. Haven't you a decent room, and a fireplace, and a proper bed to sleep in?' She huddled nearer to the smoking fire, raking at the cheap coal with a poker.

'I'm not saying anything,' she said, her head low, hiding herself from him. 'It's you who keep on nagging me and questioning me – I can't keep from shivering; it's a sort of nervousness now, and I see you get irritated because of it, and then you make me worse.'

He stared at her sulkily. Yes, she was shivering now; he could see the back of her shoulders.

'It serves you right,' he said harshly. 'I never asked you to come with me, did I?' he said. 'Why didn't you stay behind in Alger?'

She answered nothing, but he saw by the lowering of her head he had hurt her. Something pricked in his heart, like a stab of pain, and he liked it and went on:

'Don't I pay five shillings a week for this room? Had I been alone I wouldn't be spending half that sum. I could fit in anywhere. Our food too. There's not everyone would eat meat every day as we do. But I have to buy meat for you because you're so thin. Your shoes, too – I've noticed they let in the damp. I shall have to buy you a new pair, of course. God knows what they are going to cost.'

She looked up at him swiftly, biting her lip. 'I don't need them,' she began. 'I can put paper inside these.'

He laughed. 'Yes, and then go creeping about like a martyred thing, resentful of me, making out in your silence how badly I treat you. Do you think I treat you badly? What would you do if I beat you, eh? Go on, answer me. It would do you good to be beaten.'

She turned away, flushing, ashamed that he knew her so well.

'You know you can do anything you like with me. I love you,' she said.

That was it, of course. If he threw a brick at her head she would only wince and bleed and then come to him for comfort. He wondered idly how many times he had wounded her with words and she had put her arms about him.

The tedious journey on the boat, the hours of sickness she had gone through, shutting herself away from him lest he should hate her for the sight, the horror and turmoil of the ultimate landing, registration papers, the word 'Alien', medical inspection and lies, and argument and explanation with officials, and Julius using all his wits to enable them to land while she clung like a little shadow to his arm, wide-eyed, frightened, half crazy with the cold and the rain.

He could not remember one gesture of tenderness he had given her, neither at the beginning, nor then, nor now, nor at any time.

He accepted, but did not understand it, this feeling of hers for him, all he knew was that it pleased and angered him at the same time and he had no wish to put her from him.

Still, she was a tie and a drag upon him for all that. Here they were in England only to find a London that was very different from the scholastic city painted by the Reverend Martin Fletcher, a London of poverty and hardship and general squalor, the English language a medley of confusing sounds harsh to their ears, and Julius himself not so fluent as he had believed himself to be.

For again he must take every burden upon himself, Elsa had never a word but French and Kasbah patter; and he must even buy a wedding ring for her third finger before the lodging-houses opened their doors to him, and then these English shunned them and looked down their noses.

He realized he would have to depend upon himself alone in this country and expect no help from man or woman, nor did this deter him or weaken him in any way, believing as he did in himself and his own power. He would rise above these people who sneered and laughed at him; one day he would make use of them, but he would always despise them.

Little brains they had and little minds. Quickly he put his value upon them, catching snatches of their conversation from behind their doors, from the streets, from the public houses. These men were lumbering fellows with receding chins and vacant grins, who worked because they must and with no hope of rising, who fuddled themselves with beer and pored over horse-racing accounts in newspapers.

The women, idling too, leaning over area railings and spitting malice about their neighbours, droning over some question that could not matter to them, and then inexplicably shrieking their ugly laughter at a child or a dog – this English humour and lack of serious purpose that he could not understand. Yes, he hated them from the beginning, but he would make his money out of them, and they could laugh and jibe at him as they pleased; they could peer at Elsa with greedy eyes and strictly pursed mouths, unhealthy in their conception of immorality.

Julius had not bargained for this distrust shown to aliens, and work was harder to find than he had expected. That first winter was fraught with much anxiety and distress. Elsa continually with either chill or cold hardly stirred from the cheerless room in the lodging-house, while he tramped the streets for work, turned away by many a shopkeeper and salesman because of his sharp nose and his foreign accent.

'Oh! we never employ aliens; there are too many of our own people out of work'; or else: 'You're Jewish, aren't you?' and a slight hesitation. 'No, I'm afraid I have nothing for you.'

'Times are very hard, these days,' another told him. 'I expect you'll find it nearly impossible to make your living here. A foreigner, too. Why didn't you stop in your own country?'

And Julius smiled politely and shrugged his shoulders. Useless to explain that he belonged nowhere and that he had no country. A cold winter, too, for all his denial, he stamping the pavement with collar turned up and hands deep in pockets. He saved money midday by queueing up outside a soup kitchen and waiting his turn, but there was little satisfaction in soup to his belly, and Elsa would be waiting alone in Clifford Street going hungry rather than face the cold.

In the evenings he would pore over advertisements in a cheap newspaper, straining his eyes by light of a gas jet, and there would be announcements to clerks, accountants, bank assistants, positions he knew he would be able to hold with the minimum of taxation to his brain, but because he was an alien it would be useless to apply for them, and he must turn the page to the humbler columns, for apprentices, errand boys, ironmongers, shoe-blacks, any form of employment. He bent over the dirty, well-thumbed paper, seated in the corner of a public house, and the shouting and laughter of the men around the bars was loathsome to him, but he must suffer their presence because there was some warmth in the smoke-laden atmosphere and he could not return to Elsa and her white face before he had put some drink inside him and could bluff her with the lies that he was doing well.

When he became errand boy, cleaner and general slave-of-all-work to the surly baker, Grundy, in Holborn, he did not tell Elsa at first for fear she should think less of him. And when she saw that his hours away from her were long, from very early morning until late in the evening, he explained as carelessly as he could that he had found work, excellent work, connected with flour and bread-making; and when she would come to visit him in the day, proud of him, he told her that this business was far away in the City and she would not be able to find it alone. She supposed that he was making good money, and he answered her that his pay, though moderate at first, would eventually be generous; nor when she inquired excitedly the exact amount he gained a day did he attempt to turn the sum into francs, putting her off with: 'Don't bother me, little plague.'

So Julius, sweeping the crumbs from the floor of the shop, putting back the shutters, setting forth with a basket on his arm, leaning with rolled sleeves and dripping face over the bakery fires, shouted at and cursed by Grundy who, tortured by rheumatism, possessed the shortest of tempers, showed never a sign of impatience or anger, but answered: 'Certainly, Mr Grundy,' 'No, Mr Grundy,' 'Coming immediately, sir,' 'What can I do for you, madam?' softly, obsequiously, a smile on his face, but thinking: 'This is not for long – one day, one day . . .'

He would be tired, yes, but never mind about that, he did the work of three men and he had a commission on the new clients who bought bread and a percentage on the weekly orders. He possessed the quality of looking ahead, though no one might understand him. It was busy and central, that thoroughfare of Holborn; traffic would increase with the years, property would double its value, and this shop of Grundy's where he toiled as underpaid assistant adjoined other shops and other premises, buildings that could be bought or demolished, or built upon; and this fellow Grundy was an old man with no son to carry on his business, he'd be glad enough to be rid of it in a year or so. To watch something spread itself and develop under your own eyes, reaching out tentacles here and there, gathering other things into its power, and growing day after day, year after year – a business that became a concern, and a concern that made a profit, and a profit that made a fortune, and a fortune that brought power, there was a dream and a thing of beauty, a dream that held the promise of reality.

To Julius Lévy there was ecstasy in this secret life of his; the knowledge that he could not fail was like a hidden jewel worn against his skin, to be touched and caressed in the darkness with warm sensuous fingers; nor would he share the brilliance of his secret with anyone in the world. These English people were pawns in the game. Old Grundy, who called to him: 'Lévy – I want you here,' 'Lévy – do this, do that . . .' – he was like some poor old blustering fowl running hither and thither in his little span of existence.

They were nothing and no one, thought Julius, these people he jostled on the crowded pavements when the day's work was done, these lumbering carts, these plodding omnibuses with their tired horses, these mud-splashed hansoms cloppoting towards the West End with the blazing lamps and the theatre crowds. He stood amongst them, the sound of the traffic in his ears, the sharp cries of a little newsboy running forward with a late edition, this was London and he was part of it, but it could not control him; he would rise above it and use it as he wished.

'You never talk to me,' complained Elsa, stroking the back of his shoulder. 'You are always so silent nowadays when you come back. There you go, thinking, watching – what are you thinking about?'

'But leave me alone, can't you?' he would say, and throwing open the window of their poky room in Clifford Street, he would lean out far into the street, his head lifted as though there were music in the air, and a smile upon his face that was secretive and strange.

He was queer, this Julius of hers, for there was nothing beyond the open window but the ugly grey roofs and chimney-pots stretching in endless vista as far as the eye could reach, the hum and throb of traffic, the rumble of wheels, the whistles of trains, the noisy, cockney screams of children playing in the street, the hideous trill of a barrel-organ mingled with the scraping finger scales played on the piano of the house opposite.

The tumult and misery of this dwelling-place would seem to her sometimes like a weight upon her heart, and she would close her eyes and summon in one breath the sweet smells and the distant cries of the Kasbah, the amber and spice and the crushed petals of bougainvillea flowers that would never be hers again, and 'Where are we going?' she thought. 'Why must this happen to us?'

The open window drove smoke down the chimney and the cold air rushed into the room; nor did he mind, bare-headed, sleeves rolled up, lost in his dreams. She shivered, and coughed, her hand to her throat.

'Shut the window.' But he did not answer; he waited a moment, and then turned to her, smiling, the same strange smile upon his lips, and he said to her:

'Listen – can you hear it? – listen.'

He held out his arm and she went to him, and together they leant out of the little window to the street below, and all she could hear was this continuation of the hum of traffic, the ugly sound that must haunt her now for ever, and – 'What do you mean? I can't hear anything,' she said.

He took no notice of this, but drew her close against his side, and he said to her: 'Someone should make music out of this.' She leant her cheek against his.

'I don't like to think about it,' she told him. 'It's too big for me. It makes me seem such a little wretched thing. I'm only a speck amongst all this, with no will; it makes me wonder why I believe in God.'

When she said this, shyly, as though it were dragged from her, he let her go from him, and he laughed and spread out his hands as though he could gather the atoms that floated as particles of dust upon the air.

'God?' he said. 'Believe in God? Why, I tell you that all of this belongs to me and I can give it to you.'

She stared at him, half frightened, half unsure of what he had said; it was as though he had shouted his words until they had found an echo in her heart, and he stood there with his eyes blazing, demoniacal and cruel, his hands opening and shutting as one who grasps a treasure; he towered above her sinister and strange.

She backed away, startled at the change in him, the strength and the pallor of his face.

'Don't!' she said. 'Don't talk in that way – I don't like it; you look different, you frighten me. I don't want you to be like that.'

He stood over her, blocking the light from the window. He would not take his eyes from her face; he was terrible, he was changed, like someone who talks in his sleep.

'Yes, all of this is mine,' he repeated. 'I shall give it to you. Anything you want. It will belong to me.'

Now he had frightened her, now she thought he must be mad or had been drinking. Yes, she was afraid. The loneliness and misery of these months in London seemed to culminate in a great wave of despair and close in upon her heart.

'I don't want you to be like that,' she cried. 'I don't want you to give me things. I want us to be home in Alger in a little house, just the sun and the flowers and being happy, and you shall sell in the market-place and I will look after you and give you children.'

She began to cry, closing and unclosing her hands.

'Julius, my darling, my darling – let's go home now, before it's too late, away from this cold unhappy country. I've been so miserable here, so terribly miserable.'

Then he smiled; he held out his arms and pulled her to him; he was not a stranger any more but himself again, his hands running over her, his lips in her hair.

'Why, my little silly, my little absurd love, I haven't said anything. What are you chittering and whimpering about? You deserve to be beaten. I shall beat you and thrash you. You little foolish, you little nonsense.'

She thrust her head under his chin, she clung to him like a child and demanded to be comforted, and half drugged, she listened to his voice in her ear, calling her 'his love, his own Mimitte,' funny words she did not understand, but which seemed to assure her that she would be happy again.

'Are you cold?' he asked her.

'No, not any more,' she said.

'I can feel you, shivering and trembling,' he said, 'silly one that you are. Are you hungry, too?'

'Yes, I'm hungry.'

There was a thin watery soup and bread, and a scrap of butter; and then the fire must die down lest they should burn and waste the wood.

'If we were in Alger now,' sighed Elsa, 'we'd be sitting by an open window. You know how the sky is there at night. The air smells different, too, queer and spicy, sometimes moss and scent float down on it from the trees in Mustapha.'

He was sitting on the floor, his head against her knee.

'In Ahèmed's house the dancing girls are painting their heels and their nails,' he said lazily. 'Naïda is smoking a cigarette and blowing rings into the air, and Lulu is scolding one of the new girls for running away with her ear-rings. I can hear the jingling of her bangles. Down below the musicians are throbbing the drum and one of them breathes on his pipe, a thin reedy note. It would be warm in the dancing-room tonight, Elsa, all the old men huddled together and clutching themselves, and the dust rising from the floor as Naïda stamps and shakes herself. Do you want to be there?'

She would not answer. Supposing she told him the truth and he sent her back?

'I like to be wherever you are,' she said.

But he must go on with his teasing of her, hiding his laughter at her pain.

'Think of the sun in Alger, and the food, and the low divan where you used to sleep. That's better than this, isn't it? Look at this bare, empty room, and the old iron bedstead, and the ashes of that fire. You don't like it, do you?'

She would not give way, though.

'I love you,' she said. He took no notice of this. It did not come into his scheme of things at all, this business of words and protestations. She could murmur and whisper if she liked, it was all the same to him.

'At least there's one way we can keep warm,' he said, and pulled her up from the floor, thinking of Nanette with a sigh; and she said anxiously, peering into his eyes:

'You do love me, don't you? Tell me you do.'

'Of course, little idiot; be quiet, anyway,' and she must be content with that.

Later, when he woke suddenly in the middle of the night for no reason but because she had stirred against his shoulder, he thought clearly as though a cold light had broken into his brain: 'I'm hungry and poor and cold – but I'm happy – I'm happy. This won't come again.'

And as he knew this and held it to him, the thing was gone from him, out of his reach, and he whimpered subconsciously like a lost child, and fell asleep and was alone again.

The Progress of Julius

It was often a mystery to old Grundy that his assistant Lévy, this Jew fellow, should work so hard. It surely was not for the money, a low enough wage at any consideration, but with scarcely a word he seemed even from the beginning to have grasped the essentials of the business and to bear all responsibilities upon his shoulders.

The financial side of the little shop was taken in hand most admirably by this newcomer, the week's takings invariably showed a profit instead of the old deficiency. He had a good manner with the customers, too, and more than this, he had a way of arranging the shop that attracted a passer-by. He knew how to dress a window, he set the cakes and the bread to view in a tasty manner for all the world like a smart confectioner. It was a relief, when you were getting old, thought Grundy, to have someone at hand so reliable and strong who didn't fuss you, who worked smoothly, who, as it were, ran the whole concern for you. Just a Jewish fellow, a foreigner of sorts who had begged for a job two years past as though he had come to the end of his tether and demanded a charity, and now bore the whole brunt of the work and made Grundy comfortably aware that there wasn't any need for him to stir from the back parlour behind the shop. To get up late in the mornings, to sit with a newspaper on his knee and blink at it over his spectacles, to take a walk along Holborn and watch the traffic, to look now and again in at the shop and see Lévy behind the counter and customers standing, it was all very pleasant and made him feel he didn't have to think or bother about things.

So that when his assistant came to him one day, in the autumn of eighteen eighty-three, and said to him: 'Your lease is up in November, Mr Grundy; what are you going to do about it?' he stared at the fellow in amazement.

'How the devil do you know? – what's it got to do with you? I'd forgotten as it happens.'

'I thought you had. Well, it's like this, Mr Grundy. I'm very willing to buy the lease from you.'

Old Grundy could not believe his ears.

'Buy the lease? Have you taken leave of your senses? Where'd you get the money from to buy me up, I'd like to know?'

This fellow Lévy smiled; he wasn't going to give anything away. 'That's my business, Mr Grundy – enough to say that I've had the money put by. For some time, too.'

'Weren't you near to starving when I gave you this job three years ago?'

'No, sir.'

'Well – what the devil? You looked half starved, thin as a rake – seems to me you've always looked as though you didn't feed yourself. Had you the money then?'

'Yes – but I'd never touched it.'

'You let yourself go hungry, and you worked here as you did, and you had money put by – I don't follow. Are you mad, Lévy, or what?'

'I don't think so. If I'd wanted to buy your business then you wouldn't have sold it. Nor would I have made it pay. Things are different now. People know me round here, and anyway, there's no need to go into all that. Will you sell your lease, Mr Grundy?'

The old fellow was disturbed, he did not understand; everything was upset.

'The shop does very well,' he protested. 'Why should I sell up? I'm not going to turn out at my time of life. No, thank you.'

Julius Lévy shrugged his shoulders.

'Of course it's for you to say,' he said carelessly. 'It's a question of take it or leave it. If you won't sell I'll go somewhere else. I've got my eye on another business. It will mean you having to shoulder the responsibility of the shop again, that's all. These last years you haven't made much of an appearance, though. Customers have forgotten you. If I set up for myself farther down Holborn I'll take your custom with me.'

He turned away as though the matter was settled. Old Grundy was afraid. He saw the truth of these words, and he didn't like the fellow's manner. Unscrupulous, queer.

'Here,' he said gruffly, 'wait a moment. Don't be in such a tearing hurry. I'm quite willing to talk it over.'

Julius sat down at the table, a piece of paper and a pen before him, and he waited for Grundy to come to terms. For three years he had been waiting for this moment. He had infinite patience. He dipped his pen in the inkpot and looked up at Grundy, his face immobile, showing nothing of his feelings. But he was laughing inside and he knew he had won. Julius bought the lease and was the owner of 'Grundy's'. He had a new name painted over the door: 'Lévy – Baker and Confectioner'.

He took Elsa away from the wretched little room in Clifford Street, and installed her in the three rooms behind the shop. He did not tell her much of what had happened for fear she might think he had money to spend.

'We've got to be as careful as before,' he told her severely. 'It's got to be a matter of pinching and scraping. Just because there are three rooms here you needn't think I have money to burn. No nonsense over fires and food, mind.'

She shook her head gravely. Of course they were still very poor; she would be careful. How clever he was, though, her Julius, only twenty-three and this baker's shop belonged to him. She did not understand how he had managed. If he was pleased, though, nothing else mattered.

It was certainly better here in a way than Clifford Street, but the noise was worse. The traffic in Holborn never stopped rolling and rumbling past the shop. At the end of a long day her head ached so that she would want to scream. The rooms were dark and gloomy too. Very stuffy in the summer. She had much more to do now than in the old days, keeping these rooms tidy and cooking. She had to cook for the men in the bakery too, and sometimes she must come and help in the shop.

Julius told Elsa that she must busy herself with the confectionery. So now it would be that, from morning to night, late to bed and early to rise, till she was tired – tired, and had no wish for anything but sleep.

Julius's energy was unbounded; it was as though he could not understand that anyone else could be weary, that anyone should rest for a moment, their head in their hands, back breaking and throat burning.

'Oh! Julius, don't scold – for a moment let me be,' and the thought of another world swam into her tired mind half dazed with want of sleep, a world of song, and sun, and long hours of siesta, and the smell of moss and eucalyptus trees. 'Shall we ever go back?' she wondered; and his voice would call through to her from the shop: 'Elsa, Elsa, the new loaves are through from the bakery; what about those cakes? It's half past three: they ought to be ready for the shop.'

'One moment – they're coming,' and she dragged herself from the chair where she had fallen, and put her hand up to brush back her hair, and caught sight of herself in a little mirror on the wall – pale, haggard, two enormous eyes set in a sunken face; Elsa, the little girl who laughed, and clapped her hands on the dancing-floor in the Kasbah. 'I'm eighteen,' she thought. 'I'm getting old. Soon he won't love me any more.' And she took her cloth to seize the hot tray loaded with cakes and carried it out into the shop.

'They're late,' he said. 'You mustn't get slack. I don't want to tell you again.'

A customer in the shop glanced at her curiously. Elsa flushed, ashamed that he should speak to her so before people. She went back into the dark kitchen, coughing, something inside her tearing at her chest. She put her handkerchief over her mouth to stifle the sound. He would be irritated if he heard. He had scolded her for it once before.

'Keep that cough quiet, can't you? It sounds bad to a customer. Anyone would think we had an invalid in the place. Nobody will want to buy your cakes if you cough over them like that.'

She told him she could not control it: she would do her best and then it seized her again, like a suffocating wave.

'You had better buy some lozenges,' he told her. 'You surely don't expect me to get a doctor to see you? Think of the expense. It's as much as I can do to keep us both as it is.'

She assured him she wanted no doctor, that she was perfectly well.

The work was too much for her, she knew that, but she was afraid to tell him. He would say she was nothing but a slack, lazy prostitute from the south. He often said things to hurt, even when they were alone together, and he had loved her, and she was close to him. Once, lying next to him at night feeling his hands that she worshipped wandering up and down her body in a caress familiar to her and beloved, she kissed his throat and whispered happily: 'What are you thinking about?' And he yawned and said: 'I was thinking about Nanette, the coloured *blanchisseuse* –

109

I'd like to have her again.' When she pushed his hands away from her, her blood curdling, revolting, and turned her back to him, he seemed surprised and asked her what was wrong.

Now, tired from the endless baking, and her cough tearing at her, she thought that perhaps if she had a child she would not have to work. She would be able to rest for nine months. The idea of such rest and tranquillity opened itself up to her like a dream of loveliness. The longing stayed with her now continuously; she waited and watched and prayed for a sign that it should be, but the months passed and nothing happened. She realized with a sickening sense of disappointment that now it would probably never be. Perhaps her body was not fit for child-bearing. She did not know about these things. All she could do was to pray to God. Finally she summoned up her courage and casting away her pride she asked Julius why she could not have a child.

He laughed at her and said he supposed she would be bearing one every year if he had chosen to let her.

She imagined that in his way he must be like God, and she felt humble in her ignorance, and she asked him again.

'Julius, I would like to have a child.'

'What – another one to feed besides ourselves? Don't be a fool,' he said.

'A child would cost very little,' she said wistfully. 'I believe you would be happy when he was born.'

Then he hurt her once more, strangely and inexplicably, like a thrust of a sword in her heart, caring not at all how much he wounded her.

'I can't have responsibilities of that kind yet,' he said. 'Time enough years hence. Besides, you're not my wife. I don't want children by you.'

He changed the conversation and began to talk about the shop. She sat very still, not listening, but some of the warmth that he once bore her, close to her heart, was gone from her for ever.

She did not speak of a child again, often after that day she was silent with him and dull. She wondered now why it was she stayed with him when he gave her nothing of himself but his body.

After some harshness to her, some impatient gesture before a customer or an assistant, she would say to herself: 'This is the end, I won't bear it any more. I shall go from him and never come back'; and then sit white-faced and tight-lipped over their evening meal in the stuffy parlour behind the shop, while he ate hungrily, paying no attention to her mood, his mind busy with thoughts he could not share with her, and he would look up suddenly, throwing her a smile and catching her unawares. 'Mimitte has hidden herself and has put out her claws. Does she want to be loved?'

She would shake her head, her eyes grim, refusing to be drawn, and he with one touch of his lips upon her and one careless hand upon her heart would bring her weakness back to her; nor could she move nor think while he was there, laughing in her ear; but she knew she belonged to him body and soul, that her very blood and her flesh were part of him, her mind in his keeping, and she could never go from him without her own life leaving her.

'Why do you do it?' she whispered once, after a bitter word flung at her and a long silence followed by a painfully exquisite reconciliation, and she turned a tear-stained face to his, tears of happiness and distress. 'Why do you do it?'

'I don't know what you mean,' he said. 'I haven't done anything but love you. You talk too much.' And there she would be in the dark again with him forgetting her, a stranger imprisoned in her flesh.

Julius had no time for the moods and fancies of Elsa. She was only a dancing girl from Alger after all. He had never asked her to follow him. She must be sulky and strange because she was a woman, and women had no concern in the business of life as he would live it. Little problems of sex and jealousy were not for him. He had work to do. Work of absorbing interest and intense excitement to him because of his habit of looking far ahead.

Elsa imagined that because he owned at twenty-five a promising baker's and confectionery business he had reached the limit, and should be prepared to settle comfortably into the position, earning enough to keep the wolf from the door and a little over besides. So that it was only Julius and not Elsa and the two hard-working assistants, who realized the significance of a day in March, when a customer, sheltering from the rain, bought a big-sized roll of bread about midday, and being hungry ate it standing up before the counter.

The Progress of Julius

It was Julius who seized a chair and a small table from his own parlour and placed it in the shop, suggesting with a smile that the customer should have his 'lunch' in comfort.

Five minutes later a cup of coffee appeared. The customer, pleased at the attention shown to him, drank his coffee, bought a small chocolate cake and a pastry roll, and discovered he had lunched excellently for eightpence instead of spending his usual one-and-sixpence at a neighbouring tavern.

He came again, and the next time there were two other tables beside his own, both of which were occupied by people of his own type, eating rolls and coffee. The following day ham and egg sandwiches were added to the menu and fruit tarts.

The assistants, flushed and weary with the extra work, declared the 'boss' to be crazy, and a damned young slave-driver into the bargain. Elsa, her back nearly breaking from bending over the fire, outraged at the coffee and the ham she had been told to pillage from her own little private store, was near to weeping at this new departure from the normal. 'I was keeping it for our supper,' she protested stubbornly. 'Why must our own food be sacrificed to the shop?'

He was smiling that sinister secret smile of his that she feared and hated.

'Do as I tell you and make those sandwiches at once,' he said. 'Four coffees too – and bring them in right away.'

'What's the matter?' she said. 'Why are you looking at me like that?'

He did not hear her, nor was he smiling at her. He was thinking of the placid English customer sitting comfortably in front of the coffee and the rolls and the ham sandwich, and he knew with a still strange triumph that this was the beginning.

'But I don't understand, Julius,' said Elsa; 'if we are still so poor how can you afford to buy the shop next door?'

'The lease is going cheap.'

'I know I'm only an ignorant, stupid girl, but surely even a cheap lease means money of some sort. What will you do with another shop?'

'Knock down the walls between, of course, and have one large

112

space, there'll be more room then for tables. The floor overhead, too, that belongs to the same building, and comes over to me with the empty shop. I can make use of that when there's congestion below.'

'There's an old lady lives there, Julius, she's nearly blind, and only that daughter to look after all. What will they say? They won't want to move.'

'I can't help their troubles.'

'But, dear love, you surely can't turn them out?'

'Don't be a little idiot, Elsa, mixing yourself in my affairs. Of course those people had notice to leave a week ago.'

She stared at him, twisting her hands, distressed she knew not why.

'I don't know why you want to make the shop large,' she said; 'it means such an expense and the work is doubled. Why, with the savings you must have given to buy it up we could have gone away perhaps, now that the hot weather has come. Somewhere by the sea.'

'We can't afford holidays,' he told her abruptly, not bothering to look up from his paper of calculations. 'During this heat we shall have to work harder than before. August is a slack month. I've got to get all the repairs finished and done, both shops painted and re-decorated before September. We'll be ready then for a busy autumn and winter.'

Her heart sank at his words. She knew what it meant. Workmen about the place continually, the smell of paint, and they themselves doing much of the work so as to save money. Then, business starting briskly so soon as everything was finished, standing from morning till night – on – on – never ending this craze of his for efficiency, for speed, for enlargement.

Now, with the extra building and the improvements she would have help under her of course, but instead of her position becoming easier as its importance grew, she found there was more to do than before, the day's work was one endless strain, one continuous effort to keep to time. The bakery was run simultaneously with the catering for meals, and the care of the confectionery was still in her hands. Not for any moment in the day would she be away from the smell of food, from the glare of the ovens, and from the grumbling, impatient women who served under her. She could not see that this passionate turmoil was leading anywhere. They were none of them happier than before. Life was certainly no easier than it had been. Julius and she still lived shabbily and meanly in the poky rooms at the back of the building. Only two rooms now, the bedroom and kitchen, their sitting-room having been seized for 'space' for the shop. Besides her time in the confectionery Elsa had to tidy and clean these two rooms, she had to see to their own meals, frugal enough as it happened, but even so the labour was heavy on top of the work for the shop.

'Do you think, now we are doing better, I might have a woman in to clean and cook for us?' she asked.

He looked at her in amazement. 'Haven't you got hands?' he said.

'Yes – but – what with the confectionery . . .'

'Oh! I see,' he taunted her, 'you want to sit and be idle. You want to lie down on cushions and be fanned. Why don't you go back to Alger where you belong? Lazy little prostitute.'

'Julius – you don't understand.'

'I understand one thing. I never rest myself and I don't expect the people who work under me to rest. Put that into your head and don't argue. If you don't like it, you can go.'

No care, no tenderness. He considered her only as someone who worked under him. Someone he employed. Stung to anger by his sneers she let her tongue run away with her.

'Since you think of me as one of your servants, why do you expect me to work without wages?'

At this he threw back his head and laughed.

'You can go tomorrow, if you like,' he said. 'I could fill your place without the slightest difficulty. Come here.'

She went to him at once.

'Well – are you going to leave me?' he asked.

She took her hands away from him, she knew he was playing with her.

'Sometimes I believe you hate me,' she said slowly; 'it can only be hate that makes you act in this way.'

He laughed, and drew her on his knee. She hid her face in his shoulder, and he went on jotting down figures and calculations on a piece of paper with one hand while he caressed her with the other.

'Ten, fifteen,' he murmured. 'Say fifteen tables in the new build-ing and ten here, twenty – one assistant to five tables, lunch twenty minutes, tables for two, twelve o'clock till two . . . forty maximum . . . shilling charge – say one-and-three – What did you say, Mimitte?'

'You don't love me,' she repeated; 'why do you have me?'

'Because there's nothing to pay,' he said. 'Forty maximum in half an hour, two pound ten – not good enough, make tables for four, throw out two top rooms, say fifty, sixty – three, six, twelve pounds – don't cry down my neck; it bores me – can't you find something else to do?' he said.

What fools women were, only one thought ever in their heads. He watched her back as she moved away from him, drooping, dispirited, how different she was from the laughing, gay child in the Kasbah; she seemed to have no life in her nowadays. These southern girls got old quickly, always ailing too. 'You're cough-ing again,' he said, 'you'd better get another box of those lozenges. Can't have you laid up.'

She did not answer him, though. She was only like a kitten after all, she had to be coaxed and petted before she put in her claws and clung to you.

'I was only teasing you, you silly little thing,' he called softly; 'think I'd have any woman but you? I've nearly done these ac-counts and then I'll tell you things. Little nonsense – little stupid love. Don't sulk, Mi-Mi baby.'

She flung him a smile over her shoulder. He went on with his figures, forgetting her at once.

The throwing of two shops into one was a success from the start. The fresh paint and the clean appearance of the building drew the eye at once, the stock in the windows looked fresh and appetizing, and the cleverest touch of all was the low-priced menu stuck well to the front in the glass above the door. The service was quick and efficient, there was something smart about the marble-topped tables free from the last-comers' stains and crumbs, and it was a noticeable improvement to find oneself able to lunch well and thoroughly in under half an hour. 'Lévy's' was a great novelty to find in a busy, congested area such as Holborn. The numberless clerks and poorer City men who gained their daily bread in this quarter of the City were agreeably surprised to come across this place that provided a quick, cheap, midday meal. They came once and came again, they told their fellow clerks, passers-by tried it, as 'a change', and then made lunch at Lévy's a habit. The place was succeeding as Julius knew it would succeed. The upper rooms of the second shop which had been furnished as the rest with tables, chairs and counter in case of congestion below were in use almost from the outset. There was never a moment between twelve o'clock and two when one of the tables was not filled, either below or upstairs, and it was not long before teas, served between four and six, became part of the daily routine. The original bakery, from which the shop had sprung, held now a very secondary importance compared to the new café, as the owner termed it. The work continued of course; the old customers were supplied daily as before, but the back premises of the shop were extended; what had been the baking-house was now fitted up in superior fashion for cooking and serving. Julius had a lift installed to lead to the upper floor.

It seemed to Elsa that never for a moment now was the building free from workmen making some alteration. First the shop, then the upper floor, then the kitchens. Scaffolding erected in front of her bedroom window – the only spot of privacy left to her – and the sound of hammer and saw. Every month there would be an improvement to make. According to Julius, there must be greater efficiency in the kitchens, the service must be speeded up, this assistant discharged for one more capable. The two buildings were not large enough to hold the overflow of customers, he would have to take in the adjoining store – only a drapery business doing poorly. He would buy the fellow out, sell up his stock for him and make a small profit on the deal perhaps. He must have a kitchen on each floor in future to ensure rapid service and hot food. Those lifts took too long – have each floor working separately and independently but to time, with its own servers and cook. This present staff were overworked; not enough of them, he must add, improve, enlarge, change this, alter that, a new idea here, a change of policy there.

Julius never lived in the present, he was always six months, a year, ahead. The growth of his café business, as he termed it, was never too much for him. He never sat down, or paused and thought to himself: 'I'm doing very well, now stop a bit, now wait and see.' It was too easy, it was like a toy in his hands. Little simple matters like hitting on the idea of orange sunblinds let down from the open windows in the summer were a relaxation to him and an amusement, and the braziers outside the doors in winter as he remembered them, when a child in Paris, would run through his mind suddenly for no reason and be put into practice without effort.

He would stand on the big ground floor of the café during the rush hours – one o'clock till two – his eyes never still, alighting upon one thing then another and making a mental note of the fact. 'Tables a little too congested in one corner, half a dozen people were cramped unnecessarily – he must alter that. Why not stools up against that counter! – good idea – run that as a new scheme next summer when he took in the next block; keep a section for drinks and ices in the summer: run it separately and unconnected with the lunch – Elsa could surely manage that if she can't do anything else . . . Hello! – that new fellow has smashed a tray, must sack him for incompetence or give him chance of paying for damage out of his own pocket . . . Rooms upstairs filled, good – table empty in one corner; why doesn't that idiot tell 'em below there's heaps of space for anyone waiting? . . . That ham is perfectly fresh – will do very well tomorrow in sandwiches – must tell 'em never to throw food away when it can be used up differently. . . . That fellow at the pay desk looks efficient, I'll send him below. He's wasted in this smaller room . . . Who's complaining about the coffee? – too much chicory, I suppose; that's the cheaper brand, I must go back to the other, not worth fighting over two shillings. . . . Go on, you slow-witted bastard, help that customer with his coat, politeness above all things in this business – good idea – make a speciality of attention at Lévy's, start a No Gratuities with the New Year, no harm in trying . . . There's lettuce being carried out quite untouched, make a sandwich of it, sardine and salad on toast – use up these leavings and make 'em a popular feature every day; egg and cheese,

117

ham and tongue . . . That fish is off, I can smell it, no use putting that over, lose customers, silly idiot in the kitchen, give her the sack if she can't use her nose . . . Rooms are full up and a young fellow's being turned away – God in Heaven – this English climate. . . . Why can't I make a roof garden, they'd bring their women here then; tables for two under umbrellas – damn, damn, why live in London? . . . Somebody asking for sausages in midsummer, say we've got 'em, don't shake your head, you silly sheep, something can be produced to look like a sausage, never deny a customer . . . Speed it up, speed it up, fellow's finished his chop, be ready to take away the plate . . . give him strawberries and cream, we've a surplus today and they'll only rot, put it before him and disappear, he'll eat it, he's the dithering sort . . . Not enough cloakroom space, must take in more room for two extra w.c.s., somebody waiting in the corridor and getting impatient . . . There's too much water in those ices, it's flavouring they need and colour.'

On and on, his thoughts travelling like a flash of lightning amongst faces and tables and food, below, above, in the kitchens, missing nothing and being everywhere at once.

Two years, three years, four years and Lévy's growing and improving every six months, a big popular café spreading itself from a humble baker's and confectioner's. The little everyday clerks of the City who pushed each other along the pavements at midday, with their Gladstone bags and their folded umbrellas, the smug self-satisfied conventional fellows who sat year in year out on their round stools in their dusty offices, they poured into Lévy's as though it had always been – they accepted it as part and parcel of their natural lives.

Nor did they notice, so skilfully and unobtrusively was it done, that the menu eventually arrived at one-and-three and one-and-six. That besides the set course it was possible to choose dishes from a bill of fare whose price was not a whit lower than that of any other eating-house in the City; in their ignorance they fancied themselves to be saving money and time by these meals so smartly served on marble-topped tables by smart assistants who were forbidden to take tips. 'Something for nothing,' they thought, 'something for nothing,' which was just exactly what Julius Lévy intended them to think, and he pocketed his profits with a smile on his face because this whole business of exploitation and easy money was surely almost too facile an undertaking altogether.

For Elsa, who had cried with the cold in that attic in Clifford Street, the development of the café was something to be feared and hated. It was too big for her, she was swallowed up in this atmosphere of slick efficiency, of a staff working to order and to time; and she, once the humble baker of cakes over a little stubborn fire, must now be pushed out of the way to make room for skilled cooks trained to their work. She was turned over from one room to another, she was told to serve behind a counter, to attend to a certain number of tables, to look after accounts at a pay desk, and at each of these she failed in turn. She was not quick enough, she forgot the orders, she fumbled with dishes, she muddled her change.

She had never learnt English properly, and this was her great difficulty, at any sharp word or quick sentence she was lost. She dreaded the appearance of Julius, for should he come near her when she was working she became flustered immediately, she tripped over her words, flushing in distress. She made one mistake after another and dared not raise her head lest she should meet his eyes, cold and scornful, and should see that tap-tap of his finger on table or counter, the sign of his anger that she knew and feared.

'It's no use,' he would say at the end of the day when they were done. 'I can't have you in charge in the upper room. You keep everything back. I shall have to put somebody in place of you.'

She would bow her head, sensitive and wounded, unable to excuse herself.

'There doesn't seem to be anything you can do,' he said.

She tried to defend herself, but how could she when she knew he was in the right?

'It's not that I don't do my best,' she began; 'I do work – I try hard to work, but it's all so quick, and I lose myself – I'm stupid, that's all.'

'Stupidity's no good to me,' he frowned. 'I can't afford it.'

She supposed he must be nearly ruining himself over this café, how much money could it cost him, she wondered; perhaps any day he would tell her it had failed. They still lived so very cheaply in themselves, two small rooms at the top of the building. If he was making the business pay, surely he would say they could live more comfortably. It was months and months since she had asked for a new dress, and there were other little things she wanted too, stockings, nightdresses – she did her best with her needle and pieces of cheap material. She did not like to ask for clothes, if they were on the edge of disaster. He might even be put in prison for debt.

'There's only one thing left – you can hardly be a fool at that,' he told her. 'I'll put you in charge of the cloakroom. Any tips, of course, you can keep. You had better buy yourself a black dress and an apron and look respectable for once. Take those earrings off, too.'

So Elsa, the dancing beauty of the Kasbah, sat all day long as a cloakroom attendant in Lévy's café. She was too tired to mind. It seemed to her that this was the first time she had rested in five years. From now on she would only see Julius in the evenings. The management of the café took him farther from her than ever, it was as though he advanced a step forward with each alteration and enlargement and she was left behind, incapable of progress. In the evenings, over their frugal supper in the one sitting-room, cheerless and poorly furnished, he would eat in silence, his mind teeming with plans and never resting for one moment; while she, changing his plate and washing the dishes, darning his socks in a little low chair at his side, would feel like some servant with no other interest or utility to him but to see to his wants and to hold his silence.

Her duties in the cloakroom were practically negligible, she had no part in the general life and the running of the café. More and more she would become shut up in herself, unaware of this stream of vitality that passed her by, without realization of the development around her, leaving her thus stranded on the little desolate shore of her existence.

Julius was 'the manager', 'the boss', he was an unknown quantity with whom she had no concern. He moved in his own span of life in another time and their paths led away from one another.

120

In 1890, Lévy's café in Holborn was already a big three-storeyed building, comprising some three or four shops that had been knocked into one; and in the spring of that year Julius Lévy took over the entire block which brought him now to the corner of Southampton Row.

The café had sprung up like a mushroom in five years, and the only one who seemed entirely unconcerned was Julius himself, who took the affair for granted. He had known he could not fail, and far from being proud and contented with this achievement at the age of thirty, for he was certainly the envy and the thorn in the flesh of the smaller shopkeepers, he considered the Holborn café as nothing more nor less than the little fountain-head from which a thousand rivers would spring. Now that he had a capable staff working under him and need no longer himself be in constant supervision, he had time to look about him, and to gauge the market value of property, to note the growing import-ance of the West End of London as a commercial centre. The Strand, Leicester Square, Piccadilly. In ten or fifteen years' time these were the spots which would be most congested, theatres, rest-aurants, people crowding here to be fed and entertained. He had no concern with the far end of Piccadilly, of Bond Street and Mayfair; he looked towards Oxford Street as his most certain proposition. Oxford Street which would become the shopping Mecca of the middle classes, with their thick-headed, good-humoured love of a bargain, their sheep-like tendency to be driven, their grasping, inherent desire to snatch 'something for nothing', who would bring to Julius the fullest measure of pros-perity.

Every year ground rent was increasing and property doubled in value; he would have to buy early and buy quickly, he must get in first, and before the lesser sharks came sniffing at his heels. Lévy's of Holborn was serving his purpose, the profits came roll-ing in to be checked and put aside, profit to be used for the open-ing up of Lévy's of Oxford Street and Lévy's of the Strand. He knew they would be small at first, ignored perhaps, laughed at by people who fed in hotels and restaurants, but he could afford to wait, he could enjoy his patience, and sooner or later the great herd of the middle classes would come to him, and they represented, though they did not know it, the wealth and the whole meaning of England.

Nobody had heard of him yet, he was only a Jewish fellow, another of those foreigners, who ran a café somewhere down in Holborn where the clerks and office boys gobbled their midday meals. But give me ten years, he thought; ten years, fifteen years, and I'll put a chain around England that nobody will break.

Julius was a boy sailing his first boat upon a pond, he was a boy at a carpenter's bench with a tool in his hand singing as he worked, he was a child with his castle of bricks built firmly within walls. Life was a game to him, a game of pen and paper and a hundred figures jotted here and there; figures that were shaped as pounds and shillings and pence. It was a game when to win you must buy first and buy low and cheat the other fellow, when you must come first before the whole world and think just a fraction ahead of your opponent. He would not relax, not for a moment would he pause and say: 'I have done this,' but must continue unwavering and straight, reaching out to the skies like an arrow flying to the face of the sun. In one of his rare communicative moods he showed Elsa a drawing of his plans. It was a sheet of paper drawn to the scale of a map of London, and the streets and quarters were marked into divisions. Here and there he had marked certain thoroughfares with crosses. He pointed to them with his finger. 'There – that dot in the Strand, there's a site there I want for building. I shall get it in two years, they'll be sending the traffic along this side street to avoid congestion by Charing Cross. See that cross in red ink in Oxford Street? The green omnibuses stop there now and there's a row of small window-fronted shops. They'll have to come down for me. Right over there, in the south-west, in Kensington, there's property going for a song. It can wait for a few years until I'm ready. The Strand will be my first.'

He had one hand in his pocket and a cigarette hanging from the corner of his mouth. His hair flopped over one eye. He was a boy, he couldn't mean what he said.

'You haven't the money to do all that, Julius,' she said slowly. 'Why, you'll be ruined. Once you get entangled into schemes of that sort you'll be out of your depth and no one to help you.

Why can't you be content with the one café? I expect in time, if you are careful, it will be quite a big sort of place.'

He looked at her curiously. She did not seem to understand that even now the café in Holborn was a great money-making concern, that the profits this year seemed enormous for a comparatively new business and that he could, if he wished, buy his Strand site tomorrow, only he was waiting for the psychological moment. There were no original expenses here, he had bought Grundy's and the adjacent block at the lowest possible price. Something for nothing – something for nothing. He lived no more comfortably than the original baker, he had no expenses, he scarcely spent a penny – every profit went into the café. He would not let Elsa suspect the truth.

'Oh! I'll find some capital,' he said, 'even if I have to borrow or steal. Don't you bother your head about that.'

As he watched her grave face it came to him that she never smiled or was merry with him now, she was greatly changed from the old days when they first came to London. She was no longer a playful, restless, sensitive kitten who curled upon his chest, she had grown into a placid, dull little cat, a quiet, sleepy tabby cat who blinked her great eyes and was surely rather stupid. He wondered why she should be so changed. He would have liked someone beside him to share his enthusiasm, to see ahead as he did and to glory in his success. A mind attuned to his and receptive. A woman with sense and intuition who could hear him talk without bewilderment. A woman of depth and culture who possessed health and vitality. Yes, health above all things, vigorous blood in a strong body, a capacity for laughter. What had happened to Elsa? Had he outgrown her? He wanted to see her smile and chatter as she used to do. She was like an unused garment left hanging in a dark cupboard; she was dusty and stale.

'Go out and buy yourself some clothes,' he said suddenly and quite unexpectedly, surprised at his own words. 'Go this afternoon, never mind the expense. I'll pay.'

She looked shocked and uncertain, she was afraid he would mock her.

'Don't be an owl,' he said, 'I mean what I say. I'm tired of seeing you go about like a drab.'

After that she went from his mind, he had business to do, and it was not until the evening that he saw her again. She was waiting for him in the dull sitting-room, sitting nervously in a chair, her hands in her lap. She wore a pink flowered summer dress, the bodice fitting tight to her waist and the sleeves full above the elbow, as was the fashion. Her hat was large, with a single rose, and she wore it above the mass of her dark hair that had been waved and washed for the first time for many years. The excitement had brought a touch of colour to each cheek, and she glanced away from him shyly as though she were some girl he had not met before.

'Why, Mimitte,' he began in wonder, using his old name for her unconsciously; 'why, Mimitte, what have you done to yourself?'

And she answered him hastily: 'Are you angry with me? You told me I could,' like a child, afraid she should be scolded.

'No,' he said, 'you don't understand, that's how I wanted you to be – you ought to have done this before,' and he went to her and lifted her up from the chair and stood her upon it.

'Do you like me – the dress I mean?' she asked, forgetting he was the manager of Lévy's, and she nothing but a cloakroom attendant, one of his staff. 'Do you like it, Julius? – I wasn't sure about the colour, and then the price they charged seemed wicked to me, but you said never mind about that. That's scent I've put on the bodice, extravagant of me I know, but you always liked the scent of amber in the Kasbah – put your head there, smell. We used to be like this often, didn't we? It seems such ages ago. Stay with me a little, like that, holding me and your head against my breast, it's so lovely and makes me happy and queer. Why, Julius – why, Julius – so silly of me – I believe I'm going to cry.'

He stood quite still with his face hidden in her dress. The scent was the old Alger scent, disturbing and mysterious and sweet, and she felt warm in his arms and clean and good; she was once more a woman, a child, a young thing to be loved. Why couldn't she have been like this all these months and the last years? Something was wasted and gone. It could not have been his fault. He felt a tear splash on to his head, she was crying, then. He did not know how he felt, but he was stirred and touched in some way that did not explain itself.

'You funny little thing,' he said, and kept repeating it over and over again, half to himself, 'you funny little thing.'

They were together that night, and the next night, and after that, and each day she grew younger and prettier and closer to him, and was happy with a last tender rush of happiness like the late intoxicating warmth of an Indian summer. He told her she need not work any more, that was over and finished, all she had to do was to look as she did, and be with him. No work, no scolding, no insults at her, no meek acceptance of the paltry tips left on the cloakroom table; all she need do was to wear pretty clothes, and to care for her hands, and be fresh and smiling when he turned to her, and to hold her head high before company. She would have him proud of her, she thought, if she took pains to look her best, she would have him showing her off, perhaps, watching her with a smile, she would learn to be smart and clever and she would be his lady.

He began to take her out in the evenings. They went to the Lyceum and had the front seats in the upper circle.

She wore her new dress, and her cheeks were flushed like the rose in her hat, her eyes shone and she trembled with excitement.

'Is this the end?' she asked after each act. 'Will there be any more?'

And when the play was finished they drove back to Holborn in a hansom and she held his hands close to her heart.

'Isn't it wonderful?' she told him, and he laughed, for the fun of it to him had been in watching her eyes.

'I wonder why I'm doing all this?' he thought. 'I shan't want to for long; there'll be other things.' But he said to her: 'You're my lovely, aren't you?'

One day in September they rode out in an omnibus to Hampton Court, and he took her on the river, she prattling all the time in delight and trailing one hand in the water, watching the glances of other women at her dress, and he laughingly told her to put up her parasol because the men's eyes were following them and he was jealous.

The next day she was tired, she woke heavy and unrefreshed,

she found her nightgown was wringing wet, she must have sweated much in the night. Her old worrying cough had started again.

'I must have caught a chill on the river,' she thought. 'I won't tell Julius, it will irritate him.'

She felt cold and hot in turn, she had a fever, she sat indoors the whole day, rather wretched and miserable.

'You look pasty,' he told her that evening, and the next day she put rouge on her cheeks, saying she was better, and went out and did some shopping. She came back very tired again, coughing a good deal.

Julius came up full of enthusiasm and vitality, he had been discussing the price of his site in the Strand. For three hours he had argued and he had won his point, the sum was agreed – large, of course, but he could afford it – and he had only to sign the agreement and the site would be his. Building would start in November.

'Fancy,' she said, and tried to smile and show pleasure, but this silly weakness that had come upon her made her feel faint and queer. She touched nothing and watched him while he ate an enormous meal. He was in a great humour, boisterous and rough, and sweeping aside her complaint of feeling tired he made love to her.

She awoke suddenly – just before dawn – with a feeling of fear and dread that could not be explained. It was as though a blanket hung above her, and would fall at any moment and suffocate her. There was a weight on her chest, and something tearing and scratching at her, something that called out to her to cough, and cough, and yet if she did she knew a wound would open, gaping like a sponge. She sat up in bed, her head swimming, and she felt her way on to the floor and went to the washstand for a glass of water. As she lifted the jug the thing inside her broke, and a torrent of coughing rose up in her from her chest, sweeping her like a suffocating tide. She leant against the washstand fainting and exhausted, and came suddenly to her senses with the realization of the stale dull taste in her mouth, something that came from the depths of her, frothy and strangely warm, the taste of a rusty knife. She opened her mouth, shuddering, in nausea, and let it pass from her, and then she lit a candle and looked into the basin and saw the blood. She was wide awake, and her mind was clear.

126

'It's come,' she thought. 'The doctor said it would. Why did it wait so long? Why did it have to wait till I was happy?'

She wiped her mouth and sat down on a chair. Julius stirred in his sleep, and muttered something and was awakened by the light.

'What's the matter?' he said.

'I've been ill,' she told him after a moment.

'Eaten something that's sent you sick?' he asked.

'No,' she said.

'Well, you'd better come back to bed,' he said. She felt helpless and very tired. She wanted him to lift this thing from her mind and to tell her she was safe.

'There's blood in the basin,' she said, and her voice sounded far away to her, not her voice at all. 'I think you had better send for the doctor.'

'Blood?' he repeated, still heavy from sleep. 'Have you cut yourself?'

She shook her head; she began to shiver now, she was very cold.

'It came from me when I coughed,' she said; 'it's not just a little, my mouth was full. It's haemorrhage. One of the girls in Ahèmed's house had this – we used to take turns in nursing her. It isn't anything I could make a mistake about.'

He stared at her, got slowly out of bed and stared down at the basin.

'It's blood,' he said stupidly; 'it's all frothy,' and he tipped the basin sideways. 'How could all this come from your chest?'

'I don't know,' she said 'it's haemorrhage. It's always like that.'

He poured her out a glass of water. He wondered what he ought to do.

'Drink this; perhaps you'll feel better,' he said. She drank a sip and then put it away.

'Carry me to bed,' she said, and two tears rolled slowly down her cheeks and into her mouth. It was weakness, he supposed. She felt very light in his arms. Her nightdress smelt stale, of sweat. He laid her in the bed and covered her up with the blanket. 'If you lay quietly, you may get some sleep,' he suggested after a while. 'If you're not better in the morning I'll get hold of a doctor.'

She did not answer for a moment and then she said: 'A doctor will want to order in all sorts of things, there will be so much expense. Supposing he says I should have a nurse?'

'Oh! come,' he said, 'it can't be as bad as that. Just rest for a day or so, and slops to eat. A doctor will soon put you right.'

She reached out for his hand and held it between hers.

'You don't understand,' she said. 'This isn't just a little thing of resting for a few days. I ought to have started resting before – months ago; two, three years ago. I've always been near this – ready – and now it's come. Haemorrhage, I mean. To get well you would have to have sent me to Switzerland, you would have to have me nursed by the cleverest doctors in the world. It would have meant months of care and trouble and expense. You couldn't afford it.'

'You're exaggerating,' he told her stubbornly, 'it can't be as bad as that.'

'It's no use,' she said. 'We can't make things any better by pretending. I'm willing to face what's ahead. It isn't anybody's fault, it had to happen. Only – coming now, just when I was being happy . . .' she broke off suddenly, and was silent, and stared up at the ceiling. She thought of the girl in Ahèmed's house lying on the little strip of coloured blanket, and she remembered her poor face wasted and terrible, and the suffering she had endured for three months, and how at the end she had thrown her arms above her head. . . .

'I'll talk to the doctor,' repeated Julius; 'he'll know what to say. I'm bad at this sort of thing – I've never been ill, it's queer to me. I'll talk to the doctor. He'll know about the treatment, he'll tell you what to do.'

He was thinking about the agreement for the site in the Strand and how it would be signed in the morning. Why did she have to fall ill at just this time? He had to buy that site in the Strand. He had always said that nothing and no one should stand between him and his plans.

'I don't suppose it will be such a long business,' he went on; 'if you're taken care of properly you'll soon be all right again. It's this heat in late September, that's helped against you I expect.'

128

'I believe there are places in Switzerland not so expensive,' she said later; 'of course the getting out there would be difficult, and then having a nurse – it would all mount up.' She was struggling in her mind for some loophole of escape. Not the girl in Ahèmed's house, not like that.

But he was thinking of the site in the Strand. He would not give up his site in the Strand. The agreement was to be signed to-morrow.

'If it's really consumption,' he said, 'there are ways of curing that now. Anyway, it's nothing to be afraid of. Lots of people go about with consumption. My father had it for years; he was always coughing. He didn't suffer, either, not even at the end, and then it was only his heart that carried him off.' He went on talking, stroking her hand, watching the curtain to see if the light were breaking.

'You needn't be frightened, there's no suffering with consumption; it only needs rest and quiet,' and he was thinking: 'Tomorrow I shall sign the agreement for the site in the Strand.'

'No, I'm not frightened, you mustn't worry about me. I'm all right,' she reassured him, but she was thinking: 'I was with her when she died – I saw her face – I was with her when she died.'

They lay together, side by side, waiting for the morning, making a little pretence to one another that they were sleeping and were not afraid.

When the doctor came to see Elsa early the next day he sent Julius out of the bedroom and remained with her for some little time, the door closed, only the murmur of voices coming to Julius as he stood by the window in the sitting-room looking down upon Holborn.

He watched the heavy drays pass along the street Cityward, and the slow plodding omnibuses; now and then a bicycle would thread its way in amongst the horse traffic, while the pavements were already filled with people, hurrying to work. The rooms were at the top of the building, and beneath him the routine and life of the café were starting, his employees passing in at the swing doors to make themselves ready for the business of the day. Two fellows were straining to shift aside the heavy shutters, and a carter and boy were staggering into the premises with great blocks of ice.

A woman was brushing and cleaning away the dust in front of the café, calling something over her shoulder to her helper inside who, hands and knees on the ground, with a pail of water beside her, was scrubbing at the stone floor.

Julius closed down the window and glanced at his watch. Surely the doctor must have finished his examination by now. He paced up and down the room, he lit a cigarette, a thing he never did in the mornings, he turned over some papers on the table.

In the pit of his belly a pain gripped him, a pain that he would not recognize as fear; but suddenly for no other reason but that this pain must be connected with a sensation of grief, there came to his senses the memory of a little boy throwing his cat into the Seine, and the feel of the cat's claws upon his shoulders as he loosened their grasp. A shudder ran through him and deliberately he forced his mind away from the picture and began to concentrate on the wording of his speech to the owner of the site in the Strand, whom he would be seeing in two or three hours' time.

Then the doctor came into the room, and Julius turned to him, the pain in his belly gripping him once more.

'Well?' he said briskly, waiting for no preliminary chatter that would waste time, 'what have you got to say?'

The man hesitated and cleared his throat, rubbing a handkerchief between his hands.

'I gather that you must have understood the position from the first, Mr Lévy,' he began; 'after that haemorrhage of last night there could be no doubt in your mind. Well – briefly, the situation is this. In her present condition and with things as they are she cannot possibly live beyond three months – at the utmost. Another haemorrhage and everything would be over. The disease has too firm a hold on her, Mr Lévy. If I had been consulted before . . .' he broke off, searching the other's eyes. 'Of course,' he went on doubtfully, 'even now I might be able to save her, but it would mean a complete break-up of her present existence. She would have to be moved to a clinic and receive very special treatment. Possibly you have heard of Doctor Lorder, the great authority on tuberculosis, it is his clinic, I mean; only you must understand that the expense would be considerable, and again I could not guarantee the result. A year ago Doctor Lorder cured a patient in very much the same condition as your – your wife, I take it. The girl is living in Switzerland now – but there, it is for you to say, Mr Lévy; I don't know anything about your circumstances. All I can tell you is that she might – "might", I say – be saved, but at very considerable expense; the treatment would be long, you understand. On the other hand,' he hesitated again, 'on the other hand, if that is out of the question, I will do everything in my power to help her, to see that she is comfortable and that she does not suffer too much. She must have a nurse, naturally, and anything she fancies in the way of food – you see, it won't be very long that way. I am being perfectly frank with you, Mr Lévy. I am not trying to make things easier for you. I don't believe you would have me lie to you or pretend a hope when there is none.'

Julius did not seem as though he were listening. He stared straight in front of him, tap-tapping with his fingers on the table.

'That's all right,' he said after a moment; 'thank you very much. I understand the position. I want you to see that Elsa – she is not my wife – has every comfort and attention, a nurse if you wish it – but above all that she is not told she is dying. I don't see that there is any need for that. It's stupid, unnecessary. Be careful about that, will you? That's all, I think.' He moved towards the door. The doctor realized that the interview was at an end, but Julius Lévy had made no mention of Doctor Lorder and the clinic.

'Then you don't wish me to . . .' he began, reaching for his hat, but Julius cut him short: 'There is nothing more to discuss,' he said. 'I thought I had made that quite clear. I mustn't keep you, Doctor; you are a very busy man and so am I for that matter. Will you make the arrangements for the nurse to come in today?'

They moved into the passage to the head of the stairs. The doctor made a last effort in the cause of humanity. 'If you would like me to arrange a consultation with Doctor Lorder,' he said in a low voice, 'it can easily be managed. A word to him – I could let you know, about eleven-thirty this morning, he lives in Upper Wimpole Street . . .'

Julius Lévy shook his head.

'I can't manage it,' he said. 'I have an appointment. Good day to you.'

Then he turned and went into the bedroom where Elsa was lying like a pale thin child against the pillows.

'Hullo, you little shammer,' he said, smiling, and crossed over to her bed and took her hands in his; 'you're just pretending to be ill, I know you. You're a lazy little devil and you like me to fuss over you. That's it, isn't it?'

She smiled at him, shaking her head.

'What did the doctor tell you?' she asked. 'He wouldn't say anything to me. Tell me – I won't be afraid.'

'Afraid?' said Julius. 'I should think not! What's there to be afraid of? No – you've got to lie here like a lamb for about three months – fed up and petted and a hospital nurse to fuss over you – and after that, well, by then you'll be strong enough to be moved off to Switzerland. Some place in the mountains where you can bask in the sun and listen to sleigh bells. Does that suit you, little silly thing?'

'Do you mean that, Julius? Shall I really get well and will I really go to Switzerland?'

He winked at her, laying one finger on her cheek. They laughed together, and then she coughed, and had to struggle for breath on the pillows.

'Try and not do that,' he told her.

'I can't help it,' she said; 'it's stronger than me. Oh! I'm going to shut my eyes as I lie here and imagine the air in those Swiss mountains. They say the sky is always blue there and the sun shines. You don't feel the cold for all the snow . . . the horses drag sleighs at quite a pace up and down the slippery roads. I'm sure I don't know how they do it, do you? I've seen picture postcards of the Lake Lucerne; perhaps I could go somewhere near there.'

She went on chatting excitedly, patting the back of his hand, and after a while he looked down at his watch and he told her he must leave her now because he had an appointment.

'I suppose it's that site in the Strand,' she said; 'do be careful not to let yourself in for something too big for you. You'll have such a lot of expense from now on.'

'Don't you worry, Mimitte.'

'You won't be away very long, will you? There's such heaps of things I want to say. I feel much better now the doctor has been; the very thought of Switzerland makes me long to be well. Oh! dear – I'm so happy.'

'Are you?' he said, and he went off to keep his appointment in the Strand, to buy the site and to build another café.

October – November – December, the weeks passed slowly to Julius Lévy, they dragged themselves into little particles of hours and minutes and would not form together to make a definite passage of time.

The Holborn café was a certainty these days. It ran itself, the profits increased, and his personal supervision was only a matter of formality.

His interests were wholly concerned with the new café in the Strand, and building would not begin until early in the New Year. Julius was impatient at the delay. The slowness of labour in England irritated him profoundly; he felt that in any other country the excavations would already have been finished, the foundations laid, and the new structure be rising from the ground. He did not see how the Strand café could possibly be open to the public before the following autumn. Meanwhile he must wait, and waiting was not his game. He wanted to grasp things quickly that came within his reach, to create, to construct, to be for ever and continuously connected with some movement. To go from this, and then to the next thing, and on and on, tomorrow and to-morrow, his mind and his body and his soul reaching out to some hidden phase of the future. There was only one thing in life that mattered at this moment, and that was work; the satisfaction of making realities out of the starry thread of a dream; and those realities must come quickly to him because ten, twenty, thirty years were not long in the existence of one man, they would be gone from him too soon and there he would be standing with the bare threads in his hands.

There was not enough time for all he would do, not enough time to create and to hold his possessions, but because of the brute stupidity and incomprehension of those beings humbler than

133

himself he must endure the long hours of October, November, December.

Elsa, coughing her life away in the little bedroom next to him, was happy in the ignorance of death like a child who believes in God.

Time was not slow to her, the seconds passed on the crest of a wave and so out of her reach for ever.

She lived in a world of pure imagination: white mountains that stood above an azure lake, heavy branches laden with snow and the cold clear jingle of sleigh bells round the bend of the mountain. She lived in a wooden chalet amongst the tree-tops, the wide windows open to the sun, and when she leant over the wooden balustrade she would see Julius coming to her from the valleys below, smiling up at her with a wave of his hand and brushing the snow from his cap.

This nurse who cared for her and moved about the room with silent feet, shifting her pillows, mixing her food, she was only a temporary vision that swam before her conscious mind now and again; she could not disturb the happiness and the peace. Sometimes even Switzerland would go from her, and she would be in Alger once again, the street cries of the Kasbah humming in her ears, the chatter of women behind drawn curtains, a song, a note of music, and the beating of a drum. Between her hands she held the purple bougainvillea flowers, and the green leaf of eucalyptus, she crushed her face amongst the deep dark moss that grew at Mustapha. Like a breath of soft air in her nostrils came the warm lingering amber scent, and the white dust of the cobbled streets, saddle leather from a merchant's shop, the smoke of a cigarette. She would lift her head from the pillow and there would be Julius beside her, looking down at her from a long distance, and this would bring her home to the little bedroom and the sound of the traffic in Holborn. She smiled at him, for talking was an effort these days, she knew not why, and he would say: 'You're looking much better, I believe you'll be up in a week or two,' and his lies were messages of beauty to her, bringing much comfort and a drawing away of pain.

'When shall I be able to move to Switzerland?' she whispered, and 'Soon,' he said, watching her face, seeing in her eyes the pale

134

lost look that had been Père's, the look that belongs to the dying, the look of those who hug within themselves the flickering light of the secret city. Then he talked to her, made little descriptions of people in the café, till she waved her hand at him to stop, for he made her laugh too much, and laughter hurt.

'You're killing me,' she protested, wiping the tears of laughter from her eyes; 'you mustn't do it, you're killing me,' and then he would tell her stories instead, going over the things they had done together in Alger, remembering snatches of conversations, music and laughter, the words of songs:

> 'J'ai tout quitté pour l'ingrate Sylvie,
> Elle me laisse, pour prendre un autre amant –
> Plaisir d'amour ne dure qu'un moment –
> Chagrin d'amour dure toute la vie . . .'

she humming under her breath, and smiling: 'Again, Julius, again.'

October – November – December, little fragments of time that were seconds and were eternity in one, and Julius with his days spent over the new building in the Strand, absorbed in the plans for it; like an obsession it was to him, like the star to the scientist and the explorer who sees the path across the mountains. And so back to Elsa in the evening, whom life and beauty had forsaken without her knowledge, she saying to him with her child's faith:

'I'm much better, aren't I? – much better. I shall get up and look out of the window with you on New Year's Eve.'

'Oh! you,' he said, 'you're nothing but a pretence, Mimitte. You aren't ill at all. Why, you'll be flown on the air and gone from me, you'll be burying your face in the snow above Lausanne.' And he was comforted in some way that his lies were truth to her.

She died on December the twenty-ninth after another haemorrhage.

He came back about six-thirty in the evening, having spent a full long day with his contractors, and having finally arranged that work should begin in earnest on the first of January. He was in tremendous spirits and it seemed to him that life once more belonged to him in every way; he could create and control it as he wished, and this world was his own world for his own purpose. The night was clear and beautiful and cold and he walked without a hat so that the air should sting him, bitter with frost.

The pavements were filled with people hurrying home from work, the lights splashed upon their faces and lit the windows of the shops, still gay with holly and Christmas fare.

Julius was thinking: 'Next year – five years – ten years,' never at rest, never at peace, but it came to him with a glow of exultation that it was all part of his own strength, this glamour of living, his health and mind and vitality were one and the same thing, they led him in his search like the glory of a spark rising strong and bright in the darkness of the sky. He remembered Jean Blançard walking home to Puteaux on Saturday nights, his bargaining done for the day, his money safe in his blouse, singing with the sheer joy of animal living, laughing, drunk, his crazy blue eyes turned to the stars; and in his sensation of power and strength it seemed to Julius that Grandpère Blançard was with him now, alive in his blood, his great voice in his ear.

He ran up the stairs to the little poky rooms at the top of the building, caring for nothing and for no one, and the nurse met him outside the bedroom door, and she told him that Elsa had had another haemorrhage and was dying. He went into the room without a word, and he watched her as she lay with her face upturned plucking at the sheets and she tried to say his name and call to him, but her strength was gone from her.

He saw by her eyes that she knew she was dying, and that her faith was gone and she was afraid. He saw that she did not believe in God, or continuation after death, and that this was the end for her and she would never see him again. She would be a candle blown in the darkness. He saw by her eyes that she knew now he could have saved her had he wanted, but he chose to let her die, and she did not understand.

All this she told him with her eyes, but she could not say his name, and he stood beside her bed and held her hand and watched her die. She was Elsa no longer, not a woman, nor a child, but a little frightened thing with claws digging into his flesh, a thing that clung to him for safety and was thrust between the bars of a bridge to be lost for ever, and buried and forgotten.

Afterwards he went on holding her hand, empty-minded, uncertain of his feelings, puzzled at the strange impersonality of dead people, and he wondered if the horror of this would dwell within him and be part of him.

After a while he wanted food, and he went down to the café and had supper, and whatever he felt of loneliness, or grief or pain was swamped and hidden by the wave of fear and thankfulness that it was not he who lay upstairs so coldly impersonal, but somebody else, and that Julius Lévy was hungry and alive.

Part Three (1890–1910): Manhood

There was a fellow in the City who was making a name for himself. A Jew of course, but nobody knew where he came from. He spoke English perfectly, though with a French accent.

He had burst upon London from the unknown, his star rising in a night, and his two big cafés, one in Holborn and one in the Strand, drew wealth like a magnet, having seized the popular fancy of the middle classes.

Julius Lévy was making money hand over fist; he knew exactly what he wanted and went straight for it.

As he had expected, the building in the Strand was an enormous success from the start, it was a larger and more important affair than the original café in Holborn; it catered for the mass of pleasure-seeking and theatre-going public, who could not afford hotel or restaurant prices.

During the day businessmen lunched there, office clerks and salesmen, but in the evening the café took on a different aspect. There was a spirit of gaiety in the air, the large white building was brilliantly lit and an orchestra played on the first floor. It was considered rather 'fast' to dine at Lévy's in the Strand, the place was novel and amusing, and the sober, efficient, business-like tone of the day changed to something rather breathless and intriguing.

This Jewish fellow was clever enough to realize that a bad moral tone would kill his business, but a romantic and vaguely suggestive aura was sufficient to set it going with a swing.

Young earls with actresses, nervous gentlemen with other men's wives, and the ordinary sentimental cockney couple who held hands under the table, they were all of them fish to the net and very profitable fish into the bargain.

'He's not going to make it pay, he'll go smash in a year,' said the doubtful ones. 'You can't run a place on those lines and put by a fortune,' but he did make it pay, and he did not go smash, and he made more money in two years than anybody dreamed.

One man had believed in Julius Lévy since his star had first risen on the horizon. Rupert Hartmann, a director of the Central Bank, had had his eye on that Strand site, before anybody had heard of Julius Lévy, and it was while he was in Berlin on another affair that the younger man walked in and captured his market. Hartmann was disappointed, but he could afford to be magnanimous, and he found himself definitely interested in someone who had seen the advantages of that site beside himself and who had had the wisdom to buy at the psychological moment.

'Who is this chap?' he asked, and everywhere met the same reply: 'Nobody knows; bit of a mystery. Keeps himself very much to himself.'

The banker was determined to unravel the mystery. He realized that Lévy would one day be a big proposition, and besides this he was keenly interested in his fellow-men. He ran his quarry to earth in the Holborn café, where he found him living like a pauper in a couple of rooms at the very top of the building. He had imagined the typical Jew, sleek, round-bellied, immensely pleased with himself and his works, risen from the gutter and splashing his new wealth to the world by wearing a diamond ring on his middle finger, probably surrounded by a plump wife and a host of children.

He was considerably intrigued to discover a young man a little over thirty, very tall, very thin, who did not look as though he had enough to eat, whose black eyes stared strangely from a pale face, who, while he talked with the wisdom of fifty years, tapped with his fingers restlessly on the table before him, and who suddenly confessed, with the candid smile of a child, that lately he had found it very difficult to sleep.

Hartmann glanced about the room, bare and shabby, the sort of room that even a clerk earning three pounds a week would despise, the window shut for all the summer weather, dust on the floor, solitary, no sign of a woman.

'What's the idea in this?' he asked bluntly; he enjoyed breaking in upon people's private lives. 'Are you trying to be eccentric or what? The hermit of finance, eh?'

Julius Lévy looked surprised.

'What's wrong?' he said.

'Well – everything,' laughed Hartmann; 'a common shoe-black would be ashamed to live here. I shouldn't think a penny has been spent on this room for years.'

'I can't afford to live anywhere else,' said Lévy, and it seemed to the banker that this reply came from his lips like a sentence from a parrot; it was mechanical, it was something learnt by heart.

'Can't afford it?' repeated the banker in astonishment. 'Why, good heavens, man, you must be making about twenty thousand a year since you opened the Strand café.'

Julius Lévy was silent. He went on tapping with his fingers on the table, and his face was expressionless. Hartmann wondered whether he was mad.

'What are you going to do with your money?' he asked, watching his eyes – what an extraordinary fellow this was – and the younger man shrugged his shoulders. He refused to be drawn.

'Well, I suppose you've got everything all planned out ahead?' said Hartmann.

'Yes.' Still only monosyllables.

'You're a bit of a fanatic, Lévy, that's what's the matter with you. I'm not sure whether you are a devil or a saint. Tell me – to satisfy an old man's curiosity – did you have all this in your mind as a youngster?'

This time Julius Lévy laughed. He became human for a moment, and then he looked out of the window, a shadow on his face, baffling, inscrutable, as though he had reached for a secret and found it gone.

'No,' he said. 'As a boy I wanted to be a Rabbin and chant in the Temple. I wanted to make music.'

On an impulse he opened a drawer in the table and brought out a flute.

'My father used to play this,' he said: 'he never had a *sou* in his pockets, but I think he was happy. I've tried to play it, too, but I can't. Even if I had lessons it would be no good. I haven't the gift. So I build cafés instead.' Then he put the flute back in the drawer.

Rupert Hartmann felt uncomfortable. It seemed to him suddenly that he was an intruder; he had no right to be there. There was something about Lévy that he did not understand, something fatal, sinister, a quality of sadness that was strangely inhuman, that called at once upon your pity and your horror, and yet there he was with a smile on his face, a young fellow, likeable, charming, a brilliant creature who did not know what to do with his money.

The banker held out his hand.

'This isn't the time or the place to talk business,' he said; 'but I think we can be useful to one another in many ways. I admire your mind and I want to know you. If you've nothing better to do I'll be very pleased if you would have luncheon with me tomorrow, one-thirty at the Langham.'

Julius went to the Langham the following day, and that lunch was the beginning of a friendship between the two men. Hartmann had spoken sincerely when he said he admired Julius's mind; it was wild and untutored in many respects, but it was definite and it was exciting, and it was a mind that would never be controlled by another.

Hartmann was a widower, and although he had a host of friends, was exceedingly popular and went everywhere, in some respects he was a lonely man. He became attached to Julius Lévy, not only because of his brain and his brilliance which brought harmony to their business relationship, but because of his personality, and because he fancied he saw in the younger man a remote loneliness that he could understand. In his way Julius grew fond of the elderly banker, too; for the first time in his life he had met with someone whose mind and sense were not inferior to his own, and they could think alike and speak the same language. Besides, Hartmann was a Jew, he was one of his own people. Something racial, something primitive and deep drew them together. Hartmann was cultured, a connoisseur in art, literature, and music. The things that Julius had hitherto passed by were now shown to him, and his own natural instinct bade him appreciate the value of such knowledge.

'I'm going to show you; I'm going to take you about,' warned Hartmann. 'This hermit nonsense of yours has got to be stopped. You've been allowed to go your own way too long. You can't conquer the world unless you live in it. Didn't your own sense ever tell you that?'

At first the task was a difficult one. Julius was used to his own company; he liked being alone. He did not care to move out of the lonely, cheap rooms in Holborn where he sat with himself and his dreams; dreams that were never idle fancies but that came true with a swift suddenness that might have frightened another man less sure, less certain of his own destiny.

'You don't understand, Hartmann,' Julius would say. 'I've got to work – that's my life. I've got to scheme and plan and think out problems. Whether it's words with some fellow and coming to an agreement, I the winner, he the loser; whether it's a new idea for the restaurant, whether it's merely looking ahead and covering a sheet of paper with figures, it's work to me, it's absorbing – it's my life. I don't ask for anything else. I'm not young, I don't want to be amused. I tell you I've had all that.'

The banker shook his head. 'How old are you?'

'Thirty-two – thirty-three; what does it matter?'

'My dear Lévy, it's absurd to talk like that at your age. Had everything! Why, I'm double your years and every day I come across something fresh, something new. Books, pictures, men and women, the opera. I tell you I couldn't exist without interests of this sort. Making money doesn't amount to much in the long run after all. Don't you want to search and look about you?'

Julius made a gesture with his hands, and across his face came that same shadow of longing that Hartmann had discovered before.

'Look about,' he said, 'search. I'm always searching – how can you know? I tell you I'm twenty, thirty times more passionately interested in life than you have ever been. Search . . .' He broke off abruptly and lit a cigarette, and when he spoke again it was on another subject, the rise of certain shares in a new company, and whether Hartmann knew if they were worth anything. The banker took his cue, nor did he attempt to re-open the conversation; but he was more determined than ever to bring Julius Lévy out of his shell into the glare of public life.

Slowly and surely he had his way. It started with moving Julius from the sordid uncomfortable lodgings over the café in Holborn to a suite of rooms in the Adelphi.

He chose the decorations, he chose the furniture, he chose the

143

respectable capable housekeeper and her husband, the quiet, discreet valet. He arranged the whole apartment as one eminently suited to a bachelor of considerable means, and all Julius had to do was to get into a hansom in Holborn and drive there, the latch-key in his pocket.

Julius was a little disturbed by this first experience of luxury. Flash and show were needful to the success of his cafés, but he was unaccustomed to it about his person. These long, low rooms, this soft carpet, the shaded lamps, the quiet, instead of the racket in Holborn, and then the valet who laid out suits of new clothes on his bed and hardly talked above a whisper.

The peasant in Julius, the simplicity and the carelessness of living that was Jean Blançard, made him uncomfortable. He was expected to bath once a day, to change his linen, to clean his finger-nails, all surely very unnecessary and a great waste of time.

The valet put him out a clean shirt each morning, the collar of the last one hardly soiled; his laundry bills would be ruinous if this continued.

Julius was at his worst with servants; he did not know how to talk to them.

This valet was a superior fellow. He had some education and would have scorned the company of a light-hearted, drunken peasant who sold cheese in a market-place, and yet here he was waiting for orders from Julius Lévy, soft-voiced, his hands behind him: 'Yes, sir,' 'Very good, sir.'

Julius could not strike the right manner. He could only be boisterously familiar and a little vulgar or switch to the opposite extreme and become overbearing, absurdly high-handed and something of a bully.

'Treat them as you do your employees in the cafés,' said Hartmann tactfully. 'Be natural, be yourself.'

'That's different,' frowned Julius. 'I can manage my café crowd. But here – I don't know, this man gets on my nerves.'

'He doesn't like the way you speak to him,' said Hartmann. 'You order him about as though he were a galley-slave one moment, and the next you chaff him as if you both slept with the same woman.'

'Why couldn't you leave me alone?' said Julius.

'Because once you get used to this sort of thing you won't want to go back – it will get into your blood, and keep you. We're going to the opera tonight and you'll meet some charming people, pretty women, intelligent men.'

'My dear Hartmann, why the opera? And I detest the English aristocracy: they're snobs, they bore me. If you want me to have an amusing evening, let us dine in my own Strand café, drink a great deal more than we need, and then go and find a couple of women at the Empire. That's the only sort of amusement I understand. Personally, I should be perfectly content to stay here and do some work.'

But Rupert Hartmann would not be moved.

'There's a strain of vulgarity in you that has got to be cured,' he smiled; 'those hands of yours – they show breeding. But don't bite your nails. And I would rather die than be seen dining in your café. No, come with me to the opera and to Lady Foulke's party afterwards. People are excited about you and want to meet you. I promise you you won't be bored.'

And Julius thought of Grandpère Blançard after a fair in Neuilly, lying on the floor of his cart with a woman while the wheels rattled over the cobbled stones to Puteaux, breathless and laughing under a drunken moon; and it seemed to him that for all his racial sympathy and his quick brain, Rupert Hartmann and himself were poles apart from one another.

He went to the opera, though, and to the party that followed; half against his will he found himself accepting other invitations, meeting new people, and having once taken the plunge it was difficult to draw back.

Hartmann managed his introductions judiciously; he took care that Julius Lévy should meet people with some definite appeal, financiers, politicians, men whose conversation would not be of the heavy English type spoken of so contemptuously by Julius, and women possessing the maximum of charm, intelligence, and breeding.

Julius was still a little scornful of what he termed the English aristocracy. He said he did not understand them, he had no use for them, and Hartmann very wisely did not press him on this point, guessing that in time Julius Lévy's fortune and attainments would bring him in contact with just that very set he affected to despise.

Meanwhile, he was more at ease amongst those he called his own people, men who had obtained some position in the world through their own endeavour. He met some of the big important Jewish families – all of them friends and some of them connexions of Hartmann – and with these Julius felt that he was on his own ground; he was never looked upon as a foreigner or an interloper, because they were all members of the same race, and any country could belong to them. Here again, as with Hartmann, he moved amongst men and women who spoke the same language; they held in some queer indefinable fashion his great rapacity towards life, his hunger and his thirst, they did not rest in their lives, but leant out to seize the world with their hands, never satisfied, never appeased, and hiding in the core of their being a seed of loneliness and of frustration, a faint far shadow of melancholy madness. It was from his own people that he learnt to appreciate the sense of culture, beauty in the form of a painting, a statue, or a bar of music; if it was not his own he learnt the compelling necessity of possessing judgement and good taste. This was right, that other was wrong, that picture was dead, and here was the art of the future; he was told that these things were of eminent importance, and because of his flare of understanding and a little gem of brilliance within him that was genius, Julius learnt quickly and made few mistakes – but somewhere the ghost of Jean Blançard winked at him, his tongue in his cheek, cynical, calculating, and exquisitely French.

So when Julius Lévy was in the company of Max Lowensteen the picture dealer, or Jacob Glück the pianist, and one or the other turned to him, their eyes bright with enthusiasm, their warm Jewish sentiment delighted at some rare and very beautiful thing, Julius would agree with them, his head a little on one side, murmuring: 'Wonderful, wonderful.' But he would be thinking: 'Ugly or beautiful, what's it going to be worth in twenty years' time?'

It was about this time that Julius began to attend synagogue once more. He wanted if possible to recapture his mood of the old days and to climb the dizzy pinnacle of joy with the voice of the singer. He found it was impossible. He would sit still, his chin in his hands, cold and unmoved. Perhaps it was the difference in the English arrangement of the service; the rule of worship was not as Moïse Metzger had held it, and the pale-faced Rabbin in Paris was far from this minister who sang through his nose and mumbled in his beard. Here in London there was no sense of worship, no bewilderment, no pain, no reaching for the clouds, but only an atmosphere of black clothes, of fustiness, of old men peering at their books, and the irritating rustle of paper from some woman in the gallery. One Friday evening in April he went to the synagogue because he happened to be in the quarter. During the sermon he sat back comfortably in his seat, tilted his hat, and prepared to pass the time by watching the faces of the women. During the fifteen minutes that the Rabbi spoke, Julius never took his eyes off one face, and one face only. There was nothing particularly beautiful about her, but it was her air of aloofness setting her apart from the rest of the women, that and the serious devout attention she gave to the droning words of the Rabbi, that caught his fancy. It was a grave face, a pretty face, the face of somebody who was probably rather distant and cold even with her closest friends. She was perhaps extremely intelligent, she would speak several languages, she would do everything rather well and never look out of place. Difficult to know, he judged, intriguing and definitely exciting to wake, but hopeless and quite impossible to tease.

Then he thought: 'I should like to make her smile'; and he went on watching her idly, half amused, but concentrating that the pretty, serious face should be turned down in his direction from the gallery. He won. His gaze must have come to her subconsciously, for she became aware of him suddenly and flushed. She turned to her book. 'She'll look again in a minute,' thought Julius, and she did.

This time he smiled deliberately, raising one eyebrow and pulling a face at her; she flushed all over her face and frowned, biting her lip in confusion. He never withdrew his gaze, and she was aware of this; she moved in her seat, she fidgeted with the gloves on her lap. During the rest of the service it was impossible for her to be natural, his impertinent stare had destroyed her serene poise and her composure.

Afterwards, as the people filed from the Oratory, he saw her step into a brougham that was drawn up at the side of the kerb. He made a step forward and when the coachman's back was turned he laughed at her, flourishing his hat in the air; and because his bad manners deserved some return, and because she was angry, and because she knew she would never see him again, the serious aloof young lady of the synagogue deliberately put out her tongue through the window of the brougham.

Julius, of course, was delighted; he laughed, and he wondered how old she was. Twenty-four or twenty-five perhaps, not less.

Then he dismissed her from his mind.

It was some weeks later that Hartmann told him Walter Dreyfus wanted to meet him, and they were both invited to dinner at his house. 'Not a large party,' he said, when Julius yawned, 'only the family and one or two others. You'll like Dreyfus, he's diamonds you know, but he's lost a lot of money lately. Things are being difficult for him in South Africa, and of course he's a regular Boer. He says we'll have a war in a couple of years or so, but you must get him to tell you himself. Charming wife. I don't know the children.'

The Dreyfuses lived in Portland Place.

'Too big for them,' murmured Hartmann, as the footman took them upstairs. 'Walter's riding for a fall. He never was one of the big men, but he likes to live well. All show, of course.'

Their host came across the drawing-room to meet them, a little bearded man, soft-voiced, with exquisite manners.

'Dear Rupert, so good of you to turn up; we're just ourselves, you know, no formality, and we haven't asked anyone to meet you. This is Julius Lévy, of course. I've heard a lot about you. You're a very brilliant fellow and the envy of many of us. Let me introduce my wife, my sons Andrew and Walter, and my daughter Rachel.'

Julius bowed and shook hands with Mrs Dreyfus, tall and handsome, a regular Jewess, the two boys both replicas of their father, and finally turned to the daughter, whom he immediately

148

recognized with intense amusement and to her evident discomposure as the young lady of the Oratory.

'I think we have met before,' he said gravely; and 'I think not,' she answered with perfect courtesy, but turning her back as soon as good breeding made it permissible.

'This is going to be fun,' thought Julius, and at once began talking his finance with Walter Dreyfus; nor did he turn to the daughter again until they were half through dinner, when he pretended to become suddenly aware of her existence as his neighbour, and allowing for the noise of the general conversation at the table, he said to her:

'Do you make a point of putting out your tongue at strangers?'

'Only when they show themselves to be as absolutely rude as you,' she replied, flushed, still angry, and evidently believing that he was still making fun of her.

Julius was amused at her quick answer. He had half expected her to deny knowledge of the whole affair. Anger was different; he could deal with anger.

'I suppose I behaved rather badly,' he said to her thoughtfully, 'but you see, I know nothing about manners. I've lived in the South a good deal, and in that part of the world to stare at a very pretty woman is considered a compliment. That was the reason I stared at you, and you didn't understand. You seem to be looking about you rather vaguely; can I pass you something?'

'I beg your pardon,' she said, 'I was trying to catch what Mr Hartmann was telling my father – something about a picture. What were you saying, Mr Lévy?'

'Oh! then, she wasn't by any means a fool,' thought Julius. She had heard what he said to her, of course. This he supposed was a form of flirtation indulged in by young women of her class. Thrust for thrust, sword-play in words. He reflected that carefully sheltered daughters were probably brought up to believe in detachment and reserve, her mother would tell her that 'a woman should always keep something back, show herself to be mysterious'.

'I was talking nonsense,' he said, 'and incidentally apologizing for causing you any annoyance that day. The fact of the matter is, I don't care whether you were annoyed or not. I never bother about other people's feelings.'

'How lucky,' she said, 'that we can agree about that. Neither do I bother. In that way we can both of us be perfectly happy sitting silently through dinner, and you will not be offended if I listen to Mr Hartmann, whose conversation is always so brilliant.'

'I suppose,' he said, 'that this is rather a special occasion for you. You don't, perhaps, dine downstairs every evening. Do you go to school, or do you have classes at home?'

'Now that is really charming,' she said. 'How delightful that you consider me still in the schoolroom. Unfortunately I was twenty-four last birthday.'

'I was going by your manner,' he told her. 'Judging age by appearance is impossible nowadays. Women in England get old very quickly; they let themselves go to pieces.'

She was silent at this. He had obviously overstepped the mark. He wondered what exactly were the limits to sword-play in polite conversation. He supposed that in her set this sort of thing was continued indefinitely – artificial banter between two people – and the man must play his woman like a fish until she made up her mind to be caught.

'I haven't time for this nonsense,' he thought, and he said to her aloud: 'Tell me what you do with yourself all day, Miss Dreyfus. What are your interests in life?' And she told him: 'Inferior things like music and painting and books, Mr Lévy, quite incomprehensible to a businessman like yourself'; and he became suddenly bored with this armed attitude of hers, this light barrage supposedly witty that according to her standard must be treated with respect, and though he answered at once: 'Women have so many long lovely hours of indolence,' he was thinking that in his world Jean Blançard would have put her on her back by now.

He glanced down at her hands. They were long, slim, and well cared for. Hands in women are perhaps more important than anything, he thought, and he glanced sideways at the line of throat, the white shoulders, and the shape of her breasts beneath the low bodice. What he could see of her then was definitely attractive, and it was comparatively easy to imagine the rest. She would be big-boned, perhaps, and wider round the hips without her stiff corset, but she would be well covered, running perhaps to a surplus of flesh in later years. 'I adore Wagner,' she was saying. 'It's useless to talk to me about Italian opera. I don't know, Mr Lévy, if you know the duet in *Tristan* – those opening bars, that swell of mystery and enchantment. . . .' He let her go on with it, murmuring 'Yes' and 'No' as seemed to be expected; but he was considering with some hostility that the virgin daughter of a man like Walter Dreyfus could only be approached through marriage. He pushed the annoyance of this aside for a while, and soon the table was silent save for himself and his host, South Africa, diamonds, market value, England's attitude to her colonies, and then inevitably London, property, ground rent, population, the middle classes, and the wealth of the future, Julius showing his brilliance and his understanding in a parry of words with Walter Dreyfus that he had not attempted with the daughter.

Rachel Dreyfus had never met anyone quite like Julius Lévy before. At first she had disliked him thoroughly; he was arrogant, scornful, and deliberately rude, but before the end of dinner she had to admit to herself that he was clever, possibly a genius in his own way, and that there was a certain fascination in his way of talking and perhaps in his personal appearance that made her slightly excited and rather uncomfortable.

She was watching him now. He was leaning across the table to her father, one hand outspread in a gesture of explanation, his finger crooked, intent on what he was saying, and she noticed the almost unhealthy pallor of his face, the sleek black hair, the thin lips, and suddenly he glanced up and caught her gaze fixed upon him and he smiled – almost insultingly, she thought – boldly, distastefully. It was as though he could see right into her and was aware of all sorts of things. She went on cutting little slices of pineapple, but though she kept her eyes to her plate, she was certain that he was laughing at her embarrassment, for all his continued conversation to her father. She was sure that he could see inside her, and he knew that she knew he could see.

'This is very unpleasant,' she thought, her cheeks flaming; and she wondered why he should affect her in this way, because very often men had admired her and paid her compliments, and even when her cousin Eddie Soloman had tried to kiss her that time, he had not looked at her like this.

She was glad when her mother rose, and they were able to leave the dining-room, but as they went from the room she could feel his eyes on her back, mocking, penetrating, rather – well – suggestive, as if he were saying: 'I know a lot about you that you don't know yourself.'

Later, when the men joined them in the drawing-room, she sat a little apart, pretending to turn over the leaves of a book, and she half expected him to come over to where she was sitting and attempt some familiarity, odious, of course, and distressing, which would have to be snubbed, but he never once looked in her direction, taking a seat beside her mother and admiring a piece of tapestry work. She could not hear their subject of conversation, but her mother laughed a great deal and seemed to be well entertained. Her brothers, Walter and Andrew, joined them too, and were evidently delighted with Julius Lévy; so she imagined he could make himself agreeable when he chose, and had only shown the insulting manner to her.

In due course Rachel was asked to sing. She went to the piano apparently well accustomed to this ordeal, and she was glad that no one should know that her heart was beating nervously lest she should not be in voice, and that the palms of her hands were wet. She did herself justice, however, and there was the usual 'Well done, Rachel!' from her father, and a thunder of applause from the boys. Rupert Hartmann professed himself delighted, and she overheard her mother telling the well-worn story: 'You know, we thought at one time of having Rachel's voice trained – seriously, I mean. People have told us she has a great gift. But I don't know – to become a professional singer, rather dreadful, don't you think?' And for the first time in her life Rachel felt irritated at this little sentence of her mother's. After all, she only sang moderately well, and it sounded as if her family were making too much of it. Julius Lévy said nothing; he continued talking to one of the boys as though this business of singing at the piano had been a momentary and rather tiresome interruption. Rachel was certain that he was doing this to fluster her, that he hoped in some wretched, discourteous way to break down her barrier of dignity, so she went across and sat down beside her mother and Rupert Hartmann, beginning an animated discussion on the rival merits of two tenors at Covent Garden, showing off her knowledge of voice production and speaking louder than usual so that the other group should hear.

And Julius, who was really intensely interested in young Andrew Dreyfus's account of Johannesburg and the illicit traffic in false diamonds, and would have preferred to move off to the smoking-room to question him in peace, was contemptuously aware of this pantomime of the sister, and was thinking: 'What self-conscious creatures women are at all times. She imagines that I am looking at her.'

Then Hartmann broke in upon him, clapping him on the shoulder genially and saying: 'Julius shall tell us what he thinks; I've been taking him to the opera lately.' And Rachel looked up at him, her eyes bright, still on the defensive.

'Yes, Mr Lévy, I'm sure your reaction to *Parsifal* must be extremely interesting, you must have been astonished at such serious romanticism.'

'You are rather lovely in your way,' thought Julius, 'but it would do you a world of good to be put to bed.' And aloud he said coldly, speaking more to Hartmann than to her: 'I only understand two kinds of music. One, the songs without words or melody that my father used to play on his flute – he was a wretched fellow who couldn't sell a kilo of cheese without muddling the change, but he played like a god – and the other is the music thumped on drums in the native quarter of Algiers and danced to by little naked prostitutes of twelve years old.'

There was an uncomfortable silence. Even Hartmann looked embarrassed, and fumbled with his watch, the boys glanced at each other with raised eyebrows, and Mrs Dreyfus collected her manners and murmured something about 'everybody having their own taste', though she was evidently shocked.

The girl was gazing at the floor, her head low, playing with a corner of her handkerchief. Julius could imagine the revulsion of loathing, confusion, appalled virginity, and interest – yes, interest – in her heart, and he was glad. For perhaps the hundredth time he was mildly surprised at the facility with which things desirable came to him. Life is really too easy a thing, he mused; I never seem to have a fight.

And then the servants came in with coffee and cake and the

tension was relaxed, Walter Dreyfus, who had not heard the passing indiscretion, making an appearance at the same time with a portfolio of old prints to show his guests.

Hartmann shared a cab with Julius to the latter's rooms in Adelphi Terrace, and on the way he suggested, as delicately as he could, that his friend had overstepped the breach of good manners. 'The point is, that you must accept these people's standards,' he said. 'When in Rome, do as the Romans do. It is permissible to use certain words in front of married women – Mrs Dreyfus is an excellent creature, and very large-minded – but not before a girl. It is, amongst men and women of birth and breeding, quite unforgivable. They'll forgive you because you're a foreigner, and that will be the only reason.'

Julius took not the slightest offence at this scolding; he considered the matter childish and beneath contempt. He was only aware of considerable amusement.

'My dear Hartmann,' he said, yawning, 'Rachel Dreyfus is nearly twenty-five. Has she never heard of prostitutes?'

'That is hardly the question,' frowned the other. 'Never mind if she passes them in the street every day of her life. These things are not mentioned. It isn't done.'

'Extraordinary,' murmured Julius, 'the hypocrisy that goes on amongst these people. Girls like Rachel Dreyfus marry and do exactly what the little girls in the Kasbah do – the only thing is that they don't do it so well. I don't understand all this secrecy and shame. When I was a child I slept in the same bed as my father and mother and watched them as a matter of course. I found it rather boring.'

'Oh! you,' said Hartmann. 'I can believe any nauseating story about your childhood. But this is different, and I mean it seriously. English girls are brought up very strictly. Their parents believe in sheltering them from the rather coarser aspect of life.' He laughed, amused, in spite of his disapproval at Julius's social blunder. 'Wait till you have daughters of your own,' he said. This struck a new line of thought in the mind of Julius Lévy.

'I suppose,' he said, 'that a girl like Rachel Dreyfus – what is she? twenty-four, she told me – would never allow herself to be seduced?'

'Good heavens above!' Hartmann moved in the cab, seriously startled this time. 'What the devil do you mean?'

'I spoke plainly enough, didn't I? By seduction I mean making love, lying with a woman – whatever you like to call it.'

'For God's sake don't talk such utter nonsense,' said Hartmann. 'Don't you realize that I've been trying to force into your obstinate unwilling brain the fact that girls of the Dreyfus class are different – one doesn't make love to that sort of woman; one marries 'em. Poor old Walter, he'd thank me for introducing you to his house. Don't be a fool, Julius.'

'That would be very unlikely. What a nuisance it all is. Makes things so much more complicated.'

'Were you attracted by Walter's girl?' asked Hartmann, tapping on the ceiling as they drew up to the kerb. 'Here you are – I won't come in, it's too late. Tell me, though – it seemed to me you scarcely took any notice of her; you were, if anything, abominably rude. She's a nice-looking girl, intelligent too.'

Julius considered the fact a moment, the brim of his hat pulled down to his nose, his hands stuck in the pockets of his overcoat.

'Don't worry over her intelligence,' he said, putting one leg out of the cab. 'She's like any woman. Pretty enough, as you say – probably run to fat later on like her mother. Can't take a joke at the moment, but she'll have to learn. I'm going to marry her.'

Rupert Hartmann dropped his jaw in astonishment and fixed his eyeglass more firmly in his eye. Then he settled himself comfortably in the cab and folded his arms. 'Good heavens!' he said, and repeated it again: 'Good heavens! Well,' he added a second or so later, 'all I can say is that you have made up your mind rather quickly. My congratulations. When is the wedding to be?'

'September, I thought. That will give me time to fix up the Kensington deal.'

'I see. Four months' engagement. Rather short, perhaps, but quite correct. I am delighted to think of you settling down. Is she very much in love with you?'

He thought that all this was an absurd joke. He was chuckling to himself, but when he looked up and saw Julius standing on the steps of his house he could see by the smile on his face that he was serious.

'Do you honestly mean it?' he said. 'My dear fellow, I doubt if she'll have you.'

Julius laughed, feeling for his latchkey, the lamplight showing his face yellow and lined. He looked like a sinister and rather graceless faun.

'I haven't asked her yet,' he said, 'but she'll come to me, of course.' And he waved his hand and went into the house.

The episode of wooing Rachel Dreyfus counted in the life of Julius Lévy as something of a relaxation. The fact that he had met her but once and that in all probability she actually disliked him was no deterrent to his scheme; it was a little matter easily overcome and perhaps on the strength of it rather amusing. Apparently she was not to be taken casually; according to Hartmann this was impossible, because of her birth and upbringing; so if he wanted her he must sacrifice to a certain extent his freedom and personal comfort and be prepared to marry her.

Well, he was thirty-three and he had no ties, not even a mistress at the moment, love having been for the past few years neither very necessary nor very pressing. He supposed that by marrying Rachel Dreyfus she need not interfere largely with his life, but would make an effective background. It would mean a household, of course, and certain obligations, children probably, responsibilities that would have to be shouldered indefinitely. Rachel would want to be taken about; they would have to entertain. She would naturally be good at that, he imagined. She would fit in as hostess; she wore her clothes well too, and had that indefinable thing known as breeding which he considered important in a wife. Oh! yes, if he were going to do the thing, he believed in doing it well. No half measures in marriage. He would have her dress exquisitely and live in surroundings reflecting her taste; if luxury were demanded she must have it, anything in that nature she required, in fact. They would have to live a little more splendidly than other people in every way; their rooms must be larger, their food better cooked – when he came to think of it, this business of marriage made a big pattern in life.

Rachel Dreyfus should do. From the little he had seen of her he judged her brain to be just of that intelligence that would not jar –

masculine and, thank God, Jewish enough to understand his preoccupation with business; but a good percentage of femininity
that would allow her to be subservient and restful. Thinking it
over, he did not see that she could be improved upon. Set in a
suitable frame, adjusted here and there, her virginity taken from
her and something of maturity, wisdom, and a sense of balance
developed in her, and Rachel Dreyfus should make the ideal wife.

At the moment she was disturbing in her fashion, and with
initiation should prove satisfying and sufficient, but he knew that
she would never cause him furiously to dream nor would she instil
in his body that sense of hunger and thirst that was fever, and
desire, and death. As Hartmann had said in most truthful sanity:
'One doesn't make love to that sort of woman; one marries 'em.'

It was now April, considered Julius, and it would suit his plans
well if they were married in mid September. It gave him exactly
five months. She, he supposed, would be happy to undertake the
matter of finding and furnishing the house, of buying her own
trousseau. Her mother would help her. Walter Dreyfus ought to
be delighted at the whole affair. Daughters were expensive things,
and this one was nearly twenty-five. The marriage would go well
with the entire Dreyfus family. As things stood, he expected that
they would be able to announce the engagement early in May.

He had, then, a bare four weeks, during which his business, of
course, could not be neglected, in which to sweep Rachel off her
feet.

He began, naturally enough, by finding out the usual movements
of her day. Thus he learnt when she walked in the Park, when she
drove shopping, where she went for her singing lessons, and what
parties she was likely to attend. So it seemed to Rachel Dreyfus
that she was always coming across that disagreeable Julius Lévy.
It was quite surprising the way he seemed to turn up at dinner
parties and functions; at the opera in the next stall to her, although he presumed to scoff at Wagner; and even when she walked
with her maid across the Park to a singing lesson she would
suddenly be aware of him coming towards her along the path,
sweeping his hat from his head with a flourish, professing to be
mightily astonished at the sight of her, and saying with his satanic
smile: 'Hullo, Miss Dreyfus, do we meet again?' hinting, in the

most atrocious way, that she had walked that way on purpose with the hope of seeing him. He was, she thought, insufferably conceited, and he would take up a position at her side as though he assumed the right to walk beside her. He was interesting, though, Rachel had to admit that – and very amusing. He made her laugh at things she felt she shouldn't, and then he had rather a fascinating manner of making out that she was clever and lovely and nonsense like that in a new, original fashion, difficult to explain. Anyway, no other man had treated her quite in this way. Besides, when she got to know him better, and they were always meeting, it seemed, she couldn't help feeling a little sorry for him. He wasn't English and had few friends, and then living all alone like that – perhaps he was to be pitied. Of course he was terribly brilliant and slightly frightening, but he wasn't very old; and then he had that way of looking at her that after all wasn't really insulting but rather mysterious and sort of breathless as though, well ... she didn't quite know. Anyway, there it was, and she was beginning to think about him often. They kept on meeting, and first one thing and then another, it was all a little exciting and disturbing. She hoped that this was not going to affect her; it would be so ridiculous and degrading to lose her head about somebody like Julius Lévy, who was probably laughing at her behind her back, and kept mistresses and all that sort of thing – rather dreadful. He was that type of man, she felt it instinctively, but she supposed that the fact was he was clever and attractive, and this appealed to her. Then she had always been so very bored with the usual young men and boys, friends of Walter and Andrew, that this was new to her and made life different from what it had been.

'Rachel is always so serious,' her mother was fond of saying. 'She's wrapped up in her music and her books, and doesn't bother much with young people. Admirers are generally frightened off very quickly – she snubs them unmercifully.' And there would be a general laugh at this. Rachel the blue-stocking with her sharp tongue, who would not smile and blush gracefully.

'As it happens,' thought Rachel, 'I can laugh and chatter nonsense perfectly well when I choose, and as for frightening away admirers, well, I don't know about that.' And she smiled secretly to herself and looked in the glass. Funny – father said the other evening: 'Child, you're looking very handsome these days.' She wondered if it was true and why – perhaps because of this new way of doing up her hair puffed out at the sides; and suddenly she remembered dining on Tuesday with the Lewensteins and being aware of Julius – yes, first names by now, very unconventional and presumptuous of him to have suggested it – of Julius looking at her across the table and smiling, and how she had smiled back. No reason for it, but it just happened, and she could not help feeling furtive about it, as though they shared some secret; which was absurd, of course. How could they have any secrets? And yet she never mentioned to her family the flowers that arrived for her every morning, and were brought up to her room by her maid, with the card and his initials in the corner, nor the books with French titles that arrived so often, his handwriting on the fly-leaf, and which she read in bed at night. They were very advanced, but then she was nearly twenty-five, and this showed he thought her intelligent enough to appreciate them. Perhaps, then, she admitted, there was something secretive in their friendship, because neither of them mentioned these things when he came to the house and the family were present. Father had taken a great liking for Julius, which she felt vaguely was rather a good thing; the boys liked him, and mother too, so that these smiles across dining-room tables were apt to make her feel not exactly guilty, but romantically concerned in some sort of intrigue.

Sometimes she would receive letters from him, written in great haste after some evening when he had seen her, or else scribbled for no apparent reason at midnight or in the middle of the day. Short letters, but extraordinarily vital and typical of him, making out that he hadn't slept, and at three in the morning he was imagining something about her that he left her to guess – did she feel it and did it wake her up? Things like that which she supposed were rather improper and which ought to shock her, but they didn't; they only made her dress with greater care that evening if she were going to meet him, and she would try to appear unconcerned when he came in at the door.

Then it happened one morning that Andrew at breakfast mentioned casually he 'had seen Lévy at the theatre the night before with a very pretty woman', and Rachel was distressed to find that this stupid statement made her miserable for the day. She felt angry and hurt as though Julius being seen with some woman was a slight upon her personally. She knew she had no right to mind, and surely this wasn't jealousy; but her heart was beating and her voice was cold when she said to Julius the following evening at Rupert Hartmann's: 'Andrew tells me you were at the theatre a night or so ago.' And 'Yes,' he answered, 'Couldn't get out of it – I was so bored. Fellow asked me to dine – I thought it was for a business discussion – and then he developed indigestion after the fish, and I discovered I was expected to take his wife on to the Lyceum in his place. Silly little woman; bad teeth. Rachel, I wish you wouldn't wear that red dress; I can't concentrate on food or wine or the conversation of my next-door neighbour. How many men have made love to you since I saw you last? – because I shall strangle every one.' And she was happy again, foolishly and ridiculously so, and she didn't mind what he said to her; it was nonsense, perhaps, but it was he. How absurd of Andrew to have suggested for one moment that just because Julius should be seen at a theatre it would necessarily mean . . . really, she had to laugh, it was so absurd; and then she caught herself thinking what a lovely place London was in May, the beginning of the season and everything was going to be delightful. She was arranging the flowers in the drawing-room; her mother always said she did flowers well and nobody was in but her. Mother had gone off to see great-aunt Sarah at Kew, and she hummed the bars of the new song she was learning – a French song – all her latest songs were French. She wondered if Julius knew this one:

> 'Plaisir d'amour ne dure qu'un moment –
> Chagrin d'amour dure toute la vie.'

Rather melancholy words, she thought. Was it true the lovely part of love only lasted a moment and the sorrow went on for a lifetime? Still, it was just a song, and sentimental at that; real life was probably very different. However much one read and talked about love, one couldn't possibly know really what it was like until one was – well – married, and all that. People said it was marvellous and one felt utterly different. She used to think any sort of physical business must be hateful and disgusting. She didn't know how people could; she always wished men and women would just be content talking about books and music and things. But lately, she didn't know why exactly, she felt she must have thought prudishly and stupidly over various things. After all, if one was fond of a person, and he was gentle and at the same time rather overwhelming, if he took care of one and saw that one wasn't embarrassed, it ought to be more or less bearable, almost, perhaps, rather lovely.

Rachel sat at the piano, strumming with one finger in great abstraction, her eyes anywhere but on her music and her thoughts lost in some fancy, and then the door opened and Mr Lévy was announced.

Oh dear! – and she hadn't arranged her hair or her dress. What a time to call! 'Bring tea, please, Symonds, at once.' And 'Good afternoon, Julius; nobody appears to be in but me. I was just practising – come and sit down – what a lovely day.' The rush of words served, she hoped, to cover her confusion, because she felt that it must be obvious in her face that she had been thinking about him.

Julius took no notice, however; he was apparently in a hurry and slightly irritated over something.

'I was over at the new building in Kensington,' he began, striding up and down the room, 'and I suddenly realized it was the tenth of May. I've been so infernally busy this last week that the date has passed me by, confound it!'

'Why should it matter?' asked Rachel very surprised. 'Is it anybody's birthday?'

'No – but it was a month ago on the seventh that I first met you at dinner. That makes two days over the four weeks. Damn! Hartmann will win his bet.'

'I'm sure I don't know what all this is about,' said Rachel, after a pause.

'I tell you what,' said Julius; 'will you pretend that it was arranged on the seventh, only we kept it secret? That's easy enough. I'm damned if I'm going to lose that bet. Splendid. What an idea. Will you do that for me?'

'Do what? I wish you'd explain yourself.'

'Tell Hartmann that I asked you on Tuesday instead of today. It's perfectly fair. I would have asked you Tuesday, but this business has been holding me up. I bought the ring days ago, anyway, as I know to my cost. Here – see if it fits.'

He threw a small package into her lap and went on pacing the room.

'What time will your father be back? I don't think I can wait if he's not home by five. I suppose it wouldn't be the thing if you told him. Ridiculous red tape over these affairs always. Well, what do you think of the stone? I had to get a good one; your father knows too much about diamonds.'

Rachel, twisting in her fingers probably the clearest-cut diamond she had ever seen, was realizing with a sense of stupendous bewilderment that Julius had made her a proposal of marriage. No, it wasn't even a proposal; he hadn't even attempted to ask her, he was merely assuming the fact that she had accepted him. She had never imagined a proposal would be like this. He ought to be trembling, he ought to be on his knees – and all he had done was to throw a ring on her lap and complain of the cost. For a moment she wanted to throw it back in his face, she was so angry, and then it came to her suddenly, the understanding of what had happened. Julius had asked her to marry him; he loved her. It was true all the time, he had not been making fun of her. Julius and herself – Rachel Lévy. 'This is my wife . . . Mr Julius Lévy . . . Darling, I love you . . . Father and Mother, Julius and I are going to be married . . . I say, have you heard about Rachel? . . . The bride, all in white, stood at the top of the steps, her hand on her husband's arm, smiled down, radiantly lovely . . . The Italian lakes . . . How beautiful you are, Rachel; do you know you belong to me, yes, all of you; this, and that, and those. . . .'

She looked up at Julius out of a dream and she said to him haughtily, rather stiffly: 'You're taking me very much for granted, aren't you? I've never said I would marry you.'

Then he laughed. He put his hand under her chin: 'My dear,' he said, 'I wish to God I had taken you, it would have saved me a great deal of trouble. Don't be absurd, though, and unnecessarily English. I've decided we'll be married in September; it gives you time for trousseaux and all that. We shall have to find a house –

there'll be heaps for you to do, however; no need to go into it now. What's this coming in – tea? I don't want any tea. Absurd meal. What a time your father is. I shall have to go; I can't wait for him. What are you looking so prim about, with your lips pursed? Give me a kiss.' He laughed again, bending down to her, but she pushed him away.

'No,' she said firmly.

'What on earth's the matter?'

'I hate you,' she said; 'so overbearing and conceited – treating everything as settled – I don't like things like that – there's heaps to be discussed – and you behave to me as though I were anyone, a sort of girl to be kissed. . . . Symonds must have seen.'

He whistled, coarsely she considered, his hands in his pockets, his head on one side.

'Ever been kissed before?' he asked.

'No,' she said, flushing. 'A cousin tried once, very impertinently. I – I hate all that.'

'Do you?' he said. 'Then you can take it from me you're wrong.' And he put his arms round her and lifted her on to the sofa, and proceeded to kiss her and make love to her there for about five minutes, after which he glanced at his watch and saw that now he would be possibly a few moments late for his appointment.

'You need a lot of that sort of thing,' he said, 'but I can't stop now. You must wait until September. By the way, that's all settled, isn't it? We'll be married the second week, roughly the fifteenth. I can't manage it before. All right?'

'Yes,' she said.

'Happy?'

'Yes.'

He raised one eyebrow and looked down at her, lying flushed and slightly dishevelled on the sofa.

'So you damn well ought to be,' he said, and he flung open the door on to the landing and shouted down the stairs to Symonds to call him a cab.

Julius and Rachel were married on the fourteenth of September, in the year '94.

The wedding was held at the big Oratory in Great Portland Street, and a reception followed at Portland Place.

Walter Dreyfus was a well-known man with many friends, and the marriage of his daughter was therefore something of a function.

Nobody knew very much about the bridegroom Julius Lévy. He was vaguely French and rather mysterious, but heaps of money, they said, and extraordinarily ambitious and would do big things, so that everyone considered Rachel Dreyfus had done well for herself.

Her family were delighted, and Walter Dreyfus was secretly relieved that this daughter of his should be provided for, he being considerably worried financially these days. Julius Lévy was perhaps a little unconventional for a son-in-law, but he was wealthy and was going to take care of Rachel; that was all that mattered.

Once she was married, Rachel was certain she would be able to take Julius in hand and improve him.

'He needs me to look after him – he's so funny and foreign in lots of ways,' she told herself, and already she began to feel rather experienced and mature, as though she were a woman because he had kissed her. The wedding was a disappointment to her, but she would have died rather than admit it to herself. It rained for one thing, spoiling her dress as she stepped from the synagogue into the carriage, and the brilliance of the reception shone a little false. Her father seemed depressed behind his smile, and Julius was obviously so impatient at the whole affair, so wanting to be gone and away from it all, that she had scarcely time to see her friends and smile upon them and cut the cake, before he was making signs for her to go upstairs and change.

'I won't be hurried,' she said to herself, and took great pains over her toilet, closeted in her bedroom with her mother and an aunt. When she came downstairs, looking very dignified and stately in her new furs and her large hat – really married now she felt – she found many of the guests had slipped away; and there was Julius, very flushed and boisterous, with some of his slightly common business friends waiting in the hall to applaud her appearance, but they had all been drinking too much champagne.

'*Enfin*,' shouted Julius. 'We were wondering if you'd gone to bed,' and there was a great burst of laughter. How dreadful, how horrible, she thought – and one of his tipsy friends, the worst type of Jew, vulgar and fat, sang the first line of a popular song in a high falsetto voice, and Julius said something in French which she knew to be disgusting.

It was Rupert Hartmann who came to the rescue – dear Rupert Hartmann – and he kept Rachel away from the noisy crowd and saw her safe to the cab, and bundled Julius into it after her, telling him he ought to be ashamed of himself, and had he the tickets ready for Liverpool Street?

Then Julius sang French songs all the way to the station; she was thankful the cabman could not understand. As it was, he overtipped the man when they drew up at Liverpool Street and winked at him and said: 'We've just been married' – so unnecessary and coarse.

Luckily they had a carriage to themselves all the way to Harwich – the honeymoon was to be spent in Germany, doing the castles of the Rhine, her choice – but Julius spoilt all the beauty and romance of being a bride by wanting to pull down the blinds and make love to her directly the train drew out of Liverpool Street. Nothing could be more undignified or distressing; she was nearly in tears, and then when the uncomfortable, ridiculous performance was over, and she wanted to be kissed and comforted, he sat in one corner with his feet propped up on the opposite seat taking no notice of her at all, but jotting down calculations on a piece of paper.

Happily for Rachel the honeymoon, in spite of its disastrous beginning, proved a great success. Germany was wonderful, the Rhine castles all she had ever imagined; the tour was luxuriously planned, and she discovered that being loved by Julius was, after the first few attempts, a glorious, shameless experience that made the world seem more worth while than it had been before.

She returned to London and the new house in Hans Crescent, hardly wiser than when she left but considerably more human, sympathetic and indulgent, her body healthy, her mind contented, expecting neither mystery nor excitement out of life, but looking forward to a normal, regular existence as Rachel Lévy, however much the fundamental Rachel Dreyfus might be unaltered and intact.

Strangely enough it was to Julius rather than to Rachel that married life brought changes. Rachel herself was no revelation to him; he found her much as he had expected, and he had no cause for complaint. He had chosen her, she was his wife, she would do. The discovery he made was that the sensation of owning a wife, and a house, and a staff of servants, was a pleasurable one; that to order and be obeyed in his own home, to know he was master here as well as in his cafés, to entertain guests and be aware of their covetous glances at his goods, and his woman, was a thrill of keen intensity new and extremely satisfying.

It was good to watch people eat at his table and praise him to his face, people who ten years before would not have lowered themselves to glance at him in the street, they who possessed birth and breeding and he who possessed nothing at that time but incalculable ambition, a baker in Holborn. It was good to see how they hung upon his words, how they clustered round him with their eager hands and their chinless, vacuous faces; butterflies and moths swarming round a candle burning bright, and their chitter of empty voices. 'My dear Lévy,' 'My dear Julius,' 'But of course you must come tonight; no party is a success without you,' 'Rachel, insist that this brilliant husband of yours stops working for once.'

He knew that it was his money that had bought them. It was his money that drew them about his person like a cluster of flies, and because his star had risen, because he was winning, because he was a success; and he knew that their words were meaningless little bleatings in the air; they did not like him, they were afraid of him. Privately they gossiped about him in their fear and called him vulgar, an upstart, a foreigner, a Jew. He knew all this and he laughed, and he invited them to his house so that he could despise them. He remembered that they had been carefully nurtured and handled from the day of their birth; they had never known hunger or cold or poverty; and he remembered with a glimmer of exquisite pain how he had starved and frozen and suffered in the streets of Paris. It seemed to him that with every penny he made he was at the same time taking the blood and the life from the pockets of these people, that as his wealth increased so would their span of idleness and leisure dwindle and be lost to them. When he had grown to the height of his prosperity, he would have helped to smash down their class of false superiority that had lived too long.

So he sat, Julius Lévy, at the head of the long table in his dining-room, the lights from the twelve silver candlesticks reflecting the faces of those around it. He looked down at the mass of fruit piled high in the centre, peaches with a soft, luscious baby's skin, fat white grapes, the hard prickly pineapple; he was aware of the tinkle of the cut-glass fruit-bowls, the ripeness of dessert mingled with the scent of the woman on his right, the clamour of conversation, the murmur of the butler at his elbow, the pale brown taste of brandy. He leant back in his chair and watched the faces of these people, the white soft hands of his neighbour, her fingers manicured, a single diamond bracelet on her wrist; and he smiled at her voice in his ear, the smart nasal voice he hated: 'Julius Lévy, how terribly thrilling to be your wife; how I envy her those pearls. . . .' Poor fool, poor whore, thinking with her cheap pure-bred beauty she could please him, so exciting to be kept by him; and he looked at the strained harried face of another guest, an earl, who next morning would be signing a contract with him, making over to Julius a great site on his property in the West End for building purposes – another café to add to the number. And this fellow glanced up and caught the eye of his host and raised his glass, smiling anxiously, as though even yet some untoward accident should prevent the deal and he be penniless.

Both the woman and the man were symbolical to Julius of this power that money had brought to him; they were fighting for his favour, they crawled to him, they ate from his hand.

'Why are you smiling?' said someone, Andrew it was, his brother-in-law. And 'Am I?' said Julius. 'I didn't know I was. Perhaps I am glad that you are all enjoying yourselves.' And he hid his smile behind a cigar, and tapped with his fingers on the table, thinking as he had thought before after looking out over the roofs and chimney-pots of a vast dreary London: 'This is mine – all this belongs to me.'

Everything, the smell of food and wine and smoke and the

scent of the women, the clamour of voices, the movement of the servants, all that they had eaten and drunk, the chairs they were sitting on, the coverings of the room, the roof above their heads, the anxious smile of the man who must sell his property or die, all this atmosphere of unrest, of brilliance, of fever, and of excitement, had been created by him and because of him. He had made it with his own hands, his will, and his brain; from the taste of the brandy on his tongue to the body of Rachel his wife, already big with the child she was carrying, her face calm and grave between the row of glittering candles – all this is mine, all this belongs to me.

Rachel's baby was to be born in July of the following year, but August came and there was still no sign of it making its appearance. Two specialists were called in and a nurse was in attendance.

Julius, who of course gave his consent that any measure should be taken to insure the safety of his wife, was considerably astonished at all these preparations. He had always imagined child-bearing to be an easy business; women retired to their beds for three or four days to rest themselves, but the actual birth would take half an hour or so, uncomfortable, perhaps, but more or less painless. Surely, he thought, these doctors were exaggerating the gravity of the situation, they probably hoped to pocket a big fee, and it bored him to have his mother-in-law in the house treating the place as though she belonged there. The whole affair was a damned nuisance; this baby should have turned up in July and here they were in the second week in August waiting for it to happen. Rachel, poor child, looked appalling, but he supposed she could scarcely help that. Still she must have bungled things somehow to cause all this difficulty. Perhaps she had done too much in the early months, he didn't know about these things, but anyway this hanging about was trying to both their tempers. Besides, it interfered with his plans. There was a scheme afoot for opening a café in Manchester, and he was due up there for a general discussion and settlement on the fifteenth of August. It was impossible to arrange a meeting in London, neither was it practicable. He wanted to see what sort of a property site he was buying, whether it was suitable for the purpose – he didn't believe in purchasing anything blindly for all the detailed map of the district. No, he would go to Manchester whatever happened, his wife was in capable hands, after all. This baby by rights should have been alive and kicking well before this date, he had purposely put off the meeting until well on in August, chafing even then at the delay. He generally clinched a matter as soon as possible after the first proposal, got a contract written out and signed before the other fellow had time to wonder if he were making a mistake.

The start of a café in Manchester was, to his way of thinking, the first link in the chain that would eventually stretch across England, embracing every big provincial town. It was the right moment for setting about it, too. Work and reconstruction would begin during the slack months and the café be open to the public for Christmas.

And here was Rachel waiting to produce this baby, mixing his private domestic life up in his business affairs.

He would return to the house in Hans Crescent every evening from his office above the big Strand café, hoping that the event had taken place during the day, always to be met with the same disappointment, the familiar figure of Rachel lying on the drawing-room sofa, her work or a book in her hands.

'No sign yet?' he would ask. 'Look here, Rachel, how long is this going on for?'

She would shake her head hopelessly, putting her work aside.

'Good gracious,' she would say. 'If you think I care about waiting. It's much worse for me. Mother's been in to tea – she's coming for the day tomorrow, she cheers me up, and says it's sure to come soon. But I don't know . . .'

Julius strolled about the room, smoking one of his big cigars. She waved the smoke away patiently, she never liked to tell him how she hated the smell, and he never noticed her discomfort.

'What a curse it is,' he grumbled; 'if I'd known there was going to be all this trouble I'd never have let you start this baby.'

Rachel was shocked. She did not say anything. One shouldn't mention things like that – besides, it was wicked. Birth was sacred, children came to one naturally.

'Can't you do something to make it arrive?' he said. 'Move about, go for a ride in an omnibus – I don't know.'

'Of course not,' she said; 'what a dreadful suggestion. I should probably hurt myself terribly, and the poor little baby.'

He glanced at her and laughed.

'Not particularly little, judging by your size,' he said. She flushed at this, it was the sort of coarse, hurtful remark he found amusing. He would probably repeat it to one of his friends as a huge joke.

'Anyway, I can't do anything, we must just go on waiting,' she said. She wished he would sit down instead of being so restless, this tearing up and down the room was wearying to watch. Her head ached, and she was so tired of her heavy, clumsy body; she wanted to be alone, or with her mother; she wanted for some weak, foolish reason to bury her head in a pillow and cry.

'Well, I've got to go up to Manchester on the fifteenth,' he said, 'can't put it off again. You'll be all right, of course. It'll be Christmas if this hangs on much longer, the child'll be born with long hair and a complete set of teeth.'

He laughed again, his fancy tickled at the idea, but Rachel was wondering whether it was true that when a baby was late in coming it meant very much more pain.

'Don't bang the door, dear,' she called out in warning, but she spoke too late, he had slammed it behind him with a crash, setting her nerves on edge, and she heard him howling down the stairs to the butler to fetch up some drinks.

It was on the Sunday afternoon when they were sitting at tea – her mother, Julius, and the nurse – when suddenly she clutched at the table in front of her, crying out aloud, a wave of heat fanning her and little beads of sweat breaking upon her forehead.

'Oh! Mother,' she called. 'Oh! Mother, what is it?' and she put out one hand on the nurse's arm to steady herself.

'Thank God at last,' said Julius; 'this is what we've been waiting for. You'd better get her upstairs, nurse. Want any help?'

He seemed to be treating the whole affair as an enormous joke. Now he would be able to set off for Manchester in the morning and act the proud father. He was considerably put out when the doctors told him at midnight that judging by the baby's position it was not likely to be born before twenty-four hours.

His mother-in-law took hold of his hand, she, too, looked white and drawn, and there were tears in her eyes. 'Rachel is being brave,' she said, 'she is struggling all the time. You must be brave, too, Julius dear. Try and get a little rest now, because tomorrow will be a long anxious day.'

'I know,' said Julius; 'you'll have to wire me every few hours at Manchester.'

'Manchester?' she repeated stupidly. 'But you surely won't be going now? Don't you understand Rachel is desperately ill?'

'Yes – the doctors have explained.'

'Well – then you . . .' Mrs Dreyfus paused, baffled at the expression in his eyes.

'The train leaves at nine-thirty,' he said; 'you're right about getting some rest while I can. Tell them to let me know if there's any change during the next few hours. Good night.'

When he left the next morning there was no difference in Rachel's condition. He did not go in to see her, the nurse thought better not. He called to her through the door, but she did not seem to hear him. 'Poor old Rache,' he cried, 'this is bad luck – stick to it, you'll get through,' and he turned to the nurse. 'Is she suffering much?'

'Yes, sir – I'm afraid she is.'

'How dreadful.' He frowned, trying to worry it out. He did not understand pain. He went downstairs to the cab which was to take him to the station.

He arrived in Manchester in time for lunch, and then proceeded to the offices of Draxwell Ltd in the afternoon. As he had feared, the delay in the proceedings had caused the property owners to reconsider the original price; it had seemed to them, on thinking things over, that they would be making a poor bargain in letting the property go for the sum at first proposed. They now stipulated for a thousand pound increase. Julius Lévy would have none of this. He had gone, he declared, to his limit. So, they insisted, had they. This haggling continued for at least three hours, and he succeeded in beating them down to an increase of five hundred only. By this time he had missed his train back to London, nor had he yet inspected his future property.

'Are you,' they said, 'in any immediate hurry?'

171

He thought for a moment. 'No,' he said, 'I don't think so. I would prefer to see all I can today.'

They took him along to the big block where he would construct his café, and he could see at once what a fine place he would have, the excellence of the central position, the proximity to the new theatre.

Like a child with a new toy he examined the building from every angle, he pointed out what part of it should be pulled down and what should remain.

It seemed to him that it would be a novel idea to make use of the first floor in the form of a gallery, looking down upon the ground floor beneath, that this would give an impression of space and would, at the same time, facilitate service. 'You see what I mean?' he said to the elder Draxwell. 'By cutting away here and allowing for the outside walls – I'm certain it could be done. Tell me, who's the best architect here?'

They gave him some name. 'I'd like to see him,' he said. 'If he's any good I'll use him on this job. Can we get hold of him now?' There would apparently be some little delay.

'It doesn't matter. I'd like to see him if he can be found,' he said.

Then a boy came along with a telegram from Draxwell's office. 'This has just come through for Mr Lévy,' he said.

'Give it here,' said Julius, and he tore it open and read: 'Rachel weaker – strain proving too much impossible operate because of heart – situation serious – can you return at once – Martha Dreyfus.'

He stuffed it in his pocket. 'No answer,' he said. 'Look here, Draxwell, try and get hold of that architect, will you? It means missing another train, but I'll catch the midnight express instead.'

'Will that be all right for you?'

'Yes – suit me fine. Let's have a look at that ground floor again,' said Julius.

So he settled his business with great satisfaction, winding up the day with dinner at an hotel in company with the architect, and he arrived at the station with three minutes to spare before the midnight express left for London.

His café affairs concluded, he now had time to consider his domestic life, and he took out the wire and read it again.

He realized that it was well within the limits of possibility that he would return home and find that Rachel was dead. This had to be faced, nor did he shrink from it. Yes, he loved her in his fashion; at any rate, he did not want to lose her. Doctors were useless, he supposed, in a case like this, the whole thing depended probably on a woman having courage. He thought of Rachel white-faced and serious, and he stared in front of him, tapping with his fingers on his knee. He arrived at Hans Crescent shortly before five. He let himself in. Mrs Dreyfus must have heard his cab, for she was waiting at the head of the stairs.

'Well?' he said.

She shook her head. 'It's still the same,' she said, 'they can't do anything. She's so tired, she doesn't seem to be able to struggle. Oh! Julius . . .' She broke down, stretching out her hand.

'All right – ' he said, 'I'll go up to her.'

'The doctors are coming back at seven,' she told him. 'They said it was no use waiting – nothing can happen before then. Nurse and I are watching for any change.'

He went up to his wife's room. Rachel was lying very still, she stared up at him without recognition. The nurse was bending over her, wiping the sweat from her forehead.

'Will they give her an anaesthetic?' said Julius.

The nurse supposed so.

'I don't believe that's right,' said Julius, 'it will make her weaker, and take away her fighting sense. She ought to struggle.'

'The doctors are afraid of the strain, sir.'

'They don't know,' said Julius, 'Rachel isn't delicate. She's made well, she's built for this – I know her body better than they do.'

'Rachel,' said Julius, 'Rachel, look at me.' Her eyelids fluttered, she stared up at him. She cried out with the pain, twisting on her side.

'Rachel,' said Julius, 'I'm going to help you. Give me your hands.' He took hold of them and held them tightly. 'Keep your feet against the rail,' he said.

The nurse touched his arm. 'You'll kill her,' she said, 'she won't stand it.'

'Get out of here,' said Julius.

173

'I'm in charge, sir, the doctors left me in charge . . .'

'Get out of here, I say.' Then he looked down at Rachel, her hot clammy hands in his, he watched her struggle and strain, crying as she moved.

'Fight,' he said; 'go on, fight. Fight like the devil. Scream yourself crazy, it doesn't matter, it'll help. Fight, Rachel – I'm here, I won't let you go.' He saw the nurse slip out of the room, he supposed she was going to fetch the doctors.

For an age, every minute seeming an eternity, he held Rachel's hands while she pulled and struggled, paying no attention to her cries.

The doctors had not yet arrived, he looked round for the nurse, she was standing tight-lipped and aghast in the background.

'Get some cloths or something,' he said, 'we've got to do this thing ourselves.'

He bent down to Rachel. 'All right,' he smiled, 'don't be afraid. I'm going to go on helping you.'

'Now,' he said, 'fight for the last time – and let go of my hands . . .'

And so it was that twenty minutes later, exactly five and a half minutes before the two doctors and Mrs Dreyfus opened the door of the room, Julius Lévy brought his own daughter into the world, with Rachel stretched across the bed, exhausted, but alive. It was, to Martha Dreyfus, the strangest, and perhaps most terrible sight she had ever seen; this first swift vision of Rachel, torn and broken, and Julius standing above, a tall dark figure in the half-light, the lamp shining upon his face, his black hair tumbled over his eyes – and he was holding in his hands something that kicked and cried, and he was laughing.

Rachel lived, and so did the baby. They probably both owed their lives to the efforts of Julius, but his methods, though successful, were undoubtedly brutal, and it was many weeks before his wife regained any measure of strength. The girl, a great healthy child, weighing over ten pounds at birth, was nursed with a patent food and thrived well.

Rachel was disappointed that she wasn't a boy. So, apparently, were the grandparents.

'What a pity,' everyone said to Julius, 'that it isn't a son. You ought to have had a boy.'

It mattered very little to Julius what sex his child should be. She made enough noise for two, she had nearly killed her mother, and she had given him the most exhausting devilish hour he had ever spent in his life. He would look down at her in her cradle as she snorted and dribbled in her sleep; when she wasn't sleeping she was yelling for food, and there was something sensual and satisfying in her hunger and contentment, in the full pouting mouth, the flat nose, and Julius laughed at her, pinching her nose till she screamed.

'Who brought you into the world?' he said.

'I hope she'll be pretty when she gets a little older,' sighed Rachel. 'I'm afraid she's rather a lump at the moment. Baby girls ought to be pretty. Oh! dear, why wasn't she a boy?'

'Oh, I don't know,' yawned Julius; 'she's all right. All babies are funny little beasts and look like nothing on earth.'

Poor Rachel, rather a shame she should be disappointed after that appalling tussle. She would have to make the most of this baby. From what the doctors had told him privately he gathered that there was very little chance of her ever having another. This had mucked up her inside, or else it was his own unskilled hands that had done it. However, there it was. No more children. Julius was very glad, he didn't much fancy going through the business again. Besides, who wanted children, anyway?

It was, he considered, a good thing that this had happened. Rachel was religious over these matters, she didn't believe in prevention. She would, in her obstinacy, have gone on producing babies year after year rather than do as he told her. It was the one point on which she would never give way. Yes, it was a lucky solution to what would have become a very difficult problem. Meanwhile, this only child helped to make up the pattern of his background, she was a necessary ornament to his private domestic life. There was something pleasing about the possession of a wife and child, they formed another link in a chain of power.

A son would have grown up – proved difficult. A son was hard to control, and lived all the time in the hopes of inheriting money and position. There need be none of this trouble with a daughter.

175

Daughters could be managed, all they had to do in life was to look attractive.

He could not understand the minds of those men – another English characteristic, he supposed – who laboured for the inheritance of their sons. Property, wealth handed down from one generation to another with some strange instinct of pride. Fellows who, misty-eyed, showed you a portrait of their great-great-grandfather; fellows who lived like servants in one wing of an old mansion so that the place could be kept up in some sort of repair for their boy when they should die.

Possession – yes, possess the whole earth if you wanted, but keep it for yourself. What should it matter to you how your things were scattered to the winds – after you were dead? There was only one life that mattered in this world and that was your own. Even Walter Dreyfus, his father-in-law, seemed to look upon this baby as a continuation of a long line of Dreyfuses and Lévys, something solid and unbreakable in the history of two families. He did not see her as Julius did, an animal born of another animal, to eat, drink and make love in its turn, and die.

'Pity she isn't a boy,' he said like the rest and Julius shrugged his shoulders and did not answer, this preoccupation over a small child was not interesting to him.

Gabriel would, of course, as she grew older have everything she wanted. His daughter would not be restricted in any way. He would see that Rachel made it her business to bring up the child more successfully than anybody else's child. She should be better dressed, better cared for, more completely educated. She should shine more, know more, charm more than other girls of her own age, so that when she came into a room people would be aware of her at once, they would turn their heads and whisper, they would say: 'Yes – that's Julius Lévy's daughter.'

Thus it happened that from the earliest moments of her life the small Gabriel was concentrated upon that she might develop into one of her father's most successful productions. London was combed for a nurse more specially trained than other nurses, so that the child should be reared with the greatest care, receiving the best of everything and the maximum of attention. Later, this nurse would be changed or set aside for governesses of superior intellect. Gabriel should speak French perfectly, German perfectly, Italian perfectly. She would have masters to teach her to play and sing, masters to teach her to draw and to paint, she must learn how to carry herself, how to walk, how to speak, how to amuse, she would have to grow up into something finished and flawless, something so perfect that Julius Lévy would be able to say with truth: 'I made her – I brought her into the world.'

He saw her, in his mind, as a business proposition, she was another of his cafés, raw as yet and undeveloped, but when the time came she would be as he wanted her. He would be the director, he would point her the way she must go, but at the moment she was Rachel's job, the nurses' job, women were necessary in the early stages.

Yes, he liked his background, he liked his house in Hans Crescent, the white paint, the geraniums in the bright window-boxes. He liked to be pleasantly aware of Moon, his butler, waiting in the hall to receive his coat and hat, the flourish with which he opened the front door; and then the smart blue pram in its corner beneath the wide staircase; a glance at letters waiting for him on a silver salver, turning them over in his hand, then questioning Moon without looking at him – 'Is Mrs Lévy in the drawing-room?'

'I think she has just gone upstairs to change. I sounded the dressing-gong five minutes ago, sir.'

'Right. You can tell them to keep back dinner, not to serve it until a quarter past. I want a bath before changing.'

'Yes, sir.'

The swiftness of orders carried out within the second, finding his man waiting in his dressing-room, his things laid out, and the rush of hot water in the bathroom, the steam rising, the smell of bath salts. Walking into their bedroom and seeing Rachel sitting before her dressing-table, a shawl or jacket round her shoulders, and the maid brushing her hair while she polished her nails.

'That you, dear?' she asked. 'You're rather late; were you kept?'

'Yes,' he answered, 'they called me down to Holborn after

six, the manager's having trouble with the new lighting we've just put in. I'll have to have it changed. I've told Moon to keep back dinner. That's all right, isn't it? We're alone tonight.'

'Yes. Have your bath, you must be tired. I've had a busy day too. Shopping all the morning and then mother and granny to lunch. This afternoon such a large party at the Solomans – crowds of people one knew. They're dining here Thursday, and the Goldings as well.'

'Have you arranged anything for Saturday?'

'Yes – Hector Strauss wants us at Richmond. It's a big affair. I don't see how we can get out of it. Lehmann is going to sing. Mr Hartmann said something about driving down with us if we had room in the brougham.'

'I don't believe I shall get away in time. I shall be lunching with Worthing; he's coming up purposely from Manchester. However, we'll see.'

Lying back in the bath, the hot water up to his neck, stretching his legs and watching the soapy froth collect on the surface, then covering himself with a great heavy towel, rubbing his body dry; and the luxurious touch of cool linen upon his warm flesh, well dressed, well shod, the sound of the gong clanging through the house. Hot soup tasting of pheasant, and Moon at his elbow with the sherry decanter, the two tastes mingling and merging into one. Rachel leaning forward in her chair, her low-cut dress showing the curve of her breasts, the long throat slim and white with its single row of pearls – she had filled out a little since the birth of the baby; she was sure of herself, she was mature, she was a woman. A log split on the fire suddenly, throwing a leaping red flame that danced and quivered behind the heavy closed curtains. A shower of autumn rain spattering on the windows, and loud and clear in the silence of the dining-room, broken only by the calm, monotonous soup noise, the gold clock on the mantelpiece chimed the half-hour. Julius fingered the thin stem of his sherry glass, he watched the light from the silver candlestick play upon the signet ring on his left hand, and half consciously he closed his eyes the better to smell the atmosphere of this room, to breathe it deeply, to be intensely and sensuously aware of it. Hartmann was right, once you were used to this you did not want to go back, it got

178

into your blood and kept you – this voice of luxury folding and wrapping you with soft caressing fingers.

It was smooth and warm like the texture of velvet, it was cool and soothing like a linen sheet, it shone white and still like the pearls Rachel wore, and slowly, cunningly, with infinite subtlety it wove a web around your hands and feet, it cast a chain about your neck.

With the outbreak of the Boer War went the remnants of Walter Dreyfus's fortune. He lost every penny he possessed. He had been born in South Africa, his interests and his wealth had been centred there, and now at last the smash had come, finally and irrevocably. With ruin staring at him face to face, he went at once to his son-in-law. Surely, if one man in the world could help him, it would be his daughter's husband, Julius Lévy. Already the effect of the blow had been to age him ten, fifteen years. He looked bent, frail, his eyes wandered restlessly about the room and he stumbled in his speech, he could not find the right words. He kept making little ineffectual gestures with his hands. He hesitated, he searched for his phrases, the innate courtesy that was so great a part of his nature made him plead poorly in his own cause. As he watched Julius's face, pale and expressionless, it seemed to him that he had never known Rachel's husband, that it was a stranger who sat listening so impassively to his words, one hand tap-tapping on the desk before him.

It was a stranger who rose from his chair when the story was concluded, a stranger who announced briefly and firmly that he helped no one.

'I stand alone,' he said, 'I carry no burdens. If people make mistakes it is their own concern. I am sorry for you.'

He stood up, he crossed over to the window and it was as though everything had been said that he could say, that the subject henceforward would be closed to him. He waited in patience until Walter Dreyfus should recover himself. He lit a cigar and tapped his fingers on the window-pane while the older man gripped the arms of his chair and gazed at the irregular pattern on the screen.

Then Walter Dreyfus drew himself up, he stood uncertainly a

179

moment, like a sleep-walker, dazed and stunned, and he held out his hand.

'Forgive me,' he said; 'it was very wrong of me to have asked you,' and then he made some conventional little remark about the lateness of the hour, and how he was keeping Julius up. No, he did not want Julius to tell Moon to call him a cab, he would start walking, and pick one up later.

'I don't think I'll disturb Rachel,' he said, 'but would you kiss her good night for me? Apologize for my silence at dinner, tell her I was tired.'

He went down the steps of the house, his cape flung over his shoulders, his hat in his hand, and was swallowed up in the darkness; and Julius shivered a little because the night was cold. He rubbed his hands in the pleasant warmth of the hall, and he heard the solemn comforting chime of the grandfather clock striking eleven as he went upstairs to his wife and the blazing drawing-room fire.

'Father was looking seedy,' said Rachel. 'I'm so worried about him. Is it really true he's lost all this money? I can't get a word of sense out of mother. Did he talk about it to you?'

'He said a little.'

'Of course it's absurd of him to take things to heart. Heaps of his friends are losing because of this war. He's not the only one. Besides, he knows he has only to come to us . . .'

'Shall I put another log on the fire or shall we go up to bed?'

'Bed, love. I'm sleepy. Oh! dear, poor father, I wish I'd gone down and seen him off and kissed him good night.'

'Kiss me instead, Rache. D'you know, you're looking very handsome tonight.'

When Andrew Dreyfus came round in the morning Rachel had her arms full of flowers for the drawing-room, she stood at the head of the stairs looking down at him. 'Why, Andy!' she said, 'how lovely to see you – wait a minute while I put these in water.'

'Father's shot himself,' he said. 'I've got a cab waiting outside.'

'Oh!' she said, 'Oh! Andy' – and the flowers fell out of her hands, the wet stalks dirtying her dress, and she put one hand on to the banister to hold it tightly because it was a tearing momentary comfort to her, a friend, a supporter, and she looked at her brother's white face without seeing it.

'Oh! Andy,' she said. Then it was no more a passing hideous nightmare, but the blank truth, and she said: 'I must come to mother at once'; and her hat and coat were found, and she was holding her brother's arm in the cab while the tears rolled down her cheeks, and he was telling her:

'He didn't come home last night. We didn't worry, we thought you'd be putting him up, and he was found this morning, down in the City office, shot – Rachel – through the heart. I've seen him – I shan't ever forget it.'

'I didn't kiss him good night,' she said. 'I'll never forgive myself that – I didn't kiss him good night. Julius let him out, it was about eleven. Oh! Andy, what are we all going to do?'

'What did Julius talk to him about? Did you ask him?' said her brother.

'No – we went straight up to bed after he left. Julius said father was tired. And I never kissed him good night. Andy darling, he must have gone straight down to the City . . .'

'It's not your fault, Rachel, don't cry – you make me cry too, and it hurts so damnably. . . . We've got to pull ourselves together, because of mother.'

'Where's Walter?'

'He's down at the office. I left him there to come to you. Aunt Naomi is with mother. There are all the papers to go through – the firm has crashed, you know. Walter and I knew. I think it must have broken father's heart – he thought he couldn't face us all.'

'But we'd have helped, Andy – there was no need. Why, he'd only to ask Julius and everything would have been all right.'

'I don't know,' said Andrew.

Somebody had sent for Julius Lévy at his Strand offices. He was waiting in Portland Place when they arrived. Rachel ran to him at once.

'Oh! darling,' she cried, 'this is so terrible, why did it have to happen? – he was with us last, he must have gone straight down and – all alone like that – oh! why, why didn't we do something then? . . .'

'You'd better go up to your mother,' said Julius. 'Hullo, Andrew. I'll come down with you to the City right away. No use hanging about here.'

They got into the cab. 'I shouldn't have thought your father would do this,' said Julius, 'thought he had more pluck.'

'Doesn't it require pluck to put a bullet through one's heart, alone, in the night?'

'I doubt it,' said Julius. 'Not after a bottle of whisky, anyway.'

'I respected my father more than anyone in the world, Julius – this has knocked me sideways. Why did he do it, that's what I don't understand?'

'I suppose he had his reasons, or thought he had.'

'Did he ask you for help last night?'

'Yes.'

'And you refused?'

'Yes.'

'I suspected that. I kept it to myself, because of Rachel. Do you realize that it is you who have killed my father, Julius, and nobody else?'

'Don't be a fool, Andrew. A man holds his destiny in his own hands.'

'I don't know anything about destiny – all I know is that father is dead because of you. I wish I could kill you – and I can't because of Rachel.'

He began to cry, miserably, silently, the tears scalding his mouth as he stared out of the window of the cab. 'I'll have to tell Walter this,' he said.

Julius shrugged his shoulders.

'It doesn't matter to me if you tell the whole world,' he said. 'I don't think it's my affair. Your father should have managed his life more wisely.'

'You're inhuman – God! – Rachel is his daughter, didn't you think of her at all?'

'One of the first things I told Rachel was this – "I'm marrying you and not your family; remember that always." Supposing you take a cigarette, Andrew, and pull yourself in shape. This conversation won't help you. Nothing under the sun will bring your father back now.'

The crash of the Dreyfus firm and the suicide of the founder caused a mild flutter on the Stock Exchange, and a certain amount of interest in society. The crash, of course, accounted for the suicide. Nobody suspected that it might have been avoided. The two brothers, out of a strange blind loyalty to their sister, kept silence on the subject; but inevitably with the death of Walter Dreyfus the family drifted apart. Andrew went out to South Africa ten days after the funeral. He joined a Boer regiment as a private soldier and was killed at Paardeberg in February. This second blow turned Martha Dreyfus into an old woman. The home in Portland Place had been sold, and she retired to the country, where she lived in seclusion with an unmarried sister.

Young Walter Dreyfus sailed to New York, went into a large shipping firm, and eventually married and settled in America for good.

These ties gone from her, Rachel Lévy clung more closely to her husband and child. Her home was the centre of her life, to act hostess, to bring up Gabriel, to serve as that serene and charming background which Julius needed for his life.

It seemed to him that she belonged more to him since her family had disbanded. She and Gabriel were more definitely and finally his than they had been before, and he was pleased with this because possession was dear to him.

He thought of Walter Dreyfus with his heart torn from him, lying still and horrible before his desk in the office, and Martha Dreyfus a sad, solitary old woman, mooning over little flowers in a wet garden; and young Andrew hacked to pieces on a plain in Africa, and young Walter amongst strangers in a new land; and he thought, as he drew up an agreement for a new café, how strange it was that in his life things always turned to his advantage.

Now came the close of the century and the death of the Queen, followed soon by peace in South Africa, and these things also served as a milestone in the life of Julius Lévy. They marked the end of an era showing him the path to greater prosperity than he had as yet achieved. It was the beginning of a new age – the age of progress and speed and efficiency that he had long foreseen and the dawn of mechanism in all things, electricity, motor-cars, and soon flying machines in the air. The spirit abroad was one that he understood, the demon of restlessness unsatisfied, stretching hungry fingers to the skies in a superhuman effort to conquer insatiable hunger, a spirit of rapacity and greed and excitement burning like a living flame.

In this bright world that travelled too fast, Julius Lévy prospered. Success lay in a touch of his hands, wheresoever he trod; whatever he seized for himself became like particles of gold to add to his splendour, and nothing escaped him and nothing was lost.

Over twenty years ago he had arrived in England, a shabby, pale-faced Jew, who had no country and no friends; who shivered in a sordid attic of a lodging-house denying himself food and clothing, and now he was forty-two, Julius Lévy risen from obscurity, admired and envied, and sought after and praised.

The sentiments he inspired by his fortune and success were the sentiments he craved, not affection, not loyalty nor trust, for these could pass him by, these were worthless anaemic qualities, but envy and angry admiration and hatred at times and fear.

It was good to be envied by men, it was good to be feared, it was good to experience deeply the sensation of power by wealth, the power of money tossed to and fro lightly in his hands like a little god obedient as a slave. The voices around him were warm and thrilling to his heart because of their envy. He knew the meaning of the whispers and the glances. 'Julius Lévy . . . there's Julius Lévy.'

Voices, and eyes, and fingers directed towards him; wherever he walked he would be aware of them, and it was meat and it was drink to him, it was life, and lust, and glory, and desire.

Now that he had launched his cafés upon London, there were other paths that beckoned him – the lovely hidden roads of finance. He could juggle with the markets of the world, he could buy and he could sell, and his intuition was like a streak of lightning that comes before the thunder. He was first in all things; he was ready two seconds before his opponents. It was as though he calculated upon the hesitation of his fellow-men, he allowed in his mind for those two seconds of caution and reconsideration, and in that time he was away from them, he had cast his fly, he had won.

There was a fascination in this business that seized upon him with the itch of a fever in midsummer. It excited him, it tore at him, it would not leave him alone. There was adventure here and danger, and the cafés were safe, solid foundations that spread themselves and developed into mountains of success. There were Lévy cafés in all the London districts, with the building in the Strand and the new building in Oxford Street rearing their white façades and their triumphant golden signs high above the traffic and the passers-by. They were the fountain-heads and the mark of fame. While in the provinces rose others no less prosperous, no less carefully considered, each one planned and planted in firm ground by the mind and the hand of their creator.

Soon there would surely not be a town in England that did not boast its Lévy café. Each building especially adapted to the needs and peculiarities of its local population which must first be studied, but all of them bearing the style and fabric of the fountain-heads, all with white walls, white floors, white-coated assistants, and the slick smart service of a meal dispatched in half an hour at a fixed popular price, with orchestra and flowers thrown in, and no gratuities.

'Lévy's for Service,' 'Lévy's for Speed,' 'Eat more and spend less,' slogans and catchwords that caught the eye and were placarded on hoardings, in newspapers, on omnibuses, spreading even to music-hall refrains and then becoming a sure gag to a low comedian.

'The Lévy Pies,' 'The Lévy Chocolates,' 'The Lévy Cakes,' articles in common use in every household, because they were cheap and because the name and the brand had caught the fancy of the middle-class purchaser.

They were rich in experience these years of achievement. They brought an ever-increasing knowledge of life, and adventure and sensation, of men and of women; and these experiences came to him without expenditure, without affecting physically or mentally any particle of his health, his vigour, his personality, or his fortune, so that somewhere within him was still the laughing spirit of the incorrigible boy who rubbed his hands and chuckled to himself: 'Something for nothing – something for nothing.'

Apart from the passionate chase after money and profit and

'nothing to pay', that was the current and the main stream of his life, there were backwaters and branches to explore, there were hidden creeks, and undiscovered channels. There was existence in the home, there was Rachel and the child.

The house in Hans Crescent was a dwelling of the past, that had been the comfortable establishment of a rising man who had married the daughter of a small diamond merchant, Walter Dreyfus.

Since then they had moved to Bryanston Square, with a 'shake-down', as Julius expressed it, at Maidenhead because Rachel expressed a fondness for the river; and now they had moved again, this time to the big house on the corner of Grosvenor Square, absurdly extensive for two persons and a child, but built and furnished obviously for entertaining on a lavish scale, which was what Julius intended to do. And though Rachel clung out of sentimentality to the small house at Maidenhead, there was a new house down at Hove, for the summer months – a splash of modernity on the front with gay window-boxes and coloured blinds. Here part of July, August, and September could be spent, and perhaps weeks now and again during the autumn and winter to escape fogs and because sea air was good for the child; but the season must never be missed in London, nor the early spring, nor the weeks before Christmas.

The Lévys went everywhere, they knew everybody, and even if he was a Jew, and a foreigner, and had made all that money out of those vulgar cafés, surely it did not matter so very much if he were willing to entertain, and to spend that money. And besides, he was so very intelligent and brilliant, and mysterious and dangerous, and his parties were marvellous affairs, and his wife was really charming – and there it was, he was powerful, he was successful, he was Julius Lévy.

Rachel was an admirable hostess, Julius had always known she would be; and her taste was good, and her clothes were good. Yes, he knew what was said of her: 'Rachel Lévy always seems to wear the latest thing a month before anybody else,' and 'that house, my dear, quite overwhelming, positively magnificent,' and 'their food, their servants, their wine. . . . Oh! God – to be as rich as that . . .'

Why was it, people wondered, that Carlo the pianist should refuse to play at their houses and yet perform when Julius Lévy asked him? Why should Chequita, the world-famous *prima donna*, lift up her voice with naïve informality after supper in Julius Lévy's drawing-room and nowhere else? Why was it that Rachel Lévy, wearing one string of pearls, should make other women look shabby and cheap in their diamonds?

Why did they have the telephone in every room when many of the guests had not yet installed one in their hall? Why did they possess two motor-cars before anyone had properly realized that cars were vehicles at all?

Why – why – why – They resented Julius Lévy and his wealth, they protested, and they disapproved, but they clamoured for invitations to his dinners, they flocked like herds of geese to his parties, they followed him to Ascot, to Goodwood, to Henley – a familiar figure everywhere with his hat a little on one side and his inevitable cigar. Women flustered, twittering, longing to catch his eyes, and men eager, suffused, knowing that to be acquainted with Lévy might lead in some small measure to prosperity on their own account, with a handshake here, a nod there, and a word dropped carelessly at a City luncheon.

There were other parties, too, where Julius Lévy acted host, and these because they were less known were whispered over and wondered at, and nobody was sure if the reports were true or false, because the very essence of their attraction was the veil of mystery that shrouded them, dark and secret. It was said that he had a house in Chelsea somewhere, of which his wife held no knowledge, and that here he played sultan to a harem of lovely ladies whose birth and position should have taught them greater discretion. It was said that girls were decoyed here from the streets and were not permitted to depart until he had had his way with them. It was said that strangers visited the house by night and that they wore masks to conceal their identity.

Legends grew up about the habits of Julius Lévy: he was Oriental, he was a sadist, he was a pervert, he kept black women, he took opium. Story after story was whispered behind hands and nobody brought certain truth of any of these things.

Julius lived as it pleased him to live, and it mattered little to him what people said or thought. He believed that hunger should never go a-begging, and because of this his fancy fell on strange faces at times and in strange places. It would seem to him that surely along this dark river there must be something rich, and something rare; new treasures to stand within his reach and dazzle his eyes – always hungry, always thirsty, always curiously jaded.

And he searched, and he stretched out his hands, and he drank deeply of what he found, but part of him was blunted, part of him was stale, and part of him was lost for ever with the fierce sharp joy of a boy who threw stones at a washer-woman's window.

For this was worthless, and this was old, and this was like a close dank fungus smell, and there was nothing exquisite, or lingering, or dangerously sweet; and he must travel on, on, always a little farther to the next river; to the sound of uncharted waters beyond the bend, to the shadow path across the hill. In spite of disillusion, and cynicism, and the dull, stale taste in the mouth, Julius Lévy never wearied of his search. He was as tireless as the child who discovers a road beyond the garden gate, every moment in his life was a living moment of adventure that counted with him and made its mark.

He was his own god, he, Julius Lévy, and the power he made for himself. He was beholden to nothing and to no one and his destiny belonged to him.

There were moments when he stood in the Oxford Street café, the largest of all his buildings, with its great white front and its dome and its golden lettering and its glass doors, and he would watch the stream of people during the lunch hour fill the deep restaurant and the floors above; black dots of men and women like swarms of flies into a spider's web. The chatter of a thousand voices, the clatter of plates and glasses, the scraping back of chairs, the strains of the orchestra, the swift bustle of the efficient white-coated attendants, the good food atmosphere. There was life and power and excitement in this picture before him. There was vitality and strength. It brought to him the same sensuous enjoyment that the market had done long ago in Neuilly with the bargain cries, the heaps of cauliflower, onions, fruit, and cheese, the fluttering of the stalls in the breeze, the scattering litter of dust on cobbled stones.

There were moments in his office in the Strand, leaning back in the chair before his roll-topped desk, pausing a moment for a suitable phrase in a letter, which his secretary waited for him to dictate. From his window he could hear the traffic noise in the Strand below, he could see the grey roofs of buildings stretching down to the City – a dome, a spirit of a church. There was the ceaseless hum of movement that was City noise, that was working, breathing humanity. A day of ceaseless activity would spread itself before him; one glance at his calendar would insure him of this. These letters to dictate and the constant interruptions, the low b-r-r of the telephone at his elbow, switched through to him from the outer room by another secretary and therefore meaning an important call: 'Birmingham wants you, Mr Lévy' . . . 'Hullo – Hullo' – Standish, the Birmingham manager, with some essential matter to report – 'All right, Standish, I understand the situation, and I'll wire instructions.'

Going through with the letters – 'I wouldn't have bothered you with this, Mr Lévy, but there's been some trouble over in Kensington . . .' 'Well, send Kelly to me, he must go down there and take over until Johnson is fit . . .' The telephone again, the manager of the Western United Bank: 'Yes, I tried to get you twenty minutes ago. I want twenty-five thousand from No. 5 transferred to the Liverpool branch. Can you fix that? Fellow called Wilson is my representative there . . .' A tap at the door. 'Mr Conrad Marx to see Mr Lévy, he has an appointment.'

'Show him in right away.' The architect for the new building scheme in Oxford Street – a roof garden that in summer could be covered in within five minutes in case of rain. 'Look here, Marx, you've got to prove to me on paper it can be done in the time, otherwise I'm not employing you.'

More letters, more telephone calls, more interviews, and somewhere about one-thirty a luncheon with Stanley Leon and Jack Cohen across the way at the Savoy.

'I want you to see what the devil is happening at Leeds, Cohen. Complaints all the time. You can sack Frue if he's the trouble. If he isn't I'll come up myself and raise hell,' and to Leon: 'I see Holborn dropped three thousand last week, how do you account for it?' Then catching a glimpse at another table of a fellow he

189

recognizes as the director of the Bank in Hamburg, leaves his companions and crosses over to their table: 'Hullo, how d'you do, Schwaber? Tell me the truth about the Carlheim Steel. I've heard the Hamburg factory's gone up in flames.'

'How in God's name did you get wind of it?'

'I had my scouts out as usual. Sold every share I possessed yesterday afternoon. So it is true? That's all I wanted to know. Come to dinner tomorrow. Rachel's got Vanda coming, we'll get her to sing.'

Then wandering back to his own table, the servile waiters bowing before him, his big cigar between his teeth, and hearing somebody murmur: 'There's Julius Lévy.'

By three o'clock before his desk again in the Strand offices. More interviews, more telephone calls, and then at a quarter to five finding Henry waiting for him with the Rolls to take him along to the Oxford Street café, where he was kept until half past six; but his temper was good and he was looking forward to his evening. As he leaned back in the car he remembered with satisfaction his telephone message to Isaacs in the City as soon as he left the Savoy after lunch: 'Yes, the Carlheim factory's burnt. There'll be a sudden rise in Wordorf when it gets known. Start buying at once and quit when they start jumping. If they reach the old level you can sell, they won't go beyond that.'

There were moments when work could be put aside for a little space, when he was not Julius Lévy the thinker, but Julius Lévy the host. The bright sun shining in a cloudless sky, and driving with Rachel down to Ascot, she in lavender blue with a lace hat on her pile of red-brown hair, those envied pearls about her throat. And sitting in the box above the course watching King Edward arrive in the royal carriage drawn by milk-white horses, and then luncheon served by Moon and the two footmen in the room behind the box: cold salmon, chicken, strawberries and cream, champagne, the laughter of his guests, beautiful women, the shouts of the crowd warning them that another race had started. Gaiety, excitement. 'Julius, my dear, how like you to be the only creature to back the winner,' Nina, Baroness Chesborough, touching him on the shoulder in pretence of mockery, handsome, intelligent, and he looked at her until her eyes fell;

she wanted to be his mistress – and the light, and the colour, and the scent and movement of women, the thud of horses' hoofs on the turf, their bodies sleek and glistening with sweat, the patch of blue hydrangea below the King's box, a friend laughing in his ear: 'Hullo, Lévy – you've got a wonderful crowd in your party.' Another glass of champagne, another cigar, another smile at Nina Chesborough, and the whole of his pleasure concentrated in one glance on the buttons of the livery worn by Moon and the footmen, gold buttons on which the letter 'L' stood plain for all to see.

There were moments at Hove, where during the summer months he would give big week-end parties, travelling down himself late on Saturday night and finding the place full. Bridge groups, musical groups, bathing groups scattered about his house. And moments at Henley, when they drove over from the Maidenhead house and boarded the launch that had been sent up the day before in readiness, and there were more picnics, and more champagne, more laughter.

It added to the amusement and the vitality of these parties to be summoned in the middle, with the gaiety at its height, and the voice in his ear that said: 'You're wanted on the telephone, sir, very urgent,' because this was a reminder of work and of power, and a word from him on the quivering wire meant a portrayal of this power. His 'Yes', his 'No', his 'Buy', his 'Sell' was a signal bringing loss or gain to hundreds of men and women he would never know and who mattered not.

Power, satisfying and sweet.

There were moments in his home when he resolved overnight upon some decision, and his word was law and must be obeyed.

'Rachel, we'll spend Christmas in Brighton after all. I should prefer it. We'll ask fifteen or twenty people – I'll leave the invitations to you, but show me them before you send them out. I won't have Willie Kahn – he drinks too much and he can't carry his wine. Your friend Nell Jacobs? No – I don't care for her. You can ask Nina Chesborough, she'll probably refuse.'

Or it would be: 'Rachel, I'm sick of the gold walls in the drawing-room. They were amusing at first, but now they bore me. We'll have parchment instead.' And: 'By the way, I've found a

191

good-looking pony for Gabriel; it comes from the Stonyhurst stud. Time she learnt to ride properly,' looking quizzically at his daughter, a long-legged, secretive child, over-intelligent, over-precocious, unlike anybody in face – neither he nor Rachel – save for the long straight nose betraying her race, but with a mop of fair-coloured hair and hot blue eyes – Jean Blançard's eyes.

The child was always with governesses, or nurses, or tutors; he hardly knew her, but she belonged to him, and that was enough. He caught glimpses of her sometimes walking to a dancing class; she grinned at him, waving a hand as he passed in the car, or he would hear shouts of rebellion from the schoolroom quarters and would wonder with amusement if the young imp had a temper.

'Gabriel is rather troublesome,' Rachel would confess. 'Mademoiselle says she can do nothing with her.'

'Probably handles her wrong,' grunted Julius. 'I'd cope with her myself if I had the time. She's probably too clever. We'd better send her on the Continent, and she'll find her level. No child can learn anything in England.'

So Gabriel would travel with governesses in France, with governesses in Germany, and with governesses in Italy, and Julius would be aware of her from time to time flashing upon his line of vision; the best-dressed child at a children's party Rachel gave, the straightest back when riding in the Park, a pair of very long legs escaping his grasp as she ran from him up a staircase with a loud infectious laugh. A slim small figure splashing into the bathing-pool at Maidenhead before breakfast when the coast was clear and the guests were still in bed, and she, perceiving she was observed, putting her finger to her lips for silence and winking at him, which was surprising in its spontaneity. And he caught himself thinking: 'I must do something about Gabriel,' and promptly forgetting her because she would appear no more that day.

There were moments when in the still dark silence of the night sleep would not come to him, and he lay with his hands behind his head staring at the walls around him; at the warm body of Rachel by his side deep in her placid slumber. And there would come to his mind the memory of a high wistful note flung into the air from a flute like a message of beauty – a song, a whisper, an intolerable cry; and there out of the darkness was the white, happy face of Paul Lévy, the flute at his lips. And there beside him were the blazing eyes of the young Rabbin of the Temple, and the lost ecstasy of his voice, rising higher – higher, the voice and the flute mingling exquisitely in one, rising beyond the white clouds and the farthest star to the gates of a secret city.

And then Julius was troubled, then he was alone. He put his hands over his ears so that the music would not come to him, mocking, cruel, and persistent, the song that was not his, the thin high note that he had never held.

Resistance struggled within him, and he whispered like a child who tells himself stories in the dark: 'I don't want it – I don't want it.' And as he cried with the heaviness of sleep now coming upon him he was afraid of an old black nightmare with a hooded face who peered into his eyes before dawn, and who was death, and terror, and ultimate loneliness. Then the morning was brave and the sky a worldly grey, and he woke as Julius Lévy who held what he possessed, and all these fears were little sad terrors of the night banished by work and play. Paul Lévy was a white ghost who played his flute in vain. His songs were valueless; he called no tune. Julius Lévy was a magician with the world at his feet. He sat at his roll-top desk in his office above the roar of traffic and the hum of living things; he heard the rattle of typewriters, the sound of voices. He sacked one of his managers who crept from the room like a beaten cur, he promoted another in his stead, who grovelled at his feet and fawned upon his hand. He settled over luncheon for a new building to be raised immediately in Sheffield; and by afternoon the plans were on his desk and the agreement signed. He interviewed Marius from Paris, who wanted him to put capital into a café concern on the Boulevard Haussmann. He snatched an hour to drive down to the Lévy Chocolate Factory in Middlesex, which was going to be enlarged. He drove away to the sound of cheers, his workers lined up to watch him go, and he smiled, waving a hand – tapping on the glass to the chauffeur: 'Back to the office. I'm late as it is.'

Then once more, before the end of the day, with the telephone at his ear: 'That you, Isaacs? What news of Bolivian Plantation Territory? . . . Well, that's an advance in three hours, go on buying until the market closes. . . . United Havanas risen two and a half points, you say. Well, they won't keep it up, you can sell out. I've heard on good authority there's to be a textile strike in France within twenty-four hours, start selling Courtauld's right away, they're going to be hit by it. They're firm at the moment, and if you sell now, I'll have made a packet. Hullo . . . hullo . . .' Some disturbance on the line, and here was his other number being called, his private number. So while he shouted his instructions to Isaacs down one line he held the second earpiece with his left hand and listened. 'Who's there? Oh, it's you. What do you want, Nina? I feel very flattered. So you've changed your mind. Excellent. Afraid? What is there to be afraid of? No, nobody's going to see you if you get into a taxi-cab and give the Chelsea address. I'll order dinner for eight-thirty. Yes – I've been wondering when you were going to give in. Three months is a long time to wait. . . . No, I'm not laughing at you. . . . À bientôt, then.' And replacing the receiver and turning to the other mouthpiece: 'Are you there, Isaacs? I've changed my mind about United Havanas. Don't sell, they'll keep steady if they rise three points on the day . . .'

Then pushing the telephone from him, and glancing at the time.

'Ring through to Mrs Lévy, and say I won't be home for dinner,' and a message to the chauffeur that he should not be wanting the car.

Lighting a cigar and stretching himself, smiling because of Nina Chesborough and the profits of the day, and standing on the pavement before the café in the Strand while the attendant dashed to find him a taxi. Pushing his hat on the back of his head, and laughing suddenly, winking at the flickering star in the sky.

For somewhere there was a cart rattling on the high road between Puteaux and Courbevoie, and Grandpère Blançard cracked his whip at the plodding horse and said to a boy: 'One day you'll stretch yourself and wink an eye at the sky, and you'll do someone down for a hundred sous, and you'll pocket the money and walk out and have a woman. That's life, Julius . . .'

And Julius Lévy tapped his nose as he had done nearly forty years back, whistling a French song under his breath, and he was thinking: 'Ha – Grandpère Blançard, he knew me, he understood.'

On Julius Lévy's fiftieth birthday he signed a contract in which it was stated that every single provincial town in England should henceforward boast its Lévy café. He had worked long to achieve this. His plans had stretched and extended themselves to embrace north, east, west, and south, and now the ambition was realized and he had, as he had always intended to do, and in his own words: 'Put a chain around England.'

There would be no town in future days lacking a Lévy café: Lévy's was something permanent and solid, it had identified itself with the English character and because of its general familiarity had become a national advertisement.

Yes, Julius Lévy, born in obscurity, a foreigner, a Jew, who had sold rats in the streets of Paris for two francs apiece when he was ten years old, could call himself at fifty a millionaire.

It was curious that this final agreement should be signed on his birthday. It was as though his life were divided into chapters by time and circumstance, and now he had come to the end of another chapter that must be sealed, and put away and closed. He could do nothing further with his cafés, they had reached the height of their prosperity – henceforward he would look upon them as if from some great distance; they were his children, but they had grown up. They no longer needed him. Closely controlled and run by men of intelligence and understanding, how should there any longer be work necessary for the founder, and what else remained but for him to sit back and reap the immense profits?

That was the position on Julius Lévy's fiftieth birthday, and it seemed to him that in realizing his dream he had let it go from his reach for ever. For a moment, blankly, and with intense astonishment, he wondered what he was going to do. The markets of the world were left to him of course, but these had been side-tracks to his life: they were a relaxation. What else remained when your work no longer needed you? To start all over again? to escape, to hide his identity, to go on the Continent and begin life once more with eightpence in his pocket, and beg for employment as a baker's assistant in the poor overcrowded quarters of Paris or Berlin? For about five seconds he considered this seriously, and then like a flash came the vision of his house in Grosvenor Square; the great hall, the broad curving staircase, the boom of the dressing-gong, a strange hurried picture of his return home every evening.

And he knew now that he could not go back to the beginning again, that his knowledge and intimacy of luxury made the experience of any other thing a terror and an impossibility. He was caught in the web to eternity. He was more of a slave to comfort and indulgence than Rupert Hartmann – poor Rupert, dead now some years ago – had ever known. He wondered why the appreciation of these things should creep so insidiously upon a man, and why he, who as a youngster bit his finger-nails and never bothered at all, should bathe now twice a day, should hurl blasphemy at his valet if the large towel had not been sufficiently warmed upon the steaming pipes, or the shower a fraction ill-adjusted, or the water under-scented with perfumed salts.

He wondered why in the early days food had meant no more than the satisfaction of hunger – onions and a hunk of cheese being perfect fare – and now he laid his knife and fork aside if he fancied his grouse was over-cooked.

Once he had risen with his entire party from a restaurant because at the last moment plovers' eggs had been unobtainable. One became angered easily nowadays at little things. Angry that the roses were not in bloom at Granby Hall during a wet week-end in June – why keep an estate in Buckinghamshire if the gardeners were not efficient? Angry because the Paris *modiste* had turned Rachel out in a dress that fitted loosely round her hips. One suffered much from irritation, from dislike of people and places. The week-ends at Granby were not, after all, so very amusing. People became bores after twenty-four hours, and one wondered how it was going to be possible to endure them for another twenty-four. By avoiding them one merely wandered about the estate by oneself and then one was lonely.

It would come to Julius in these moments that he had no friends. There was no one he cared about who brought a warmth to his heart or a sensation of excitement to his loins. Rachel – yes, but then Rachel was like a chair or a table about the house – she belonged, she was there, she was the necessary furniture.

No, he had no friends. Sensations these days were rare. He failed to be moved by wit or beauty. Once there had been the amusement of the Chelsea flat, Nina Chesborough, Lottie Deane, and others. Lottie had been a beauty at that time. He remembered the box that was taken in his name every night of the eight months her play had run, and how she had sent for him, exasperated and angry, ready to cover him with abuse, and she had gone out to supper with him instead. Nina, jealous, a fishwife, a whore like many ladies of the land, sending anonymous letters to Lottie, and Lottie in her turn jealous because he turned from her to Mary Annesly, wife of Bill Annesly the polo player.

Scenes, jealousy, fierce loves that lasted a year and a day, and the fun of giving women presents, plastering them with jewels; and then the sordid discoveries of husbands who lived on these wives one kept. Husbands who did not hesitate at blackmail. Husbands who demanded compensation because their third child had not been begotten by themselves.

And now one had become a little weary of all this. The sensations were always the same. One fancied, in the secrecy of the heart, that women no longer gave themselves for love, they acted a little like one acted oneself, their sighs were forced, their cries were insincere. They wanted that diamond bracelet very much more than they wanted one's person.

Niti Lokala had been the last – over two years ago too – nobody since then. She had bored him very easily, and he hated her lies.

No, he had no friends. Parties and functions and entertaining had only been amusing because of the woman of the day. There had been the constant show and display, the glittering parade of what one could do.

The fun of Rachel as a wife whose charm and beauty baffled his mistresses, that had been good; they had always felt themselves to be slightly insignificant beside her. Now Rachel without a rival was merely herself. His wife, one of his belongings. She was getting big too, she had put on a couple of stone last year. She was fond of bridge. She had plenty of friends; she lived her life. She had never been a very amusing companion.

The child was in Italy, due home soon, he supposed. This week, today, he had forgotten. She was nearly fifteen. Lumpy and awkward, he supposed. He hadn't seen her for ages.

No, he had no friends. He was a millionaire, he had cafés all over England, and his work was gone from him. He could, he supposed, spend a year or so amusing himself. He could travel. But he did not want to travel. People and places everywhere were very much the same. Natives in New Guinea beating drums – he had seen the dancing girls in the Kasbah – where was the difference? If he went to Italy it meant he would be obliged to look at pictures or float about in gondolas – well, he had pictures worth many thousands at Granby Hall, and at Maidenhead he had his own electric canoe.

Rachel and he had gone down to Monte Carlo for a few weeks during the winter, and he had found it dull. Blue skies – and people chattering, people squabbling, people smiling at one because of one's money. Travelling to new places was not worth while, it meant being without one's accustomed things, one's way of living. Besides, travelling alone. . . . He could, perhaps, go in for racing. Get advice, buy a crop of yearlings, and start a stable. He would need someone though to share the enthusiasm, and that applied to every hobby; work was the only satisfying business that could be achieved in solitude. His fiftieth birthday – and he had had everything that he had ever wanted. Surely there must be something somewhere that was not exhausted?

His fiftieth birthday, and he was bored, irritable, and lonely. He was going back to a solitary dinner at Grosvenor Square, and a solitary night. Rachel was down at Granby. He would have gone down himself but for the meeting that was over at last. He knew his evening – the perfect dinner served at eight precisely, he himself changed as though people were dining, and Moon, getting rather old and deaf, standing behind his chair. Silence, and the clock ticking, and the coal settling in the fire. Sitting alone over a glass of brandy and a cigar, and wondering what things, if any, in his life had been worth while.

He began to hate the thought of his evening, it was a menace. It challenged him, it was the finish to the life that had been, it was the beginning of the one to come. He did not want it; he was afraid. He crossed to the window and looked up at the sky. A white cloud passed above his head moving swiftly like a wreath of smoke and was gone.

Down in the street Mander waited with the Rolls, a small figure at the wheel in his purple livery, reading an evening paper. The two things were like symbols to Julius: the car below waiting to take him home, and above the white clouds flying.

He slammed the door behind him, and stepped on to the landing, and pressed the button of the lift. Mander jumped from his seat when he saw his master in the street and crushed his paper out of sight; then he flung open the door, touching his hat.

'Where to, sir?' he said.

Julius hesitated, wondering for one moment if there was any place upon the earth he cared to take himself, realizing with a sense of ridiculous frustration that possessing his wealth he could command trains, boats, cars, hotels – he had only to say a word and his word would be obeyed. Supposing he said now: 'Mander, we are going tonight to Timbuctoo,' the man would touch his hat and say: 'Very good, sir.'

Julius glanced up and down the street – the same ceaseless traffic, the same endless stream of passers-by – and he said: 'Home, Mander.'

He sat with his chin balanced on his stick, he gazed moodily out of the window. He thought of the big library at Grosvenor Square – ladders placed against the walls to reach the highest shelves – and how he never read. Did anybody bother about those books? he wondered. Surely not Rachel; she bought the new novels. Perhaps under-housemaids browsed amongst those shelves. He never went into the room himself. It struck him forcibly that his life was a sublime piece of irony, that all his money was a gigantic parade to no purpose. Because nobody cared. Nobody was interested. He was Julius Lévy, aged fifty today, and what of it? Perhaps it was not so very interesting after all.

The car drew up to the house. Before Julius could lean to the door Mander had opened it, had whipped the rug from his knees. The footman, listening for the sound of the car, was already standing upon the steps. Moon was waiting in the hall.

'Shall you be wanting the car again, sir?' Should he? No – to what end? 'Not tonight, Mander.'

There were letters waiting on the salver. Useless to glance at them because his secretary would go through them and answer them for him. There was no work he need do of any kind. Menials performed every service.

The Progress of Julius

It was extraordinary he reflected, that the process of washing one's hands and relieving the burden of nature still remained to one. They were, perhaps, the only things to remain. He went through the hall, and along the passage, and across the farther corridor to the privacy of his own room. His study, his sanctum, where in days gone by he had worked late in the night, time being too short, the day too quickly sped. And now for the first time in his life time would hang heavily on his hands. He paused before opening the door, because it seemed to him that even from those sound-proof walls he could hear something. Something faint and thin, like a note of music. Yes, there again, a call, a cry, a whisper flung into the air. It was the sound of a flute. Somebody was playing Paul Lévy's flute. He opened the door and now the note came clear and strong, piercing like a challenge. And it was not the far-flung sob of mystery and pain and spiritual distress that Père had sung; it was not the whisper of immortality beyond the clouds, of things unseen, of things unknown, of pale and lovely unsubstantial dreams; this was a song of life and love and passionate beauty, of laughter unafraid, of adventure on the hills, of a ship on the sea, of danger in the deep woods; it was a song of triumph, and brutality, and joy. He looked into the room and he saw her standing by the window with the flute to her lips, watching the white clouds pass across the sky. She raised herself on tiptoe as though by drawing herself up she could throw the notes into the air, as though she would break the silence, disturb and torture the dumbness of the dark room.

Her curls were brushed behind her ears, forming a clump at the back of her neck, golden and thick. Impatient and careless, she tapped with her foot upon the floor.

Disturbed by the opening door she turned, and then flung a smile over her shoulder, her eyes watching his eyes.

Julius did not smile back; he looked at her, her face, her body, her hands on the flute, the colour of her hair; he looked at her figure outlined against the window, and a fierce sharp joy came to him stronger than any known sensation, something primitive like the lick of a flame and the first taste of blood, as though a message ran through his brain saying: ' I for this – and this for me.'

It was Gabriel.

Part Four (1910–20): The Middle Years

It seemed to Julius Lévy that the discovery of Gabriel was the most exciting thing that had ever come to him in life.

It was stimulating, it was crude; because she was unknown to him though part of him the realization of her was like a sudden secret adventure, tremendously personal to them both, intimate in the same absorbing fashion as a disease is intimate, belonging to no one else in heaven and earth, egotistical and supremely self-obsessing.

She had come at the right time. He knew that he had reached a period in his life that was stale and unprofitable, a mass of work and achievement lay behind him, a wealth of experience and knowledge that tasted dry as dust.

He had trodden so many paths that had led him nowhere, they were all alike and they had brought him nothing. It was as though he had eaten too much and drunk too much, and the mixture of years had destroyed the quality of his palate.

The joys of youth had long been lost, the early restless excitement, the ambition, the lust for work. He had had all that, he had passed them by, and now that he could stride the world as he wished because of his own money power, the charm was gone, the charm and the will-to-want, and the desire.

He was fifty, his body and his mind were undergoing some organic chemical change – he needed a tonic. So here was Gabriel at fifteen, with an abundance of youth and health and vitality which she must give to him because she belonged. He would use her as a boy uses his dreams, and a man uses his work and his mistress.

He had brought her into the world and now he was ready for her.

This voracious passion for his daughter that started so swiftly was like a match giving blaze to a high explosive; only the explosive burnt up and around, stretching further and beyond with flaming tentacles, and was not extinguished. He concentrated upon Gabriel to the exclusion of everything and everybody; subconsciously it seemed to him that he must have foreseen this moment in his life fifteen years back when he brought her into the world with his own hands.

He had given her health and beauty and intelligence; he had created her for his purpose.

This sudden devouring obsession burst like a thunderbolt upon the house of Lévy and on the social world in general.

And Rachel, cool, calm, level-headed Rachel, whose life had run so smoothly during the past years for all her husband's indiscretions, which had not touched her nor broken the serenity of married life, Rachel was disturbed and a little bewildered by this upheaval in the family, this pushing forward of Gabriel, this encouragement of precocity.

Rachel was devoted to her daughter in a placid conventional fashion. Gabriel was clever, Gabriel was attractive, Gabriel had been studying so well in Italy and emerging naturally and gracefully from a strong-willed, mischievous child to a well-mannered, sensible girl. Governesses and masters had spoken highly of her, and Rachel enjoyed the holidays spent by Gabriel's side, encouraging little talents such as her dancing, her music, her knowledge of languages, and then the pleasure of dressing her well and having her in the drawing-room during afternoon At Homes and musical evenings. Playing a round of golf with her on the private course at Granby, chatting with her about books in the schoolroom where she had her eight o'clock supper, kissing her affectionately, suggesting the advisability of a coffee-lace afternoon dress rather than chiffon velvet – velvets were too old – and all this while looking forward in her mind to Gabriel's coming out in three years' time, when she would have a dance, of course, and would do the season properly, and would enjoy everything with a fresh naïve curiosity – Rachel to guide her. And perhaps in a year or so meeting some eligible successful young man – one of their own race, naturally – and a suitable period of engagement, and a big wedding, and Gabriel radiantly happy in her new home with babies of her own.

Then this lovely, simple vision to be spoilt by Julius's sudden absorbing interest, his insistence in pushing the child forward before her time, spoiling her, indulging her, encouraging every craze and every wish expressed.

At first it had been so pleasant, she thought; Gabriel home again and Julius being so delighted with her, Julius down at Granby where he complained of boredom generally, and the pair of them riding together, chatting, laughing, such good friends. It would, she hoped, bring the three of them closer to one another. Rachel would have once more the somewhat lost relationship of being his wife and companion and not merely his hostess and his background; the pleasure they shared in Gabriel their daughter would be the strengthening bond between them.

But none of this happened at all. His way was not her way. He was like a fanatic, obsessed with a new religion. And Gabriel was not the gentle, cultured, unsophisticated girl that Rachel had hoped to mould; she was someone who had grown up to strange maturity during those months abroad. She was no schoolgirl, charmingly *gauche*, a trifle shy, earnest over literature and music, leaning upon her mother for counsel; nor was she even the sullen, difficult adolescent, puzzled and easily irritated, rebellious of authority. Rachel could have coped with this by the judicious use of tact and gentle persuasion. No, the Gabriel who returned home needed no counsel, asked for no advice; she had emerged from a child into a vivid, flamboyant personality with a depth of knowledge in her eyes, as sure of herself as though she were a woman grown, no movement of awkwardness, no blunder in speech, instinctively wearing the clothes that set off her hair and her figure to advantage, speaking with the low soft voice that was no longer a child's, laughing, lifting an eyebrow, shrugging a shoulder, using already the little tricks and gestures of sophistication; and these qualities coming from her naturally and unforced, so that they were part of her and could not be repressed. They were not the silly play-acting of an unfledged schoolgirl but the realities of her hitherto hidden self.

Rachel was hurt; she did not understand. Something within her was shocked. She felt that Gabriel at fifteen knew more than she did at forty-five, and yet how could she? – the child had been carefully brought up and strictly attended, never out of the company of governesses at home or abroad. It was not acquired knowledge then, it was born in her; it had risen from her, and somehow it was doubly distressing to Rachel that her daughter could be such a stranger so far removed from her. She felt herself shadowy and ineffectual beside her, and for the first time middle-aged.

She watched Julius brush her aside for Gabriel, making the girl into a rich flaming background for himself while his wife was no longer needed, was a screen thrust into a corner, scarce acknowledged, ignored, and tolerated as a piece of furniture that has served its time.

Rachel had to watch them, both so dissimilar physically and yet like to each other in blatant intimate fashion: the same laugh, the same brilliance, the same swift understanding and appreciation; and one was her husband and one was her child. And with a strange intelligent intuition she saw herself as the machine that had brought them together.

They were exactly alike in their supreme blind egotism, and as they wanted the same things their temperaments never for an instant clashed.

They knew one another so well. Rachel saw it in every boisterous laugh, in every glance, in every swift-as-lightning conversation, all starting from that first evening when Gabriel returned to England, and the pair had dined alone together for the first time.

They had motored down to Granby the following day. Rachel remembered the car coming round the sweep of the drive while she waited on the steps, and Gabriel leaning back in the car, her arm through Julius's arm, kissing the tip of her fingers to her mother in greeting, saying something to Julius and Julius laughing back. And there they were both of them, side by side, Julius excited, possessive, gallant as though this child were a prize he had won, his eyes never leaving her; and Gabriel cool and collected, very smart in a sky-blue dress that matched her eyes, and a new ring on her finger, and a smile on her lips – too old, too wise.

A flash of misgiving ran through Rachel's mind as she thought of the room that had been redecorated for Gabriel, so girlish and suitable, pale pink, of course, and the sitting-room in the same tone, the neat desk, the row of leatherbound classics on the bookshelves – and now she was following the child upstairs after the first warm embrace, Gabriel talking rapidly and giving a vivid account of the accident they narrowly missed *en route*, telling the story amusingly – too amusingly, thought Rachel, too self-confident – and here was Gabriel at the threshold of her little suite, an eyebrow lifted quizzically and a glance at her mother: 'My dear, what have you been up to? Why this nun's bower?' And Rachel, shocked and slightly embarrassed: 'Don't speak in that tone, darling; it sounds so vulgar. And I hoped you'd be happy having this all to yourself.'

Then Gabriel kissing her on the cheek, so like Julius, rough and overwhelming, and throwing down her coat untidily on the bed and kicking off her shoes. 'Don't worry, I'm happy anywhere. Aren't those lazy hounds going to bring up my things? I want a bath and a change. I suppose Louise is going to maid me . . .'

Yes, there again, the same overbearing manner with servants, shouting at them if they were not on the spot, and yet treating them with unaccustomed familiarity at odd moments; as now, for instance, when Louise the maid came into the room: 'Hullo, Louie my girl, put on a stone in weight, have you?'

Rachel left the room murmuring something about tea, only to find Julius behaving in much the same manner in the library, shouting at the butler, who was getting very deaf: 'God in heaven, you old bastard, haven't you any authority over these bloody servants? Tell someone to bring me a whisky and soda – have I got to yell myself hoarse?'

'Julius – Julius – please – I can't bear that sort of thing,' said Rachel. And then he must make things worse by patting Moon on the shoulder, forgetting his anger, laughing at him in sudden confidence. 'What do you think of Miss Gabriel? Isn't she a beauty?' – Moon bowing his way out, avoiding Rachel's eye. She thought how impossible this sort of thing would have been in the old days at home, in the Dreyfus circle, and her own poor father with his exquisite manners. She was uncomfortably aware that she was not looking forward to the evening. Dinner would be unbearable if Julius and Gabriel said anything dreadful in front of the servants. It had been unwise, perhaps, to suggest Gabriel dining downstairs.

Rachel, wishing for solitude, shut herself up in her boudoir between tea and dinner; she had some embroidery to finish, and then she allowed herself a quiet hour with the *Thoughts of Marcus Aurelius*. Anyway, it would be nice discussing books and pictures with Gabriel, and as the gong sounded and she went along to the south wing to dress, she heard voices and laughter coming from beyond the hall, and the click of a cue against a ball. They were playing billiards.

When she was dressed and downstairs in the library waiting for the second gong, she wondered what Gabriel would wear. She tried to remember her various dresses, but perhaps the child had bought herself some little frock in Italy.

Julius appeared first, usual velvet smoking-jacket, of course. He seemed in an excellent humour and was humming under his breath.

'Where's Gabriel?' he said.

'She'll be down directly,' said Rachel, vaguely irritated, and went on: 'Can't you bear her out of your sight for a single moment?'

'No,' he said, and laughed, the sarcasm wasted on him.

Here she was at last, three minutes after the gong had sounded. Rachel tried to frown tactfully and glance at the clock, but she could only gaze at Gabriel, this child, this daughter of hers who looked so incredibly lovely in black velvet with a string of pearls round her neck, her red-gold hair brushed away and two pearl ear-rings just showing – quite unsuitable, of course – and the dress to her ankles – much too old; she looked eighteen at least.

'Oh! you supremely beautiful thing; what am I going to do about you?' said Julius – ridiculous words to say to a child – and Gabriel smiled, walking towards them languidly. Rachel felt she had staged her entrance well, and Gabriel said: 'D'you like it, Mummy? I think the waist ought to be higher, and it could be narrower round the hips.'

'You look very sweet, darling,' said Rachel, 'but it's years too old for you. Now, if you have it several inches shorter and then perhaps a little band of velvet round . . .'

'Oh, rot!' interrupted Julius rudely. 'Nothing's too old for Gabriel. She looks absolutely right. I won't have it altered. She's not a child.'

'She's only fifteen,' said Rachel.

'My dear,' said Julius, 'in Alger girls of fifteen have generally had half a dozen lovers.'

Gabriel laughed. 'Not guilty, Papa.'

Rachel said nothing. Coarse of Julius to speak in that way, but Gabriel hadn't even blushed.

'Shall we go in?' said Rachel. 'We're five minutes late already.'

Rather to her relief, because of the servants, much of the conversation at dinner was spoken in French. Gabriel's fluency was a great delight to Julius. They spoke so rapidly to one another that often it was difficult to follow, although Rachel had always considered herself a fair scholar.

This was no scholarly French, though, that they were speaking; it sounded like the commonest slang.

'Not French all the time,' she pleaded. 'I can't get a word in. Let's hear some more about Italy, Gabriel. I want to hear what you thought of the Uffizi in Florence. Did you see those lovely Fra Angelicos?'

'I don't care for primitives,' said Gabriel; 'they're too formless and too cold. None of the Florentines appealed to me at all. I like colour above all, and flesh that is flesh, and something that looks alive. Titian and Correggio, for instance; and there's someone who gets hold of the richest glorious reds; what's his name – Giorgione.'

'I see. I really must rub up my *History of Art* when we're in town; we'll go to the National Gallery together. Did you think the Forum very wonderful?'

'I liked Rome,' said Gabriel. 'That's where I got this dress, by the way. Oh! the Forum. I don't know, I can't get interested in dead things. It seems to me so useless, that sort of knowledge. Of course we went into every church and every gallery – Signorina wouldn't let me miss a thing – but when you say the word "Rome" it doesn't make me think of St Peter's, or Raphael, or the

Colosseum; it brings up a picture of a very mad evening – the carnival night before Carême, you know, and I'd made friends with an Italian girl called Maria; we gave Signorina the slip and mixed with the crowd. We wore masks, of course, and we clung to each other in case we were separated. I've never been drunk in my life, but I had the feeling of being drunk that night. Imagine a thousand people jostling together singing and shouting – such a warm, rich smell of flowers and wine and excited bodies, and the night very dark, a black sky like velvet, with torches tossing a yellow glare from the crowd. I remember a girl leaning out of a window with dark eyes like sloes, and she threw a scarlet flower to a man below, and he laughed and climbed up to her, and they shut the window. I know so well what they were feeling.'

There was a silence for a few moments, and then Rachel said 'Fancy!' rather brightly, and wondered if her daughter knew what she was talking about. It all sounded a little odd, but Julius was looking at Gabriel across the rim of his glass as though he understood.

'The best thing in Italy was Venice,' said Gabriel, 'only we were there too early. Take me there some time, Papa. You'd be very good in Venice.'

She treated him, thought Rachel, as though she were his equal.

'Yes, we must do that,' agreed Julius. 'Venice, and the Greek Islands, and the Dalmatian coast, and Central Europe, and the Mediterranean – we might plan out a tour this autumn and winter down south, perhaps. Would you like it?'

'Julius, my dear, don't fill her head with such nonsense,' put in Rachel. 'It will be lovely for Gabriel to do all those things when she comes out, but you must remember she hasn't finished yet. I thought Paris in September for a year.'

Julius laughed. 'I'll show her Paris; she'd have a very good time, I assure you.'

'I think,' said Gabriel, raising her eyebrows, 'that it would be most amusing to be finished by Papa.'

They both of them laughed, aggravatingly intimate, and Rachel said sharply, distressed at her own irritation: 'Don't play the fool, Julius; Gabriel has at least two years of lessons and classes before she begins to be grown-up.'

And this time Julius did not laugh; he looked at his wife with his eyes narrow and his thin lips pressed together, and he began to tap on the table with his fingers.

'This is my affair,' he said rapidly. 'I've decided that Gabriel has had all the education she needs. You've looked after her up till this moment – from now on she's mine. Don't argue – I know about these things.'

Rachel dug her nails into her hands to control her anger. She knew by the way Julius spoke that this was final. Of course he would spoil Gabriel, ruin her completely; they would be a laughing-stock to all their friends, a girl of her age brought forward in this way! And suddenly her anger left her. She felt weak and depressed – she knew that the headache that had been threatening all day would be splitting before long – and she was tired, and she was aware that neither Julius nor Gabriel would mind if she went up to bed early. They did not care, they did not want her; she was rather a bore, in fact, tiresome, in the way and spoiling their fun.

She rose from her chair, her voice breaking in spite of herself. 'I've got a wretched head, I'm going upstairs,' she said, but they were not aware of her; they had forgotten her already, and Julius was leaning across the table reaching for Gabriel's fingers. 'Give them to me,' he was saying. 'What an amazing thing heredity can be; you've got hands like my father's. But the rest of you is Blançard, pure Blançard.'

During the next three years Julius Lévy gave himself up to an orgy of expenditure. In spite of his wealth he had never before experienced the lust of pleasure that comes from wanton, reckless extravagance. He and Rachel had lived grandly, even pompously. He was a millionaire and believed in keeping up such a state because of the malicious delight it afforded him to watch other people's envy.

With the discovery of Gabriel, any remnant of his youthful miserly instinct was thrown to the four winds; she could make a bonfire out of a thousand-pound bank-note for all he cared and if it amused her.

She expressed a wish to hunt that first autumn, so the Grand

Tour was naturally postponed. A house was bought in Leicestershire and Gabriel had her choice of a dozen hunters in the stable. Sometimes Julius went with her, sometimes he followed by car. Melton became the Lévy headquarters that winter, and Julius's business visits to London were on rare and only urgent occasions.

With the spring came the start of the flat racing season, and Gabriel must now declare herself in strong favour of owning racehorses, and as she expressed herself firmly to her father: 'Now, Papa, we've got to do it on the grand scale. The best trainer, the best jockeys, the best horses. Otherwise I'm afraid it isn't going to amuse me. Do something about it, will you?'

And Julius, in a fever lest she should be bored, bought up the entire stable of the Duke of Storborough, whose heir was an idiot and in the care of a keeper; and as Julius told the Duke brutally: 'Your boy doesn't know the hind legs of any animal from its head, so you may as well sell me the lot, and then shut up your estate and spend the money I give you at Monte Carlo,' which the Duke was glad to do.

Thus was founded the famous Lévy stable, and – soon widely familiar to every race-goer in England – the Lévy colours; and being Julius Lévy, of course, no working up into a position but starting with a splash and a bang right away; an owner on the grand scale, as he had promised his daughter.

So now there was a house down at Newmarket, for Gabriel to be on the spot whenever she wished, up at six in the morning to watch the gallops. She was horse-crazy during that first year and a half, talking horses, dreaming horses, living horses, and giving Julius some of her own enthusiasm, instilling into him a desperate interest that was not his by choice, but of which he forced himself to partake so that he could watch her face under its hard felt hat, her eyes intent on a gallop a mile and a half away, breathing shortly, her lips compressed, and he watched the long line of her leg pressed close against the flank of her animal, and her hands slender and firm upon the reins.

'You do feel it, Papa, don't you?' she said, leaning down to him, her hand on his shoulder. 'You're not pretending; it does get you, doesn't it, like me? Because we've got to have the same things, you must see with me over everything. There's never been a thrill like this – listen – do listen, that thud, thud, over the hill beyond that mound. They'll be round the bend in exactly half a minute – here they come. You couldn't have anything more alive than that, could you? As I thought, Red Deer is leading; he's a perfect devil when he gets away – faster than I expected, though. Follow Me shouldn't be two and a quarter lengths behind – I thought this was a trial, not a morning gallop. What's that idiot boy doing? – why did Follow Me swerve to the side of the track? Red Deer's slacking, he's a sprinter, of course. Follow Me has double his stamina, but Red Deer'd send 'em all to bed over five furlongs. That little chestnut in the second string just coming along now has a lovely head, don't you think, Papa? But he's nervy – damn sight too nervy ever to be a certainty. I think we ought to breed from him – those looks alone are worth a fortune.'

She rattled on, never expecting an answer, while Julius patted her horse's neck and leant against her knee, aware only that the morning was sharp and fine, a haze of early summer across the heath, a bee buzzing close to his ear, and the fact that Follow Me had more stamina than Red Deer mattered little to him; he liked the warm breath of a horse upon his hand, the smell of horse-flesh that was a mixture of sweat and leather, the sun and the air and the feeling of Gabriel at his side – her health, her laughter, more alive than fifty race-horses. These were the things that mattered to him.

Rachel did not join in the crazes of her husband and daughter. She knew little more about horses than did the idiot son of the Duke of Storborough. Occasionally she dragged herself to a race meeting, and from pure pride put in an appearance for formality's sake at Melton during the hunting season, but both were an effort to her. She disliked the hunting crowd and the racing crowd, they were Philistines and alien to her; they knew nothing about music, her sort of music, they never read, they didn't care for pictures. All these things formed a great part of Rachel's life. She was bitterly disappointed that Gabriel shrugged her shoulders at any form of art, and at the same time had an instinctive flair for the value of any object, invariably picking out the best from the mediocre with the inevitable phrase on her lips: 'What's it worth?' No love in her heart, though, no true appreciation. She had one talent uncannily inherited from Paul Lévy, and this was self-taught without guidance from any master – she played Paul Lévy's flute as though the knowledge of it was part of her blood. Rachel could not bear to listen to her. The flute was like the symbol of some evil thing; she would go to the other end of the house and shut the doors between them. In her mind, and she was intensely musical like all the Dreyfuses, the flute should be an instrument of intense purity, a high single note rising into the air with piercing sweetness and restraint together mingled, suggesting in some strange fashion the unbroken voice of a young boy.

In Gabriel's hands and against Gabriel's lips the cry became a summons of a different kind, a call out of the earth, a beckoning, mocking whisper like a night-bird from the woods; and there was one jerky persistent note that started from a mere breath of suggestion and grew into a leaping, discordant rhythm, harping its way into the brain with maddening power – a wild, fantastic tune hopelessly unsuited to a flute, a savage, ugly note, a jungle note.

The continuation of this seemed to Rachel like the ceaseless and senseless banging of a stick on a hollow drum, and with her nerves torn to shreds she would call down to Gabriel: 'Not that appalling thing, for pity's sake. Can't you play music, real music?'

But Gabriel only laughed, for Julius would be lying in a long chair with his feet propped up on the mantelpiece and his hands under his head, the crazy, jerky rhythm beating upon his senses like the lost hidden music of Alger, mysterious and alive, and he said to his daughter: 'You play the flute like my father would have played it if he'd sold his soul to Satan.'

So Gabriel smiled and tapped her foot on the floor, and, 'What do you call this, then?' she asked, drawing a breath, and breaking into a note that was a query, an unbalanced quiver of suspense, that ran unevenly along a broken trail as though it had lost its way, and then mounted slowly, higher and higher, swooping in circles to some unattainable summit, like the relentless climbing flight of a bird of prey – soon lost, soon vanished in the glaring rays of the sun.

To Julius with his eyes shut it was like the song that Père had sung to him as a child and the whisper that led to the secret city, but this was another whisper and another city; this was not the enchanted land beyond the white clouds, so melancholy, so beautiful, for ever unattainable, a land of promise unfulfilled – for there was a sudden swoop and a turn and a plunge into the bowels of the secret earth, heart beating, wings battered and scorched, and this new-discovered city was one that opened and gave itself up to him; there were eyes that welcomed and hands that beckoned, all mingled in extravagant confusion of colour and scent and ecstasy.

'Do you like that, Papa?' said Gabriel, and he was in the room again, back in the world, startled as though with the first shock of waking, the sight of her standing there so cool and undisturbed jarring upon him who felt dissatisfied and unrefreshed, an odd taste in his mouth, and a sensation in mind and body that was shameful and unclean.

'You're an odd creature,' he said, staring at her. 'I don't believe you ever feel anything, do you? Are you fond of your mother? Do you like me? Do you care about anyone?'

She laid her flute down upon the table. 'I don't know,' she said carelessly. 'I like doing things.'

'You won't always be like that,' he insisted. 'Some day you'll feel something, surely? I believe you're still a child in lots of ways. All this – the flute, and hunting and racing and driving, it's just a game to you, isn't it?'

She shrugged her shoulders.

'We think alike over everything and enjoy the same things,' he said. 'We're together almost always. But you don't let me get at the core of you, do you? Why don't you? Is it that you're such a child?'

She frowned, drawing patterns with her finger on the table.

'I don't know,' she said.

He rose and began walking up and down the room.

'You'd tell me if you weren't happy, wouldn't you?' he said.

'Yes – I suppose so.'

'I'd give you anything, you know.'

'Yes.'

'Sometimes,' he said, 'you look so old and so wise, a curious kind of wisdom. I wonder what you are thinking about.'

'I don't often think,' she told him. 'There's nothing to be curious about.'

'You're so terribly alive, and yet terribly inhuman in a way,' he said, standing and looking moodily out of the window. 'I'm not like that; why should you be?'

'Don't nag at me,' she said. 'I'm what I am. If I'm inhuman it's your fault; you made me.'

'That's true enough,' he said. 'Sometimes I think I ought to have left you. You'd have been born dead if I hadn't worked at you.'

'Don't be silly,' she said. 'We have fun, don't we?' She took hold of his hand and crumpled up his fingers, squeezing them against each other so that his signet ring cut his skin and he cried out.

'I like your hands,' she said, 'they're the best things about you,' and then she dropped them and moved away, humming a tune.

'There you are,' he said, 'that's what I meant. Are you a child or do you do it on purpose?'

'I don't know what the devil you're talking about,' she said.

'You're a bloody liar,' he said.

They were silent for about five minutes. It was getting dark. He could scarcely see her face. The fire burst in the grate and shot up in a quiver of flame, lighting them to one another.

'I'm sorry,' he said abruptly. 'I don't want you to be angry.'

She crossed over and pinched the back of his neck.

'I'm not angry.'

'Is it that you're a child and are happy like that?' he said.

'I expect so.'

'You'll tell me, won't you, when you begin to feel things? You'll come to me?'

'You'd know without me telling you,' she said.

They laughed, and she reached out for his hand.

Then there was the sound of a footstep in the hall.

'Here's Mother,' said Gabriel softly. She moved away swiftly from the fire and began to turn up the lights. Julius looked at a magazine upside-down, whistling, and fondling the ears of a spaniel that had awakened with the flooding of the light. 'What makes you think that Lorelei can't be beaten in the 2.30 tomorrow at Epsom?' he said, and then broke off suddenly as though surprised: 'Hullo, Rache . . .'

It was perhaps inevitable that Gabriel's enthusiasm for racing, born so swiftly without warning and developing into an interest, extravagant and obsessional, should as suddenly receive a check and be in danger of bursting like a bubble. The passionate enjoyment of horses was still part of her, but a race meeting was no longer a thrill; there was a sameness about it. She had allowed herself a surfeit of it, had plunged too quickly and too deeply, and was now exhausted.

Gabriel looked about her for something new, and the next craze was yachting.

'You see, Papa, I've set my heart on this; we're got to shine like we do on the turf. No half measures, no dawdling about on the Norfolk Broads; we must start with the best and go in for first-class stuff. Why not take a house at Cowes for the summer? – I don't mind missing Epsom and Ascot this year. I want to learn to sail, and I want to be taught by the best yachting skipper you can find. Do the thing properly, Papa, start coping now. You'll have to pull strings to belong to the right yacht clubs, but it oughtn't to be difficult with all your money. Let's make a splash.'

And Julius Lévy did as he was told.

The idea was another shock to Rachel, who had scarcely accustomed herself yet to the endless race meetings and hunting seasons and houses at Newmarket and Melton, and people and conversation concerning themselves with no other subject but horse-flesh.

'What – not yachting on top of all this racing and hunting?' she protested. 'I don't see how you'll have time.'

'Yachting's only from May to September; don't be absurd,' said her daughter. 'You know one doesn't hunt in the summer and I'm off racing for the time. One must do something. Anyway, yachting's the most terrible thrill.'

'Julius – aren't we being ridiculously extravagant?' argued Rachel. 'We never used to do all these things. I often feel nowadays that people are laughing at us; we're overdoing it. It's – well – almost vulgar, this show of opulence.'

Julius flushed angrily.

'Don't talk such awful muck,' he shouted. 'People laughing at us – what in the name of God do you mean? Why should they laugh at us? I'm as good as anyone else, aren't I? A damn sight better – what? I could buy up the whole bloody yachting and racing crowd if I wanted to. Extravagant? It's my money, isn't it? I've worked for it, God knows. Worked a damned sight harder than any thick-headed Englishman.'

'Oh! don't shout like that,' said Rachel wearily. 'I don't want to argue with you. I notice things if you don't. That's all.'

'What things?'

'When Gabriel was a baby we lived very happily without all this fuss and showing off. We lived very well, we had interesting people about us, we gave lovely parties. And there was something digni-fied about those days. I can't explain. You're spoiling it all now.'

'Dignity, eh? You're a fine one to chitter about dignity. I sup-pose you thought your father was dignified when he blew his brains out after he'd made a mess of his life?'

'That's unnecessary, Julius, and very cruel.'

Rachel turned away, pale, her mouth trembling.

Julius laughed. 'Oh, don't be a wet blanket, Rache. I don't interfere with you much. You enjoy your concerts and your books and the highbrow talk of your intellectual pals. Let Gabriel and me alone to enjoy our things. We're different.'

Rachel turned before leaving the room, her hand on the door.

'You don't know what a mistake you're making,' she said slowly. 'Gabriel's barely seventeen, and before she's twenty-one she'll have had everything. What sort of a life is it going to be for her – after that? Have you ever thought?'

Julius shrugged his shoulders.

'When I was twenty-one I was starving in a garret and working fifteen hours a day as a baker's apprentice. I want my daughter to hold the world in her hands.' There was a silence, and then:

'Sometimes,' said Rachel, 'I'm very sorry for you both.' She hesitated a moment as though she would say something more, and then she went out of the room.

Julius yawned and stretched out his arms.

'What's wrong with her?' he said.

Gabriel laughed softly and reached for a cigarette. 'Jealous,' she said.

'D'you think so?' Julius sat up. 'Oh! hell, that's funny, isn't it?'

The idea excited him. He pulled the box of cigarettes away from Gabriel.

'Don't smoke,' he said.

'Why not?'

'Not until you're eighteen.'

'Don't be silly,' said Gabriel. 'I do as I like,' and she lit a cigarette.

'You've never done it before,' he said. 'What's it mean?'

'A gesture,' she said, blinking her eyelids, and blowing a cloud in his face.

'If we get this cruising boat,' he said, 'we'll go down to the Mediterranean, shall we? Down to Sicily and up the Adriatic, and you shall show me Venice.'

'Yes – some time.'

'Not this summer?'

'No – I want to sail at Cowes.'

'We might go down in the winter.'

'I shall be hunting this winter as usual.'

'The following summer?'

'Oh!' She rose in irritation. 'Don't harp at me, it bores me so. I'll go with you when I want to and not before.'

He flushed under his skin, hating her.

'You're such a bitch,' he said.

She took no notice of him. She was looking at a yachting paper.

'By the way, I forgot to tell you I was in Cartier's yesterday and chose a bracelet for you,' he said; 'a double row of diamonds, twisted. I told them to alter the clasp, it didn't show up enough.'

'Thanks,' she said, and went on reading the paper.

Julius wondered whether she was sick of bracelets. She would perhaps have been better pleased with him had he chosen a necklace instead. He made a mental note to order a necklace in the morning. Meanwhile he poured himself out a drink and waited moodily until she would be ready to be friends with him again.

The five months of yachting passed swiftly for Gabriel. She threw herself and her boundless energy into this new sport with the same fervour that she had given to horse-racing. Here was racing of a different sort – the thrill of a narrow-built, slender cutter heeling in a trough of a sea, the tall mast straining, the stiff breeze whistling in the huge spread of canvas, the lee rail awash, the thud and kick of the helm.

The skipper who trained Gabriel was a Clyde man, one of the most experienced yachtsmen afloat. Julius spared no expense to find the best teacher. The boat, a brand-new six-metre built that year, was named *Adieu Sagesse* – the suggestion of Julius.

Then there was the cruising yacht, a schooner of nearly two hundred tons, a beautiful thing of bravado and extravagance; one of those luxury vessels all white paint, scrolled gold, and polished brass, with a deck like ballroom parquet. *Wanderer* she was called. She wandered between Southampton and Cowes and no farther. The Lévys used her perhaps half a dozen times that first summer. Gabriel could not be dragged away from her six-metre. She was racing mad – she spent all day and every day at the helm of *Adieu Sagesse*, the Clyde skipper at her elbow and Julius a passenger, generally in the way.

Julius, crouching in the cockpit that sloped at an angle of forty-five, wondered if all this was safe, and as he looked at Gabriel with her frown of concentration, her teeth biting her lip, and her hair swept by the wind, he was seized with a terror lest they should founder and drown, and he would only have had two years of her, paltry and insignificant. Only two years of companionship and so little to show for it; she still self-contained and a stranger in many ways. He thought of the passion that had been hers for riding, and now this fever for sailing that had taken its place. And he wondered with a curious sense of excitement what would be the next craze of her impetuous will, into what channels would her stream of energy wander, and whether this flow of spirits was the advance guard of high pressure that would be rapture and emotion and ecstasy.

It was an endless sensation of pleasure to him that he was able to do the things that she did, that his health and energy equalled hers, and that his fifty-odd years were no burden to him. He might have been without wisdom and married late, and then grown old before she was ready for him. Rachel had been decorative and helpful as a wife, but her utility was over now. Gabriel would make as good a hostess when she came out next year. She was modern, too, in advance of her age.

Rachel was getting fat like her mother before her; she had the set, heavy, Dreyfus look about her. She could not progress, she was early-Edwardian. He was conscious that Rachel's expression irritated him now; it was sullen, discontented; he was aware that he did not want to see much of her. She did well to stay down at Granby or in Grosvenor Square. He was genial to her, but no more than this; there was little friendship and no intimacy between them.

Rachel, for her part, joined her husband and daughter at intervals from a motive of pride. She could not bear that her friends should pity her. She knew instinctively the gossip that touched them – Julius, Gabriel, and herself – the slight contempt that clings about a neglected wife, the lies, the curiosity. The absurd rumours of divorce, the cheap newspaper minds of men and women.

She loathed this sort of publicity, the indignity and squalor attached to any knowledge of people's private affairs.

So she appeared now and again on board the *Wanderer* and in the house at Cowes, and later up at Melton during the autumn, tactful and calm, her face a mask, studiously agreeable to Gabriel and Julius and their friends, knowing in her heart that her presence was a blind convention of her own, and that they all laughed at her behind her back.

She, too, waited for Gabriel to pass to the next craze, hoping with bitter, grim tenacity that the girl of eighteen would wake up suddenly and throw away her crude, unbroken, dangerous charm and fall in love and lose her individuality. Then only would she be harmless and natural; the wife of some man or even his mistress – Rachel did not care – and lead her own life in her own way, possessed and held at last. Rachel would see the man as a saviour, whoever he should be. Then Julius would understand what a fool he had made of himself these last years, he would realize his age and his whitening hairs, he would come back to Rachel and Granby, and their old interests together. Side by side they would drift into the serenity of their middle years.

So Rachel, like a prisoner who awaits the final verdict, bided her time amongst the roses of Granby, reading Schopenhauer, petting her griffon, worrying herself over a pain in her side that was sometimes imaginary and sometimes real.

The yachting season finished at the end of September, and the boats were laid up for the winter.

Gabriel looked forward to a good time at Melton. Papa would be there, of course, and the house always filled with a crowd. Not Mother, she hoped. Mother brought her disapproving personality and stifled the house in an atmosphere of gloom. She always wanted to talk about books and music, and made such a fool of herself in front of the hunting crowd. Nobody felt at their ease. Papa would go sulky and red under the skin like a schoolboy; he was always difficult to manage when Mother was around. He seemed to think Mother would be continually listening at doors or peeping through keyholes.

'What the devil does it matter if she does?' Gabriel would say, losing her temper, and then he would cross silently to a door and fling it open, hoping to surprise Rachel in the act of eavesdropping, and find nobody, of course.

'Don't be such an idiot,' said Gabriel; but Papa would run his hands through his hair and become temperamental. 'I can't stand it – I'm going up to town,' and he would rush away and shout at the servant to tell Mander to bring round the Rolls, he was going to London.

Gabriel lit a cigarette and shrugged her shoulders. If he liked to behave like a criminal fleeing from justice he could for all she cared. She knew there would be a wire from him in a couple of hours' time, sent off from some post office in the Midlands, and then another wire from London when he arrived, and then the telephone the next morning before breakfast.

'I'm coming back,' he would say, his voice faint on the long-distance call. 'I can't stand this.'

'All right,' she would answer.

'I'm going down to the City this morning to see what's going on, and then I'll be right back. Did you sleep?'

'Like a top – I always do.'

'It's more than I did. Listen: do you want anything?'

'No.'

'I'll find time to go into Cartier's and see if they've got anything good.'

'Oh, don't bother.'

'Yes – I want to. It makes an interest. It's damned cold in town. Would you like another fur coat? – you were twittering about a chinchilla the other day – here – are you there? – are you there? – don't cut me off.'

'I've got to go, Papa; the horses are waiting, and I don't want to be late. Good-bye.'

She hung up on him, laughing to herself. God! what a crazy man. She was glad he was coming back. And crossing the hall she would see the figure of her mother standing in the doorway of the breakfast room, making a pretence of glancing at the morning paper, then looking up. 'Was that your father?'

'Yes – he's fed up with town.'

'Didn't he ask to speak to me?'

'No – he was in a hurry.'

'I wish he wouldn't be so restless, always chopping and changing about. It makes arrangements so difficult. Besides, he dashed off yesterday without even telling me.'

'I shouldn't let it worry me, if I were you,' said Gabriel. 'He's always doing things like that. I never let it interfere with my plans.' She flicked her boot with her riding crop and crossed the hall, whistling to the dogs.

Typical of Mother to moon about and imagine household arrangements were being disturbed. As if it mattered whether people were early or late for meals, or whether the numbers were odd, or if the servants were put out. Servants were paid, weren't they? She resented her mother dealing with the Melton staff. Gabriel felt they were her own property and responsibility. She couldn't think why Mother bothered to traipse up to Melton, anyway. She obviously did not enjoy it. Everything ran so smoothly when the household consisted of Papa and herself alone. Guests did not matter one way or the other.

It was a great relief when Mother finally developed a severe pain in her side and, taking alarm, at once declared she must return to

Grosvenor Square and undergo some treatment. Gabriel felt as though she had been living under some strain and could now breathe and be herself again.

Rachel sensed the obvious relief of her husband and daughter when she told them she was motoring up to London. As she stood on the steps, while the suitcases were put into the car, and her maid fussed round her with her rug and her dog, it was as though she were a guest being sped away who had made too long a stay. A guest in her own house. And Gabriel was the hostess, hatless, at her ease, belonging there, giving the order to the chauffeur that Rachel herself should be giving: 'There won't be room for those flowers inside, Mander; they'll get crushed. They'll have to go in front. Look out . . .'

And Julius, too boisterously cheerful, saying without sincerity: 'Now, Rache, take things quietly in London. Don't over-tire yourself. Get that fellow to put you right, and don't stand any nonsense from him. Good-bye, dear.'

The duty kiss, first Julius, then Gabriel, the climb into the car, exhausting with so many rugs and coats, and the dog, and her hot-water bottle. The maid in front with the chauffeur.

'Good-bye.' The forced smile at them through the window, the wave of her hand, and then the car gliding away down the drive. She craned to look back through the window, but they had turned already up the steps, dismissing her from their minds, Gabriel with her arm round her father and he calling the dogs. They had their day in front of them, cut and divided from hers.

Rachel tried to picture the anticlimax if she suddenly tapped on the glass and told Mander to go back, she had changed her mind. She wished she had the courage. And as the car drove out of the gates and on to the main road Rachel thought of the long dreary drive that lay ahead of her until she reached London, with the straight unhelpful backs of the maid and the chauffeur in front of her, her only consolation the water-bottle that eased the pain in her side, and the warm body of the griffon on her knees.

But to Julius and Gabriel left behind it seemed as though the air were free once more and the house welcomed them in the old way; the hall was wider, clearer, most beautifully theirs again;

even the dogs jumped and wagged their tails, barking loudly at Julius, who flipped at them with his stick.

The sun shone from a placid sky. It had rained in the night, and the harsh white frost that had stopped hunting for a whole week was turned to soft mud and gravel and rich damp turf.

'If this blessed weather holds, we can turn out again tomorrow,' said Gabriel. 'Come on, let's wander along to the stables.' And they set off round the corner of the house, holding each other's arms, keeping the same step, singing the same song:

> 'Two lovely black eyes—
> Oh! what a surprise!
> I got them for kissing another man's wife –
> Two lovely black eyes.'

So the winter passed and the early spring, no dull moment to Gabriel, whose entire life was spent in the saddle.

Once more hunting came to an end, and it was good-bye to Melton and the trek south to Newmarket at the beginning of April – racing again, and the Spring Meeting at Epsom – Gay Lord driving Gabriel to fury by failing to win the City and Suburban, and her temper restored again because Follow Me proved his stamina the next week at Newmarket.

Then May came along, and for the next few months of the summer Gabriel could not be dragged away from the Island except for the Derby and Ascot week in June and Goodwood later. And her time was spent at the helm of *Adieu Sagesse* or in luxurious idleness in a deck-chair on the *Wanderer*, gramophone at hand, a crowd of young people about her.

Whether it was because the summer of 1913 was notoriously wet and sailing conditions were seldom ideal, rain and gales day after day in July, or whether the very atmosphere at Cowes and the life on the water held no longer quite the same thrill for her because the novelty was gone, Gabriel found herself losing interest in regattas and races, she began to weary of the one topic of conversation on the lips of her yachting friends.

What was the fun in *Adieu Sagesse* when a half gale made sailing impossible, or, worse still, when a flat calm and a steady drizzle made sailing merely a dragging and a boring pastime?

The Island was ugly in the rain; there was nothing to do. It was absurd to go across to London, because at that time of the year London was dead.

Granby? Mother was down at Granby. Ill again – she had a nurse on hand now. Nobody knew quite what was the matter with her. It occurred to Gabriel that her mother must lead a strangely empty existence, never caring much about things. Odd of her. She supposed it was middle age. And yet Papa was several years older than Mother, and nobody could call his existence dreary; he was always so enthusiastic, so terribly alive. He had a personality that stood out above everybody else's; he made other men – young men especially – look so stupid, so callow and inexperienced. Papa was young too, but in a different way. Subtle, queer, there was a glamour about him.

Perhaps one of the reasons she was feeling restless and bored was because Papa had been spending more time in London this summer. He was gambling in the City again, and getting the same thrill out of it that she had got last year out of sailing. She had driven down to his offices once, when she was passing through London, and he had not been expecting her, of course. He was busy. She had been told to wait in some room as though she were nobody, some creature without an appointment. And she had not been able to stand that; she had walked straight through into his private room without knocking. He was speaking through the telephone. He had looked up when she burst into the room, and instead of throwing down the receiver and leaping up from his chair as she expected, he put his hand over the mouthpiece for one second and said to her: 'Sit down – don't talk,' and then on with his rapid, unintelligible conversation. He was smiling, but it was not because she had come into the room. For the first time in her life Gabriel realized that this was power and Julius Lévy held it between his hands. She watched him speaking into the telephone, and as she looked at him who was so deep in his game, taking not the slightest interest in her, it was as though the faint imprint of a hand touched her and lingered indescribably, mysterious and pleasing, a new sensation that was disturbing and exciting at the same time, curiously physical like a pain in her body, and it had never come to her before.

When he had finished and turned to her, smiling for her once more, glad that she was there, she was abrupt and careless to him, coolly lighting a cigarette and leaving him after a few minutes, pretending a composure that she did not feel.

She had crossed over to the Island that afternoon, and in some dim inexplicable fashion the memory of those few minutes remained with her unchanged, mingling and becoming part of her dissatisfaction with the weather, and Cowes, and yachting. She was restless, bored. She wanted new things and she could not put a name to the things she wanted.

People irritated her suddenly, especially young men, they were such fools. Life seemed empty for no reason that she could see. One moment it had been exciting and breathless and fun, and now it was none of this – the charm had gone.

She felt as though there were no definite scheme of life awaiting her; her will was blunted for the time being and she was a blank page ready to receive some impression or suggestion.

In August she would be eighteen. Papa was giving a dance for her. He said he was going to make the whole of Cowes look like a carnival at Venice. Everybody would be there, of course. It was the finish of Cowes week and people who might otherwise have left would stop on because Julius Lévy was giving a party.

'This dance is your official appearance in the world,' he told her, laughing. 'I believe they call it coming out.'

'I thought I'd been out for three years,' said Gabriel.

'Yes – you and I think so. But convention likes to make a thing of a girl's eighteenth birthday. Anyway, we'll have a splash. We'll give 'em something to remember us by. Rather fun, eh?'

She shrugged her shoulders.

'Oh! you're just a *blasé* young woman nowadays,' he said. 'What's wrong? You know *Adieu Sagesse* ought to have got an easy first on Wednesday and you were well beaten; you weren't trying. I was watching you through my glasses. You were thinking of something else.'

'Oh! go to hell!' she said suddenly, and went out of the room.

For a moment Julius was startled; he crossed to the window and saw Gabriel jump into a car and drive away at a ridiculous pace. Restless, eh? Bad-tempered and funny about something.

Then he wondered if there was any difference between a boy and a girl at that age, and whether they went through the same identical means of ridding themselves of superfluous energy. He had a sudden vision of himself as a boy climbing through Nanette's window and he laughed.

Too much, too soon. Was it, though? Had it spoilt life for him in certain senses? He was never quite sure. Besides, it was all so long ago. He had forgotten what it felt like to be a boy. The present was the only thing that mattered to him – the present and the future. The future seemed very close to him now, the white clouds passing near. He would not have to reach out for those clouds, they would come to him.

Julius went outside on to the wide veranda stoop, and chose a long easy chair in the full glare of the sun. He stretched out his legs upon another chair and placed two cushions under his head. Then he lit a cigar and closed his eyes, his mind and body relaxed, a faint smile playing on his lips.

Rachel came over to Cowes for Gabriel's eighteenth birthday. She rose from a sick-bed at Granby and came across to the Island without a nurse in attendance, making a supreme effort of will-power for the occasion. She was constantly in pain these days; her mysterious disease whispered vaguely as 'something internal' was in reality the beginning of cancer. Nobody had told her, but she knew. There was something in the too-cheerful outlook of her nurse, the hearty manner of her doctor, that warned her like a red lamp of danger.

She bought books about cancer and read them when the nurse was not with her. The books all agreed about the ultimate inevitable pain in the death that followed. There was no certainty as to the length of time a growth took to strangle the life-force, and this frightened her and made her feel as helpless as a child groping in the dark. To her cancer was a name of dread, something that must never be mentioned.

She must cover up her knowledge and pretend to a forced cheerfulness with the nurse who waited on her.

She thought that if she stayed in Granby when a dance was given for Gabriel at Cowes there would be two stories mingled horribly in the minds of their friends. 'They don't live together any more. She has had to give way and let him lead his own life; terrible for her.' And then, in a lower tone, hardly above a whisper: 'She's ill, too – they say it's cancer.'

There would be two shames for her to bear – knowledge of her husband's indifference and knowledge of her disease. Whatever the cost might be to herself, Rachel shrank from the ugly glare of publicity, the sting of gossip, the pity born of curiosity.

It was a duty she imposed upon herself to hold high the standards of convention and decency bred in her bones. And beneath all this, right at the core of her trouble, was a little crushed seed of hope that struggled for existence. She wanted Julius. He was her husband, and bound up with her for all the layers of ice between them; she had known happiness because of him, and her life had been his; they had been young together and Gabriel had been their baby. She remembered how he had been tender with her many times, and proud, and he had told her lovely things. She had stood by his side through all that meteoric rise of his to power and position. What knowledge she possessed of the world and men and women had come to her from him. She wanted Julius, he was her husband. If there was anyone beyond God that should know of her illness and her suffering it should be him. He was bound to her in so many ways.

So Rachel came across to the Island to act hostess at her daughter's dance, and nobody must guess that the colour in her cheeks was rouge to hide the pallor, and her eyes were bright only because of the rouge. Her dress was new for the occasion, and she wore the Dreyfus diamonds at her throat, and a diamond tiara in her hair.

She stood at the head of the stairs to welcome the guests, a figure of great dignity and grace, lending by her presence alone a suggestion of ceremony and distinction that waved proudly like a single standard amongst the parade of ostentatious glitter conjured up so sumptuously by Julius, who stood by his wife's side flaunting his wealth in a cloud of glory.

That party that Julius Lévy gave at Cowes has never been forgotten; it was like a crazy, dazzling theatrical display, bursting upon the world in a night for one performance only, lit by a thousand lights that flashed scarlet and silver and gold.

The Progress of Julius

Every room in the house had been cleared for dancing, and on the lawns was a dancing floor. There were two bands in the house, a band in the garden. Upstairs, downstairs, amongst the roses, under the trees the dancing couples clung to one another, jostled, excited, laughing half-hysterically at this wild hum and call of music from which there was no escaping, finding each other with new eyes and new colours because of the constant change of the streaming, flickering lights that played upon their faces.

There were tables set for supper in every corner and space of the garden not taken by the dancing floor, and waiters who appeared mysteriously from the trees with a supper that came from God knew where – surely the whole cuisine and staff from Claridge's itself – impossible, untrue; and all the time the never-ceasing throb of music from the three bands, the splutter and hiss of fireworks rising in the air and exploding in a hundred glittering stars, the stamp of feet, the bewildering chatter of voices and the movement of dancers, and champagne, and more champagne.

It was a panorama of intoxicated splash, a reeling, tumultuous exposition of everything that is riotous and exuberant and crude; and Julius Lévy himself in the background, a magician with a wand conjuring new sights and new sounds without pause or relaxation until his guests surrendered to his mood in complete abandon, finding themselves crazy in a crazy world, so that they went on dancing whipped and stung by the music and the lights and the shooting stars, forgetting who they were and what should matter, a circle that tossed and twisted round a living flame.

And Gabriel was the flame, dressed in gold like a sheet of armour, her dress the colour of her hair. Her party, her guests, her music, the whole wheel turning because of her and Papa cracking the whip that set the wheel in motion – Papa, who had invented this night for her as though it was his wish to make her drunk for the first time, drunk with the glorious wanton waste that he was powerful enough to give her. She danced with her head thrown back and her lips parted, unconscious of her partners, who they were and what they said to her, aware only of this music that never ceased, sending her nerves a-jangle and beating against her brain, the glare of lights from the house and amongst the trees

228

in the garden, the sudden burst of an explosion when the fireworks broke in the sky above her head blazing a path to her feet.

She had no will of her own now, no consecutive thought, no power of concentration; she was being dashed and hurtled into a chaos that blinded her, some bottomless pit, some sweet, appalling nothingness.

A little trailing question flashed into her half-conscious senses: 'Am I drunk? Is this being drunk? Am I lost? Am I dead now?' And then no time to fix upon some determination because she would be swept away on another wave of sound and light, borne by this terrible music across the dancing floor, aware of Papa who watched her, Papa who smiled at her, Papa who played her on a thousand strings, she dancing to his tune like a doll on wires – Papa who harped at her and would not let her be. He was cruel, he was relentless, he was like some oppressive, suffocating power that stifled her and could not be warded off; he gave her all these bewildering sounds and sensations without pausing so that she was like a child stuffed with sweets cloying and rich; they were rammed down her throat and into her belly, filling her, exhausting her, making her a drum of excitement and anguish and emotion that was gripping in its savage intensity. It was too much for her, too strong.

She felt as though she were a dry stack in a deep wood, and he had put a match to her and was watching her burn.

She passed next to him once, he was standing by the steps of the veranda, and he looked down at her and said: 'Are you enjoying it? Do you want it to be over?' And she laughed back at him, shaking her head: 'I don't want it ever to be over' – afraid of the sudden flat calm that would come when the music stopped, the garish pallor of day when the lights were extinguished, the odd dark silence when the couples melted away, and she would be left with her restlessness and discontent and indecision. After the party the old life once more, the same string of happenings that could never be the same again. And yet she wanted the party to be over, because otherwise the turmoil and the clash would wear her down; she would stand up amongst them all, and scream and scream.

The end came suddenly with a whirling beating of drums and

a last spluttering rocket that shot a crimson star. The intoxicated, hysterical crowd of dancers were stilled to attention by 'God Save the King'.

It was over, as swift to die as it had been born, the mad party that Julius Lévy gave for his daughter, and the bands were silenced and the guests were vanished as though they had never been, the house and the garden strangely empty like a haunted place disturbed by the coming of the day.

Gabriel shivered, cold suddenly in the grey light, and she and Rachel and Julius made their way without a word to the launch that waited at the landing-stage to take them on board the *Wanderer*.

The yacht loomed white and clear on the still water against the grey light of the early day.

'We'll have some coffee brought up into the deck-house, and we'll watch the sunrise,' said Julius.

Nobody answered. Rachel was looking at Gabriel, and Gabriel was leaning against the side of the launch with her eyes shut.

'Are you tired?' said Rachel.

Gabriel moved, and opened her eyes.

'No,' she said slowly. 'I don't think I've ever felt less tired in my life.'

'Why did you shut your eyes?' said Rachel. Gabriel did not answer.

The launch drew alongside the gangway of the yacht. Julius was humming a tune under his breath. 'You can feel more things with your eyes shut,' he said; 'isn't that right?' He laughed, but he was the only one.

Rachel looked grey, he supposed she was feeling ill again.

They went on board and into the deck-house above the companion-way.

Julius shouted to the steward to bring them coffee.

Rachel sat down on one of the settees, pulling her cloak around her, drawing the heavy fur collar close to her throat. She was cold, chilled by the short journey across the water in the launch, and the pain in her side was like a dull gnawing toothache. It seemed to her that this weariness oppressing her was no ordinary fatigue, it was the ultimate surrender of a general whose last battle has been fought, who hauls down his torn fluttering standard and as he does so turns his sword into his own side. She felt as if she had waited for this moment for a long time, building her barriers against it, knowing in her heart that they would not stand.

Gabriel stood motionless at the opening of the deck-house, leaning her back to the door, her profile outlined against the sky.

The crazy bewilderment of the night had gone from her now, she was no longer enchanted and possessed. She was free again, at liberty to do as she pleased. Free in a new way. For a moment she had been troubled, and exquisitely sad, but now she was happy again; she was no longer afraid.

She knew that whatever happened to her henceforth it would be because of her own will and because she wanted it to be so.

She would be the victor, she would never be possessed. Nothing could hurt her now. In her life she would go out and do as she pleased and take the things that waited for her. She and Papa were two branches on a tree, and he had tried to see if he was stronger than she. He thought he had won. He thought he had beaten her down and she would let him go on thinking this as long as it suited her. She would keep him by her side and draw upon his strength; his life was her life, his flesh and blood were her flesh and blood, but it would never be he who was master. She held him between her hands and he did not know. When two forces came against each other and struggled and battled for supremacy one of the two must suffer and be hurt. People were like that in their relationship to one another. She and Papa. Papa would be hurt. This knowledge came to her as she stood by the doorway of the deck-house, looking out upon the water. She put her old life behind her as one who puts away childish things.

The steward came up the companion-way with the coffee tray in his hands. He laid it on the table and went below.

Julius poured out the three cups, slowly, methodically, taking his time. He no longer made any attempt to hide his smile, he was so sure of his future now, so blindly certain of success. He was taking a cruel deliberate interest in the situation he had created. He was aware of this tense, strained atmosphere between the three of them, Rachel on the settee, Gabriel at the doorway, himself by the table pouring out the coffee. All the fences were down between them now. He handed them both their cups of coffee and they drank in silence. He knew that Rachel would be the first to speak. It was as if she were a character in some play he had written, and the laying down of her cup in the saucer was her cue to speak. He was not prepared for what she said though.

'You may as well know the truth, Julius, about my illness. I've kept it from you up to now because I thought there might be a grain of hope somewhere – I don't mean of my recovering, but of you coming back to me again. Now of course I see that it won't be possible.'

She spoke very calmly, choosing her words carefully, speaking as though the subject were impersonal to her. She hesitated a moment, summoning her courage to use the word she hated.

'I have cancer,' she said.

They both turned and gazed at her, Gabriel with wide-open eyes of astonishment, Julius with disbelief. Rachel made a little ineffectual movement with her hands.

'Oh! no,' she said, 'I wouldn't try to deceive you. What would be the use? I'm not a fool. You may have thought me so, Julius, but you were wrong.'

He was not listening to what she said, he had only caught at the one word. 'Cancer?' he said. 'Who says you have cancer? That fellow Isaacson? Perhaps he's diagnosed you wrongly. Are you sure?' and then realizing by her smile and her shrug of the shoulder that she was speaking the truth, he let escape from him without caring the one question that mattered to him.

'Cancer!' he repeated. 'How long d'you suppose it's been going on? Is it contagious?'

She did not look at him now lest she should see the light of fear in his eyes that she knew would be there. She did not want to despise him. But Gabriel broke in swiftly – 'Oh! Papa,' she said scornfully, 'as if that matters – haven't you any pity? For God's sake don't make a fool of yourself.'

Then she looked at her mother again. 'I'm awfully sorry,' she said; 'I've never known pain of any kind, it must be terrible. Please believe me when I say I'm sorry. Can't anything be done?'

'That rather depends on you and your father,' said Rachel.

'Oh! but of course Papa's influence can get you the best doctors and treatment in the world,' said Gabriel. 'There must be somewhere in Germany or Switzerland – I don't know why one always thinks of those places, but surely . . .'

She broke off, she saw that Rachel's eyes never left her face.

'Your father's money isn't any use to me,' said Rachel. 'You know perfectly well I didn't mean that. Why beat around the subject?'

Gabriel drew back into herself. If her mother chose to throw away the sympathy she was offered it was her affair. She must suffer alone. She would not succeed in staging a battle.

'I'm not trying to evade anything,' said Gabriel, losing interest. 'I don't see that I come into this. It's between you and Papa.'

She turned her back once more as though she dismissed the idea of any form of discussion. She ignored the last bitter wave of antagonism. She leant against the door and watched the light breaking in purple and silver patches on the water.

Rachel looked at her husband.

'Well?' she said.

And even as she spoke she knew that she was not the central figure in the scene, she never had been. The question of her illness had scarcely touched the fringe of this atmosphere so tense, so still, it had brushed the outer layers of it, and struggled there impotently for the space of a moment, seeking to gain admittance. And now once more it had been wafted aside and she was nothing but a mute spectator, a poor shadow thing, watching some silent duel that held no relation to her, that admitted nothing and no one but the two locked and interwoven forces themselves. They were living their own lives on another plane, seeking the key to their own interests, pushing their way beyond her and losing themselves indefinitely in the white clouds. She was dead to them already. Rachel did not wait for the answer that never came, she got up from the settee where she had been sitting, holding to the cloak that slipped from her tired fingers, and she walked past Julius and Gabriel as if she were truly the ghost she saw herself to be, and she felt her way down the companion-way to her cabin like a spirit in a world of its own.

They heard the door of her cabin close.

Julius moved from the table, lighting a cigarette, and he went and stood by the side of his daughter looking out upon the water. Neither of them spoke for a moment. The hard rim of the sun was rising above the dark grey sea.

He said: 'I've been worried about you lately. You've been restless, disturbed about something. I knew what was the matter but you had to fight it out alone at first. It will be all right now, won't it?'

'Yes,' she said.

'We mustn't be serious about it,' he said, smiling. 'From now on everything's going to be like the party last night, only without the jingle and the glare. You're going to be happier than you've ever been. You must make up your mind to that.'

She smiled too. 'I made it up a long while ago,' she said.

'Did you? When?' he asked, curious, surprised at this.

She shook her head, she would not tell him. She would always keep some things to herself.

'What shall we do?' he said. 'Shall we make any plans? Is there anything you have in mind?'

'We might do the cruise you suggested,' she said. 'We'll go south in this boat and not bother to come back until we want to. I don't want hunting or racing now. Not for a long time, anyway. Shall we do that? Would you be bored?'

'Don't be an idiot, I'm never bored,' he said. The sun was rising higher out of the water, soon the whole dull orange body would appear, and it would not be the odd grey light any more, but the beginning of a new day.

Gabriel stretched her arms above her head and yawned, sleepy suddenly, contented, the strain and tension lost with the new dawn. They laughed at each other. He caught hold of her hand and swung it about in the air.

'We're going to have terrible fun,' he said.

Down below in her cabin Rachel was pouring five, six, seven little grey pellets from a bottle into her hand. She went to her washbasin and filled a glass of water. Then she swallowed the pellets one after the other, and swallowed the water from the glass. She opened the porthole by her bed and saw the sun come up over the water. It seemed strange to her that her last conscious thoughts should not be of those two on the deck above, but of

Walter Dreyfus, her father, sitting alone at his desk in the City, a revolver in his hand.

'That time when you came home from Italy,' Julius was saying, 'and you said at supper you'd like us to go to Venice, I believe you were thinking of this.'

Gabriel laughed.

'Were you?' he said. 'In the depths of your mind – were you?'

She made a face at him.

'Oh! Papa – you know me too well.'

He glanced at her, hesitating, biting his thumb-nail, and then exclaimed in annoyance, as though irritated, brushing the air away with his hands: 'Don't call me Papa.'

The following morning Rachel Lévy was found dead in her cabin. She must have been taken ill in the early hours of dawn, and perhaps called to her husband, and he had not heard.

Julius Lévy wired to his own doctor in London as soon as the tragedy was discovered – he would not let anyone from Cowes see his wife – and this doctor was brought down to Portsmouth in a fast car and a launch met him and brought him right over to Cowes without delay, and on to the yacht.

It was heart failure, of course, so the news was given out; no need for a post-mortem or an inquest. And then a few hours afterwards the *Wanderer* left her moorings with husband and daughter on board, taking Rachel Lévy home to Granby to be buried.

It was hardly to be wondered that Julius Lévy and Gabriel should decide to go abroad after the funeral. They were to be away some seven or eight months, and would not return for the hunting at Melton that winter. Nobody could remember Julius Lévy being out of England for so long before. His wife's death had probably broken him up. It was a good thing that he had such a companion in his daughter. Rather odd, perhaps, that they should choose to travel to the Riviera in the *Wanderer*, the yacht in which Rachel Lévy had died, but perhaps being a Jew and a foreigner he was funny about certain things. He might even have some sentimental attachment to the yacht because of his wife.

So Julius and Gabriel left England, joining the yacht at

Southampton one morning towards the end of August, and they did not come back to England until the beginning of April.

News of their travels came through to England from time to time, Julius Lévy keeping in touch with business and happenings in the City, but it was understood that he was taking the first real holiday of his life.

When he returned at the beginning of April looking very bronzed and fit it was decided by all who welcomed him that he had successfully recovered from the shock of his wife's death. He seemed in splendid health and in terrific spirits, looking not a day older than forty-five. If he was a trifle on the big side, his neck bulging ever so slightly over the back of his collar, it suited him. His hair, thick and growing white at the temples, was most distinguished.

And Gabriel of course was lovelier than ever, older perhaps, a little more self-possessed and sophisticated than before, but quite lovely. She had such abounding vitality, such terrific enthusiasm for life. She was like her father in that way. She was her father over again. She was vivid, amusing, brilliant in twenty ways. She did things well, she was talented. Wherever she was, and in whatever company she invariably made that place and those people more vital because of her. The word most used to describe her was 'attractive'.

'Gabriel Lévy?' people said with a certain depth of interest, smiling a little. 'Oh! yes, decidedly attractive,' and they would put a world of suggestion into their toning of the word 'attractive' as though it held infinite possibilities. It became a meaty word, a significant word. She was also 'mysterious', and 'intriguing'. 'Intriguing' used perhaps by women with an unmistakable tremor of envy in their throats. Yet no one was able definitely to discover the secret of her personality. No one was able to return home and say: 'Well, now we know what she is.' She defied interpretation. It was finally admitted that the truest statement made about her was by a young man hardly out of the nursery whose knowledge of life was limited, and yet because of his very simplicity was able to see straight. He said, flushing to the roots of his hair: 'You know, I think she's terribly attractive, but when you dance with her she makes you feel she doesn't want you. It's as if she were tremendously alive and you were a piece of wood. And that's all wrong, because she obviously must hate pieces of wood – she has such hot eyes.'

So there was Gabriel Lévy seen by a boy, and soon by everybody else, too – she was baffling and disturbing, and finally explained as 'Yes – very odd, keeps one at arm's length and God knows why – she has hot eyes.'

It mattered very little to Gabriel what people thought of her. She went her own way, choosing as companions those who amused her and who did the same things; who danced, and rode, and sailed boats; but though she laughed with them and gave to them the warmth of her personality she was intimate with none of them. She enjoyed the company of a large collected crowd, she did not want the close relationship of individual friendship. At the moment she was eminently satisfied and happy in her way of living. It seemed to her that her world could continue in this fashion for a long time. There would not have to be any changes.

Julius was happy, too. He thought he had reached a place in his life in which it would be pleasant to dwell for ever. He had climbed a hill, and as yet there was no pressing need to look down upon the further side. If he chose it would be easy for him to rest here continuously, his back turned to the future. He would make the future into the present. Nothing had ever been too formidable for him. His past, seen in perspective, made an interesting picture to look back upon. He took a pleasure these days in reviewing his past. He had come to a time when there was a certain relish in conjuring up old lost sensations. It seemed to him now that his life had been rich in many ways. There was a zest and a flavour about it that stung and was good. The old early restlessness and striving for achievement were enjoyable to remember now that he was satisfied. There had been doubts and indecisions in his youth that were his no longer. Even those fears and night terrors that had come to him throughout his life even three and four years ago, were banished now. The faces of dead people did not haunt him. Death itself was a bogey in a dark cupboard, locked securely, and tied by the feet. Paul Lévy was not a mocking figure in the silence of the night, but a poor ghost vanished into the air. And the old beautiful intangibility of the secret city had gone up in smoke and dust and ashes. In its place had risen a city of reality, of scents and of sounds, and he dwelt in this city holding the key in his hands.

It was a new and wonderful sensation to be without fear and to have confidence in the night. There was no spectre of loneliness lurking in the shadows, no dreaded whisper in his ear – 'Why? – Where now? – to what end?' All that was gone. He had come upon a new land and he was satisfied.

During the eight months he had travelled Europe with Gabriel his outlook had been that of a boy, fresh and unspoilt, open to every new impression, ready to receive each sight and smell and sound with enthusiasm and appreciation. There had never been a moment of boredom, no listless yawn, no rebellion at the surfeit of impressions. His energy was boundless, it was impossible for him to tire. Gabriel was the ideal companion, the other self, the ridiculous denial that they were in reality two persons. She was a vital necessity, a limb, an artery, the sap of the tree. It was incredible to him that there had been a time when he had lived alone. They understood one another. They were happy together. He knew that he was content and that this was no phase. He knew that he would never more want anything in life but this relationship.

The war of 1914–18 was the means of breaking up the scheme of things that Julius Lévy had intended for himself. The pleasant relaxation of living could be his no longer, the idle enjoyment of body and soul must give way before the terrific onslaught that shook the security of Europe.

It was imperative that his interest should be held firmly, from the first angry mutterings and rumbles of the approaching storm.

It was impossible that he should remain untouched. Here was a new field of venture open to him that he had not expected and for which he was unprepared, but which nevertheless he must turn upon and use for his own purpose.

War to him was no waving of banners, no departure of troop-ships overseas laden with men ready to sacrifice their lives for their country, no horror of carnage, no desolation of empty homes; but a game that must be played with great caution and subtlety by people who were never seen, who like himself were ready to gamble on the financial resources of that nation whose powers of endurance might be expected to last longest.

A European war, if carefully watched, need not necessarily bring ruin to those who meddled with it, and in a country like England, on whose shores it could safely be assumed there would be no actual fighting, he saw no reason why the state of war should not be the means of producing a source of profit. Profit to men such as himself. It was, perhaps, a welcome interlude in his life, coming at an opportune moment when he had been ready to allow his mind a certain laxity.

It happened that the situation was one which called for immediate action and he was determined not to miss the chance of exploiting this war for his own ends. It was, he reflected, an extremely lucky thing that war was with Germany and not with France. It might so easily have been the other way. Even to be an Englishman of over thirty years' standing was no help to one whose name unfortunately happened to be Goldberg or Bernstein. As a Lévy he was safe, as a proud possessor of French blood he was safer still. He was glad that he need undergo none of the uneasiness and embarrassment suffered by so many of his friends, Jews of German origin. Their method to avoid detection afforded him amusement. There was a lack of dignity in the scramble to change the second syllable of a name, a certain infantile air of dressing-up for charades when any of them appeared in uniform. Some fellows had the misfortune to be interned. The war would not be a source of profit to them unless they had the intelligence to employ reliable agents to look after their affairs.

However, their worries were not his worries, the awkward position of the German Jew only left the field clearer for himself.

Sometimes he permitted himself a small particle of personal satisfaction in the thought of this war against Germany; he closed his eyes and turned his mind back to the fear of a child forty years ago who was driven from his home. He thought of Grandpère Blançard shot before his eyes. He thought of the bare garret in the Rue des Petits Champs and the sound of the shells falling upon Paris. He thought of the guttural voice of a Prussian soldier in the silence of the night, and he remembered his own heart beating and his hands sweating as he crouched in the rail wagon. No, he had been through his experience of war. It was the turn of other people now. In England they had turned their backs on his suffering forty years ago, they had sat tight and secure in their little island, stretching no hand across the Channel. He wondered how they would enjoy the experience of bombs falling upon their precious homes. He wondered whether they would wriggle when the price of food grew dear. These things would be interesting to watch.

Meanwhile, the very herd instinct of these people made them easy to lead. They were like so many sheep in a pen. The shepherd whistled, and they flocked at his bidding. There was only the need to cry: 'England, my England!' and they rose to a man. The clarion call of patriotism was a lovely tool. Enthusiasm and a loud voice, shining eyes and a warm handshake, vigour, personality – Hip-hip-hurrah with a tearing ring and a sob at the back of it – these little qualities were useful.

More useful still were factories where women stood for several hours a day to make munitions. Women who must be fed, too, who must queue up to meals in their hundreds and in their thousands if their endurance was to last.

Never should it be said that the women of England failed their native land because of empty bellies.

Rather let there be depots in their hundreds and canteens in their thousands to satisfy this tide of hungry women. And what could be better for them, what more likely to put muscle into their honest English sinews and health into their stout hearts than Lévy's Bully Beef?

Those boys who marched on Salisbury Plain, those children who waved their caps at Waterloo Station, weren't they all trained on Lévy's Bully Beef?

That line of trenches silent and black in the early dawn, the bunch of grey-faced men waiting for a signal, the officer with his eyes on his watch, the scramble and the shouting, the wild, desperate run and the last limb kicking. Victory or Defeat? No matter, these men were fed on Lévy's Bully Beef.

Kitchener wants you. Yes, but you can't serve your King and Country until you fill up with Lévy's Bully Beef.

Why is Fritz frightened? Because Tommy has that Lévy look.

And that poster on every hoarding, of the Emperor of Germany caricatured as though in terror, his spiked helmet awry, his moustache twisted up in fear, his hands upraised in a gesture of surrender while towards him advance a regiment of red-faced smiling tin-hats – 'When Kaiser Bill said Kamerad – He learnt that British Troops were Fed on Lévy's Bully Beef.'

There was the song on everybody's lips, first sung at the Empire, and afterwards yelled and whistled on route marches:

> Bully Beef'll take you back to Blighty.

A household word, born in a night, started by nobody knew whom, and made of nobody knew what – horse, dog, cat – it scarcely mattered – the full flavour, the rich stout blood-making quality of Lévy's Bully Beef.

The originator of the boom moved amongst the munition workers and the land girls and the raw recruits, the wounded Tommies, the departing troops, and the W.A.A.C.s and as he watched them he smiled and thought of a boy in Paris forty-five years back who had sold rats in the street for two francs the piece.

Something for Nothing – Something for Nothing. 'It is men like you, Mr Lévy, who are helping England to win through.' The warm handshake, the bright eye, the excited cheers of five hundred munition workers.

> For he's a jolly good fellow
> And so say all of us.

Then 1916, 1917, the dreary hammering monotony of war, and Julius Lévy wondering whether Bully Beef had played itself out, and turning his mind to another vital necessity – Boots.

'Given time,' he decided, 'this war could be won on boots alone.'

It was easy enough to flood the market with an unending supply of strong Army boots – but they had to be cheap, and they had to look light. They had to have just that extra touch that would make them the smallest bit different from any other boot. The Lévy Boot. Wear Lévy leather and march to Berlin. Could the British Army wearing Lévy leather and eating Bully Beef fail to win the war?

'I tell you, sir, it's war-time that brings out the best in every-body. That fellow Lévy is a patriot. He may be a foreigner and a Jew but he's putting all the brains God gave him into this business. He's showing up these chaps in the War Office and in the Government. He knows what the men in the trenches want. Three cheers, all of you, for Mr Julius Lévy.'

Take Granby Hall. Granby was a full-blown Military Hospital, the gallery and the drawing-rooms had been turned into wards, the terrace and the gardens were sprinkled with bath-chairs and men in blue. Julius Lévy, the millionaire, had given up his beauti-ful country seat for the wounded sons of England. The house in Cowes was a convalescent home. The hunting-box at Melton Mowbray was shuttered up, furniture in dust-sheets. Surely there was no end to the sacrifices made by Julius Lévy and his daughter for England. They lived in only half of the big house in Grosvenor Square, their brief holidays were spent at Brighton. No racing now, no yachting in the Solent. Gabriel appeared in a bewildering array of uniforms. At first she was a V.A.D., she scrubbed the floors of hospital wards, she carried bloodied refuse from operat-ing-rooms. Then she went on the land, she wore breeches for a brief period and lifted hoes on her shoulder and bundles of hay, she milked cows, she fed pigs. Her next appearance was to serve in one of her father's canteens, in cap and apron, pouring tea (Lévy Tea) into cups and cutting slices of beef (Lévy Beef) on to plates. Breeches once more, she drove vans and lorries, this new occupation coinciding so well with a suddenly developed passion for cars. Then the organization of bazaars for the blind, and entertainments for the wounded, and concerts for men home on leave. Her picture appearing endlessly in the weekly papers – 'Gabriel Lévy, one of our most ardent War Workers.'

And finally, when all these exertions began to pall, the realiza-tion that the war work most appreciated and most satisfactory personally, was to take for lingering drives in Richmond Park officers who were not too badly wounded, and then to change one's dress and to dance somewhere with officers home on leave who were not wounded at all.

'That girl of yours is doing splendid work, Lévy. So noble of her, giving up all her fun, her yachts, and her horses. Aren't you proud of her?'

Julius, shrugging his shoulders, making a vague gesture with his hands as though none of this counted.

'Nonsense – we must all do something to help the country,' winking at Gabriel over somebody's shoulder, and later driving back to Grosvenor Square in the one Rolls that had not been commandeered, glanced out of the window as they passed the big café in Oxford Street, the basement of which had been turned into a vast cellar to accommodate frightened crowds during an air raid, and Gabriel said yawning, resting her head against his shoulder: 'Oh, darling, what a hectic life we lead. How on earth did we manage to amuse ourselves before the war?'

Julius Lévy was made a baronet in 1918.

'Such a waste, a baronetcy. I ought to have been a boy. Why on earth did they give you it, anyway?' said Gabriel.

'How the devil should I know?'

Buy Lévy Leather – Buy Lévy Bully Beef. Three cheers for Sir Julius Lévy.

'I tell you what, Gabriel. We'll get rid of the *Wanderer* if this war ever finishes, and buy a steam yacht about a thousand tons. The *Wanderer* is a bit cramped.'

'I know. I've been thinking about that, too.'

Three cheers for Sir Julius Lévy, one of the most patriotic and powerful men in England today.

Who'll buy rats, big plump rats, *deux francs la pièce – deux francs la pièce?*

Something for nothing!

By the time the Armistice was signed in November 1918, Julius Lévy, baronet, had augmented his fortune by exactly three-quarters of a million. The profits that had come to him from Bully Beef and Boots, in addition to the colossal sums he had gleaned from his cafés throughout the country and from his private speculations in the markets of the world, had made him probably the wealthiest man in England. The four years that had passed, bringing misery and horror to most people, had merely doubled his success.

The Great War had been an interlude to him, a passage of time fraught with keen interest and excitement. He had lived intensely during these last years, every moment had served a purpose, and had been used by him as a fresh experience.

In his blood always had run the desire for action, and now he had been able to give vent to this desire to its fullest extent.

For years he had lived ahead of his generation, and with the swift changes brought about by the war it was as though he stepped into his own time. This new restless way of existing at high tension was his way, this nerve-racked atmosphere of rapid movement, sudden destruction and startling creation was his atmosphere. He understood mushroom growth and the craze for speed, he loved all things born in a night. This past war could be no nightmare to him who had no brothers, no sons, and no friends. England was not his country, France was not his country, the sufferings of many millions of people would never be able to touch him.

The actual monetary value of his gains meant little to him. He accepted the knowledge of the added three-quarters of a million with a shrug of his shoulder, it was the fight that had counted with him, the satisfaction he had gained in using his brains, and seizing his advantage where others had failed. He had nothing but contempt for those men who had allowed themselves to be broken by the war, who gave way and were beaten morally, who appeared now as shadows of their former selves. So many of his contemporaries had proved unequal to the strain. So many had been bewildered, and had shrunken and grown old. They had not possessed the intelligence to progress; in their curious timidity and super-sensibility to the horrors of war they had weakened and stood aside, they had not made the slightest effort to reach out for the prizes that lay close within hand of every thinking man.

Now they were pushed and shouldered out of the way, they were good for nothing but their morning papers in their fusty clubs. His contemporaries, old fellows, shrinking from noise, disapproving, muddle-headed fools. In two years' time Julius would be sixty, and he still felt forty-five. This war had made no mark upon him. Like Gabriel, he wondered how he had lived before.

Nothing would ever be the same again, not in the old way. Interests had changed, people too. One no longer wanted the same things. Racing, yachting, hunting, the parties at Grosvenor Square and down at Granby, would they be able to take them up again in the old way? Did they not seem slightly wearisome now, out of date? Four years back he had been on that tour round Europe with Gabriel, and he had said to himself he would never want anything more than that. Then the war came. And now that the war was over he knew that neither he nor Gabriel would enjoy these things in the same way again. Something had gone because of the four years. A little seed of dissatisfaction had sprung into being. It was as though a voice unnamed whispered inside him: What now – what next? The war had stopped too soon for him, his energy was baulked. His power and his vitality had been arrested half-way. Now that there was no direction for this to find an outlet the stream would turn inwards towards himself. He would be at a loose end, he would look about him with uncertainty.

Gabriel had a new passion. She was dance-mad like most of her generation. She thought of nothing else. At first Julius went with her and was her partner, she taught him the new steps. Then he found he became bored, there was something absurd about jigging round a room hour after hour.

It seemed to him there must be an appalling waste somewhere to have used his brains for four years and then at the end merely to arrive at this jigging round a room.

Gabriel laughed at him: 'You're lazy,' she said, 'you're getting fat.' And she was whirled off in some young fellow's arms while Julius watched, faintly irritated, drumming his fingers on the table, yawning, his mind a blank. Something to do, to do, to do. . . . Of course there were politics. He wondered vaguely if there was anything to be gained from politics. There seemed to be a glimmer of light in this thought. Politics. A Coalition Government was in power. On a sudden impulse he resolved to stand as Liberal at the next by-election.

'Why Liberal, darling?' said Gabriel.

'Why not?' he said.

He didn't care. When Commander Ainsworth, a Conservative,

resigned his seat of West Stockport for reasons of ill health, Julius Lévy, baronet, contested his successor and won the seat by a majority of twelve thousand. He liked the fight. For the short space of time preceding his election he enjoyed the same sensations as he had experienced during the early years of the war. He was up against something, it was a little battle of its own. He made a good speaker. He took all the shine out of the other fellow, an honest, thick-headed Tory, with a mind like a cabbage. The other fellow was nowhere. Because of his work in the war, Julius Lévy was popular; no one doubted for a moment that he would win his fight.

'It's men like you the Government want, sir.' The same old story. It was easy enough to go around amongst the working classes of West Stockport and tell them how he had worked his way up from a baker's apprentice down in Holborn. They liked that, they cheered him, they shook him by the hand. 'Good old Ikey,' they said. He was familiar with them, his coarse humour was received with roars of ribald laughter. 'I'm a plain man,' he told them, 'no airs about me. You won't get any long speeches, I warn you. Want a tip for the two-thirty at Newmarket tomorrow?' His tip was luckily correct, and gained him probably a thousand extra votes.

Then he left them, waving his hat, throwing the red carnation he wore in his buttonhole to a woman standing on the top of her area steps (another vote) and he walked to where the Rolls was parked discreetly several blocks away, and drove off to address a meeting for the benefit of the West Stockport gentry; different methods then, different gestures.

Lucky business that West Stockport was an important ship-building centre, he was able to have the new steam yacht *Gabriel* of eleven hundred tons built there. The keel was laid during the election fight and invitations were broadcast for anyone who cared to see the first bolt driven. The champagne was free. Never before nor since had West Stockport known such exquisite extravagance. The streets were hilarious that night, and the lock-ups were full. The invitation cost Julius an unmentionable sum and probably won him his majority. The Conservative candidate could not afford champagne. When the result of the poll was known, Julius Lévy appeared on the balcony of the Queen's Hotel, and smiled down upon the crowd gathered in the square. The balcony was draped in the colours of his racing stable, an unpardonable piece of vulgarity which delighted him intensely.

'Well, that's that,' he said, aware of disappointment now that the fun was over, and he thought without interest of his approaching status as representative for West Stockport in the House of Commons where he would merely be one of six hundred and fifteen members. Something to do, to do. . . .

His next movement was to buy secretly a combination of newspapers, including the *Daily Watchman*, the *Evening Post*, and the *Weekly Gazette*.

These papers had been suffering a big drop in circulation owing to bad editorial staff work, no particular policy, and poor advertising space.

It seemed to Julius Lévy that there must be a future in journalism.

He turned the *Daily Watchman* into a twelve-sheet paper, four complete pages of advertisement, and the two centre pages given up to the latest news – the more sensational the better. People wanted sensation. They wanted thrills. They lived to read about the private lives of actresses, the intimacies of divorce courts, the feelings of murderers in condemned cells, the reactions of mothers whose children had been raped. They wanted to know the number of street accidents per day, the quantity of bargains purchasable by post, and the truth about the earl who slept with his cook.

Julius Lévy gave them all this in the *Daily Watchman*. In six months' time, with the aid of football and racing competitions, his circulation had increased by over ten thousand. The papers were set, they had only to go straight ahead. The staff were competent and keen as mustard. The Lévy newspapers were in control like the Lévy cafés, and the Lévy factories, and the Lévy stables.

Everything was so easy. He had only to stretch out his hands. Something to do, to do. . . .

When Julius Lévy was driving home from the House of Commons on the night of his sixtieth birthday, there came to him suddenly, like a flash of light in a forgotten corner, the memory of his fiftieth birthday ten years ago.

The evening was much the same, dull and colourless, the many sounds and scents of London were unchanged; even Mander waiting for him in his purple livery, holding the door of the car, was the same silent Mander of ten years back.

Julius remembered his mood of depression, that odd blank sensation of having reached a milestone in his life. He had returned home to find Gabriel, aged fifteen, playing Paul Lévy's flute by the open window of the study.

Ten years ago. Oh! the uncharted seas, the untrodden ways, the undiscovered paths across the mountains – yes – and the waters under the bridges since then.

'Mander,' he said suddenly, throwing his hat and his stick into the car, 'I can't make up my mind whether it makes a penny-worth of difference being sixty – or forty-five – or twenty-one.'

Mander smiled: 'A woman is as old as she looks, a man is as old as he feels, Sir Julius. You know the old saying?'

Julius settled himself in the car, drawing the rug over his knees.

'All damned nonsense, Mander, you poor mug. A man feels twenty one moment and eighty five seconds afterwards. Matter of temperament. Heigh-ho!' he yawned, settling himself amongst the cushions. 'I don't regret a thing, Mander, not one bloody thing.'

The chauffeur waited politely, his hand on the door. 'Home, sir?'

'Yes.' The door was closed, Mander climbed to his seat.

'What does he care?' thought Julius. 'What the devil do I matter to him?' He began to go over in his mind pictures of things that had happened, scenes scattered here and there across his track of memory. Gabriel in a black velvet frock coming down the stairs at Granby, Gabriel on horseback at Melton, Gabriel at Venice, Gabriel dressed as a V.A.D., Gabriel driving officers in Richmond Park – Gabriel – still, that sort of thing could go on indefinitely. She was nearly twenty-five. He was sixty. H'm. . . . 'Look out, Mander, you bloody idiot, what d'you think you're doing?' Nearly ran over that woman, silly fool. She was young and pretty too, he turned to look at her through the window in the back. Bad legs. Where was he, though? Oh yes! – ten years, fifty to sixty. Rachel, poor old Rache. Always thinking about her health those last years. Malignant, the way she had put an end to things. There might have been a nasty scandal at the time. He had been too quick, though. Gabriel in Corsica – she used to wear a pair of sailor's trousers and a scarlet sash. . . . The war, you couldn't get away from the war, thinking back. It seemed to loom over everything. It cut out the memories of the days that had gone before. Buy Lévy's Bully Beef – and then a title on top of it. Sir Julius Lévy, Bart. No sons. Who cared? – the whole thing was just a lot of . . . Gabriel dancing at that Victory ball, she wore gold. She was best in gold, it was her colour. Vote for Sir Julius Lévy, the man who gets things done. His maiden speech, 'one of the best maiden speeches of recent times'. Somebody said that, didn't he? Or was it he himself in the *Daily Watchman*? It all came to the same, anyway. Those papers were the envy of Fleet Street, the crashing answer to out-dated journalism. Give him time, he'd show the world. Show them what? Did he care? Did anything matter? He yawned once more, he was tired, he wanted to get home to supper, the comfort of a dressing-gown and slippers and a last cigar, and Gabriel coming in to chat. His sixtieth birthday. They ought to celebrate it.

Home again, and the door opening, and the car driving away, walking upstairs slowly, because his back was aching and there was something wrong with his right knee, he must see Isaacson about it, and so on into his suite of rooms, supper all ready for him.

'Clear out, I'll wait on myself. Where's Miss Gabriel?'

'I couldn't say, Sir Julius.'

'Well, go and find her.'

That's better, dressing-gown and slippers, a glass of champagne, cold salmon, early strawberries from Granby.

'Miss Gabriel is not in, Sir Julius.'

'Oh, very well.'

Damn her, where to now? Dancing again, always this infernal dancing. What in the world did she see in it? Silly business – jigging about. Bored him stiff. What energy she had, never still a moment. Always on the go. He had been the same at her age. Her age, that's bad – twenty-five, sixty. He must be tired to keep thinking of that. Funny how one changed; one didn't care to do the same things as one did ten years back. This was good, lounging in a chair in front of the fire; it was cold for May, one needed a fire, and he was enjoying his supper. Why didn't Gabriel come, though? Midnight, 1 a.m., 2 a.m., might as well wait and ask her where she's been. But weary, damn weary, head nodding slowly, the paper falling from his hands, mouth open wide, a long spluttering snore. . . . Hullo – waking with a start, the sound of a car below in the square. God damn and blast the girl, it was 4 a.m. He rose from his chair, his legs stiff, he crossed to the window and looked from behind the curtain at a small, closed car drawn up in front of the house. That was she, he could see the glimmer of her white cloak. Why the devil didn't she get out? Was she talking or what? Two minutes, three minutes, five minutes, eight minutes – damn her, damn her, what were they doing in the car, why didn't she get out? Why didn't she get out? His hands had gone clammy cold, his fingers twitched at the curtain. He kept passing his tongue over his lips, and then swallowing. The door of the car opened at last and Gabriel stepped out on to the pavement. He couldn't see her face. Some fellow with her – never mind about him, though. He didn't count. At the bottom of the steps Gabriel turned, catching her cloak round her, and then the fellow leant forward and took her face in his hands and kissed her. Julius saw this quite plainly. He saw Gabriel throw back her head and laugh, and reach out her hand to the fellow's throat and draw him towards her and kiss him. Then they disappeared under the pillars of the porch, he could not see them from his window any more.

Julius crept from his room and crossed the corridor to the head of the main stairway. If they came in he would be able to watch and listen from the head of the stairs. There were no servants about. He understood now, they probably had their orders. They were used to this. Once more he swallowed and passed his tongue over his lips. He heard the key in the lock of the front door. He crouched back in the shadows, his eyes fixed upon the dark hall below, his mouth open so that he should hear better. The door slammed. Gabriel had come in alone. There was the sound of the fellow starting up his car. Julius backed away from his cramped position, and reached out for the switch. In a moment he had flooded the hall with light. Gabriel looked up, startled, she was fiddling with her bag. Her hair was untidy, and her cloak was slipping off one shoulder, a shoulder-strap of her dress showed. He saw all this in a glance.

'Hullo! – it's you,' said Gabriel. 'Why such a scene with the lights? You gave me a shock.'

He did not answer, he stared down at her, white and trembling in his dressing-gown.

'Darling, are you ill?' she said. 'You look terrible – what's wrong? Why aren't you in bed?'

He looked her all over as though fearful that something should escape him, and when she joined him at the head of the stairs he spoke:

'You bitch!' he said. 'You bitch!'

For a moment she gazed at him, thinking he must be mad.

'What on earth . . .' she began. He did not give her time to continue.

'I saw you,' he said. 'I saw you from the window. Out in the square with some fellow. You were in that car eight minutes. I timed you, eight whole minutes, and then you got out and I saw him kiss you. You bitch!'

She burst out laughing.

'Good God, was that all? I thought you were in terrible pain. Your silly face is grey, darling. Go along to bed and don't be so absurd.'

'You can't make a fool out of me,' he said, and he reached out his hand to her arm, and shook her.

She wrenched herself away.

'Don't do that,' she said. 'Are you drunk, or what? I've never heard such bloody nonsense in my life.'

'Come along to my room,' he said. 'I'm not joking with you.'

She followed, shrugging her shoulders, switching out the lights in the corridor.

'I'm tired,' she said. 'I've been dancing since ten this evening. I'm not going to stay.'

He dragged her inside his room and shut the door.

'How long has this been going on?' he said.

'What the devil d'you mean by "this"?' she said. 'Why so melodramatic?'

'Don't talk like that to me,' he said.

'I shall talk as I damn well please,' she said.

He took hold of her wrists.

'Why did you let that fellow kiss you?'

'Because I like it,' she said.

'Has he done it before?'

'No – as a matter of fact. No. I only met him tonight.'

'You let him do that, and you've not met him before?'

'Yes – darling.'

'Do other men kiss you?' he said.

'Yes. If I'm attracted by them.'

'On the mouth?'

'Good heavens, where else do you suggest?'

'Don't play with me,' he said. 'How long have you let men kiss you?'

'Oh! darling, I really can't remember. I suppose it started during the war.'

'Those fellows you danced with?'

'Yes.'

'Whenever you go out do you always let them kiss you?'

'It depends – please don't be so damn idiotic. I want to go to bed.'

'Do they only kiss you, or do you let them do other things?' he said.

'What d'you mean by "other things"?'

'You know,' he said.

'Oh! I don't sleep with them, if that's what you're getting at,' she said.

'D'you expect me to believe you?'

'Yes.'

'How can I?'

'Because I wouldn't lie to you,' she said. 'If I ever want anyone, I'll tell you. As it happens, I've never felt like wanting anyone up to date.'

'You bitch!' he said.

He sat down, passing his hand over his mouth, his hand trembling.

She looked at him thoughtfully.

'Why should you mind?' she said.

He brushed the remark away.

'How do you think I'm going to live if I'm never to be certain of you, day or night?' he said to her.

She shrugged her shoulders.

'It's not my affair if you choose to make a fool of yourself,' she told him.

There was a pause and then she said: 'You might have known this would happen. I'm nearly twenty-five, my life's my own, after all.'

'No,' he said slowly. 'No, that's not true. You have no right to say that. You're part of my life.'

'Don't shout, the servants will hear,' she said. She picked up her bag from the table.

'I'm going to bed, all this is very boring. You've probably had a tiring day and will feel better tomorrow.'

She went to the door.

'Gabriel,' he said. 'Gabriel . . .'

She glanced at him over her shoulder and shook her head.

'No,' she said.

He gazed at her sullenly, gnawing at his finger-nails, hating her.

'I'll stop you going to places,' he said. 'I'll have you watched, I'll see that you aren't left alone with anyone – you needn't imagine you can fool me, nobody has ever fooled me yet. Take care.'

She considered him a moment, her eyes narrow, making a study of him in her mind as he crouched in his dressing-gown, biting his nails, his shoulders hunched, his neck bulging over the collar, his white hair rumpled.

'You know what's the matter with you, you're getting old,' she said. Then she went out of the room.

Julius sat in his chair staring at the closed door; and as he waited there numbed and cold, too weary to drag himself to bed, it seemed to him that he could see faces watching him from the shadows, and could hear voices whispering in the corners, and he was no longer Julius Lévy, but a traveller who had reached the summit of a mountain and must now go down into the dark valleys below. The white clouds had passed from his reach, the music of the heights was lost to him, and the gates of the secret city were closed.

And as he sat there alone, he knew that never again would he have any sensation of peace or contentment, that never would his days or his nights be free from anguish and bitter distress. Because of what he had seen and heard that evening he would be driven tormented to mental horror as yet unknown to him and feared, there would be no rest for him until he had crushed and hidden and made secure into eternity his own creation, possessed for ever or returned to the place from whence it came.

The weeks that followed were hideous in their monotony. The days came up and passed Julius by, giving him no respite from his mood of bitterness and despair. He must watch and wait, and listen, despise no trick as unworthy, steam open her letters, peer amongst her things, sit with doors ajar, steal from his room at night-time to hearken outside hers.

Her secrets would not escape him, she would not break away.

It was the height of the London season and Gabriel was for plunging into it, and doing everything as they had done before the war, only with greater freedom now, and luxury and abandon, because the war was over and she belonged to this new generation. Very well then, she should do as she liked, but he would follow her. Every function, every race meeting, every party – he would be by her side. He would dance with her night after night, however much he loathed it, he would know minute by minute every movement of her day when business in the City or attendance in the House kept him from her. She must introduce him to all her friends, he would know in a glance which ones to fear. He would not let them get to her. He would drive with her in the car back from her parties, he would see her to her room. Even then he would listen outside the door. Never left alone, never trusted for a moment, unless he knew for certain her plans. If she announced a hairdresser appointment he would verify this, he would ring that hairdresser himself and find out if she were really there. Even then, the man might have lied, and to satisfy himself he would have to go in person, and walk into this shop and say: 'Is Miss Lévy here? I am her father.'

And even with all these precautions, could he be certain? How was he to be sure?

She would say: 'People are coming in to bridge this afternoon,' and he would answer: 'What time?' And when she told him he would remember this, and if he could not be back he would telephone her from wherever he should be, asking to speak to her personally, counting the seconds she took to reach the telephone, listening if her voice should be breathless as though she had been surprised.

'Who is with you? How many of them? How long will they stay? What are you all doing?' and then, lying cunningly to her: 'I shan't be home before eight-thirty,' so as to give her an opportunity to deceive him, and then returning stealthily at seven, going silently upstairs, flinging open the door, and finding her with her friends, playing bridge, calm and unconcerned. Was this a blind? How could he be sure?

When she smiled or talked to anyone, was there something behind that smile, a double meaning in her words? Why did she glance over her shoulder at that fellow, was there some reason in it?

He would watch her dancing, never taking his eyes from her for a single instant, and surely it would seem to him there must be some intimacy between her and her partner, her hand resting thus on his shoulder, her face upturned. What were they saying now, why did she laugh?

He would question her when she returned to the table. 'What was he saying to you?' And she, flushed and happy from her dancing, humming the tune: 'Saying to me, when? I don't remember.'

Surely she was lying.

'Why do you like dancing with that boy? What does it do to you?'

And she, angry: 'Oh! don't harp like that. You'll drive me mad.'

'Dance with me, then,' he said, and they would get up and

dance together, he miserable, she bored, holding herself from him until he said to her: 'Why do you keep away from me? Do you hate me?' And she wearily: 'Don't be so ridiculous, why must you always be in this mood? Can't I ever have any peace?'

A sullen silence, and then another scene, and then silence again. The drive home in the car.

'I suppose you want to be in a closed car with some boy, the lights turned off, under the trees in Regent's Park,' he said, and she, yawning, replying absently: 'One's not allowed to draw up in Regent's Park,' and he fiercely, seizing upon her words: 'Ha! So you've tried, have you?'

Then she laughed. 'God! What a fool you make of yourself.'

No understanding, no love, the old companionship gone. No intimacy, no trust.

'Oh! Gabriel, this is such damned hell. Don't let's be like this.'

'But it's you,' she said helplessly. 'It's nothing to do with me. What have I done?'

'You think I'm old, is that it? I'm not young enough for you. You think I'm just an old fool, and you're sick of me – is that it?'

'When you behave in this way you might be senile,' she said.

'No – no – let's finish that, let's begin again. Tell me everything is just the same, Gabriel; tell me you'll never be any different.'

'Oh! of course,' the sigh of exasperation, the silly half-hearted reconciliation, he groping for her hand, blubbering, murmuring nonsense in French, sentimental like an old drunkard, aware of his own fatuity and loathing it, and she so cool and impersonal, suffering him, her eyes somewhere else and thinking what? Thinking of whom? No peace ever. Day after day, night after night.

He would give her presents after one of these scenes. Bracelets, ear-rings, a ring, a new hunter for next season, another boat, but whatever he gave her he knew it was but a temporary branch of truce, and meant little to her, she had so many of these things already.

'Suggest something you want, I'll give you anything,' he would say, and she speaking straight from her heart: 'Leave me alone, don't harp at me – that's all I ask.' And this he could not do.

So the summer continued, the long drag through the little, petty events of the London season, dances, charity balls, dinners, garden parties, Epsom, Ascot, Wimbledon, Lord's, Henley, Goodwood, Cowes – one after the other came and went, Gabriel professing herself to be amused by them, and Julius must therefore accompany her, otherwise she would deceive him, and escape, and go her way.

The City did not matter to him, nor the quarterly meeting with the managers of his cafés, nor the reports from his factories, nor the sales of his newspapers, nor the events in Parliament; there only remained to him this shadowing of Gabriel, this ceaseless vigilance that must not be relaxed.

She pretended she did not care, but he knew he was wearing her down. His was the stronger will, before long she would surrender and admit she could stand no more. He would have crushed the antagonism between them, and there would be no other course for her but to be subservient to him in all things. He had it in his mind that she took no pleasure in her days now that there was a barrier dividing them, her gaiety was a mask. He too, at her side, was like an actor playing a part, the happy father and the devoted daughter. It came to him sometimes that they were two dolls in a puppet show grimacing before company, but within they were lifeless, cold, and stuffed like dummies. They would go to some big party together, she radiant and lovelier than ever, wearing those many jewels he had given her as though they were service stripes; and he at her elbow, tall and distinguished, bowing and smiling to their friends, calling a joke over his shoulder to someone who passed, and always a little buzz of excitement wherever they went: 'There's Julius Lévy and his daughter, isn't she lovely! Oh! to be as rich as that. Mustn't it be marvellous?'

No longer a fierce pride and a triumphant amusement because of their envy, but desolation, and emptiness, and a bitter feeling of contempt for their ignorance.

Those pitiful remarks: 'You are a lucky fellow, Lévy, you've got everything in the world you want.' And: 'Hullo! Lévy – good man, you turn up at all these parties – gosh! You've got more capacity for enjoyment than any youngster,' and then he must nod and smile and play his part, while Gabriel with her brilliant mask forced a smile in her turn, waved her hand to some friend who gazed at her in admiration, who called to her: 'Hullo,

Gabriel – you look wonderful. Having a marvellous time as usual, I suppose?'

The clatter and screech of voices, the senseless patter of footsteps, little trills of empty laughter and loud guffaws, the thumping jazz band rattling above them all, and a fellow with a blackened face shouting to the moon.

While the end of all this would be the return to Grosvenor Square, the house for all its art treasures and exquisite furniture like a cold barracks, the servants in their livery, dumb and immobile as doorposts, Gabriel sitting down before the dressing-table in her bedroom, and pulling off one by one her bracelets and her rings, turning to glance over her shoulder at Julius, who stood in the doorway. And she would yawn, tapping her foot on the floor impatiently, her face hard and her eyes cold, saying: 'Well, what now?' then not waiting for his answer, she lost control of herself, pushed the bracelets away from her, ran her hands through her hair in a frenzy of irritation and said: 'Oh! God – if you knew how you bored me . . .'

He asked her if there was anything in the world she would like to do, and she said she did not know, she had had everything, there was nothing left to do now; and when he suggested some fresh party or amusement, some new sport, motor-boating or flying, she shrugged her shoulders, she did not care.

He waited then, wondering if this was his chance, and he said gently:

'Let's go south in the yacht, we haven't cruised since the war, wouldn't you be happy doing that?'

She thought a moment, she would not commit herself, and: 'Perhaps,' she said, and reaching for a file began to cut her nails.

'Shall we just be ourselves?' he began, but she broke in on this as though it delighted her to hurt him, and she said: 'My dear – how deadly. What would we do? No, let's have a crowd.'

He knew then that life on board the yacht would only be a repetition of the present summer, and so there would be no peace for him.

When Cowes week was over the big steam yacht *Gabriel* sailed from Southampton bound for Cannes, a party of fifteen, besides

Julius Lévy and his daughter. This yacht was the luxury ship built at Stockport – she was like a miniature hotel.

When they were on board, Julius had some measure of security, Gabriel was too close here to elude him. She was therefore under his eye continually. Her state-room adjoined his on deck, separated only by a bathroom; if he slept with both doors ajar, he could hear every movement. The rest of the guests slept in state-rooms below, and the men of the party in separate quarters to themselves. To go there anyone would have to pass along the deck outside the window of Julius's state-room, and he would see them. He was pleased with this arrangement of the cabins, he had thought it out with the greatest care.

When they arrived in Cannes surveillance became more difficult. It was so easy for people to slip away at the Casino, to disappear from the ballroom into the gambling-rooms, and then out perhaps, undiscovered, hidden somewhere. He trusted none of Gabriel's friends, he disliked them all. He felt safest when she was playing bridge, or actually dancing – then he was able to watch.

When he was making a fourth himself and she was dancing on deck to the gramophone, he would keep his ear awake to the sound of the tune, and if it was stopped and a pause came before another one started he would move restlessly in his seat, wondering the reason. He could hardly conceal his impatience before the rubber was over to make some excuse, and jump up from his chair and climb the stair to the upper deck to see whom she was with.

Daily he grew more apprehensive, more highly strung, and she seemed to notice none of this. Whether it was the air of Cannes and the change from London, he did not know, but as his anxiety for her increased, so did her spirits improve, and her old true gaiety return, and she was happier than she had been for many months, singing, laughing, the old Gabriel, but for the mute antagonism between them.

Either this meant an approaching surrender and a going back to his way of living, or it foretold a new departure. He did not know, he could not tell. His doubt was like a fever within him.

The yacht had left the harbour at Cannes and had come to an anchorage between the islands of St Marguérite and St Honoré. It was very hot and still. Here there was none of the glare and dust belonging to the baked, white streets of Cannes, nor clatter of sound, nor forced bright gaiety.

Here the silence was odd, unnatural, it was like the quiet of an enchanted land. The pale blue waters of the sea were motionless, they made no splash upon the shingle stones of the beaches, and the thick heavy trees in the wood never moved, they clung together and were still like sleeping things.

Day after day the sun shone from a sky blue-black and shimmering with heat, and a thin white haze spread from the sea between the islands and the mainland.

The only sounds of life came from the yacht herself, and there was something wrong and harsh in these sounds, breaking so abruptly upon the silent air. The clanging of the ship's bell, the run of the engines, the voices and laughter of those on board, and that ceaseless blare of the gramophone were intrusions to which the sleeping islands held no welcome.

Sometimes a flitting brown figure of a monk peered furtively from amongst the trees on St Honoré, wondering at the great white yacht that lay across the channel, and then he would creep back to the monastery, his eyes downcast, his fingers fumbling at his beads.

Every morning the party from the yacht would land at St Marguérite to bathe. Avoiding the deep woods that held themselves aloof, mysterious and mosquito-laden, they would scatter into little groups and then lie on the beaches close to the water, the sun tanning them mahogany brown. When the glare became a torture, they would stretch themselves, yawning, and slip into the sea swimming lazily, turning over and over, splashing with their hands.

Julius never bathed amongst them. Because he was sixty in some half-conscious way he feared their ridicule. But he would watch them through glasses, or pull out from the yacht in a boat, or even land and walk away amongst the trees, and then turn to see if some opportunity was taken in his absence. He discovered nothing, no calls, no beckonings, no sudden swift departures. Perhaps they were too clever for him.

One night it had seemed to him, with a queer upward lift of his heart, that Gabriel had smiled at him in the old way. After dinner she had played the flute on deck, silencing that gramophone he loathed, and she had looked at him across the heads of those fools as though she were saying: 'We know, don't we? We have nothing to do with them.' Perhaps she was tired now, perhaps she wanted to come back. This morning it was she who had suggested coming alone with him in his boat; she sent the others to the usual beach, while they were to row round the farthest point. 'There's some deep water there, I want to dive,' she said. And the others were too lazy, they said they would follow later.

Julius pulled across the channel with slow, methodical strokes. Gabriel lay back in the stern, gazing at the sky. As he watched her he wondered if this was really a wish of hers, wanting once more to be alone with him, or if it was another change of mood. It seemed to him so long since they had been alone together. They chatted of little unimportant things, and he knew that this was not the real purpose of their being with one another, it was a subterfuge. His heart beat loudly, he smiled to himself, and he hummed a song under his breath.

They landed at the point, leaving the boat, and walked until they came to a strip of land where the sea ran deep and the trees came to the water's edge. They sat down, pretending to watch the colour of the water and the reflection of the trees, and then she moved away from him suddenly and began unclasping her bracelets.

'I'm going to bathe,' she said. He reached out his hand to her.

'Gabriel,' he said. 'Gabriel,' looking up at her, pulling her towards him, but she shook herself free and went on with her undressing. And now it was she who smiled, and she who hummed the tune. When she had finished, she kicked her clothes on one side and stretched, her arms above her head.

'Oh! darling, I'm so happy,' she said.

He made no answer, and then she said: 'I have a new thing about living, it's not going to be the same any more. It's going to be more wonderful than anything has ever been. I'm so happy.'

'What do you mean?' he said.

'Oh! You can guess, can't you?' she said, and she was laughing at him. 'You know everything there is to know about me. I said

I'd tell you if I ever wanted anyone. Well – it's happened at last. I'm not going to be me any more. I'm going to be somebody else, Gabriel will go for ever.'

She looked at him a moment, and frowning she said: 'This will hurt you, of course, but – I can't help that. I can't think of anyone but myself when I'm happy. You said I was always to think of myself.'

Still he said nothing, and she went on: 'I shan't tell you who it is yet, because that would spoil it. I've been clever, haven't I? Nobody would know! I can't tell you what it's made me feel – all young again, and unspoilt, and as though I didn't know things. You won't recognize me soon. I'll be domesticated and subservient and humble, and talking about chintz curtains and servants and babies' napkins.'

She laughed again, and threw a handful of sand in his face. 'Say something,' she said. 'Don't sit like that. Oh! I'm in that mad drunk mood when I want everyone to be happy because I'm happy. Can't you see? I'm sick of my old self. I want just to get away silently and be lost and nobody to find out. D'you understand? Say you understand. It's going to spoil everything if you're against me.'

Watching his face it seemed to her that he could scarcely have heard a word of all she had been saying, because his expression had not changed, and his eyes were cold. She wondered if he were thinking of someone else. Then he looked up and he said: 'Père was not a clever man, he left traces in the Rue des Petits Champs and had to run away.'

'What are you talking about?' she said. 'Haven't you been listening?'

'Yes, I heard you,' he said, and he got up and went to the water's edge and looked towards the point. There was no sign of the rest of the party.

'Aren't you going to bathe?' he said.

She hesitated. 'Yes – of course,' she said. 'But what's the matter, are you angry with me?'

He shook his head. 'Not with you,' he said. 'But angry with myself for bringing you into the world.' He held out his hands. 'With these,' he added.

She smiled. 'You act all the time,' she said. 'You're never yourself for a moment. I'll talk to you later.' She waded in and began to swim out into deep water, her back to the shore. It came to him then how lucky a thing it was that nobody had ever seen him swim. Never in thirty, forty, fifty years. Swimming belonged to his boyhood. He went in after her, swiftly, silently, fully dressed, not even kicking off his shoes. Round his right hand was twisted a handkerchief. She did not hear him until he came up behind her, and she turned on her back and cried out, astonished, shaking the water from her hair. He was on her before she could move, seizing her throat in his right hand, bending her legs with his knees, pressing her down into the water beneath him. She fought in his grip, but was unable to free herself. She opened her mouth: 'Papa – Papa . . . Papa . . .' a last cry, a last choking struggle for breath. As he held her beneath the water her frightened blue eyes flashed up at him in a moment's recognition. She looked like his mother. He was thinking: 'Père never thought of a handkerchief, he must have left his fingerprints on her throat.' He went on holding her beneath the water, beating her legs with his knees, and he wondered how long it would be before her body sagged under him, and grew limp, and was lost to him. . . .

Part Five (1920–32): 'And After'

Julius Lévy went to live in Paris after his daughter was drowned. It was the only place that suggested itself when he awoke to realization. He had been very ill those first weeks, he had taken chill from having been so long in the water, the doctors said. He must have gone in without a thought of his own danger, hampered by his clothes and because he was unable to swim he could not get to her. The party from the yacht told how they had come upon him up to his neck in the water, shouting at the top of his voice like a madman. It was appalling. Nobody who was there would ever forget.

It was a mercy that he should be taken ill, he was spared the dreadful aftermath of discovery, the finding of Gabriel's body, the necessary details involved. One of the members of the party took all this upon his shoulders. He did everything, he made arrangements. Julius Lévy questioned none of this, he lay in bed on board his yacht and would see nobody.

Only his doctor came to him.

When his secretary, summoned from London, tried to induce him to make some statement as to his wishes, he sent him away, he would not see him. 'I don't want to know,' he said. 'Do what you like. Make what arrangements you like. I don't want to know. Leave me alone.'

They feared for his reason. They left him undisturbed. This was bound to be, they said; this was the shock, the reaction. No one knew how it would ultimately affect him.

The party dispersed, of course, immediately after the accident, and Julius Lévy was left alone on the yacht.

Gabriel's body was taken back to England. She was buried beside her mother at Granby.

Julius did not ask where they had carried her. It was as though he would cut all memory of her from his mind.

And the yacht waited at her moorings in the harbour at Cannes, with Julius Lévy, her owner, below in his cabin, never coming on deck, never moving, the door closed. Alone, seeing no one.

There was no other topic of conversation in Cannes but Julius Lévy, and how long he would remain. His secretaries, his doctor, his crew could tell nothing of his plans. They waited, wretched and distressed, shaken by this tragedy that had fallen so swiftly upon them all, and they listened to the silence that struck forcibly now there was no laughter, no song, no sound of music, and all the while the hot sun blazed down from the hard sky upon the yacht still and quiet at her moorings.

Then one morning Julius Lévy came up on deck. He climbed up to the bridge of the vessel and stood for a moment looking out towards the sea. He stood awhile, the breeze playing in his white hair, his hand resting on the canvas that protected the bridge, and then he turned suddenly and called to the captain, who was watching him from the window of the chart-room.

'Will you get under way as soon as possible?' he said.

The captain came out on to the bridge.

'Certainly, Sir Julius. We can get up steam and be off by noon if you wish it.'

'I do wish it,' said Julius; and then the captain hesitated a moment, coughed, and said: 'Where are we going, Sir Julius?' He paused awkwardly, wondering if he had been tactless, pre-suming, and then Julius Lévy laughed and shrugged his shoulders. It was terrible, the captain said afterwards, to see him shrug his shoulders, and then the way he pulled out his cigarette-case and tapped it and offered him a cigarette. It was callous, strange.

'Plans?' he said. 'I have no plans. I'm finished with plans.'

And then he went down the ladder to the deck below, half laughing to himself and muttering aloud:

'Plans? Why the devil should I be expected to make plans?'

At the bottom of the ladder he looked up and called: 'You'll put me ashore at Marseilles, and sail this ship to the South Seas for all I care. I'm not going back to England.'

The captain stared after him, worried and perplexed. He did not understand his orders. He thought Julius Lévy had gone crazy, and he was afraid. All this was too much responsibility. He would have to consult someone, the secretary, that doctor, the manager who had come down from London, anybody.

Julius Lévy repeated his orders, however. He gave notice all round that he was leaving the yacht at Marseilles.

'Take the yacht back to Stockport and sell her,' he said. 'Do what you like. I can't be bothered with those things.' And then when his secretary tried to tell him of the business that awaited him, all the mail accumulated, the messages, the cables, the people who wished to see him, he waved his hands, he swore, shouting aloud: 'I tell you I've finished with all that. I don't want to think any more. Get rid of people; don't answer letters. The whole lot of you can go to the devil.'

Then the secretary, in desperation: 'Where are we going, Sir Julius? Are we going to stay in Marseilles?'

'Marseilles? No, you poor fool. We're going to Paris. Back to the place where I was born.'

Everyone was bewildered and upset. Nobody understood what he meant. Arrangements were made, though. There were three cars waiting at the quay in Marseilles to take Julius Lévy and his personal servants and his luggage to the station. There were three compartments reserved for him in the train *de luxe*.

He was settled in a corner with cushions and papers, his food being brought to him from the wagon restaurant.

It seemed to him that there were a dozen officials fussing about him, rubbing their hands, bowing from the waist.

'Can't you leave me alone?' he said.

He drummed with his fingers on his knee, and he remembered how the last time he had travelled this route he had walked by road from Dijon, his clothes in rags, and Père had played upon a flute like a beggar. That was over fifty years ago.

When they had made up his bed, and he had washed, and was undressed, and lay stretched between the sheets, it came to him that he would be lying thus when the train passed through Dijon, and from Dijon to Paris he would be rocking gently in this bed staring at the dark sky, never sleeping. And once he had lain amongst stones in a truck, bruised and bleeding, unconscious and safe, close to Paul Lévy's heart.

All night long he tried to keep his mind on these things, and he was thinking: 'I want the road back. I don't want to go forward any more. I want the road back.'

When the train drew in at the Gare de Lyon there were several people waiting to meet him at the platform. There was the managing director of his cafés, there was Isaacs from the City, Brunt, editor of the *Weekly Gazette*; there was Max Goldheim – the whole crowd. He was bored by them. Why were they there? Somebody was saying something about his usual suite at the Crillon.

As he leant back in the car, his managing director beside him talking gently, nervously patting his arm – he didn't listen to a word – he supposed he was going to the Crillon, because he had generally gone there when he had visited Paris on business. All that seemed very long ago, though, as if it had happened to a different man.

He peered from the window, his eyes dazzled by the morning sun, his ears full of the sounds, the cries, the turmoil that was Paris; in his nostrils the old familiar smell of dust and cobbled stones, *tabac* and dark burnt bread; and as the car rattled through the streets he felt that this Crillon Hotel was not his, it did not belong to him. They should be taking him eastward, across the quays to the old houses and the narrow byways, back to the garret in the Rue des Petits Champs.

He decided from the very first that he would never return to England. England belonged to another time. He had had all that. It had been possessed, and locked away. It was finished now. His people could make all the arrangements they pleased. Sell his estates and the whole of his property. None of those things interested him any more. He did not want to think again, nor to use his brain in the smallest matter. He wanted to be quiet and still; he wanted to sit at a window and watch the people passing in the streets. No more effort, no conversation. Just to sit at some window and bite his nails. . . .

It was this new sensation of feeling tired that he did not understand. He had never been tired before. It must be the result of that chill he had taken. He found that it was very pleasant to rise late in the mornings, a little before twelve, and then after his bath to stroll a little while and return to luncheon at one o'clock, to have his meal served upstairs in his suite. Then after lunch he would rest and fall asleep, and if he was lucky this afternoon sleep would endure some length of time, so that there would not be too long a gap between his waking and his time for dinner.

He was afraid of the time of waking. He was afraid that his brain would start to work in the old way.

Food became a matter of intense interest, therefore, and he began to eat and drink much more than he had ever done in his life. He found that the more he ate the heavier he slept. And that was good. He put on flesh, he grew very big around neck and shoulders – big in the belly, too. This was increased because he did not bother to take exercise. His walks were nothing; he went everywhere in a car.

During those first months in Paris he would be driven about a great deal. He would sit comfortably, leaning against cushions, his arm through a strap-hold, a rug about his knees, warmly wrapped in a thick overcoat, for the autumn days were cold, and a warm bottle for his feet. It was incredible to him how Paris had changed. He wondered why he had never considered this on his business visits to the city. He supposed he had been thinking of other things. But now, in these days, he kept expecting to find the Paris of his boyhood, and it was gone from him. The fortifications were no more, they had all been destroyed; what had been the outlying suburbs was now Paris itself, fully grown and developed. He could not find any of the places he had known.

Once he told his chauffeur to drive to Puteaux, and in place of the straggling village where he was born, there was a mass of tall factory chimneys and warehouses; trams rattled over the bridge and the rough high road was a broad avenue with houses and shops on either side.

It was hideous, overgrown and cheap. A thousand workers poured from the factories, wagons and lorries thundered in the streets.

Neuilly was a vast district, part of Paris itself. Round and about, backwards and forwards, he told his chauffeur to drive the car, and wherever they went there was nothing of what had been. He might have been a stranger in a foreign land.

And he thought, startled by this suggestion: 'I'm old, that's what it is. I'm old. This has all grown up since, and has no business with me. It's changed, it's passed me by.'

The car turned into the new Avenue du Roule, and opposite the Église de St Pierre that he had not known they came suddenly upon a long line of stalls set up upon the pavement, and through the open window of the car were blown the cries and the smells that he knew, that would never be lost: cauliflower and leeks, and rich ripe cheese, cotton-stuffs and leather, the sound of many voices excited and shrill, the bustle of a crowd who jostled each other, girls without hats, old women with baskets on their arms, even a little sharp-eyed boy at the pavement's edge who held a sprig of flowers in his hand and cried: '*Cinq sous la botte – approchez-vous, messieurs, mesdames – cinq sous la botte.*' It was the market. The same as it had always been. Familiar, known, unchanged.

Julius Lévy tapped on the glass in front of him and the chauffeur drew up. Then he got out of the car and stood by one of the stalls, leaning on a stick, and he listened and breathed those scents and sounds that had not come to him for more than fifty years, the first things he had ever known, and he wanted to tell these people who sold in his place that he belonged here and was one of them.

He thought that they must surely recognize him as one of themselves, and it was strange to him that no one called in his ear or tapped him on the shoulder, no one whistled to him from that stall across the way, no one shouted: '*Eh bien, c'est toi, mon vieux.*'

Then he heard a fellow laugh at the stall by his side, and this was followed by a shrill titter from a woman who was wrapping a slab of cheese in greasy paper, and one of them made a joke about the old monsieur in the fur collar who seemed to be looking for a lavatory.

He hated them then, he hated their misunderstanding, their lack of recognition. He hated their denial of him. He wanted to shout at them: 'You fools, you damned blind fools. I knew your trade before any of you were born. I've had everything in the world and you'll never rise above your own dirty cheeses. You fools.'

He turned sharply away and the driver helped him into the car and settled the rug over his knees.

270

He lit a cigarette, his hands trembling.

'I'll show them,' he was thinking. 'I'll show them.' But the smell of the market was strong in his nostrils, and in his ear rang the old cry: '*Approchez-vous, messieurs, mesdames, approchez-vous donc.* . . .'

It was after this visit to the market that he formed his project of building a house in Neuilly, a house that he would fill with treasures, a house like a palace. In his mind the idea was a defiance of the people of the market, and the answer to his own doubting fear. This palace would prove that he was right and they were wrong. He would live in his palace beyond price, and know that it was his, and he would think of them in their poor sordid hovels; and it would be a satisfaction to him, this thinking of them so inferior, so dulled.

The birth of this plan brought back to him some of his lost energy; he was almost well again, he forgot to be tired. Those people of the market had made him remember that he was Julius Lévy.

Julius Lévy – he was Julius Lévy. He was the richest man in England. Hadn't he been that? Wasn't he still? Surely he could have that name in France too. He could buy up anyone if he cared. He could own the whole of Paris; he could possess the world.

The fools around him, the poor blind fools. He would not be swayed by fashion or taste in the building of his palace. Everything should go into it, marble, glass, and precious stones. One period jostling against another; one style mingled with the next. He had never cared for simplicity of form; now he could pile together everything of value that belonged to him, lump them, crowd them cheek against cheek like so many lots, and he would know that all of that had come because once he, too, had called: '*Approchez-vous, messieurs, mesdames, approchez-vous.*' Only he had not been a little gutter rat with his nose in the mud; he had risen because he was himself, a Lévy, a Jew.

So he started to build his palace, and every morning his car would take him from the Hôtel Crillon to the site he had chosen by the Porte de Madrid, and he would drive across the broad Avenue de Neuilly past the market stalls with the old familiar

271

clatter and smell, watching them from the window of his car, his arm through the strap-hold, a smile on his lips.

This daily vision of the market affected him in many ways. It was as though the indifference of these people reacted as a slap in the face, quickening his blood. He took their attitude as a challenge. They would not recognize his superiority. If it was thus with the peasants who sold in the market, it would be the same with the rest of the world. They would imagine Julius Lévy was a broken man, that he was growing old. He would show them that this was false. He began to take stock of his appearance, those sagging lines, those pouches beneath his eyes, and the paunch in his belly. He had a masseuse visit him daily at the Crillon and waited anxiously for the result to be obtained from the strong, slender hands that worked upon him. He wore a belt-supporter, he visited a clinic and sat for violet-ray treatment. He endeavoured to diet, to restrain his desire for rich food. This was difficult; food had become important to him.

He dressed extravagantly, eager for that admiration that had been his for so long and which might soon be lost to him; and because he possessed no discernment nor valuation in this, his appearance was overdone. He was no longer distinguished; he looked flashy – vulgar. An old fellow, a flower in his buttonhole, with waiters laughing at him behind their hands.

The building of the house in Neuilly and his settling in Paris caused much discussion and excitement. He was still a public figure of great importance, whose wealth was fabulous. Once it became known that he was to live permanently in Paris invitations and introductions were showered upon him; he was asked everywhere, all classes of society wished to receive him. They wanted a share of his money, his personality mattered little to them; and he, accustomed for so many years to adulation, flattery, and praise, began to go about once more, to dine, to sup, to receptions, attending these functions without any real interest or desire to mingle socially with his fellow creatures, but acting from a motive of self-pride. He feared if he did not go people would say he was old, he was finished.

Julius Lévy – finished – burnt out.

They must not say that.

So he dressed himself with greater care; he tightened his corset belt, he suffered silently for an hour under the probing fingers of his masseuse.

He rested during the day so that he should not become too tired in the evening. This new, hateful sensation of fatigue never before experienced, now always at hand, waiting around the corner. It would come upon him sometimes when he was dining out or standing at some reception, an overmastering clutch of sleepiness wrapping his brain like a blanket; and he would fight against it, knowing that it would dull his brain, make him rusty, make him unable to continue a conversation with his usual intelligence.

It would swamp him, blunt his brilliance and fine perception, and he would not be Julius Lévy any more, but any old fellow who had dined too well and wanted his bed. An old fellow – a bore.

He must try to keep his mind from wandering; he must show these people that he was still himself. So he would talk, he would discuss some topic of the day, endeavouring to hold the conversation as he had always done, and for all their good manners and their tact, a light of instinct within him would warn him that he could not hold people as he had done. Their smiles were false, their eyes looked past him.

Then he would check himself, he would pretend to fumble with his food, and for all his instinct he could not tell himself where his mistake had been, he could not see where his words had failed, but he knew that something within him was not the same; something was blunted, was lost to him.

Fellows chatted amongst themselves, they did not ask his opinion. He told himself that this was a new generation growing up, indifferent, rude. They were fools.

And women – women had greatly changed. Their manners were atrocious, they only thought of themselves. They did not bother to listen, they made excuses to disappear, they would get up and go off dancing with some fellow. He did not dance these days; he would find himself sitting watching the dancing with some intolerable old bore of a chaperone aunt, and he would wonder why he was there, sitting so stiffly with a flower in his buttonhole, smothering a yawn, thinking of his bed.

He used to pass the time speculating on the relationships

between people. That girl with the legs and curly hair dancing with that boy: were they lovers? What would they do? Would she be cold, would she be lovable? He would imagine the intimacy between them and the imagining of it gave him an odd tingling sensation that was pleasant, that stirred him. He would like to hide in a room behind a curtain and watch those two.

His mind would ramble on, going over the picture, adding a piece here, a piece there, and part of him would seem near to sleep so that his head would nod, the room become hazy about him, and he would be startled suddenly by a voice in his ear: 'Good evening, Sir Julius . . .' And 'H'm – who – what?' he would mutter, coming to with a shock, stifling that yawn, and: 'Oh! how do you do? Very pleased to see you;' thinking to himself: 'Who the devil's this?'

Then the rest of the interminable evening until he was back at the Crillon again, his stays off, his clothes flung from him, lying between the cool comfort of sheets, a hot-water bottle at his feet, and he would think that sleep was the only desirable thing remaining in the world; sleep, and food, and drink. He could not keep strictly to the diet recommended by his doctor, it required too great an effort.

Food was a pleasure, he would not go without this pleasure.

Soon the one interest he had when he went out to a party was that of wondering what he would be given to eat. The men and women about him seemed poor lifeless things compared to the food on his plate and the wine in his glass. Food filled him with some measure of content.

While he ate he need not bother to talk and to impress people. It made him too tired, this business of conversation and impressing people. He would watch the courses appear, his eyes intent, scarce listening to the claptrap of his neighbour that buzzed in his ear, giving no reply to the man opposite who questioned him on the causes of the inflation of the franc. Something was going to be served with a rich sauce; it smelt good, it would taste better, no doubt. He asked the waiter for more sauce, and he mashed it up with the meat, turning his fork over and over. 'The inflation of the franc, my friend,' he began, loading his mouth, 'is due, of course, to – to . . .' And he hesitated, pondering the matter, then continued some lengthy rambling, off the point, muddled and confused, his questioner already bored and talking to some woman. Julius Lévy laid down his fork, glancing about him to see where the servant had gone with the sauce, and he was aware of a warm full sensation, the only sensation that mattered now. He stifled the wind that rose in his throat, and reached out a hand for his glass. Over the rim he noticed a young woman watching him; she was lovely, very fair. He smiled at her, raising his eyebrows. He would talk to her afterwards. She was lovely, his type. Women still looked his way, then. They knew, they could always tell. He went on smiling to himself, picturing some scene between them. He would show her things; he would make her feel she was alive.

He lifted his glass to her, he nodded, then he looked over his shoulder for the servant. 'Bring me some more sauce,' he said.

And the girl said to the man at her side: 'Who is that old Jew guzzling at his food? He keeps staring at me.'

'That's Julius Lévy, one of the richest men in the world. They say he's an insufferable bore.'

'Look,' she said, 'he's got a splodge of sauce on his chin.'

Julius heard every word they said. He felt something seize at his heart, as though a hand was touching him there, twisting and turning it about. A wave of colour mounted in his face, up to his temples, at the back of his neck, in the roots of his hair. He pretended to go on smiling, to go on mashing his food into a soup. But the sauce burnt his tongue, it drew the water in his eyes. He laid down his fork, he crumbled a piece of bread with his hand.

He felt very old suddenly – very tired.

Originally Julius Lévy had intended to entertain in his palace at Neuilly. He had had visions of great dinner parties, the huge rooms filled with men and women. And he the centre of the crowd, smiling to himself, aware of their envy.

Now he decided that he did not want any of that, something had made him change his mind. A snatch of conversation overheard at a dinner, words not intended to reach his ears, they had sunk deeply into his mind. He would not forget them. He despised these people, he hated their little vacuous brains, their futile wandering train of thought. They would like to see him make himself ridiculous, they would grovel at his feet for an introduction to his house, and they would criticize, they would snigger behind his back. He was determined, therefore, that they should not have this pleasure. He would live alone in his palace, with no one but his personal servants, and the rest of the world would be shut outside, would struggle vainly for admittance.

They would picture the beauty of the place they did not know, and they would imagine him there living like some emperor, with ways and tastes superior to the common herd of men, a strange figure of secrecy, exciting wonder, awe perhaps, looked upon as someone apart from the rest of mankind – like a god. There would be a dark veil of mystery about him that no one should ever break.

Thus when his palace was ready to receive him Julius Lévy entered upon a new way of living, an existence that once he would have believed impossible and fantastic; suspicious of everyone and resentful of criticism, he shut himself up within the walls of his incredible mansion, fast keeping to his plan of solitude unnatural to him and appalling at first in its stark novelty, and then accepting it as a refuge and screen hiding him from the curious sceptical eyes of the world he had grown to hate.

This last phase was like a play to him, in which he, the leading actor, played the lone, important part.

He was Julius Lévy, the great Julius Lévy who had chosen to retire from the world, and the things he did and the way he lived should be an everlasting subject of inquiry, so he thought, a ceaseless, feverish discussion on the lips of the people without. It pleased him to picture their envy. They would tell each other stories of his wealth and lament upon the pitiful insecurity of their own luckless lives dependent on the morrow.

There would be a slackening of conduct for him now, he realized. No need to groan under the hands of his masseuse, no longer must he wear that restraining corset, nor watch his diet. He would be able to let himself go and no one would know. He was able to act as he pleased. With the wealth of the world in his hands and possessing no ties, he told himself that he held greater liberty than any man alive. He was free. Few people could boast such freedom as was his. And the world could chitter if it liked how fallen he must be, how sunk, how lost, how prematurely aged, how battered of intellect; but they would have no proof.

The laugh was on his side.

He gave himself up entirely to his imagination. Little by little the fear came to him that his wealth might depreciate in value. For all he knew secret forces were at work to rob him of his possessions. Trickery was afoot, his agents were bribed, thieves probed amongst his papers. He trusted no one, he knew his world too well. His very servants were false maybe, waiting their chance, covering their schemes with feigned attempt at service. Rigorously he began to cut expenses. He curtailed his staff to a minimum, he supervised accounts himself. In this way he was able to control every centime that went out of the house. He checked each item paid. The experience was of absorbing interest to him; it was like returning to the work of long ago.

He understood these things.

'What is this?' he would say, tapping a bill with a pencil. 'Why the sending of all this linen to the *blanchisseuse*. Can't we wash the necessary things here? I gave no orders for my bed linen to be changed so frequently. We must see that it lasts longer.' And then frowning, spreading out his hands: 'So many francs a week for kindling-wood is monstrous. Isn't the Bois itself across the road? Why doesn't the gardener gather faggots free? In that way there will be nothing to pay.'

He moved about his house peering through keyholes, listening on landings, bursting without warning suddenly into the kitchen quarters, expecting to find his servants discussing him. He was loathed and feared, and he knew it and he did not care. It mattered little to him if they all deserted him one by one; it would mean less to dole out in weekly wages.

It was profoundly irritating to him when the franc was stabilized. Hitherto his agents had been able to gamble effectively on the exchange. It had been his favourite old game of something for nothing.

Apart from the control of his household, Julius Lévy lived mostly in a world of dreams. He had no company but his own thoughts, and he fell into the habit of talking to himself aloud. His mind ran in channels varied and intermingled, carrying him back to the past mostly, some sixty years or more. It was hard for him to realize that he was older now than Jean Blançard, that Paul Lévy when he died had been his junior by over thirty years. The fact of this left him perplexed, it muddled his pictures. He would see himself as a boy of ten dressed in a little blue cloak and clogs on his feet, stamping along the cobbled streets to the bridge across the Seine. The memory of those early days was vivid now, it was as though a curtain had risen from part of his mind, showing him these scenes painted in bright colours. The intervening time was swept away. Once more he wanted to hear music, once more he wanted the unreality of dreams.

Sometimes he would listen for a whisper in the air, the echo of a voice that was beautiful and sweet, and he would see the face of the young Rabbin who had sung to him of the enchanted city.

Once he ordered his car, long disused and idle in the garage, and he was driven to synagogue. Only this time it was not the bare temple of his boyhood, but the great oratory in the Rue de la Victoire, where the wealthy Israelites of Paris worshipped, wrapped in their furs. An elderly Rabbin ministered, his voice powerful and clear, and there were violins in the choir, and there were harps, and great sonority of sound, but there was no melody of beauty that rose like a bird in the air.

Julius came away disappointed, bored. So this faith was meaningless after all; it gave him nothing. Once more he must rely on himself for supreme understanding. He would not go to the synagogue again nor to any other place. Paris as he had seen it that day depressed him, made him want to shrink back in himself, take cover behind his screen. He had lost contact with people for too long. That night he looked at his reflection and saw himself as he had grown to be. It was one single moment of lucidity that came upon him as he gazed at his reflection in the glass, a momentary escape from fatigue and a freedom from excess in food and drink. He saw the heavy face, the loose lips, the dark pouches beneath the eyes, he saw the bowed shoulders and the trembling hands. He saw his childhood, and his youth and his manhood in a single flash of penetration; his struggle, his victory, his burning progress like a meteor in the sky; he saw the face that stared at him now, ugly, degenerate and old, and he knew that his life counted therefore as nothing, that no achievement lay behind him, no battle won, no beauty possessed; that Julius Lévy was a name already vanished and lost in the sky, that had never been, that would not go on; and he wondered if there was no continuation of life, no future, no treasure beyond the stars, and if in reality there was neither God nor man, nor any world at all.

The house was like a palace built by some crazy emperor of long ago, some lonely king of Babylon, with its columns of marble, its steps of stone, its windows of vari-coloured glass. Gargoyles crouched at odd angles of the roof, and about the gardens there were statues of satyrs and little twisted fauns.

On the terrace a fountain played and was never still, the jet of water rising high in the air with a cool splash and a shiver of sound, and from the smooth hard lawns below the peacock would come to the fountain to drink, spreading his tail of glory to catch the rays of the sun. Then he would glance about him, standing on one foot and scratching his feathers, his eye cocked to the western end of the terrace, where he could see the great aviary of birds, and from here came the whistle and sweet song of their hundred voices, a mingled chorus lifted to the air. He spread his tail, and there was colour there of purple and blue and gold, and colour amongst the wide scattered rose-beds, too thick and too full-blown, and colour of dazzling crimson from the richly planted shrubs.

The great white house with its turrets and its pillars stood like a mausoleum amidst the splendour, the long windows were shuttered, the shutters were barred.

There was a high wall built around the palace and its grounds, and beyond this wall were the trees of the Bois, while the road ran away to join the Porte and the Avenue de Madrid.

The house was a vast museum. The marble hall with the gallery above was surely set for such a purpose with its pedestals and sculpture, and on the walls of the lofty rooms there were tapestries and pictures beyond price, and cabinets containing china treasures of great worth.

To anyone who wandered here there would be but one thing lacking, and that was the attendant on his chair by the door, coloured catalogue in hand, a war pensioner with medals on his breast leaning heavily on a stick and reciting one by one the objects by their name in rapid monotonous recitation.

And instead of this there was no one; not even a spectacled tourist from the States, nor a yawning, adolescent girl from a convent school, but only the rooms themselves with their shuttered windows, the air fuggy yet strangely cold, and the unseen chairs and furniture grouped together in stiff familiarity. They knew nothing of daylight beyond that which stole into the rooms murky and grim. Only sometimes they were visited, and this in the silence of the day or the night that were the same, and at these times their owner came, flashing suddenly the horrible yellow glare of electric light; and he would wander amongst his treasures in doubtful interest, caring for none of them, but remembering with uncanny precision the worth of that picture and the value of that chair.

It seemed that these occasional visits must afford him strange and singular satisfaction, for he would smile sometimes, with a recollection of a bargain, and he would look about him whistling under his breath, touching a canvas with his finger-tip, caressing the texture of a china vase.

Then he would go once more, leaving the rooms and the treasures they contained to the old solitude, and walking down the wide marble stairs, his feet echoing hollow as they stepped, he would wander towards a shuttered window giving on the terrace, and drawing aside a bolt, turn the creaking shutters sideways, and stand for a while screened by them looking upon the terrace and the blazing shrubs.

Perhaps a gardener would pass on his way to the rose-beds, watering-can in hand, looking neither to right nor left, and the owner of the palace would instinctively draw back behind his shutter for fear he should be seen, muttering to himself, passing his hand over his mouth. Then unobserved he would watch the working man, taking note of the measure of his labour, reckoning the hours of work against the wages paid. And every movement, every bending gesture of the man would be an interest to him, the way he set down his can or lifted his rake, so that he would stand there for many stretches of time, his hand against the shutter.

When the gardener moved from his rose-beds, and disappeared once more round the lower edge of the terrace the owner would wake from his strange immobility and pad through the hall to a little room at the end of a long passage, a room stuffy and untidy, redolent of that peculiar pungent food smell that clings invariably to a single living-room. The windows were tightly closed, and the room was unbearably hot, although the fire in the grate burnt low. A leather chair was pulled close to the fire, and near to the chair was a table covered with a baize cloth, and upon the cloth a tray bearing a plate of sausage and half a piece of cheese, a long thin loaf of bread, and a bottle of red wine. Part of the food smell came from this tray, and part from the canary in a cage hanging against the wall; he sat on his perch pecking feebly at his seed, and the seed-jar was upset, some of it spilled on the floor.

The owner sat down to the table and carved off a large piece of garlic sausage, for he was hungry, and as he loaded his mouth with the sausage and the cheese he reached with his other hand to a piece of paper and a pencil, and he jotted down figures, reckoning the wages of his gardener. Some of his food escaped from his mouth and trickled down his chin; he had a smear of sausage at the corner of his mouth.

Once he felt something warm and furry twine itself round his legs, and glancing down he saw the cat – a big, fat cat, over-fed and lazy – and the cat began scratching at him, purring and humming, and then suddenly leapt into his lap and settled, closing its eyes.

The owner finished his sausage, and felt in his pocket for a packet of cigarettes. There was one left in the crushed packet, and he broke it in half, placing one end in his mouth and the other he returned to the packet.

The cat moved on his lap, and lifting a leg above its head began to scratch, the irritation proceeding to his owner, who half consciously dug his nails under his left armpit and scratched in company.

'You give me your fleas, you little filthy thing,' he said, and the cat gazed up solemnly into his face, caring not at all. It was a big heavy cat and its breath smelt of fish.

There was a tap at the door later, and a fat, undersized boy came into the room, carrying a scuttle of coals. He had little round eyes at the top of his head, idiot's eyes, and a silly, vacant smile. His hair was thick and curly.

The owner looked up from his notes. 'What do you want, Gustav?' he said. The boy put down his scuttle, giggling, and shuffled away towards the door.

'I told you not to bring more than one scuttle a day,' came the command. 'Have you no idea of the price of coal? Do you want to ruin me?'

The boy said nothing, his eyes blinking foolishly.

'Come here,' said the owner. The boy advanced, his loose mouth drooping, and when he stood before the chair the man slapped him twice across the face. He smiled as he did so, liking the contact and the sting against the flesh, and because he liked it he slapped him again.

'Get out,' he said. 'Get out.'

The boy crept from the room, sobbing loudly, and this little scene appeared to have given the owner fresh appetite, for he cut off another slice of sausage and another slice of cheese, and mashed them together with crumbs of bread, and then, reaching for his wine, he poured some of it on top. In this way he could make a soup of his food.

After his meal he loosened his trousers, and settled before his fire, leaning forward first to grasp an old, greasy newspaper that was tucked away at the back of the scuttle. It was a week-old newspaper, torn across the middle, but this he did not seem to mind, for all news was alike to him, and he read in detail every scrap of printing that was upon this newspaper, from a speech in the Chambre des Députés to an advertisement for impotence.

Presently his grip on the paper relaxed, and his chin dropped; soon his head lolled at a foolish angle and his mouth hung open.

He slept for two hours perhaps, breathing heavily, snoring from time to time, and when he awoke his fire was out and darkness was beyond the windows. For a moment he was startled, his heart hammering in his chest; he did not know where he was or why he should be there. Was he alone, was he himself, had not there been a dream, and the sound of a voice, and a cry in the night? Was that the whisper of a flute in the air? Had someone tapped on the ceiling overhead, and were those footsteps echoing away, down the dark passage, lost and then hushed into silence?

A whimper escaped from him, and he fumbled at the table by his side for matches. When he struck a match and the feeble light showed him the room, and the drooping canary, and the sleeping cat, it was as though a finger laid itself on his brain and closed down a shutter. He was all right, he was home. He had been dreaming. He was reassured to find himself in safety, but as he groped down to the fire to blow at the fallen grey embers, he was aware of a dull blank pain in his side colder than the airless chill of the room, a pain that was born of an old longing and a dead thought. He knew that when he was asleep he did not suffer this pain, but walked in a land he had once known and which belonged to him.

It was soon after his seventy-second birthday that Julius Lévy fell victim to a stroke. Nobody knew how it had happened, but he was found one afternoon lying face downwards on the terrace, close to the door of the aviary. He must have been listening to the birds singing, so the gardener said – it was the gardener who found him there – and then been seized without warning, and stumbled and fallen without having the time to save himself or to utter a cry.

At first the gardener thought he was dead, but when he had summoned help and they had carried the great unwieldy body to his room, they found that he was still breathing.

The servants were flustered and very much afraid; nobody seemed to know what should be done for the best. Then a doctor was summoned, and as soon as he came into the house order reigned amongst the scattered staff, there was discipline where there had been confusion, a feeling of regularity was theirs, a return to normality after the madness of many years.

Nurses were in attendance night and day. The tone of the solitary, unkept mansion changed to a brisk hygienic atmosphere; it was like the sudden installation of a hospital, brisk and coldly efficient. Windows were flung open that had been closed now for so long, and the warm June sunshine poured into these lifeless rooms, bringing the scent of flowers and songs of birds, bringing also the distant clamour and movement that was Paris.

Julius Lévy stretched upon his bed felt none of this. The stroke had rendered him powerless and dumb. He would lie through the endless days and nights with his eyes closed, the breath coming through his open mouth harsh and loud. The doctors could not tell how long he would endure. It might be hours, they said, it might be years.

Because he was still living, he must be washed and fed, and tended regularly like a baby just born into the world; and he was as helpless as a baby now, as pitiful, as weak.

It was nearly three months after he received his stroke that Julius Lévy returned to partial consciousness.

One day the nurse found that he could open his eyes, a little later he was able to move his hands. Whether this was the sign of eventual recovery or whether this was the last flickering effort of life before the end, no one could tell. He remained in this state for several days. He noticed the faces round about him, the nurses who attended to his wants, and he smiled at them like a baby smiles, grateful for the nourishment they gave him, the gentleness of their touch, and for the security with which they took his body into their keeping.

It was supreme relaxation. It was a negation of life and a returning once more to the beginning.

One lovely summer's afternoon they wheeled him on to the terrace so that he should feel the air blow upon his face and should sleep under the warm rays of the sun. He did not sleep, though; he was too interested in the colours of the garden, in the scents and sounds, in the movement of things. His eyes moved restlessly from side to side, and later – tired by all he had seen – he lay still again, his eyes turned upwards to the sky. He would watch the white clouds passing across the face of the sky. They seemed so near to him, surely they were easy to hold and to caress; strange moving things belonging to the wide blue space of heaven.

They floated just above his head, they almost brushed his eyelids as they passed, and he had only to grasp at the long curling fringe of them with his fingers and they would belong to him instead, becoming part of him for ever.

Not yet did he understand, for a puzzled look crept into his eyes, and he frowned his ancient baby frown of an old man, while from the innermost part of his being came the long-drawn pitiful wail that can never be explained, the eternal question of the earth to the skies: 'Who am I? Where from? Where to?' The sigh of the baby, the cry of the old man.

The first cry and the last.

He cried to them and they did not come. They passed away from him as though they had never been, indifferent and aloof; like wreaths of white smoke they were carried away by the wind, born of nothing, dissolving into nothing, a momentary breath that vanished in the air.

His last instinct was to stretch out his hands to the sky.

Paris, January–Bodinnick, November 1931.

Daphne du Maurier

'Has no rival' *Sunday Telegraph*

Rule Britannia 40p
US Marines land in Cornwall, and Mad – a world-famous
retired actress, autocratic and irresistible – rallies her family,
friends and neighbours to defend their heritage.

'Du Maurier's bestselling novel is a political thriller' *Daily Mirror*

My Cousin Rachel 50p
Ambrose married Rachel and never returned home. His letters to
his cousin Philip hinted that he was being poisoned, and when
Philip arrived in Italy, Ambrose was dead . . .

'A Jane Eyre-ish quality of suspense and hovering tragedy'
The Lady

The King's General 50p
A brilliant re-creation of the love shared by Sir Richard Grenvile
– at once the King's General in the West and the most detested
officer in his army – and Honor Harris of Lanrest, as brave as she
was beautiful, during the years when Cornwall echoed to the
brisk tattoo of Royalist drums and the alien challenge of rebel
bugles.

The Ferdinand and Isabella Trilogy
Jean Plaidy

Castile for Isabella 40p
With fifteenth-century Spain rent with intrigue and threatened by
civil war, Isabella became the pawn of her ambitious, half-crazed
mother and a virtual prisoner at the licentious court of her
half-brother, Henry IV.

Numbed with grief and fear, Isabella yet remained steadfast in
her determination to marry Ferdinand, the handsome young
Prince of Aragon, her only true betrothed . . .

Spain for the Sovereigns 45p
With the might of Portugal humbled, the Court of the
Sovereigns saw the rise of Torquemada, the establishment of the
dreaded Inquisition, and the coming of Columbus who left the
woman he loved to make a dream reality.

Daughters of Spain 45p
During the last years of Isabella's reign it seemed there was a
curse on the Royal House which struck at the children of the
Sovereigns.

Tragedy followed tragedy – the Infanta Isabella, a broken-
hearted widow; Juana, driven to madness by her husband's
philandering; and the sorrow of parting with young Catalina,
destined to become Katherine of Aragon, wife to Henry VIII and
Queen of England . . .

I Heard the Owl Call My Name 40p
Margaret Craven

The gentle bestseller that is sweeping the world.

'Margaret Craven's novel gives an epic quality to the old tribal ways . . . an entrancing chemistry' *New York Times*

Mark Brian, a young Anglican priest who has not long to live, is sent to the Indian village of Kingcome in the wilds of British Columbia.
While sharing the hunting and fishing, the festivals and funerals, the joys and sorrows of a once proud tribe, Mark learns enough of life to be ready for death.
On a cold winter evening when he hears the owl call his name, Mark understands what is to come . . .

A first novel of poignant beauty which reflects the author's perception, wisdom and warmth of human insight, giving her unique story the quality of a legend or a fable.

'A rare clarity and simplicity. It is a long time since I was so moved by a story, touching in its dignity and wise in its folklore'. *Daily Telegraph*